The BookSeller

The BookSeller

Johnny Fry and Jinx ~ Book 2

Skeet Will

The BookSeller
Copyright © 2021, 2025 – Skeet Will
ISBN: 979-8-9986565-3-8

JK Press
Oregon, USA

Dedication

To Mary, for many years Wendy to my Peter Pan,

And To Bev, who was there for me every step of the way.

Book One

Chapter One

Lemuel Waters screwed the lock shut on the door to the wagon and turned to gaze around at his noisy surroundings. The building yard of the Pony Express Construction Company was overpoweringly loud, but he felt completely at home in the midst of it.

His father had been a carpenter, and from age eight they worked together building things. He still loved to do it, witness the wagon behind him—a product of his own hands and mind. Nothing felt more normal to him than the smell of fresh cut timber and the sounds of carpentry were in his blood.

In front of him, four men were maneuvering a roof truss onto a special wagon for shipment to a job site in Sacramento. To his left was the saw pit and a half a dozen men, each sawing at his own rhythm and rate, made a continuous racket which still wasn't enough to drown out the sound of hammers driving nails.

With Brutus, his year-old British bulldog, trotting beside him, he crossed the yard, nodding to men he passed and entered the big door that led into the supply shop and office. Through the windows he could see Bill Fry talking to several of his drivers, so he waited, and when they left, stuck his head around the door and said, "Hi Bill. You busy?"

Bill Fry looked up and his face split into a toothy grin. "Hey, Lemuel," he said. "Not busy, just got things to do. What's the plan and when are you leaving?"

Lemuel seated himself across the big desk while Bill and Brutus exchanged greetings, after which the dog came to lie down beside his chair. "Tomorrow morning," he said. "The books will leave a couple of days later and we hope to be open within a week or so after they get there."

"How many books does it take to open a bookstore?" Bill asked, leaning back in his chair, wondering in his voice.

Lemuel laughed. "Depends on how big the store is I guess, but we're going to have a little over a thousand to start. If things work out like we plan, we could have an inventory of ten thousand or more but that's a way down the road."

"Johnny tells me he's going to be putting in some things he learned from his dad," said Bill. "Tack and saddle work and gunsmithing and such."

"Your young nephew has quite a head for business it seems, and he's putting up a good-sized chunk of the money we need to get started," said Lemuel. "We've found a good spot in what they call the Marina section of town, on Chestnut about ten blocks from the bay. There's no telling how long it will take for business to get up to what we need to pay our bills, so it will be nice to have his resources to fall back on if need be."

"His Pa was a pretty good businessman, apparently," said Bill. "Truth be told, you know Johnny Fry better than I do. You've been around him these last six or seven months and I haven't seen him since he was just a squirt."

"Even at nineteen, a man couldn't ask for a better partner. We've got some good plans for the future and if they work out, we should be OK."

Lemuel stood and extended his hand. "Thanks for all your help with the wagon and tell the men I appreciate it. The wagon is important to our plans. You know, Johnny told me once he felt it was alive because it was always changing and growing. I think it might finally be finished, grown up, so to speak."

They shook hands and Lemuel walked out onto the main street of Hangtown Crossing.

Hangtown Crossing was a small place just east of Sacramento. It had gotten its name in the days of the Gold Rush because it was where the road from Hangtown to the state capital crossed the American River. In 1854 church and civic groups rallied behind a new name for Hangtown and it became Placerville, but this was still Hangtown Crossing.

Watching Lemuel walk down the street it was easy to misjudge him. He was slight for his height and a little stoop-shouldered with shoulder length blonde hair, turning dark as he aged, and bright blue eyes that shone with intellect. He was thin and wiry and looked as though a strong wind might blow him over.

The fact he had ridden with Sherman and Sheridan through four years of war, been wounded twice and came home a major, invariably surprised people. Someone who pushed him usually found out quickly about his temper and the sawed-off twelve-gauge double barrel scattergun he kept within reach in the wagon.

Halfway between the yard and Sacramento where his friends were staying, was a small café where they sometimes met for coffee and occasionally breakfast. For the last couple of weeks, he had been spending most nights in the wagon, and it seemed natural to meet somewhere in the middle to talk, plan and relax.

He constructed the wagon so he and Greta, his soon to be fifteen-year-old daughter, could sleep comfortably, and indeed live comfortably in it for weeks at a time. They had done so during the three years they meandered across the west from Missouri, selling books in towns and on farms and ranches, indeed, anywhere they found someone who wanted to buy a book.

Greta had risen magnificently to the challenges of travel and life that came with being blind from a childhood accident. She would be joining him in the wagon again for the trip west. For the last month she had been working at the clinic Annaliese and her father, Dr. Crawford, had opened to serve the Mormon population of the area around Sacramento. She usually slept at the clinic or at the cottage Annaliese and Johnny had rented nearby.

As happened, most of the time when he thought of his daughter, he thought of her mother. The day he found his wife dead on the floor of the backroom of their Kansas City bookstore shattered his life. She had been his other half, the one who brought love and books to him.

As a carpenter he learned to read but only just enough to do the job. She opened a new world of books to him, and he embraced it.

The year after Greta was born, they came into a small inheritance and opened the bookstore and reading room in Kansas City.

The need to care for his daughter brought him out of deep mourning after his wife's death, and to the realization that helping Greta learn to use the senses she had was more important than spending his life grieving about something lost.

He believed a new life would open her to new things, so within a month of Mary's death, he began to build the wagon. Three months later they left Kansas City in a bookstore on wheels, designed and built by a damn good carpenter.

He began with a box nine feet long by four and a half wide by two and a half deep. Across the top of that he built a hinged floor that swung up allowing for storage below, and when closed provided the floor for living space in the center of the wagon.

On either side he built bookcases facing outward to display his inventory with sliding doors in place to protect the books when they were on the road. He framed the front and back walls with iron, planked them with hickory and hung doors in both with the forward one hinged so it would fold to open and close accordion style and, like the rear door, could be barred from the inside. The inside height was five feet seven inches, just high enough for them to stand without a stoop.

The frame and box were made of oak, but the rest of the structure was of lighter woods. Even so, it was very heavy and needed two good draught horses to pull it comfortably on the plains. Since they weren't in a hurry and many times stopped for days at a time the horses got plenty of rest.

When they began to rise into the foothills of the Rockies, he bought two more horses. Depending on the ground he had to cross, he would either alternate them - one day on - one day off or harness them in tandem to pull steeper grades or tough terrain. He carried enough good fodder to keep them in shape so when he needed their strength it was there.

The wheels were also of oak and an extra two feet in diameter which gave better clearance on the many poorly maintained roads they traveled. Even so, there were times he needed to use his tools to clear the way for their passage.

The extra height also allowed for swinging storage beneath the box, and along the sides were numerous containers and barrels attached for flour, cornmeal, water, tools and other necessities.

Both axles were reinforced, and all pivots and joints were of heavy construction and had good access for greasing and repairs. The roof was pitched toward the rear allowing water to run off and extended over the driver's seat to provide protection from the weather.

It was painted green with white trim, and on either side the legend "The BookSeller" was painted in large gold letters. The first thing most people thought when they saw it was "it's a fort on wheels".

In the three years since they began the trip, he constantly added things, improving access and space. Every year they stopped somewhere for the winter, and he used the time to make changes until he had now reached the place where he felt happy with it.

His basic construction included a kitchen apparatus that folded down in the rear with drawers and cubby holes on shelves for spices and things. A canvas canopy over the kitchen kept off the weather, and canvas awnings rolled out over the sides to protect the books from the weather, as well as the customers while they made their selections.

Brutus led the way into the café. Lemuel found a place by the front window and settled in to wait for his friends.

Hilda, the waitress, poured him a cup of coffee, petted Brutus, then set the pot on the table.

"I'm going to miss you all coming in for coffee and to visit with your friends," she said, "especially your daughter. She's so clever and such a nice person. I've always been amazed at how much she knows about things, seeing as how she can't see and all. It's not like she went to school or anything."

The bell over the door tinkled and she turned away to greet new customers, leaving him to think about Greta again. She was amazing, and he liked to think he had a part in it.

Before Mary died, Greta was one of a circle of people around him. He was concerned for her and committed to finding ways he could help her get along in the world, but she was just one of many things and people around him. Suddenly she was the only thing in his life that mattered, and this led him to seek new ways to help her cope with her disability.

He had read of Denis Diderot, a Frenchman, who wrote how the blind could learn to elevate their other senses and so compensate for the loss of the one.

Using that as a guide of sorts, Greta and he had begun a pattern of living where he read to her every night after dinner and chores, whether in the wagon or wherever they happened to be. In the three years they had been on the road, he had read her almost every book that passed through his hands and answered her constant questions about them.

To help her develop her mind, he would ask her about things they read days before and was amazed at how retentive her memory was. She not only remembered things but understood them, and her grasp of complicated ideas and concepts amazed him time and again.

He also asked her how things felt or tasted or smelled, trying to help her develop her other senses. It was gratifying how much she had grown in the three years they had traveled, and he was constantly reminded how proud of her he was.

She had a peculiar way of listening when he read to her. She would cock her head so her right ear was toward him and sit very straight in her seat with her chin lifted and thrust forward. When she sat that way, he knew she was focused intently on what he was saying, and he would remember to make the book or idea the topic of a future conversation as they whiled away the hours riding in the wagon.

Because she was not born blind but lost her sight in an accident at age eight, she had visual memory of many things, and he always tried to help her use those memories by describing the country they passed through so she could paint a picture on her mind and file it away to be recalled at will.

Though there were not many hours when he didn't miss Mary and what she had brought into his life, he was happy now and felt he and Greta had forged a new life, one Mary would have been happy to be part of.

He had missed Greta on the trip across the desert. She had come west on the cars from Salt Lake City with Annaliese and her father, and since they had been in Hangtown Crossing, he had only seen her occasionally. He was proud of the way she learned her duties at the clinic but missed their time together and felt a little resentment at the people she spent time with now, even though that time was a good thing for her and her future.

She was growing up and that meant one day soon she wouldn't need him so much. She would look to someone else for her happiness and security, and it made him sad and a little jealous.

It was beginning to look like Jed was the thing he was most worried about. He liked the boy and appreciated the part he might play in their future, but sometimes when he saw him for what he was, a rival for his daughter's affection, he remembered his resentment. Now he quickly pushed it to the back of his mind and stood to greet them as they came in the door.

Chapter Two

Johnny Fry had decided he liked being married. Since he and Annaliese had gotten married just a month before, he found all sorts of benefits he had never thought about. Like waking up and seeing first thing her beautiful red hair shining in the morning sun, or the taste of a pink tipped breast before breakfast, or the fact he could touch and feel and taste her whenever he wanted. Then there was the warm, moist time when the world disappeared, and everything was good; that was best.

As for this last one, he tried to arrange it before breakfast that morning but had been reminded of a breakfast date he had with his friends, and her need to go to work. Of course, tomorrow morning there'd be time. He was going away for a couple of weeks, and they'd need to before he left, maybe twice.

On the morning after their wedding, they stood by the bed, locked in an embrace after a long kiss, and vowed to begin every day with just such an embrace.

This morning, they stood in the small kitchen of their small rental house, looked into each other's eyes for a time, and after the promised embrace and an ardent kiss, he decided to try again. No luck, and within five minutes he was being pushed out the front door to begin his day.

Jinx was a small black cat who was also a part of this new life. He didn't understand some of it but seemed to accept the changes around him without much of a problem. He had traveled across the country with Johnny and was now riding on his shoulders as he walked down the main street of Hangtown Crossing.

Everyone who knew Johnny Fry knew Jinx. From his birth, the rant of a litter born in the hayloft of Fry's Livery Stable in Junction City, Kansas three years before, to his presence at the Justice of Peace's office when Johnny got married a month before, they were seldom far apart. Fortunately, Annaliese accepted this and was perfectly fine having him in the middle of her life. Actually, she tolerated Jinx, as he did her, to keep Johnny happy.

The livery stable was on the way, so he stopped to pay his bill, and when he came out onto the street again, there were two horses and a mule tied next to the clinic wagon at the little café down the street. That meant his friends, people who had come into his life at various times in the last year, were there waiting for him. Five left Salt Lake City with him in March and he could see four of them drinking coffee at the front window table.

The horse belonged to Jason, and the mule was Wash's. The mule's name was Master, and the irony wasn't hard to figure. George Washington Moore was born a slave on a rice plantation in South Carolina, 45 or so years before; he wasn't sure exactly of the date. He felt nice riding Master instead of master riding him.

He reached up to scratch Jinx's ears. "I'd say your buddy Brutus is here. Think you two can keep out of trouble till we get through?" Jinx jumped onto the hitch rail and to the boardwalk and waited for Johnny to open the door. When he pulled out a chair, the cat was already rubbing up against the bulldog in greeting.

"Morning boys," he said. Jason Redbird grinned at him and jerked his head at Lemuel and Wash, who were arguing over the best way to lubricate the sliding doors on the wagon. Jason was unusual among Indians because he smiled and laughed more than most. They all got a kick from the way Lemuel and Wash bickered over the wagon.

"Before we start talking," Johnny announced, waving an envelope, "we got a letter from Rebecca yesterday. She says they're fine and getting used to Saint Louis and the show. They are probably on their way to Chicago by now. According to her, Handy dresses up in buckskin with sequins and wears a ten-gallon cowboy hat during the show."

They all laughed. "Just what he needs," said Wash, "something to make him look taller."

Handy, whose full name was Hansford Robert Josephson, was the other member of the company. He was blonde, broad shouldered and six feet eight inches tall. He and his wife, Rebecca, had recently joined William F. Cody's Wild West Extravaganza and Congress of Rough Riders, and were currently on a tour of the country and getting paid for it.

"If you want to read the letter, here it is, but I warn you, it's mostly women talk." He tossed it on the table and looked around at everyone.

Except for the fifteen-year-old Jed Travers, at nineteen, Johnny was the youngest of the group, but for some reason he had never been able to understand, they saw him as their leader. Now he cleared his throat, and everyone looked at him.

"It looks like everything is ready and we should be ready to go in the morning," he said. "The plan is for us to meet at the clinic, pick up Greta, say goodbye to everyone, and be on the trail by about ten o'clock." He looked at Lemuel. "Are you going to need help getting ready?"

"Wash and Jed are going to stay over with me to help, and we should be there right on time," he answered.

The clinic had been open for just two weeks and setting it up was the reason Annaliese and her father had come to Sacramento. The new doctors and nurses were ready to take over and Dr. Crawford had left the day before, glad to be getting back to his little hospital in Salt Lake City.

The road running south out of Sacramento passed close by the clinic and was also the route to Stockton, about fifty miles south. There they would swing west to pass around the south end of San Francisco Bay and then north on the peninsula to San Francisco.

The route around the bay was chosen because Lemuel didn't want to trust his precious wagon to a boat when there was another way to get there. His memories of problems crossing some of the great rivers of Virginia during his time with Sheridan's Cavalry during the War had soured him on boats and large bodies of water.

Johnny had decided to turn north at Fremont on the east side of the bay and head to Alameda, where he would catch a ferry across the bay to the terminal at San Francisco. He would get there several days before the wagon and he planned to have the books delivered from the train station and uncrated before the others arrived.

Greta would have to do most of the work arranging them on the shelves so she would be able to find them at need. If all went as planned, they should be open for business by the end of July.

Johnny grew up above a livery stable in Junction City, Kansas, and while working with his father learned to work with leather and guns. Now he wanted to add a leather goods store and gun sales and repair shop to the bookstore. But that would come later, after the bookshop was up and running.

The second floor of the store was a small apartment where they planned to live until they could find the quarters they needed. It would be a little crowded, but since it was for just a short time, they figured to tough it out.

Johnny awoke the next morning with mixed feelings about leaving. On the one hand he was always excited about traveling to someplace new, having new experiences and meeting new people. On the other, he had no desire to be away from Annaliese for two or three weeks or at all, for that matter.

He turned on his side and Jinx came to lie against his chest. This was something they did every morning. Jinx would crawl up against his chest and lie there and Johnny would love and pet him and feel the rumbling purr and heat from the little black body.

Next, they'd race to the outhouse, Jinx leading the way, and on the way back complain about not having indoor plumbing, Jinx as loud as Johnny.

When they got back Annaliese was usually awake, and they'd discuss how the place they rented in San Francisco would have indoor plumbing.

Their embrace this morning was especially long and warm.

"I'll miss you, ya know?" he said looking into her green eyes. He began to count the freckles on her nose with his tongue, then kissed one eye and then the other.

"What will you miss?" she asked, her head on his shoulder.

"All sorts of things," he answered," but mostly standing here in the mornings and looking at you, knowing we're married and can do this every day for the rest of our lives."

She lifted her head and looked into his eyes.

"I sure am glad you fell off your horse and landed in my hospital," she said with a grin. "Now let go of me so we can get going. We've a lot to do today."

Black, his big black gelding, was saddled and ready for him. He tied his bed roll on behind the cantle, lifted Jinx onto the saddle, grasped the mounting strap and pulled himself up. Black was a tall horse, and Johnny needed an assist from the strap to get aboard.

Annaliese turned her wagon toward the city and the clinic while he aimed for the rendezvous with his friends.

He could see them coming down the street, four outriders and the wagon. The number puzzled him for a minute, until he saw the extra rider was his Uncle Bill riding alongside the wagon talking to Lemuel, who held the reins.

Bill met him with a big smile and a handshake. "I'm glad you came. Hope you realize you'll always have a place in my home," he said. "I'll ride a ways with you. I have to stop at city hall about a bid for a bridge the city wants me to build."

A little farther on he stopped and said, "here's where I leave you." To Wash and Lemuel he said, "You two fellows ever need a job, you got one at the Yard. I like the way you work together." So saying, he rode off with a wave.

Chapter Three

Annaliese Fry shook water from her hands and dried them on a towel. Already she had seen five patients, and it was only nine o'clock. It looked like it would be a long day.

There was a soft knock on the open door of her office, and she looked up to see Greta standing there.

"Can I talk to you for a minute?" she asked.

"Shut the door and have a seat," Annaliese replied, and the girl came in and found the chair without fumbling. She sat silent for a minute, so Annaliese asked, "What did you want to talk about?"

Greta hesitated and blushed noticeably. She mumbled something, cleared her throat, and finally said, "I want to ask you some things about being married."

Annaliese smiled and then, realizing Greta couldn't see the smile, asked, "Are you thinking about getting married?"

"Well yes, I guess I am," she replied, "and I know you'll tell me I'm too young, but I'll be fifteen this month and that's not so very young." She hesitated for a moment and continued. "You see, I never thought I'd meet someone to marry or to fall in love with, but I have, and I want to find out about it so I have an idea what to expect if it happens, we get married." This last came in a rush as though she knew what she wanted to say and had to get it out before she lost her nerve.

Annaliese didn't say anything for a moment. Instead, she sat thinking about how and how much to answer this pretty blonde girl who would never see the man she loved.

"Jed?" she asked.

Greta nodded her head and smiled. "Yes Jed. Of course. Who did you think?"

"Well, it's possible you've got someone locked up in the barn." They both laughed.

"I think he loves me, but he's shy and won't come out and say it. But he treats me the way I've heard you treat someone you love."

"How do you feel about him?"

"I think it's love although I don't know what it feels like. I mean, I love Papa, but I don't feel these things about him."

"What things?"

Greta took her time answering. "Whenever he's around I get out of breath really easy, and I feel like I'm blushing all the time. When we touch each other accidently, I feel a shock." She stopped for a minute and then went on. "And I feel funny down there, you know, between my legs, whenever I think about him."

This last she mumbled with her head down.

"Well, it sure sounds like love to me," said Annaliese. "So, what is it you want me to tell you?"

"I don't know what to do about it. I just want to grab him and kiss him or hug him or something, but I don't know what's OK and what's not."

"From what I know of Jed you'd probably scare him to death if you did those things to him out of the blue," said Annaliese. "Do you ever hold hands?"

"We have twice. We were by a creek in Salt Lake City, and he took my hand so I would be safe and once when it snowed and it was icy, he helped me down some stairs."

Annaliese looked out of the window and said slowly, "you want to know about lovemaking? Is that it?"

"Yes." The word shot out of her, and she blushed a deep red.

"You see, I've heard women talk about it when they didn't think I was listening, and most of them talk about it like it's something they don't like but do because it's part of being married and having families."

She paused for a moment and seemed to sit up straighter." When I'm around you and Johnny, I can tell you really like that part of it, and I guess that's what I want from it, but I don't have any idea how to go about it." She giggled. "Sometimes I can hear you two when I'm in the backyard hanging clothes and it sure sounds like you're having fun."

It was Annaliese's turn to blush and then she laughed. "Well, it is fun," she said. "In fact, it's more fun than anything, especially with someone you love. Of course, I've only done it with two men, and I loved them both, at least I thought I loved the first one."

Through the window they heard voices, the sounds of the wagon stopping in front of the clinic, and of men dismounting.

"Let's do this," Annaliese said, getting up, moving around the desk and taking Greta's hand. "I'll be coming to San Francisco not long after you get there, although Johnny doesn't know, so keep it to yourself. When I get there, we'll go somewhere and sit and talk. Then I'll have some time to figure out how to handle this, so I get it right. Can you control yourself and not jump on him until then?" she asked with a chuckle.

Greta smiled. "I think so, but it's not easy." She paused. "I asked Papa about talking to you and he said it was a good idea. I'm glad I did." She followed Annaliese out to greet the men in front waiting to say goodbye.

The first town they passed coming out of Sacramento was Elk Grove, and the thing they noticed right away was it didn't smell. They had gotten so used to the odors from the river in the capital city they ceased to notice. Now, fifteen miles south, the air was fresh and clean. They breathed deeply and cursed the mine owners whose filth defiled something beautiful just so they could make themselves a little richer.

They camped for the night south of Elk Grove and enjoyed the cool of the evening. The day had been hot, and everything seemed to droop from the heat and humidity.

"It feels damp because we're getting close to some of the rivers of the delta," said Wash. "The San Joaquin River runs west of here and there's a bunch of small streams feeding it running east to west. We'll have to cross some of them, but some we can go around." He drew deeply on his pipe and blew out a cloud.

"Tomorrow, we get into some marshy country, and with the heat and all, we'll probably run into clouds of skeeters. No way around it so we just have to keep moving at a good pace so they can't keep up."

"If you stop, look out. I've seen a man's arm from elbow to wrist covered so's you couldn't see the skin in less than a minute. And they'll drive a horse crazy, so he'll start to run."

He gestured toward the wagon. "That could be a problem, as slow as it is. I'd say we harness all the horses in the morning and once we begin to see them, push as fast as you can. The skeeters will probably last for ten or fifteen miles or so. Then the ground rises some and we won't see so many."

The next morning, they started early, planning to take a break after they got to the higher ground. But first they had to get through the bugs.

Johnny couldn't really imagine it would be a real problem, but that idea faded when they encountered the first cloud and he saw Wash hadn't exaggerated. There seemed to be millions of them, and they all seemed to come after him.

He quickly lifted Black into a gallop, and with Jinx holding on to the saddle horn with all claws, fled the area as fast as he could, both for his sake and for the horse's.

From behind him he heard Wash yell, "no use trying to swat them; just ride."

The wagon lumbered along behind, team straining at the traces, but was quickly outpaced. Lemuel had buckled it up as tight as he could and with the effort of the horses he seemed to get ahead of the worst of the horde.

By the time they all gathered on a low hill after crossing several small streams, the team was sweat-covered and blowing, and they were all covered with bites.

Greta had been riding behind Jed and had the fewest, but Lemuel's hands and face were covered with red splotches. Wash soaked them in vinegar, and it seemed to help for a while, but the itching returned.

Wash alone came through with almost no bites. He grinned at the rest of them and said, "either my skin is too tough, or they don't like the way I taste. Whichever is fine with me."

"Now I know what it's like," Lemuel remarked, "I think I could get through better if we have to do it again. Gloves and scarves would have helped."

They rested in the shade until evening, then took to the road again and stopped for the night several miles short of Stockton. Although Jinx rode with Johnny most of the time, occasionally he would jump on the wagon seat to visit with Brutus.

Stockton, California was founded in 1849 because its location at the head of navigation on the San Joaquin River made it a natural place for a supply depot for the mines that lay to the north. It was supposedly the first town in California to have a name not Mexican or Indian. Though at ten thousand or so people it was half the size of Sacramento, it was spread out along the river, so it took a while to get through. South of town the trail began swinging to the west toward the south end of San Francisco Bay.

They quickly fell back into the routine that marked their first trip as a company across the desert from Salt Lake to Carson City. All accepted the idea there were things that needed doing and set about doing them. It was assumed Lemuel would do the cooking and the rest of them would rotate among all the other chores. With Greta along, the cook didn't need an assistant like before, so they would miss out on the little treats that were part of the job. Jinx was Greta's assistant, so he and Brutus still made out.

Wash, on the other hand, was the scout, riding ahead to see what they faced round every curve or over every hill. Their nights were usually safe and comfortable because he had done his job.

Though they were all part of the circle round the campfire at night, it was accepted Greta and Jed were a little apart. Most nights they would find somewhere to walk by themselves and somewhere to talk, and he would answer her questions about what he could see and what they could hear.

Once, during their time in Salt Lake City, Johnny suggested Jed write her a letter and read it to her. He liked the idea and spent the intervening several months composing, rewriting, and correcting one.

Finally, it dawned on him that it didn't need to be perfect, and he was just afraid, so that evening, he took a deep breath, and began to read.

"I don't know what I'm supposed to do when I want to tell you how I feel, so I'll just tell you, and if I make any mistakes, don't be mad at me. I think about you most of the time. I believe you are special, and I would never find anyone nearly so special no matter how long I looked. When I wake up in the morning the first thing I think about is you and when I see you, I know it's going to be a good day."

"I'm not sure what love is but I think I love you."

"If you feel the same about me, I believe we should get married and spend the rest of our lives together."

"If your answer is yes, I will ask Lemuel tonight and we can get married whenever you wish."

While he read this to her, she was sitting on a blanket in a clearing by a little stream. She sat very straight with her head cocked a little to the right and said nothing for a moment and then said, "Would you like to kiss me?"

"Yes," he breathed, "but I don't know how to go about it."

"I don't either. Maybe we could learn together."

Chapter Four

George Washington Moore, Wash to his friends, sat on the big ornery black mule he'd named Master, and surveyed the view of San Francisco Bay in the distance. At the foot of the hill where he sat, he could see the trail coming down from the north and the joining where it met the one they were moving west on. Here's where Johnny would leave them and head north to Alameda and the ferry to cross the bay. Wash was a little nervous about the trip round the bay and hated to see someone as handy with a gun as Johnny ride away when they might need him on the week-long journey up the peninsula west of the bay.

The City by the Bay had a long history of rambunctiousness, and though law had come to the city itself, there were still places along the approaches to it where bad men rode and tried to steal what they could get away with. The wagon was a likely target, and with Johnny gone, it would be his job to get the company there safely. He felt the weight of responsibility a little more heavily on his shoulders than usual. On the other hand, he'd learned early in life he could only play the hand dealt him, so he was resigned to handle it the best he could.

He was born a slave on a rice plantation in the low country of South Carolina. He was not sure when, but believed he was about forty-five, and he had lived a lot in those forty-five years.

In New Orleans with a trader in 1862, he was waiting to be sold at a slave market when the Yankees came to town. Shortly thereafter he joined the Union Army, fought with Grant and Sherman throughout the War, and later became a Buffalo Soldier and served on the western frontier.

In 1874, when he mustered out, he came to the mountains of the west and spent the next ten years roaming them with one group of men or another. He was at loose ends in Casper, Wyoming when he was somehow drawn to the two young men passing through who seemed to need his help. Since then, he had traveled with them, and it just seemed natural to keep doing so.

Though he planned to help them with the journey and the bookstore, he had his own reasons for wanting to go to San Francisco and they mostly revolved around Woman.

Her name was Woman. She had come to the city from Australia with her father and two older brothers and helped them establish and work a claim on a creek north of Sacramento in 1849.

When her kin were all murdered by claim jumpers, she was left alone and gradually worked her way back to San Francisco where he met her several years before.

Life was hard for a while, but she established a friendship with a woman of means, Hannah by name, and began working for her. With Hannah's assistance, she lived a good life in a small cabin on one of the hills overlooking the bay.

In the camp after her family was killed, she found herself the only woman among eighty or so men and began to dress in pants and overlarge shirts, wear men's boots and carry a Bowie knife in a sheath behind her back

The knife had dripped blood more than once before they learned to leave her alone. Though there was no longer any need, she continued to dress in her peculiar way and carry the Bowie and didn't hesitate to use it when she felt the need.

It was in the camps she was first called The Woman, and she clung to the name to mark herself as different and dangerous. Men soon learned she was that and unpredictable too. She chose a man but would not let herself be chosen, as though she reserved the right to decide.

She was striking looking rather than beautiful; short, stocky built with bright blue eyes, long dark hair, a large sharp nose, and dark skin she acquired working in the sun panning for gold she never found.

Wash had met her three years before and was anxious to see her again. For some reason he never figured it out, she was attracted to him, which was unusual. Not an attractive man, he was very black with white hair and a leathery skin from working the rice fields in the broiling low country sun as a young man.

He was born with a twisted spine and was short and stocky with a large chest and shoulders, very bowed legs and an unusual gait that involved swinging his body forward when he took a step with his right leg.

Years before, in a fight with another slave, he had been slashed with the point of a needle-sharp dagger and the scar ran from above his left eye across his mouth to his right jaw just below the ear. He almost lost the eye and there was a cream-colored line across his face and lips where the skin had peeled back. He once heard a learned man use the words 'grotesque looking' to describe him and though he didn't know exactly what it meant, he knew it wasn't handsome.

Though Woman was in her middle fifties, she had a strong sexual appetite, but only with some men. With him she seemed insatiable and though he had a little trouble keeping up, he loved trying. Though the Lord hadn't been kind to him in most ways, he had one large advantage, and she loved to play with it, kiss it and use it until she tired.

He could see the wagon lumbering along the road below him and rode down to join his friends.

Three days later Wash was scouting the back trail of the wagon when he came across fresh tracks of someone who seemed to be interested in the company. The tracks led to one promontory after another, each one with a view of the wagon and the route they were traveling. Finally, they led off to the north and he followed, careful to stay far enough behind to be out of sight.

It was evening when he smelled their smoke, and moving carefully forward, heard conversation among several men squatting around a fire. Listening, he soon realized he and his friends were the subject being discussed and this group outnumbered his by more than a few.

Pulling carefully away, he rode swiftly back to where camp was set up for the night.

"These fellows are after what's in the wagon, and they've got some ideas about what it is and aim to have it and the woman too." He looked at Greta and then Lemuel. "There's only one thing this kind understands. If we make them pay with enough blood, we may get out of this. We need a plan."

Lemuel spoke for the rest. "Tell us what you think's best and we'll do it," he said.

Wash was quiet for a full minute, thinking.

"They figure you aren't going anywhere fast with this wagon," he said, "so they won't be in a hurry which means we've got time to get ready."

He lit his pipe and sat down on a log near the fire. When they were all seated around him, he began. "We've got a half-moon so we can see to travel, especially going back where we've already been. The place where we nooned today would be a good spot to wait for them. We'll park the wagon close to the rock wall on the other side of the creek so they can't get around behind us too easy."

"If I counted right, we're outnumbered about ten to the four of us. Jason and I will be in those rocks. When the show starts, we can likely lower the odds a bit or I'm no judge." He drew on his pipe and blew a thin stream out while he sat thinking.

"Lemuel, it's your wagon, what do you figure's the best way to handle it?"

Lemuel sat looking at the dirt between his legs where he was drawing circles with a stick. Finally, he looked up. "We've had some situations in our travels, and I've always sat on the front seat with the twelve gauge in my hands and talked to them. Only twice did I have to use it, but it sounds like this may be one of those times."

"I'd say that's right," replied Wash. He looked around the circle. "Make no mistake, these men will do whatever they want to you if you let them. The only way to stop them is shoot to kill, and with the odds as they are, we need to empty some saddles at the start of it."

"The safest place for Greta is in the wagon box," said Lemuel. "It's got enough oak around it to stop most bullets, so I want her in the wagon. Let's put Jed in there with the ten-gauge and let him use one barrel on the first face he doesn't know who opens the door. Then reload and wait. Maybe by then the price will be too high for them and they'll leave; maybe not. Either way, I'll be on the seat with the twelve gauge, just like always."

He looked at Jed. "Ever fire it?" he asked, indicating the ten-gauge shotgun. Jed shook his head. "If you do, make sure the butt is tight in your shoulder as it can be, or the recoil is liable to break it."

Looking at Lemuel, Wash said, "You know you'll be a prime target if anything starts."

It was a statement, not a question. "This is my home and she's my daughter," Lemuel replied.

Chapter Five

They came out of the woods the next morning a little after dawn, a file of men spread out into a skirmish line of sorts; four men in the front rank, six more behind. Ten to four, just like Wash said and the formation showed some among them had likely been in the army.

When they came close enough, Lemuel could see them looking around. They had been told there were others but all they could see was him, a dried-up old man sitting on the seat of a large wagon holding what looked like a shotgun across his lap.

Lemuel smiled to himself. The leader was obviously the one in the middle of the front rank just like in the army. He shifted the twelve gauge in his hands so it pointed directly at the head man's chest. The fellow didn't like this, and he reigned his horse a little left. The twin barrels followed him.

"How can I help you gentlemen?" asked Lemuel with a smile.

By then they had all reigned in and sat waiting for the boss to speak.

"Where are your friends?" he asked. "Bob here tells us there were four or five of you last night."

"We'd kind of like to know what you got in the wagon," he continued when Lemuel sat silent. "With those deep tracks you leave, we figure it's something valuable, maybe gold or coin."

"My daughter and I are traveling to San Francisco to open a

bookstore. All that's inside are supplies for living and traveling. And a few books." He paused and added, "The wagon leaves a deep track because it's heavy, not because of what's inside it" he added after a pause.

"We'd like to check for ourselves and maybe meet this daughter of yours."

The cocking of the double hammers was loud in the still morning air. "Mister there's a Sharp's fifty, a seventeen shot Henry and a Winchester aimed at you right now." Lemuel's voice was calm. "Now, I heard Phil Sheridan say once there's a time to talk and a time to shoot. If you take one step towards the back of this wagon, I'll blow you right off that horse."

The bandit's horse shied sideways. "You be careful with that thing, old man," the man yelled and made to draw his gun.

About that time Brutus came on the scene. He had been shut inside, but the year before Lemuel cut a door in the floor where the puppy could go out. Brutus had somehow gotten it open and now exploded from under the wagon, growling, snarling, and snapping at horses' heels. The horses went wild, bucking, twisting and crow hopping.

Out of the corner of his eye Lemuel saw a man reach for his gun. He pulled one trigger, saw the leader's chest dissolve into a bloody mass and swung toward the man who had drawn. Too late. The bullet hit him in the shoulder. He heard the boom of the Sharps and suddenly there was gunfire all around. He felt another bullet strike and fell backward off the seat.

The pain in his shoulder woke him. There were hands lifting him and it hurt. Even with pain shooting bolts through his right side he realized it was quiet. No gunfire. That meant it was over, but what happened? He lifted his head, which made the pain worse, and felt someone lifting his shoulders while Jason lifted his legs. They were moving him onto a bed in the wagon.

When he opened his eyes again Wash was bending over him tearing a piece of cloth into strips.

When he realized Lemuel was conscious again, Wash said, "I've got to stop the bleeding and to do it will likely hurt you some more. This bullet went through, but you also got one in the hip that didn't. It's not bleeding so bad so it will have to wait. We should be close to San Mateo in the morning so we can get you to a doctor and get that slug out of your hip.”

“What happened out there? And when?” he managed to mumble.

“They decided what was in the wagon wasn’t worth it after all, so they left. Those of them able to, that is. If I counted right, they left five on the ground and two rode away with lead in ‘em,” replied Wash. “We’ll talk later. I don’t want you to get excited and get to bleeding again. Lie back and rest. We’ll have you to a doctor by morning. We’ll have plenty of time to talk.”

He blew out the lamp and Lemuel fell asleep feeling the wagon moving beneath him.

Chapter Six

Johnny had seen it before, but when he stood on the dock in Alameda and looked at the lights of the city across the bay, it still took his breath away. He had left the wagon the day before and was now anxious to get across the water to get on with what he had to do.

"Ferry leaves at 6:00 AM sharp," said a man's voice behind him. He turned and could see the sailor's cap outlined against the lights of Alameda behind him. "It's probably best to get your duffel aboard tonight so you can just jump on in the morning."

Johnny looked at him for a moment. "And if I'm late in the morning?" he asked.

The man chuckled, "It'll be waiting for you on the pier in Frisco, of course."

"I'll do my best to be on time," Johnny replied.

The man turned and matched strides with Johnny back along the pier.

"Name's Jim Steyer. I'm the first mate on the ferry." He held out his right hand and Johnny shook it as best he could.

"Johnny Fry," he said. "Hurt my arm last year. Used to be right-handed but had to switch."

"I saw you in the dining room at the hotel. Your holster looks a little different than most. You make it?" asked Steyer.

"Yeah. I do some leather work and when I had to switch hands, thought I'd try something new." He patted the canted holster on his left hip. They walked on for a while. "So far it's worked out pretty good."

They climbed the steps to the hotel porch. "I'm going to have a drink." Steyer nodded toward the saloon next door. "Care to join me?"

"Don't think I will. Too many bad things happen in saloons" said Johnny. "Figure I'm better off if I stay out of them."

Steyer stood looking at him a moment and then chuckled. "Sounds like good advice. If I followed it, I'd surely be richer than I am and have fewer scars." He laughed and slapped Johnny on the shoulder. "See you in the morning."

If Steyer noticed Jinx on his shoulder, he hadn't commented. Now Johnny leaned over a chair and the cat hopped down and led the way into the lobby of the hotel.

The next morning, carpet bag in hand, bread and cheese in his pocket from the hotel kitchen, and cat on his shoulder, Johnny watched Black loaded onto the ferry and was the first passenger over when they put down the gangway.

Jim Steyer was on the bridge and waved a hand. He leaned over the rail. "Best be careful with the cat. If he goes overboard, he's lost," Steyer called down. "The captain won't stop for him."

Johnny raised his hand and said, "He stays pretty close to me, so I won't worry too much."

They found a spot on one of the long benches that lined each side of the boat, dropped the carpetbag, and stood at the railing watching the ferry get ready to depart.

He nuzzled Jinx. "What say Little Buddy, feel like a swim? I hope not, cause I don't swim so good." He could feel the claws get a little tighter through the leather vest he usually wore when the cat was on his shoulder. "Guess not, huh?"

They remained at the rail until the ferry was underway, then returned to their seats.

"Is this one taken?" The speaker was a tall man in his forties with silver hair and a smile showing all his teeth.

Johnny gestured and the man sat down, squeezing in next to a young lady.

"This your first trip to our fair city?" he asked.

"No, I was here a few weeks ago with some friends. We were

looking for premises for a store we want to open," replied Johnny.

"I'm a storekeeper myself," he responded. "Did you find a place?"

"Yes, we did, as a matter of fact. On Chestnut Street on the corner of Scott. It's a few blocks from the bay," said Johnny.

"Well, what do you know? My store's on Chestnut, at Pierce, about three blocks down from there." He held out his hand." My name's Frazier Knobloch. I'm a greengrocer and in dry goods. It's not the best location, but we do alright. What about you?"

"Books," said Johnny, "and a couple of other things. We won't be competition for you."

"That's just great," he said. He seemed to be one of these fellows who was enthusiastic about everything and enjoyed talking. "Opened up a couple of years ago and just last year brought my wife and daughter out on the cars all the way from Boston.

"When do you plan to be open?" he asked.

"We've got the books and supplies at the train station. Tomorrow I'm going to have them delivered, and we'll go from there. Shouldn't take but a couple of weeks to get ready, so I'd say the first week in July. My partner should be here later this week. He's bringing a wagon around the bay from Sacramento."

"Sounds like a strange way to get here, in this day and time, what with the railroad and the ferry and all," said Knobloch.

"He doesn't like boats, and it's a really special wagon he built himself, so he's really careful with it."

During this conversation Jinx was trying to talk the lady next to Johnny out of part of her lunch. After he succeeded, he jumped into Johnny's lap to take a bath.

"Never saw anyone travel with a cat before," commented Knobloch. "With all the rats around here, he'll probably stay pretty busy keeping them out of your stock."

"He's a bit small for rats. Usually sticks to mice," Johnny said.

"Plenty of them around too." An hour later they were standing at the rail watching as the big ferry was maneuvering into its berth, and he was still talking; about the city and his business, about his wife and daughter, and about anything else that happened to cross his mind.

Johnny listened and learned about the city which would likely be his home, for a few years anyway.

Since Knobloch was a frequent passenger, he knew Jim Steyer, and the first mate met them at the gangway.

"I see he's been talking your ear off," he said to Johnny. "He does that, but he means well." He joined them for a cup of coffee at a café on the pier while they waited for Black to be unloaded.

When the big black horse came down the gangway everyone close by stopped and looked.

Steyer whistled. "Wow! He's big. Is he fast?"

"I don't really know," Johnny replied ruefully. "Since I've had him, I've never let him run all out. Tell you the truth, he makes me a little nervous. But he's good natured and I couldn't ask for a better."

"You'll have people around here who'll want you to take him to the track and run him. They're quite a racetrack crowd here. Nearly every week there's something running out at the track. Keep a close eye on him and a lock on the stable, or he could disappear."

It was just after noon when he rode up to the store and dismounted. The door was open. He could hear hammering in the back and saw someone sweeping up sawdust in the front room. As he stepped through the front door, he saw a dress whisk out of sight which looked vaguely familiar. He stood for a moment trying to remember where he'd seen it, and Annaliese walked in carrying a broom and dustpan.

Johnny's mouth fell open and he stood staring, not quite able to believe his eyes.

"Surprise," she said with a smile.

He grabbed her, hugged, and kissed her before she could say another word.

"Trying to catch me with another woman, were you?" he said, and she laughed.

"No" she said, "I didn't see any reason to stay when they didn't really need me, so I decided to come early to help you get things ready."

"When we first saw this place, one of Lemuel's friends said he would get some furniture for upstairs. Did he?" Johnny asked.

"There are two beds and dressers in the big room upstairs and a few other things we will need," she replied.

"Beds?" he said.

"Yes, beds," she replied. She looked at him sternly. "You aren't one of those young fellows who's constantly looking for reasons to get some poor girl in bed, are you?"

"Yup," he said with a leer.

"Well, you can just put that out of your mind, young man," she said. "We have work to do, and besides, there are two carpenters in the back room."

She leaned forward and patted him on the front of his pants. "Later" she whispered, her mouth close to his ear.

Having it on his mind made it difficult to work around other people the rest of the day.

The back room was stacked with crates delivered from the station earlier, and she put him to work opening them and stacking the books alphabetically by category so Greta could begin putting them on shelves when she arrived.

Lemuel had described her method of shelving them so she could put her hand on any one she wanted, any time. He kept a list of every book sold, and she was able to keep track of everything in the inventory as it came and went. Johnny was eager to see how she did it.

The carpenters left early, and it was still light in the sky when Johnny put down the broom, snuck up behind his wife and grabbed her. She struggled playfully for a little and then relaxed, turned to him, and had just begun a passionate kiss when someone knocked on and stuck their head in the open front door.

"Welcome to Chestnut Street," said Fletcher Knobloch, coming in with a smile. "Since I didn't think you'd be up for visitors quite yet we decided to invite you to Mattie's Cafe down the street so you could meet some of your new neighbors."

Annaliese's face was twitching to cover a smile, and Johnny had an exasperated look, but he smiled graciously when he turned to meet his friend from the ferry.

For the next couple of hours, they met the people who would become their friends and fellow merchants on Chestnut Street. Johnny was talking to Mr. Green who owned a livery stable and blacksmith shop across the street from Fletcher's General Store when he noticed a small man sitting with a young fellow near the door. That the man was Chinese was evident by his dress and appearance.

Mr. Green noticed his glance and said, "That's Mr. Li and his son Jimmy. Their family runs a laundry and small restaurant and store here on Chestnut. The boy and his sister live above the laundry. Some people in the city aren't happy they don't live in Chinatown. But they have some friends in our community, and they provide a convenient service, so they are usually left alone."

He paused and continued. "Of course, it helps they rent their place from a rich widow who has many friends at city hall and is not afraid to stand up for them." Johnny nodded at Mr. Li and his son and stepped forward to introduce himself.

"Mr. Li," he said, "I'm Johnny Fry. My partner, Mr. Waters and I will be opening a bookstore here in the next couple of weeks, and we plan to be a participant in all the affairs of business here on Chestnut Street. We will hold an open house when we are ready to begin operations and hope you and your family will honor us with your attendance."

The old fellow nodded slowly, and his son spoke for him. "Though he understands, my father does not speak English well. We will be honored to attend, and we plan to use your business to add to our growing library. Thank you for the invitation."

"We hope we can use your family as a resource to help us learn how to navigate the ins and outs of business in San Francisco," said Johnny. He shook hands with the son. He never did learn the old man's first name. He remained Mr. Li.

Later Fletcher told him a bit more about the Li family. "The back room of the restaurant is a gambling place for Chinese sailors and local Chinese. He also controls a large pool of labor he can use to help anyone he chooses to. He's a good man to have on your side in dealing with City Hall."

"In addition, they run a Chinese Emporium down on the docks that caters to Chinese sailors when their ships are docked here. He has two other sons, but they live and work elsewhere in the city. Jimmy runs the operation here."

"Li is a sharp old fellow," put in Mr. Green. "Not much happens in this city he don't know about."

Fletcher went on. "About dealing with City Hall. Why don't I come by tomorrow and the two of us can sit and talk? It can be a little sticky if you don't know your way around."

"Jimmy looks a little young to be his son. Looks more like a grandson," remarked Johnny, looking pensively at the door where the two men had departed.

"You need to know some of the history of the Chinese hereabouts. A big bunch of them came here to find gold in '48 and '49. Eventually they were too successful and were pushed out of most of the mining camps. Many of them settled here afterwards. Women didn't come with them because most planned to go home with their gold."

"Of course, when they came, there were no Chinese women here. One of the men volunteered to return to China and bring some women back. His fees were paid by the men here and most of the ones who could afford the price were older. Mr. Li, like most Chinese men hereabouts, was a little old when he married. It's like they skipped a generation."

Chapter Seven

"Some of the city's Supervisors run a game where they sell you insurance for protection against potential violence." Fletcher was sitting on one side of a barrel in the back room of the BookSeller and Johnny and Annaliese were on the other.

"And if I choose not to purchase their insurance, what then?" Johnny thought he knew the answer but asked anyway.

"You'll probably get a visit from some of Sunny Jim's bully boys," said Fletcher. "That's the name of the Councilman, Sunny Jim O'Hanlon."

Johnny looked at his wife. She was staring at Fletcher; her mouth open in amazement. Things like that didn't happen in Salt Lake City. The Saints wouldn't have allowed it, and she was surprised it happened here.

"And you pay them?" she asked.

"Every month. We all do. We, meaning everyone on the street and in his ward I guess, although I don't know about Chinatown." He shook his head. "It's probably impossible to figure out who owns what down there. But I bet they pay too, maybe a bit different than us, but they pay."

"By the way if you ever go down to Chinatown for anything, make sure you carry a gun and have someone with you, or else you may not come out in one piece."

"Getting back to this 'insurance' thing," said Johnny, "with

Wash, Jason, Jed, Lemuel and myself, we can handle the bully boys."

"Then they'd find another way to get the message across. Might be broken windows in the middle of the night or an attack on someone around you. I'd keep a close eye on your cat if I were you."

He grinned. "Of course, if I were you, I probably wouldn't have the cat in the first place." He scratched his chin. "Come to think of it, I could probably use a couple to keep the rats and mice out of my fresh stuff."

He went on. "A couple of times they started fires, but it didn't take them long to see that starting them was easier than putting them out. Once they started one, and it burned three city blocks, and if it hadn't started raining, they might have burned the whole damn town, so they don't do that anymore. Mattie, down the street, has only been open a few years on Chestnut. Her first place went up in that fire."

"So, what is the going rate for their insurance?" asked Johnny.

"It seems to vary. But usually, it starts at twenty a month. As business gets better, they'll want more. Someone will stop by after you've been open for a few weeks and give you the sales pitch. After that, a collector will stop by every month. Cash on the barrelhead."

"Anyone ever fight back?" asked Johnny.

"Every once in a while, but they usually realize you can't keep watch twenty-four hours a day. There are too many of the bully boys for the average business to handle. If we could organize, we might do something, but when they hear of such happening, they find a way to break it up."

"From what I've heard, most of the big businesses pay too, and so do the whore houses, gambling halls and opium dens. I guess you can't fight city hall especially by yourself. It's easier to pay than to fight a losing battle."

A couple days later Johnny and one of the carpenters, with Annaliese directing from below, were hanging a sign from the roof of the front porch when they heard a horse gallop up to the store.

When they finished with the sign, Johnny was through the window and down the stairs in a hurry to see Jason standing, dust covered, inside the front door.

Before he could get out a word, Annaliese came out of the back room with her black bag and said, "Lemuel's been shot. Jason left them about three hours south of here. They told him they would stop at the South entrance to the Long Bridge and wait until we got there."

She put her bag on the counter and took Jason's arm. "Let me get you something to eat and drink while he gets the buggy hitched up and his horse saddled."

In anticipation of the coming of the Transcontinental Railroad, the city of San Francisco built the Long Bridge across the marshy land around Mission Bay south of downtown. The idea was to open the area up for what was inevitable industrial growth they could see from the changes happening on the east side of the bay.

For the wagon, heavy as it was, crossing the bridge would be rough on a wounded man and make it hard to keep the wound from opening and bleeding, so Wash pulled it on to a graded parking area at the south end and waited for Johnny and Annaliese. He was in the wagon redressing Lemuel's shoulder when he heard them arrive.

Annaliese was out of the buggy and up the steps of the wagon before Johnny stopped.

He stood near the patch of light streaming from the wagon and listened to Jed and Jason tell him about the fight and how Lemuel had been shot.

"Any of the ones left on the ground still alive?" he asked.

"I didn't have time to check," said Wash, who had come out of the wagon and was sitting on the steps. "Lemuel cut down the leader just when they opened the ball. I figure the man on their side who started things wanted the headman's job. He had to know what Lemuel's twelve-gage would do to him when things got started."

"We needed to get Lemuel to Annaliese as soon as possible, so we left them where they lay. Maybe their friends came back to help them; maybe not. Didn't see it as my problem."

Annaliese stuck her head out of the wagon door and said, "Johnny, you and Jason go back to the store and get everything out of the little room off the front. Get a bed in there from somewhere and have some soap, hot water and bandages handy when we get him there." When she was in that mood Johnny just jumped to obey.

Her head was filled with her patient's needs and everything else was irrelevant.

Though a doctor in San Mateo had removed the bullet from Lemuel's hip, the constant, shuddering jolts over the uneven wooden floor of the bridge made the trip across difficult. However, Annaliese was able to staunch any new bleeding and give him enough laudanum to keep him asleep.

Even though they felt the need to hurry, it was still four hours before he was in bed in the small room they had planned to use for an office.

Later that night Annaliese closed the door to the sickroom behind her and stood leaning against it for a moment to clear her senses. She glanced down at the watch pinned to her dress and saw two o'clock.

When she moved out into the store, she was surprised to see everyone sitting there, apparently waiting for her to come out and tell them what was going on behind the closed door they had been staring at for the last several hours.

"Well," she said, "with the bullet out of his leg, we got the bleeding stopped for now. The wound in his shoulder is in an awkward place to get a tight bandage on, so we had to hold it, turnabout for a while until it stopped seeping blood. Greta and I will take turns sitting with him tonight and I'd like someone out here to give a hand if we need help."

Jed stood up. "I'll volunteer," he said. "I'm too worried to sleep anyway."

Johnny smiled to himself. "And besides it's another way to be around Greta," he thought. He took a deep breath and asked, "So how does it look? Will he be OK?"

Annaliese shook her head. "I have no idea whether he'll live or die right now. All we can do is watch for infection and keep his blood from running out. Whether he'll make it is something we'll have to wait to find out. Eventually we will have to get food and water in him, but not for a day or two."

Wash stood and stretched. "I've got a place to sleep tonight, so I'm going to head over there to try to get a couple hours." He looked around. "Jason, why don't you come with me now so you'll know where it is and can come get me if need be before morning?"

Jason picked up his Winchester and stood ready. Given his experiences with this part of California in the last couple of days, it was easy to see why he wanted it with him when he moved around the city.

After they left and Jed had gone in to sit with Greta, Johnny stood facing his wife. "I have a feeling it will be lonely in our bed for the next little while."

She stepped close and hugged him, stood feeling his heartbeat for a moment. "I'm afraid so, at least for the next couple of days."

He pushed her away and held her at arm's length. "Darn," he said, "just when I'd gotten used to having you there all the time."

She took his hand, and with Jinx leading the way, guided him to the stairs. "Come on," she said. "I'll tuck you in."

Chapter Eight

Johnny didn't sleep much that night and he woke up early, took Jinx on his chest and lay thinking. All the plans they made for the move to San Francisco and opening the store were based on Lemuel's experience and knowledge of the business. He was to guide Johnny through the startup and teach him how to make it work so Johnny could open and operate a store of his own one day.

Now it looked like it was all on him to get things up and running. There was some money in the bank, but it was going out fast and with nothing coming in, it could soon be a problem.

When he sat down for breakfast at Mattie's the next morning, he was anxious to talk to Annalise, but she was with Lemuel.

By the time he finished breakfast he had decided to let her know they needed to talk and right away. He needed someone to help him decide what things needed doing and solve what problems needed solving. He saw her as his savior.

Unfortunately, she didn't see it that way.

"In the first place, I've got to stay focused on Lemuel until he gets out of danger," she said. "And second, I didn't come to San Francisco to help you open a store. I came here to get admitted to medical school and to do what was necessary to become a doctor."

"When we first talked about marriage, I warned you what it would be like. So now we're married but this is your crisis not mine. I will help you as much as I can but right now it's not the first thing on my list of things to worry about." They had been sitting across from one another at the barrel in the back room. Now she stood and looked at him for a moment.

"Johnny you've got friends to help you and you're a pretty smart fellow. If you all put your heads together you can surely figure things out."

He was sitting, looking at her with his mouth slightly open and his brow furrowed, not believing he heard what he had heard. Now he watched her walk to the door of the sick room, stop, and look back over her shoulder. "I'm sorry," she mouthed at him, and disappeared inside.

He sat stunned, staring at the door for a long moment, then shook his head as though to clear it. What did she mean, 'it was his crisis not hers?' he thought. They were married, after all, and he needed her help. He could feel himself getting angry, really angry at his wife for the very first time. He stood up suddenly and Jinx, who was in his lap, hit the floor with a thump.

OK, he was standing up. Now what? What did he need to do next? He wanted to storm into the sick room and confront her, but there was a badly wounded man in there and his bedside was no place to have an argument. He wanted to storm out the front door and walk fast somewhere, but where and why?

After a minute of standing looking through the front door of the store at the sunshine of a pretty morning, he smiled.

"OK, so she was right," he thought.

His Pa always told him, don't decide anything when you're angry, so the first thing he needed to do was to calm down. So, he did what he always did when he needed to think; he picked up Jinx and settled into the only comfortable chair in the place.

He was still sitting there, Jinx asleep in his lap, when Annaliese looked out two hours later.

Since he was now a businessman, Johnny carried a pocket watch with a nice chain stretched across his vest. He looked at the watch now and saw it was a few minutes before Wash showed up with their guest.

It was a week since the patient was installed in the sick room, and they were making good progress on solving the problems of opening the store, though Annaliese still wouldn't let any of them talk business with Lemuel.

"He doesn't need to worry about anything at this point," she said. "Give him another week, or at least a few more days, and then we'll see." When it came to her patient there was no arguing with her, and he had enough sense not to try.

Since his fruitless conversation with her about helping him, he had brought Greta, Wash, Jed and Jason into a discussion about what was necessary to getting the store open and making money, and among them there were enough ideas to move things along pretty well.

Jason had gotten a job working at Mr. John Green's Livery Stable and Blacksmithing Shop down the street, and Jed spent three days walking around downtown to learn his way around the area and so qualify for a part-time job delivering messages. This meant they could pay their own expenses for a while and let him focus on the business.

They agreed to divide the responsibilities of helping with Lemuel and walking Brutus. The demands of the sickroom were enough that Annalise, and especially Greta, needed help in moving him and turning him from side to side.

By this time there was no need to have someone with him all night, but there were still times when his needs kept them up after everyone else was in bed.

With Jed's help, Greta stocked all the shelves and set up a system for keeping track of sales so she would always know what books were on hand.

She also opened Lemuel's business ledgers so they could see how he kept track of income and outlay, and how to go about ordering new volumes and where to get them.

Both Jason and Johnny had a little experience with bookwork at the livery stables where they had worked, and between that and looking over Lemuel's books, were able to set up a temporary system so they could know what was coming in and where it was going.

After the first couple of days Johnny sat everybody down after work and they talked about ideas they had and what they had learned so far about the business of selling books.

Greta was a big help with new ideas. She remembered some ways Lemuel and her mother promoted the business back in Kansas

City. She suggested open houses where they could serve coffee and pastries and have discussions about books or lectures on all sorts of topics.

This led Jed and Johnny to clear out a space by the large bay window fronted on Scott Street and furnish it with easy chairs and tables with lamps where people could sit and read, and a lectern where someone could speak. They spent part of a day tacking up signs around the neighborhood announcing the Grand Opening tomorrow and the first open house the following Thursday.

This meeting tonight wasn't about selling books, though. Wash's friend, Woman, knew a lot about the people in charge and the way things worked in the city. Johnny had invited her, Fletcher and Mr. Li and his son to discuss and decide the best way to deal with a problem they would be facing sometime soon.

"So, tonight is when I meet these friends of yours." Woman was standing in the door to her cottage in a night dress. The light behind her showed all her curves to good advantage. "The ones you followed across half the country."

She came back inside and stood behind him, leaned forward and pressed her breasts into his back. "You sure you wouldn't rather stay here and do something else?" she purred into his ear.

"Lord, Woman," he said, "don't you ever get tired?"

She laughed, and after a minute he did too, and took her in his arms.

"Tell me again how you met them," she said.

"Went into a little café in Casper, Wyoming," he said. "Theirs was the only table with a seat. They invited me to join them. When a fellow objected to me being there with 'the white folks', Handy drew out his pistol and laid it on the table. I've been with them ever since."

She looked at him for a moment then asked, "Why?"

As usual he took his time answering.

"I guess because I can trust them. I mean really trust them; with anything."

She looked at him for another moment, then smiled and slowly nodded her head.

Rather than take her in the front door at the store, he led her into the alley behind. They stabled their mounts and as they walked up to the back door, she grinned at him. "They make you use the back entrance?"

"No, but I feel it's probably best if no one sees you meeting with them," he answered. "Don't want you to have any problems with the bully boys from City Hall."

She stopped and when he turned to face her, she said, "Haven't you figured it out yet? I'm not afraid of them; they're afraid of me."

He looked at her for a moment. "I just bet they are," he said.

Annaliese met them at the door and led them into the storeroom where, somehow, they had rounded up enough places for everyone to sit, even if it was on a box or small barrel. Fletcher came in while introductions were in progress and almost immediately the Li's followed. A young woman with them, and Jimmy introduced her as his sister, Sun Li.

When everyone was seated, refreshments in hand, Johnny began by summarizing their readiness to open and then asked, "So, what information and advice can you give us about operating a business in this fair city?"

For the next two hours they talked. Questions were asked and answered. Woman watched them, making her own judgments about who to trust and how much.

Johnny was the leader, though he was also the youngest, but the one who impressed her the most was his wife. It didn't take long to realize how intelligent she was. She appeared quite a bit older than him and spoke with some authority. The questions she asked made sense and led to more information being exchanged.

"They call him Sunny Jim but don't be fooled by the name," Woman said. "He'll do whatever is necessary to keep this ward and city under his thumb, up to and including murder, if it comes to it. The smile's just an act." She watched their faces while they digested this and went on. "Once you're open for business he'll be around for his cut, you can count on it."

"Has anyone ever said 'no' to him?" asked Johnny.

"Not successfully. The problem is the resistance is scattered and unorganized. The minute someone stands up to him, he comes down on them hard. It's always one man against a bunch of them." She shook her head. "They find out about anyone meeting to organize and then . . ." She shrugged and chopped down with her open palm.

Johnny looked at Mr. Li and asked a question with his eyes. The old fellow nodded and said in a low voice, "The lady is right. These men are dangerous and will not hesitate to injure you and your friends if you oppose them."

"Do you pay?" Johnny asked.

"We pay for the business here ourselves," said Jimmy and the Tongs pay for all Chinatown. It is a cost of doing business here, an informal tax if you will."

Fletcher spoke up. "Everyone on the street pays, more or less, depending on business. We've all thought about fighting, but it's difficult to coordinate with anyone, so that means you stand alone. Most of us have families and we don't want to endanger them or our businesses."

"This is why we pay," said Sun Li. "They would hurt a child or a woman. It's easier to pay than to defend against so many."

"So," said Annaliese. "Is it a strategic decision based on safety? It's better to pay than to fight, especially since you'd likely lose anyway."

All nodded.

"How much are we talking about?" asked Wash. "Is it a fixed amount?"

Woman spoke up. "It varies. It seems to depend on how long you've been in business and how good business is. I'd guess for you it would probably start at about twenty a month. Then they'd watch and see how you do. When they think they can, without driving you out, they'll boost it. The more you've got to lose the more it costs to protect it."

Fletcher interjected, "Sometimes when a business competes with one of their interests, they'll force someone out. I don't think you have to worry about that. Somehow, I can't see them wanting to go into the book selling business."

"There's a man who will probably come to see you in the next week or so," said Woman. "His name is Terrance O'Donnell. He's Sunny Jim's collector in this part of town. He'll let you know the terms, and don't make the mistake of thinking they're negotiable, they're not. Knew a fellow down in the Mission District who tried. Ended up paying more after they broke all his windows one night."

That night in bed, Johnny and Annaliese discussed the whole

situation and agreed paying was the only sensible answer, at least at this time. If there was ever a chance to organize against City Hall, they would lead the charge, but for now, they would pay.

Wash and Woman discussed the meeting in bed and came to the same conclusion.

"She seems to be special," said Woman, speaking of Annaliese. "How old is she? He looks to be about twenty but she's closer to thirty."

"Good guess. He's nineteen and she's twenty-eight. She was his nurse when he had a bad fall from a horse and things just happened from there."

He rolled over to douse the lamp, and as darkness settled over the room he said, "Her father was Johnny's doctor and he taught her a lot about medical things. She's here because she wants to be a doctor and plans to go to school."

"Hmmm," she said, almost to herself. "I might be able to help her with that."

Chapter Nine

Wash was nervous, and that didn't happen too often. Woman came out of the bedroom with her broad brimmed black hat on, sliding the Bowie into its sheath in the back of her belt.

She smiled at him. "Are you ready?"

He nodded and followed her out the door. In the distance, maybe a couple hundred yards away, he could see the lights of 'the mansion' as Woman called it.

It was built in the days after the Gold Rush by a very wealthy man who died several years later, leaving the house and his fortune to Hannah Grimes, his charming wife, also known as 'Madame', with the accent on the second syllable.

She had been the most successful madam in a city with many such ladies and was well off when she married him. She was the kind of woman who wouldn't have married him if she hadn't been.

It wasn't love. They enjoyed each other in bed and enjoyed wielding the power inherent with the money they had but had nothing else in common. When he died, she missed him, but life went on and she was happy without him.

She met Woman one night when she and some friends were out on the town and two men accosted them with robbery on their minds.

Suddenly this short, stocky whirlwind came out of nowhere, Bowie knife in hand. She flicked it across the face of one of the robbers and the other took to his heels and disappeared.

It was only when the figure turned into the light she realized it was a woman. She watched, fascinated, as the woman plunged the knife into some turf to clean the blade then re-sheathed it behind her back.

"Darling, you people shouldn't be in this neighborhood this time of night." So saying, she touched the front of a dark, broad brimmed hat with a single finger and disappeared into the night.

Madame was enthralled. She spent the next few days seeking information about this fascinating person, and when she got it, wrote a polite note inviting the woman to visit her at the mansion.

The next day she met Woman and offered her a job. The offer was accepted, and this was who Wash was going to meet tonight and the reason he was nervous.

"What's the matter?" Woman asked when he stopped at the back stairs and stood looking up at the house.

"Well, we're not really dressed for dinner at a place like this," he answered.

She snorted, "I've eaten meals here with less on than this." She didn't bother to explain this strange remark but came to the foot of the stairs and took him by the arm. "Come on," she said, almost dragging him up the steps.

In the kitchen she said a friendly 'hello' to several people working there, continued into the hallway beyond and up two flights of steps, stopping in front of what was clearly a bedroom door.

She rapped, and momentarily it was opened by a tall man wearing what Wash took to be a butler's outfit, though he couldn't recall ever seeing a butler since he left South Carolina. They passed through a room with the largest bed he'd ever seen in the middle of it, and into a dressing room. Sitting by a bay window overlooking the bay in the distance was a small woman in a dressing gown.

When she saw them, her face broke into a smile and she came toward him with her hands held out. "You'd be George Washington Moore. I'm so glad to meet you at last. Woman has talked of nothing else since you got to town." When she stood, her gown fell open and the leg he saw didn't look like it belonged to a woman of sixty.

She kissed Woman on the cheek and gestured to the two seats at the table in the alcove.

"Won't you join me for some dinner?" When they assented, she turned to the man who admitted them. "Gray, tell Hattie we're ready to eat."

"Will you pour us some wine, Woman dear," she said, and while that was done, she turned to Wash. "I understand you have been to San Francisco before."

"Yes Ma'am. I was through here about three years ago and stayed around for a while." He was almost stammering, disconcerted by his surroundings and by the deep cleavage displayed when she leaned forward to offer him something on a small tray.

"I don't see how you could stand to leave this fascinating woman, but you must have had a good reason".

Woman set a tall glass in front of him. Madame offered a toast. "To absent friends," and drank most of her wine in a gulp.

Wash sipped his, felt it tickle his nose, and watched the two of them talk. Madame's face was filled with warmth and good humor. There were many laugh lines at the corners of her eyes and her behavior toward Woman seemed to be more like a friend than an employee. "How much more?" he wondered.

The two women seemed to have much in common. Both were independent, Woman from the force of her personality and Madame from the wealth she wore so lightly, although he had a feeling she was like this when she ran the fanciest whorehouse in the state.

Looking at Woman he sensed her complete comfort with where she was and began to relax himself. After all, if he did something stupid Madame could just throw him out, not have him arrested. Or could she? Woman had told him of her political friends and her connections with everyone who mattered in the city's pecking order.

"So, tell me about these people you traveled here with. I'm curious to know someone in the book selling business. And Woman tells me one of them is a woman who wants to be a doctor and is here to go to school for it. Is that right?"

By the time he finished talking about his friends, he had drunk two glasses of the bubbly wine and was surprised to feel it affecting him.

"I imagine with his partner recovering he's having a rough time getting his ducks in a row, isn't he? I mean, how old did you say he was?"

"Well, he sat us all down and we talked, and he got some ideas, and he's put it all together, so we'll be opening this next Thursday," said Wash. "His partner's daughter's been a big help getting things set up and ready, and by the way, he's nineteen and a very smart fellow.

"Woman told me about her. She's blind, isn't she, the daughter? How can she help in a bookstore when she can't see?" Her glass was empty again and Woman poured her another. Though she was drinking two to his one, he was woozy, but she seemed unaffected.

"You'd need to meet her to understand," said Wash. "When she and her Papa were traveling to get here, he read to her every night and helped her to train her memory. She can lay a hand on any book in the shop. She put them all on the shelves and can remember where every one of them is. When they sell one, they put it on a list, and she can work each sale into her memory of what's left on the shelves. She really is amazing."

"Sounds like I want to be at this open house you're talking about." She looked at Woman. "Are you free that night?"

"Of course, and I'll bet I can find a fellow to escort us." She grinned at Wash.

"I'd be honored," he said, inclining his head. When he stood to leave a while later, he was unsteady on his feet and needed to use the furniture to get out of the house.

Later in bed his head cleared somewhat, and they talked about Madame.

"She's like me in a lot of ways," said Woman. "She goes for months without a man and then someone from her past will show up and they're in bed most of the time until he leaves."

"That's a lot like you," he said, laughing.

She punched him in the ribs. "You complaining?"

"Not a bit," he said and reached for her.

Later while they were making love she whispered, "I've told her about you."

Wash stopped what he was doing and listened.

"She'd like for you to join us some evening if you're interested."

"Join you for what?"

"Come along and see," she said.

Chapter Ten

Johnny was talking to Wash in the back room when he heard the tinkle of the bell over the door. When he came into the store, Jason was standing by the counter breathless.

"You better arm yourselves," he said. "A gang of toughs has Jimmy Li down at the stable. They're fixin' to hang him."

Johnny turned to Wash who handed him the ten-gauge from inside the storeroom door and picked up his Sharps, always close at hand. Jed was buckling on his gun belt and picked up the Henry.

As they went out the door, Johnny called to Annaliese. "Lock the door and don't let anyone in you don't know. Make sure Jinx is inside." She came out of Lemuel's room just in time to see the last of them go out the door.

"My Winchester's at the stable," said Jason, and he led the way down the street to where they could see torches.

As they approached the livery stable, Johnny motioned Wash and Jason into the loft and spoke in a low tone to Jed.

"You cover my back. Don't let anyone get behind me."

Then he stepped up on the boardwalk and hailed the gang of men crowded around an old oak close by the front of the stable across the street.

"Can I help you gentlemen with something?" His voice rang out and several of the men turned to face him, opening the crowd to where he could see two men trying to work a noosed rope over one of the branches on the oak. To one side, two more men were holding the slumped body of a man he presumed was Jimmy.

"Not unless you want to help us hang this damned Chinaman," said a man standing watching the operation."

"What did he do to deserve hanging?" Johnny asked. He didn't need to hear it, but he wanted to give his friends time to get in the stable loft.

"We were trying to cut off his pigtail and he hurt Charlie there." The man waved drunkenly at another man sitting on the ground holding something against an obviously bloody nose.

Johnny had the ten-gauge cradled in his left arm. Now he moved the two barrels slowly across the crowd and said, "I don't think I'm going to let you do that," and when he cocked both hammers all movement came to a halt.

From the shadow under the tree a man spoke. "Are you going to do that all by yourself with just the popgun?" He stepped out of the shadow and Johnny could see he was not as drunk as the others.

"First off, this is a ten-gauge, loaded with double ought buckshot and second, you don't really think I'd be dumb enough to come down here by myself, do you? Right now, besides this shotgun, there are other guns looking at you."

Several of the men looked around and the drunk one in the middle said, "Aw he's bluffing."

"No, I don't think he is," said the man from the shadows.

"I'd call that a right astute observation," said Johnny with a smile.

"Astute observation?" said the man thoughtfully. "You wouldn't be the fellow who's opening the new bookstore down the street, would you?"

Johnny just looked at him. "Let him go. Now!" he said, and when the two men moved away from him, Jimmy slumped to the ground. Immediately a young girl darted forward from the shadows near the stable and embraced him protectively.

The crowd around the tree began to break up, leaving the man from the shadows and his drunken companion standing alone by where the girl was helping Jimmy.

"We'll be around to see you soon," the drunk said. "We work for Sunny Jim, and he won't like this."

Johnny carefully eased the hammers forward and leaned the

shotgun against the building. He turned to face the two men, pulled his coat back to expose the canted holster and said, "That sounds like a threat. I don't like threats. Maybe we should settle this now."

The man from the shadows put a restraining hand on the drunk. "So, you're a gunnie," he said.

"We know how to take care of them, don't we boys?" the drunk said. He turned to his friends and suddenly seemed to notice they had all disappeared into the dark.

As the two men walked away the man from the shadows said over his shoulder, "There'll be someone by to see you soon."

"Tell him to make sure he's sober," said Johnny to their retreating backs.

By the oak tree, Jason and Jed joined Jimmy and the girl who turned out to be Sun Li, his sister. Jimmy struggled to his feet as Johnny approached.

"I thank you Mr. Fry," he said. "I am in your debt."

"My name's Johnny," Johnny replied "and you don't owe me anything. Just try to be there if anyone's ever trying to hang me." He put his hand on Jimmy's shoulder. "Are you all right? You know my wife's a nurse?"

"I will care for him and get him home," said his sister. She was looking at Jason and she smiled shyly at him. "Thank you, Mr. Redbird. Without your help it might have been too late."

Jason smiled and nodded. "Glad I was there to help."

"Is everything alright? Is Jimmy OK?" asked Annaliese when they came in the front door of the Bookseller. Behind her Jed embraced Greta and she buried her head in his chest.

"Everyone's fine, although if Jason hadn't acted the way he did, we might have had a much different outcome." Johnny replaced the shotgun by the storeroom door and embraced his wife. "But I guess all's well that ends well."

Behind him Wash cleared his throat. "I'd say it hasn't ended. When they tell the story down at City Hall tomorrow, we may find there are still things to deal with."

"What did you do down there?" Greta asked. They were sitting on two upturned boxes in the cluttered storeroom.

"Johnny was holding the ten-gauge and he talked to them,"

replied Jed. "Wash and Jason were up in the loft of the livery stable and Johnny let this bunch know he wasn't alone. They decided to leave, and we came home."

"I know it wasn't as simple as that," she retorted. "What were you doing while this was going on?"

"I was covering Johnny's back, making sure no one got behind him," he said.

"What would you have done if someone tried?"

"I'd have let him know I was there and shot him if I thought he was going to hurt Johnny."

She sat quiet for a while then asked, "Why do men behave this way? Why do there always have to be so many guns and people trying to hurt others?"

"I asked Johnny one time, and he said, 'I don't know, but if the bad guys have guns, we must have them too. Maybe one day it won't be so, but right here, right now, it is.'" Jed paused. "I would do anything to keep Johnny Fry safe," he said. "And if that includes shooting, even killing someone, I will."

She lay awake for a long time in bed thinking about what he'd said.

Woman's thoughts the next morning were the same as Wash's. "From what you said the man in the shadows was Herschel Grieve, one of Sunny Jim's men. Jim might have been sending the Lis a message. It could be he won't take kindly to your interference."

She poured him a cup of coffee, and sat across the kitchen table, frowning at him.

"Johnny felt it needed doing and I agreed with him," said Wash. "Those fellows were bully ragging Jimmy and when he fought back, they were just drunk enough to get out of hand." He looked at her for a moment, his tongue playing across his bottom lip. "You reckon Sunny Jim wanted Jimmy killed?"

"Probably not, likely he just wanted to get his father's attention about something," she replied. "There are many who don't like any Chinese living outside Chinatown, so it's possible Ike and the boys just took it on themselves to teach him a lesson. Maybe Sunny Jim didn't know anything about it, although with Herschel there that ain't likely. Herschel is Jim's eyes and ears, and he don't usually act independently."

"You think there'll be trouble over it?" he asked.

"Just have to wait and see," she replied. "Maybe Jim will want to find out more about you people before he acts. I mean, you all are an unknown quantity, and he usually likes to know what's what before he jumps."

Chapter Eleven

Johnny came in the back door of the store with Jed, took a towel hanging there, wiped the sweat off his head and neck, and handed the towel to Jed. The sun was warm, and they had been practicing with Colts down by the bay. Since he arrived in the city, they hadn't been able to work with the guns much, but after the problem the night before, he thought it might be time to start again. In addition, he enjoyed it, and it was good time to spend with Jed.

The boy seemed to have a knack for it. They would toss pieces of wood into the bay, draw and fire at them until they were shot to pieces, then toss in another. In the two weeks since they had practiced, neither had lost any speed or accuracy.

While Jed joined Greta at the counter, Johnny stopped by the door of Lemuel's room and watched his wife and Wash help Lemuel into an easy chair. Wash had put caster wheels on the chair the day before, and after Lemuel was settled, he moved it to a place by the window.

Johnny watched as his partner sat with his eyes closed, letting his breathing return to normal. There was no blood on the shoulder dressing he could see beneath Lemuel's dressing gown. This was the one so hard to dress properly. But since they had finally stopped the bleeding, healing had begun, and his face already showed better color than yesterday.

Annaliese looked at Johnny and nodded. "Just a little while," she said. "He still gets tired very easily."

Johnny sat in a chair, leaned forward, elbows on his knees, and waited until his friend's eyes were open again. He grinned and said, "Well, day after tomorrow's the big day. We've got everything set up in the store and between notices in the newspaper and placards we've tacked up around town we hope to be busy."

"Greta's been telling me what you've been doing." His usually robust voice was little more than a whisper. "How can I help you?"

"We're getting low on cash, so I need some help from you," said Johnny. "I think we've got enough to open with and to cover most expenses, but it would be nice to have access to some if we should need it in a hurry."

Lemuel's eyes closed momentarily. When he opened them again, he said, "If you can get a lawyer in here tomorrow, I'll sign a power of attorney to Greta, and she can handle it from there."

Johnny glanced at his wife who was watching them like a hawk. "Since we have no idea how much business we'll have the first week," he said, "Greta has helped me put together an order for new books which should allow us to restock so we won't run out of things we need." He reached out to touch his partner's knee. "That is where we miss you the most, but Greta knows enough about ordering to get us by until you're back on your feet."

He looked up at Annaliese hovering behind the chair, lips compressed into a thin line, and decided to bring things to a close. "I think we can get by till then. You just think about getting better, OK? We'll take care of everything else."

Johnny and Greta had furnished the new reading room with chairs, and he and Wash sat and waited for Annaliese to join them.

"He seems to be improving," said Johnny as she sat down. "Any idea how long till he's up and around?"

She looked at them thoughtfully for a moment. "Maybe two weeks. Wash is going to take a kitchen chair and make it into a wheeled chair he can maneuver around, but it will be a while before he's strong enough to handle it."

She sat for a moment chewing on her bottom lip. "We're still not out of the woods. His wounds are healing, but there's still the risk of infection and especially of pneumonia. Until he's up and around we must watch for that. At his age, it's especially a problem and if he gets it, he won't bounce as fast as you did. "

Johnny remembered his own bout with pneumonia and how exhausted he felt just getting up and into a chair. It didn't seem to him he'd bounced fast at all.

Later that afternoon Annaliese was sitting at her desk writing in her diary when Greta knocked on the door.

"What's on your mind?" she asked. Greta came in and deliberately closed the door.

"First, what is a power of attorney?"

Annaliese pushed her diary aside. "Sit here," she said, and the girl reached forward and felt her way into the chair by the desk.

"A power of attorney is a paper signed in front of a lawyer which gives someone the power to conduct the affairs of an injured person or someone who is incapacitated in some way. Your Papa will be telling the lawyer you have control over his affairs until he can handle them himself."

"So, if Johnny needs some money, I can go to the bank and tell them to give it to him?"

"That's right. Johnny will talk to you about the things he would talk to Lemuel about, and you decide what's best for Lemuel's interest."

Greta sat in the way she did when digesting information, then said, "OK, I understand. Now I want to ask you when we can have our talk you promised to have about marriage and all."

"I was wondering when you were going to bring it up," said Annaliese with a chuckle. "I don't want you to think I'm putting you off, but I wanted to think about how to tell you what you want to know. It's the kind of thing a mother usually talks to her daughter about but, since you don't have one of those, I'll do my best to help you."

"Where did you learn about it?" Greta asked.

"I tell you what," said Annaliese, ignoring the question. "Everything is ready for the open house Thursday, and the fellows can keep an eye on your Papa for a while, so let's you and I take a picnic tomorrow and find a place to sit and talk."

"Oh, yes," responded Greta, a little breathless. "I'll get

everything ready. What time?"

"Apparently as soon as possible," said Annaliese with a laugh.

Though Annaliese was comfortable on horseback, Johnny had bought a small sorrel mare named Dolly trained to a buggy and about noon the next day, with a hand from Jason at the livery stable they got in the buggy and were soon on their way into the Presidio.

The Presidio, originally a Spanish possession, came into Mexico's hands after the Revolution, and finally to the United States after the Mexican War. It was a military reservation occupying a large piece of the south side of the Golden Gate and was anchored by Fort Point, a brick-and-mortar fortification built to protect the entrance to San Francisco Bay during the Civil War.

When Annaliese stopped the buggy and led Greta to a good spot to lay the blanket down, they were right above Fort Point in the distance. They set their lunch basket aside and promptly forgot about it.

"Tell me what you see," said Greta, hugging her knees and moving her head to catch a noise she didn't recognize. "What's that noise?"

"It's the ocean waves crashing on the rocks near the entrance to the bay," said Annaliese, "and if I told you what I saw, it would take all day. Let's just say it's the perfect place for two girls to talk about boys."

"Oh good," said Greta, a little breathless again. She sat quiet for a minute, apparently gathering her thoughts. "Remember when we talked in Sacramento and I told you how I felt when I was around Jed?"

"Yes, I remember. You told me how he made you feel funny."

"Well, while we were coming here, we ran into a great swarm of mosquitoes. We had to ride very fast to get through them and away. Wash and Johnny lifted me onto Jed's horse and I rode behind him until we got past the bugs." She laughed. "I'll bet he thought I'd squeeze him to death."

She shook her head. "Anna, I never felt anything like it before. It felt so strange, it scared me. When I finally got down, I couldn't stand up. I was so dizzy and out of breath that Jed had to hold me up for a while."

Greta was still hugging her knees and now she was rocking back and forth. "When I caught my breath, I just wanted to grab Jed but I didn't have any idea what I wanted to do with him."

She was quiet for a moment and then, "I guess that's what I want to talk about. What do married people do when they feel that way?"

"Usually grab each other," answered Annaliese with a laugh.

They sat silent for a minute listening to the waves and then she began. "Making love is about wanting to make the person you love feel good. You do that in different ways, usually by touching or kissing them somewhere it feels good." She paused waiting for Greta to ask a question but when the girl sat silent, she went on.

"What you felt was how people who love each other feel when they want to make love." Again, she waited for a question, but the girl sat mute.

Finally, she asked, "Is that when he puts it in you?"

"Well, sometimes, but there are things you can do to make it feel even better when he does. Things like touching him in places he likes or kissing him where it feels good."

"Is there any place I shouldn't touch him or kiss him?"

Annaliese was a little surprised at the question. "No there isn't, but he might feel shocked if you are too bold, and maybe a little frightened too."

She paused for a moment. "I've only been with two men in my life, and I loved them both, at least I thought I loved the first one, and I guess it's the same thing. When Johnny and I did it the first time I was the one who led the way. He didn't really know what was happening until I showed him." She chuckled at the memory.

"Tell me about the first one," Greta said.

"He was a patient at the hospital. As he got better we talked and he teased me. His name was Jean Paul Moreau, which I always thought was a romantic name. He was French and I thought he was beautiful. I was seventeen and, when he invited me into his bed I didn't think twice."

"He was older, I think about thirty-five and he knew a lot about love making. He taught me and I loved learning. When he got better and left the hospital, he stayed close by and we met at a place he found in the canyon."

"When I look back on it, I am amazed I didn't get pregnant, but I didn't. I haven't with Johnny either. I guess I'm one of those women who can't have children. I'm sad when I think about it sometimes but from a practical point of view it would make becoming a doctor more difficult, so I guess it's for the best."

"Anyway, when he left, I was crushed. I think I cried myself to sleep every night for a month. About the time I got over him, he showed up again and stayed through the winter. He left again and I heard later he drowned at a place called Klamath Falls up in Oregon."

"Does Johnny know about him?" Greta asked.

"Oh yes, he wanted to know where I learned all the stuff I taught him," Anneliese answered, "plus I let him read my diary which had all the good parts in it."

"Was he jealous?"

"He didn't seem to be," answered Annaliese. "When I asked him if he was the jealous type he said, 'I don't know, I've never had anything to be jealous about'."

She went on. "Being jealous doesn't mean you love someone. It just means you're afraid of losing them. From what I've seen, if you asked Jed to jump off a cliff, he'd probably do it, so I don't think you've got to worry about losing him."

"Just remember, when you begin go really slow and gentle and make sure he does too. After a while you won't want to be slow and gentle anymore, but you'll know when it's time.

"An important thing to remember is he can love you with his eyes too, even though you can't love him the same way. Never be ashamed when he looks at you, especially in the moonlight. That's the most romantic and when it's the most romantic it's usually the most fun."

"You know it will probably hurt when he enters you and you will likely bleed some, but from what I remember it stops hurting after a few minutes and the blood washes out in cold water.

"Have you thought about waiting till you get married?" she asked.

Greta sighed. "I know I'm supposed to, but with Papa sick in bed and everything going on, I don't want to wait. We can get married when Papa's better, but to tell you the truth, I think I'll," she paused and then blurted, "go crazy if I have to wait much longer."

"Well, we're invited to a get-together at Mattie's tonight. I'll stretch it out and keep Johnny and the rest of them out of the way for a while if you want to take him upstairs. I can keep them busy for a couple of hours anyway."

Greta looked startled, "Does it take that long?"

Annaliese burst out laughing. "Well, the first time it might not, but if you wait a little while you can probably try again."

She was still chuckling when they got back to the store. A short time later, Greta approached her in the back room.

"I whispered to him when we were by ourselves and told him to come up after everyone was gone," she said. After a moment she asked, "Is there a full moon tonight?"

Though he couldn't tell which was which, Jed was extremely nervous as well as very excited when he knocked lightly on her bedroom door. He took several deep breaths before she opened it but was still having trouble breathing. She backed away and stood between him and the window. Through the thin nightdress her body was outlined against the light behind her. As he watched she pulled the night dress over her head and stood naked. She leaned forward and whispered, "Tell me what you see."

He was speechless. He licked his lips several times, took another deep breath, reached for her and folded her into his arms. After a long kiss he stepped back and began to undress, never taking his eyes off her.

When he took her in his arms again, she could feel his insistence against her tummy and when she reached down and took it in her hand it grew even more rigid, and suddenly he moaned, and his sperm was hitting her breasts and running down her body.

"Oh," he gasped. "I'm sorry. It just happened."

She pressed against him and muttered into his chest. "I love you Jed and I'm glad I make you so excited."

She led him to the bed, got a towel from the nightstand, and they gently wiped each other clean. For a while she lay in his arms and then they found Annaliese was right, about that and about so many other things. It *was* the most enjoyable thing she ever did.

Chapter Twelve

Dear Johnny and all,

I know I should have written this letter before now but here it is.

We are both fine. We were walking around Chicago yesterday and came across a public library. Looked around and found a nice little corner where we can sit and write letters, so we've decided to find a library in whatever town we're in and write a letter.

The first few days after we got to the show, we got our costumes fitted and all the get up that goes with them. Then Bill told us to go to the show a couple times and just watch and we could learn a lot about what we were supposed to do. It's nothing hard to catch on to. Mostly just standing around. Shoot a lot of blanks and ride my horse some. We were supposed to let the others teach us, and it didn't take long and we were in the show.

When we got here, they put us up in a hotel, but we decided we liked it better on the train with all the other folks. There are over eight hundred people with the show doing one thing or another, and most of them live on the train in cars especially made for the show. The rooms are kind of small, but we make do.

The different jobs it takes to make this thing work would make your head spin. There's a kitchen right on the train and a lot of cars set up for all kinds of things. Would you believe we have over a hundred fifty horses, a dozen buffalo, a bunch of cattle and some mules and burros that travel with us? Takes ten men to take care of them all, and the fellows sleep in the cars with the stock.

The horse I ride and some of the others get special treatment and they wash them every couple of days. Speaking of which, I used a shower for the first time in one of the hotel rooms. Good way to get all over clean real quick.

Got one car set up as a laundry and every morning they bring your costumes around for the day's show.

Most of the crew eat in one of the three dining cars. They fix breakfast and dinner and when we're in town we find our own lunch. They do serve lunch on days we have shows. They have a smoking car but there isn't any whiskey or beer allowed.

On the way here from St. Louis we played two-night shows in several smaller cities and I watched the crew set up and then later take down the big tent. There were thirty-eight men working on the tent and they had it down and on the train in about three hours. Johnny, you wouldn't believe how big the tent is, but they had a system and it was really something to watch how organized it was.

This whole setup is big and complicated, so I'll tell you more about it next time I write.

I told Bill when I started it was for a few months and then we would talk about it and decide if it was for me. He agreed and we set a date for November first. Even if I decided to leave, he'd like it if I could stay until we finish in New York which would be around Christmas.

I guess it means if I come home at the end of the season and decide I don't like it, I won't come back. There are things about it I like and things I don't, but I'll talk about that next time.

To finish up, Rebecca thinks if she gets pregnant, she'll come to San Francisco. Sarah also wants to come out there to live so she can be around the kids, including grandchildren whenever we have any. We'll talk about how I feel about that when I see you, but if Rebecca's happy usually I'm happy.

She's not really happy right now. She has gotten to be friends with some of the Indian women and doesn't like how they are treated in the show. She has become even more beautiful, and they want her to wear costumes she doesn't like. Personally, I think they look great on her but don't tell her I said so.

I see Bill every once in a while. He's good to me but I've heard some things about his drinking and some of the problems it's caused. He's married but his wife lives on the ranch in North Platte. He's on the road most of the time and there sure are a lot of women around.

My father has been sick, and my brother thinks I should come to see him before he dies so I may go by home on the way out this winter.

My hand has a cramp in it, so I'll close for right now. Hello to everyone there.

Your friend,
Handy

PS. I don't think Sarah's told Jed she's coming out so don't mention it to him.

Chapter Thirteen

Johnny was sitting in one of the easy chairs in the reading room, Jinx in his lap, looking out the bay window at Scott Street, holding Handy's letter in his hand and thinking.

He missed his friend. Handy could cut to the root of a problem quicker than anyone Johnny knew, and right then Johnny was facing a problem that needed Handy's kind of sharp instinct.

The store was already so busy he had trouble keeping up with everything that needed doing. Having Greta and Jed there to prop him up was a godsend, especially with Lemuel down and Annaliese tied up with his care.

Their roaring good start had brought a note from Mr. Terrance O'Donnell asking for an appointment to discuss some matters of mutual interest. He knew the powers in City Hall had noticed The BookSeller and knew how successful their first weeks had been. Now they were going to inject themselves into his life and he was powerless to stop it. His partner was too weak to really be a part of decisions about the store's affairs, so it was up to Johnny.

He talked to Wash and Woman about it, and the consensus was he should listen much, talk little, and tell O'Donnell he would discuss it with his partner and come to City Hall by the end of the week with an answer.

Though the answer was a forgone conclusion, he could be reasonably certain they wouldn't have a problem with the suggestion. It would give Lemuel a little more time to recover, and he hoped by then time would allow him to bring his advice to bear on the issue.

The bell over the door tinkled and he rose to face a short, stocky red-faced man who looked to be in his fifties. At first glance he looked like a jovial fat man, but something around the eyes made you look again, and the way he moved seemed to indicate more muscle than fat.

On his right hand there was a ring on every finger, and they seemed to have a purpose. A right hook could be damaging, and Johnny recognized the implied threat. The man was dangerous.

Johnny had been wearing the gun on his left hip every day since his fall the year before. He still practiced regularly, and the feel of it there seemed so natural he never thought about it. Now O'Donnell's glance at the canted holster made him suddenly aware it was there. He was sure the man knew the story of the encounter with City Hall's bully boys over Jimmy Li, and he was also sure O'Donnell knew of the firepower marshaled on Johnny's behalf at that confrontation.

"Mr. Fry?" he asked, and Johnny assented and shook O'Donnell's extended hand. "I'm Terrance O'Donnell. I just wanted to stop by and offer you greetings from Supervisor O'Hanlon and discuss your success in this new venture." He glanced around the store while Johnny was leading him to the reading room.

When they were seated in the chairs at the front window, O'Donnell asked, "Do you mind if I smoke?" He held up a cigar with a questioning look on his face.

"Well sir, I'd rather you didn't. My partner is recovering from some serious wounds, and the smoke makes him cough. We don't want him to start bleeding again." Actually, Lemuel's wounds were far beyond that stage, but he didn't want the meeting to last any longer than necessary.

"How can I help you, Mr. O'Donnell?" he asked.

The man took his time replacing the cigar in a silver case and finally said. "You've chosen an unusual place to open your store. You're just a few blocks from one of the most dangerous parts of the city. We offer a service to protect you from the bad element so you can go about your business in peace." While he was talking, he fiddled with the rings on his right hand in a most threatening manner.

Johnny recognized the implied threat but chose to ignore it. He sat silent waiting for the man to continue.

"For a monthly fee, we will make sure these people leave you alone and protect your establishment from harm." He looked Johnny in the eye when he said this.

"Actually, we're able to handle that kind of thing ourselves," said Johnny. "I have some friends who came west with me and they are usually close by when we need them."

"That's what I've heard. In fact, I know you had a little problem with some of my men recently. Something about a Chinese fellow who lives down the street?" O'Donnell cleared his throat and waited for an answer.

"The fellow was the son of a friend. Your men were preparing to hang him over a trifling thing. My friends and I stepped in to stop it." Johnny made sure he spoke distinctly so O'Donnell could not mistake him.

"The son of a friend? What friend?" asked O'Donnell. "You mean old Li?"

"Yes, Mr. Li and his son operate a business on the street, and I believe they also pay for your services. It appears your men got a little out of hand. In fact, I think they were quite drunk." He sat quiet for a moment then continued. "Mr. O'Donnell, if we pay for your services, will we have this kind of problem with these same men?"

"No, no," he answered hastily. "I can guarantee there will be no problems with them."

"Just how much are these services you're talking about?"

O'Donnell took out his cigar case, then remembered and put it back in his pocket. "Let's say it starts at $25.00 a month. Of course, if your business continues to thrive, it may go up."

"Why would it go up?" Johnny knew the answer but wanted to hear the man say it.

"The more you make, the more you'd have to protect. You might say it's like a tax on the value of your business." He heaved himself to his feet and turned to Johnny. "I have a meeting with the Supervisor on the hour, so I must go. When can I have your answer?"

Johnny stood and shook O'Donnell's proffered hand. "I will need to discuss it with my partner. Can I let you know on Friday?"

"No later," he said, put on his hat and left.

Later that evening he was standing on a stepladder replacing a globe on the chandelier when Annaliese called from the back room.

"It's almost six, Johnny, and you need to change your clothes."

He grunted in reply, descended the ladder, and stuck his head around the door of Lemuel's room where Wash was sitting on the floor working on the wheeled chair for Lemuel. Wash had created it from a kitchen chair and a couple wheels from an old-fashioned baby carriage. It would allow his partner to attend the Open House and participate in the business of the store for the first time.

"Will you fellows need help getting him in that thing?" he asked.

His wife came up behind him. "In case you hadn't noticed, I am not a fellow," she said, and he had the good sense to duck.

He caught her arms, held her squirming, and kissed her soundly. She struggled for a moment, then grinned and began to kiss him back.

"OK, OK," he said. "I seem to remember you're not a fellow."

"Ahem," said Wash, and when they turned, he was standing next to the bed looking at them.

"Go get dressed," she said and smacked Johnny on the butt. "I've been doing this sort of thing for years."

Upstairs he stripped off his shirt, and after a sponging with cold water, selected a new one from the closet. It was a bookcase they'd put a rod in, but it worked. Much of the space available in the building had gone into the store, so the living quarters were a bit cramped, and they needed to be creative.

Jason now lived above the livery stable where he worked, and Jed had moved in with Greta the week before. Lemuel seemed to accept the inevitable when they told him and even congratulated Jed on his engagement.

As he stood buttoning his shirt and looking out the window, his mind went back to the meeting with O'Donnell. He didn't like the situation, but at this time, acceptance seemed the only rational choice.

Before they could ever hope to affect changes in the power structure of the city, they must establish themselves and it would probably take a while, assuming of course they ended up establishing themselves at all.

Even having been open for only a week, The BookSeller had

attracted several people who Johnny could sense wielded power of a certain sort.

He hoped the biweekly open houses would attract more of the type of people who might be interested in changing the way things were. Then at some time they could organize and change the system. For now, they must accept in the short term what they could not immediately change.

Mr. Li, Jimmy and Sun Li had attended the opening the week before. In their conversation things were hinted and implied, and all knew they would talk again, probably sometime soon. In Mr. Li, he sensed power and influence, masked by his quiet manner and nondescript appearance.

Another person who impressed him was the woman who attended with Wash and Woman. Madame seemed drawn to Annaliese, and they had a long conversation about his wife's plans to become a doctor.

Madame was very rich and seemed, at first glance, to be younger than she was. Her easy self-confidence was relaxing, and her social position was not part of her personality, though he thought it might be if she needed it. She was not someone who could be pushed around, and he bet it would be dangerous to try.

In that sense she was much like Woman. In fact, they were alike in more ways than one, though Madame got the effect without the Bowie in the sheath on her back belt. Neither was the kind of woman to be pushed around.

He was fascinated with the obvious attraction between the two of them, and it was easy to see they were more than friends. "How much more?" he wondered, not realizing he was echoing Wash's very thoughts on the same subject.

When he came down the steps, Annaliese was pushing Lemuel out into the store in his new chair so he could see how things were arranged. She helped him into an easy chair by the front window, and wherever he was in the store, Johnny knew she'd be watching.

Greta and Jed were behind the counter. Greta's ability to take in money was limited by the greenbacks that replaced specie since the war. She could feel the difference in coins, but the paper money baffled her, so Jed was there to take in the cash and she to greet the customers and help them find what they wanted.

Johnny and Jason circulated among the bookshelves helping

customers make choices and find books. This gave Johnny a chance to meet and get to know a little about a lot of different people and, though he had trouble remembering all the names, he tried to remember the faces. Some of them impressed him and he hoped he'd recognize them the next time they came in.

What made it easier was learning their interests by helping them find books on things they liked. He helped one man and wife find a volume on gardening, feeling all the while he knew the fellow.

Turned out he was the young lawyer who'd brought the papers for Lemuel to sign for the power of attorney they needed. The lawyer's name was Nathan Jones, and they stood and talked for a while, until Johnny had to help another customer.

Madame came in with Wash and Woman, and immediately sat down to talk to Lemuel in the reading room. While they stood watching them talk, Johnny leaned over and said to Wash, "That chair works really well. Where'd you learn to do that kind of thing? I know you didn't learn it as a Buffalo Soldier."

Wash laughed. "No, I learned it in another life." He was quiet for a moment, then continued. "Before the war I was on a plantation in South Carolina. I helped an old fellow who worked with metal and fixed things around the place, machines and tools and such. When he died, I just sort of inherited the job."

Johnny waited for him to go on and when he didn't, said, "Well it sure comes in handy at times. Pa taught me some blacksmithing and such, but you just seemed to have a knack for it."

They stood for a minute and watched Annaliese join Lemuel and Madame.

"So, tell me about Madame," said Johnny.

Wash looked at him quizzically. "What do you mean?"

Johnny chuckled. "You don't mean to say you think she's an ordinary, run of the mill rich widow, do you?"

"No," Wash agreed. "Ordinary is not a word I'd use when I talk about her." He stood quiet for a time, as he was prone to do.

"I'll tell you what; ask me that question in a month. Right now, I don't know how to answer it."

Chapter Fourteen

Johnny was still standing puzzling out what Wash had said when a man touched him on the elbow.

"Excuse me, Mr. Fry." He was close to Lemuel's age but an erect, stocky, vigorous-looking fellow. "I just wanted to congratulate you on this wonderful addition to our city." He grasped Johnny's hand and gave it a firm handshake.

"Well thank you sir," Johnny replied. "You know, I remember seeing you last week at our opening, but I didn't get to meet you."

"John Willoughby Smith," he said with a big smile. "I'm as original a resident of this town as you're liable to find. I was here when the war with Mexico began. Came out here in '45. They put me in jail when the war started but then let me out the next week because they needed me."

"Well, you must know Madame. It seems to me she said she came out in '46," said Johnny.

"Indeed, I do," he replied. "Knew her when she ran The Pink Slipper. We're old friends. In fact, I spent a lot of money in her establishments over the years."

Johnny grinned at him. "So, how's your business doing? You must have been here in the panic of 73."

"Yes, yes I was," he said, "but we bounced back from that one OK. Right now, business stinks," Smith said with a smile.

"Oh, I'm sorry to hear it," said Johnny.

"No, that's good," said Smith, "and call me Will. Everyone else does."

Johnny's face wore a puzzled frown. "It's good when business stinks?" he asked.

"For me it is. You see, I clean out people's privies for a living." Smith was still smiling broadly. "Well, actually my company does."

Johnny was having a hard time keeping a straight face. Finally, he exploded in laughter and turned away from Smith to catch his breath.

Smith's broad smile had grown into a grin. "It's always good for a laugh," he said.

Madame and Annaliese turned around at the sound of Johnny's laughter, and when the widow saw Smith, she jumped up. "Hi Will, how's business?" she said loudly.

"It stinks," he replied just as loudly, and all three dissolved into laughter, leaving Annaliese standing with a puzzled frown, wondering what was going on.

Jed, Jason, Greta and Wash had all come to see what was so funny, and Lemuel woke up from a doze and was craning his neck, trying to see what the fuss was about.

After everyone was filled in on the joke and calmed down, Will looked at Johnny and said, "I'll bet the next time I come in here you'll remember me, won't you?"

"I'd say yes to that," said Johnny.

Later after the store closed and they drew the curtains in the front window, they sat with some of the guests and talked.

"Will's a great fellow and he knows a lot of people in the city and in Sacramento," said Madame. "He's one of the few in town left from when I first came here. I don't know what the city would do without him."

"Considering how fast the privy fills up, I can see that," said Annaliese.

"I wonder what he does with all the stuff," said Jed. It was easy to hear the wonder in his tone.

Wash knew a little about the process. "With all the water around here it's not hard to figure." He looked at Woman. "Is he the only one in the city?"

"No," she replied, "but he has most of the business north of Market, except for Chinatown. I guess they handle it themselves."

"I hear there are more than two hundred thousand souls living in the city now and quite a few living close by," said Madame. "If that's true I can see why there's more than one company.

"Will surely has enough business to keep him busy. He has a lot of men working for him. He owns all the land for a long way around his wagon yard simply because the land is so cheap. No one wants to live close to the place because of the smell, so he bought it all up. It's south and east, not far from the bay, which is probably where a lot of the stuff goes."

"He also has men and wagons who go around the city and pick up horse droppings," said Jason. "I talked to a couple of people who work for him the other day and they tell me he sells it to farmers south of here. Sometimes he sends whole boatloads of it across to the north side of the gate."

"Well, I can tell he loves this place, and since his office is right down the street, you'll probably see a lot of him," said Madame. "He's a good friend to have. Over the years he's done many things for many people, including some who are very important. When he needs something, he can call in favors from more than a few places."

They found the talks after making love were the best, and that night Johnny and Annaliese had plenty to talk about.

First was the store and how good business was. It was fortunate the books they ordered from Kansas City had arrived, because the trade in their first week created large gaps on the shelves. In the morning Greta and Jed would begin filling in those gaps, and already she and Johnny were making out another order to keep them ahead of what was going out the door.

They never ceased to be amazed at how Greta could keep the inventory in her head. She rarely made a mistake and could take a customer right to a selection almost as easily as Jed or Johnny.

"She seemed interested I was planning to go to medical school," said Annaliese, speaking about Madame. "She says she has many friends at the school who can introduce me around and help me get admitted and settle in. From what Wash and Woman say she knows about everyone in town and is one of the most influential people around."

They were each lying on their side, leaning on bent arms to talk. Jinx was lying on his pillow at the foot of the bed, his bright eyes going from one to the other.

"I wonder what her relationship is with Woman," Johnny mused. "Wash says she works for Madame but watching them I see something more. They seem to be close friends and equals rather than one working for the other. I asked Wash about her and he said to ask him next month. Apparently, he doesn't know what to think about her yet."

"Sounds like Wash," said Annaliese. "He'll think about it and after a while he'll tell you what he thinks and when he does, as he says, 'you can take it to the bank'."

"What did you think of Mr. John Willoughby Smith?" she asked.

Johnny blew his breath out audibly. "He was right about one thing. I'll sure remember him when he comes in again." He chuckled. "I'll bet the two of them have been doing that 'Hi Will, how's business?' routine for years."

"Likely," she said. "It sure is a great way to say hello."

They lay quiet for a while and she said, "Johnny, I don't like having to pay those people for protection." She waved her hand when he started to protest." I know, I know, it's all we can do right now. But I still don't like it." She punched up her pillow and rolled on her back, looking at the ceiling.

"You know this store is a good place to build a resistance to the power of those people."

She looked at him for a moment then continued. "There were some important people here tonight and last week at the Opening. Over time we could get to know some of them and find out how people feel about forcing a change. The BookSeller could become the center of a reform movement." She kissed him goodnight and turned over.

For a good five minutes he lay there, propped on his arm, thinking. "Damn it," he thought. "Now I'll never get to sleep."

He must have because Jinx woke him up by tapping him on the nose. He turned on his side, drew his little buddy close and lay for a while, listening to him purr and thinking about what his wife had said. He didn't really see himself as a crusader, but if ever he saw a situation which needed one, this was it.

It needed thinking though, and care. Overt opposition would

probably bring a violent response, and his responsibility wasn't just to himself and Annaliese but also to the others who'd hitched themselves to his wagon.

Before they approached anyone to enlist against City Hall, they must be sure, not only of their opposition to Sunny Jim and his cohorts, but of their trustworthiness. He wasn't even sure there was such a word, but nevertheless he knew what he meant.

He wanted to talk to Wash and Woman about it, and maybe Madame. What about John Willoughby Smith? He knew Fletcher Knobloch was against the protection game but was he enough against it to endanger his family and his business to set it right?

He was so involved thinking about it he hurriedly threw the covers off and stood up suddenly, inadvertently throwing Jinx to the floor. The cat walked stiff legged to the door and stood waiting for Johnny to pick him up and apologize.

There were several people waiting at the front door when they opened the store that morning, and while Johnny was working in the back, he heard Will Smith laughing and talking to Greta up front. When he emerged, Smith was introducing the short, broad figure of a woman standing beside him to Greta and Jed where they stood behind the counter.

He turned, saw Johnny and repeated the introduction. Mrs. Smith was younger than and seemed a quiet counter to her somewhat boisterous husband. Johnny was soon talking to them and showing her around the store while her husband trailed along behind.

With Annaliese's words from the night before in his mind, Johnny focused his attention on getting to know the two of them to see if they might fit what he saw was the beginning of a group that would try to change San Francisco for the better.

Chapter Fifteen

Annaliese was working in Lemuel's room when Jed came to the door and said, "There are two women out here to see you." When she emerged into the front of the store, one of her visitors was talking to Greta at the counter and the other was looking at some books displayed on a table.

"I'm Annaliese Fry," she said. "How can I help you?"

The one talking to Greta turned, removed a glove, and extended her hand to Annaliese. "I'm Doctor Lucy Wanzer and this is my associate, Doctor Catherine Brown."

The woman by the table came forward and also extended her hand. "We have heard you are someone we should meet and talk to." Doctor Brown was shorter than Annaliese, and though she looked only in her forties, her hair was a striking silver.

Annaliese noticed this because she was standing with her mouth open in surprise, staring at her unexpected visitors. She recovered quickly, and after a glance at the cluttered back room, invited them into the reading room.

"Can I get you some refreshment?" she asked, "although a cup of tea is all I can offer."

"Thank you, no," said Dr. Brown. "We came because our good friend and patroness, Mrs. Grimes, told us you intend to pursue admission to the medical school here in the city."

"Mrs. Grimes?" Annaliese shook her head. "I don't think I

know her." Then it dawned on her who they meant. "Oh, you mean Madame."

"Yes, Madame," said Dr. Wanzer. "I understand that's how she's known to her friends."

"We're not really personal friends of hers," she continued, "but she has been a great friend to the Medical School and especially to the Children's Hospital. Whenever we get into a bind over money, she always rides to the rescue."

"So, you want to be a Doctor?" asked Dr. Wanzer.

"Since I was ten years old," replied Annaliese.

"Tell us about yourself," said Dr. Brown. "Mrs. Grimes told us you worked with your father for a number of years."

Over the next hour the three women talked, and Annaliese relaxed, telling them of her life and ambitions. When Johnny came in from walking with Jinx and Brutus, he was introduced and had enough sense to retire to Lemuel's room and leave them to talk. On the other hand, Jinx stayed, and the women thought him wonderful as usual.

"You know you'll be in for some hazing and such ridiculous behavior?" said Dr. Wanzer. She was stroking the cat while she talked. "I went through quite a bit when I first started and most women doctors I know had to deal with it. It's not as bad as it was in '73 when I began but some of the professors are old fogies and let you know they still don't believe women should be doctors."

She laughed. "Old Doctor Jennings, our anatomy professor, told me 'any woman who wants to be a doctor should have her ovaries removed'." All three women laughed. "I told him that was fine if the male doctors had their testicles cut off.

"But I must admit, the old fellow treated me fairly in the end. He was one of those who protested when I was blackballed at the San Francisco Medical Society and when some of us were admitted to the state society a couple of years later, he sponsored my re-application to the city group."

"I understand you're newly married?" asked Dr. Brown. "How will your husband handle the demands of school and your profession?"

"We discussed it at length before we married and he understands where my priorities must lie," Annaliese replied.

"What kind of practice do you want to establish?" asked Dr.

Wanzer. "We can always use new doctors at the hospital if you're interested in children."

"To tell you the truth, I haven't thought that far ahead yet. One thing at a time. What I've done to this point has been just taking care of whoever comes in the door, like my father." She paused. "Johnny and I have talked about moving to South California, maybe around Los Angeles or even San Diego."

"We have a friend and colleague down there, Dr. Elizbeth Follensbee. She would welcome you and help you in any way she could," said Dr. Wanzer. "She and I started together but she got fed up with the way she was treated and went back east to finish school and then returned. She was one of the founders of the Children's Hospital here and it was her idea to start the Nursing School. Her health didn't agree with the weather here and she left about two years ago."

As the two women gathered themselves together to leave, Dr. Wanzer took Annaliese's hand in both of hers. "We want you to call on us for help with any problem you have with your application, and after you're admitted we'll be here for anything you should need. Welcome to San Francisco!"

For a while after they left, she sat gazing out the window seeing nothing. There were so many thoughts running through her mind they almost chased each other in a circle. When Johnny spoke, she jumped.

"Well, I'll bet that was interesting," he said. "Madame and probably Woman had something to do with them being here. Wash told me they talked about your plans."

"It surely was a surprise," she said distractedly, and resumed looking out the window. Johnny took one of the easy chairs, stretched out his legs, and sat looking at her until she was ready to talk.

Her mind was filled with her life, both past and future. She saw the hard work needed for her to reach her goal and remembered the hard work that brought her to this point. These women had invited her to step on the path leading to where she'd always dreamed she'd go. It was exciting, even thrilling. They would help her to achieve in the same way the Doctor had helped her, and her brother George had helped her, by believing in her even when she didn't believe in herself. She took a deep breath and looked at her husband.

"They told me Madame had given them my name and my ambition, and they wanted to reach out to help me achieve it." She stood and held out her arms and he was in them. Head on his shoulder she said, "I'm a little scared."

He pushed her away and held her at arm's length. "I didn't know you could be scared."

She smiled weakly. "Oh, yes. What if I can't do it? What if all I've learned isn't enough?" She was talking into his shoulder now and he could hardly hear her. "I know the Doctor would be disappointed."

"The Doctor will love you if you do it or not, just like I will; just like all your friends will. Doctor or not you're still Annaliese which is all I need."

She pulled away from him and said, "You're just trying to get on my good side so I'll take you to bed."

He looked at her, speculation in his face. "Now that you mention it, I've always wondered what it would be like with a medical student."

"So, when is she going to apply?" asked Lemuel. "Do they have regular terms?" They were sitting in the office the next morning.

"As far as I know, she will apply for admission to the class beginning the first of the year," answered Johnny. "The ladies suggested she let them work with her on the application because there's always some man looking for a reason to keep her out. I think it means she should start working on it right away, so she'll have time to fix any problem before class begins in January."

"Well, she doesn't need to worry about me anymore. With the wheeled chair Wash made me, I should be able to get around OK until I get strength back in my legs." Lemuel stretched his back. "Although it will be a while before I can spend the day in this chair. It bothers my back some."

"I wanted to talk to you about a special role I'd like you to fill when we have the open house," said Johnny. "I think it will give our customers a new angle and give us more regulars."

Lemuel forgot his aching back and leaned forward in the chair, interested.

"I'd like to set you up in the chair you like in the reading room and have you answer questions and talk to customers about books. You've read almost everything we sell so you can talk to them about the ones they've read and ones they want to read. It would be something new, and I think the customers would love it. You'd be like our oracle on books." Johnny sat back and scanned his partner's face.

Lemuel's face lit with an eager smile. "Yes, I'd love that, and it would give me a chance to get involved in the store without one of you fussing over me all the time. I don't know how long I could do it at first, but let's try it and see how it works this week."

He sat quiet for a moment and said, "It would be a great way to get to know the readers of this town. That's a wonderful idea, Johnny."

"Well, it was Jed's Idea, so why don't you talk to him and see what you two can come up with on how to make it work? I'll ask Greta to sit with the two of you. She always has great ideas."

That night Johnny and Annaliese talked about her meeting with the two doctors and what would be her first step toward admission. She asked Johnny to go with her to the school and make sure she got there alright. Since she arrived in San Francisco she had spent most of her time at the store and didn't know her way around the city yet.

Because Lemuel was still her patient, Johnny was a little reluctant to bring up the new role he and his pardner had discussed. She could be possessive when it came to her patients and he was not sure she would feel Lemuel was ready for the job but she liked the idea and believed it would help him get active again and interested in the store.

"Truth be told, I think he feels you don't need him anymore," she said. "You, Greta and Jed have done so well in getting things up and running, he doesn't feel he has a place. This will put him in the middle of things and that's probably better for him than anything I can do."

Chapter Sixteen

Wash was really nervous this time and for the same reason; they were going to visit Madame again. He could tell Woman wanted him to ask her more about why. Indeed, after the first time she brought it up, he had done so, and she gave him an enigmatic answer: "Come along and see."

For the last week she had dropped hints, but he refused to take the bait. Now he was about to find out.

He stood on the landing of the staircase leading to Madame's room and watched Woman's derriere sway while she climbed the steps. At the top she turned, saw he wasn't behind her and smiled down at him.

She held out her hand and said, "Come along and see."

He looked up at her for a moment, then began to climb the stairs, his eyes on her face, her smile. It looked different, a little impish and very appealing. He took her hand, and she led him down the hall, through the door of Madame's bedroom to the room beyond, where Madame was sitting in her chair looking out at the lights of the city.

It was dim. Two candles flickering in the bedroom cast a low light into the sitting room and he could just see her stand and turn as they entered. When she did her gown fell open. She was naked, and in the wavering shadow, he could see her tummy, and just below, a hint of darkness; and he could see most of her pendulous, dark tipped breasts which swayed a little as she came to meet Woman.

He stopped, but Woman moved on, and Madame embraced her and kissed her on the cheek, then the lips; and Woman slipped her hands inside the dressing gown touching and caressing. He stood watching, and when they separated, Madame held out her hand and said in a low voice, almost a whisper, "Come and join us, won't you?"

He wasn't surprised, but he didn't quite know what to do, how to act. Something far back in his mind told him this was wrong, unnatural. Yet this was Woman, his. . . his what? His woman? No, she was more. His mate? No, not even close. She was no one's anything. She was her own and no one else's, so what were they to each other?

As he stood and watched Madame help her undress, it dawned on him; he felt whole when he was with her. If this gave her pleasure, he wanted to be a part of it. That was reason enough for him, and besides, it would probably feel good. As he moved to join them, he felt the heat and swelling in his groin and knew it would.

It did.

Afterward, they talked. Woman sat cross-legged, naked between them while he and Madame lay turned inward, facing each other, also naked.

"Well?" asked Woman. "Tell me what you're thinking."

He lay still and thought for a minute. "You mean what do I think about you women tempting me into sinful and unnatural behavior?"

She closed one eye and squinted at him balefully while Madame laughed heartily.

"I never could see what women could get out of it before, so I learned something tonight," he finally said.

"What made you believe it only felt good when a man did it?" asked Woman. "Of course, I remember teaching you a few years ago and I must say you learned well, but a woman, now that's different."

"How?" he asked.

Madame smiled and reached out to touch Woman's lips. "A woman knows better what feels good to a woman and a woman's hands are softer, gentler, her skin is smoother. She tastes and smells different. It's quite different."

He rolled over on his back and said, "Show me." And they did, touching, and kissing and rubbing him the way they loved each other.

For the next two hours they pleasured him in new ways and new places, and he learned new things. Before long they were all excited again and he mounted them, one and then the other, and it was different and more exciting than he would have believed.

When he woke the next morning, his first thought was it had been a dream but when he looked at Woman, she was smiling the kind of smile that told him it wasn't.

Chapter Seventeen

Greta was sitting in her Papa's room waiting while Jed helped him into his wheeled chair. Usually during this routine chore, she was focused on what was happening, but today her mind was elsewhere.

She wanted to talk to Annaliese. Since their original talk in the Presidio, she thought of her friend as a confidant, someone she could talk to about all things female; things she couldn't talk to Jed about and certainly not Papa.

She felt Jed pass her and touch her hair on his way out of the room. Lemuel's voice startled her. "Do you ever think about Mama?"

She sat for a moment bringing herself back to the present. "I think about her a lot." Her mother's image came into her mind, smiling at someone from where she stood behind the counter in their bookstore in Kansas City.

"I sometimes think about how she'd feel about our life since she's been gone," he said. "I mean we've lived in the wagon and in someone else's place for almost four years now." They sat silent for a minute, each in their own thoughts. "Do you think we'll ever have a place of our own?" he asked.

"Don't you like it here, Papa?" she asked.

"Well, to tell you the truth, I don't really know," he answered. "Since I came in the door, I've spent most of my time in this room and in this bed. It's just this week I've done much besides lie here.

"I'm really proud of the way you all have taken hold and made the store go like it has, but I don't feel like I've contributed much at all.

"Do you ever think about going back on the road selling books again?" While she sat thinking with a puzzled look on her face he continued. "I really enjoyed doing that. It felt like something I was meant to do."

"What do you think about Johnny's idea—you sitting in the reading room, talking to people about books?" she asked. "Johnny told me you liked the idea."

"I did. But the more I think about it, the more I believe it's just make-work to keep me happy. If I'm to be a partner here I need to be an important part of things."

"Papa, I think you need to give the idea a chance," she said. "Jed has handouts on the counter, and he said people seem to be interested in the idea. Also, Johnny has put something about it in a couple of the newspapers."

She moved behind him and pushed him to his place beside the window.

"Why don't you see how it works the next couple of weeks," she said. "By then we can see if it's good for you."

Lemuel watched her walk out of the room. It was amazing how she managed to move around the store without a problem. He knew everyone was careful to leave everything in its place so she wouldn't stumble, just like someone was always around when he needed help with something. These people they had hooked up with in Salt Lake were special. It was as though he and Greta had joined a family, a group of different people who seemed to have one thing in common; one of them was always around when you needed help.

With Jed and Greta together and soon to be married, he believed Jed's mother would probably join them before long and he looked forward to seeing her. Sarah was closer to his age, and he liked spending time around her. For now, at least, he felt all their lives would revolve around The BookSeller, and that made him smile.

For the last week he felt he was rejoining life. While he was recovering, he was doing just that, recovering. Recently he felt he had crossed a line and gradually felt both aware of and ready to join the world again.

Watching Greta as she went about her day's work gave him a feeling of pride, the feeling of a job well done. For the first time since her mother died, she was going to be living a life with someone else at its center, and like always, was handling it well. It was all part of growing up, but nonetheless, he felt the loss.

Jed was a nice boy who seemed to be willing to join their lives instead of taking her away, and he was grateful for that. On the other hand, the idea he was no longer the most important person in her life made him feel a little lonely.

Annaliese looked up from a letter she was writing and was a little startled to see Greta standing in the doorway.

"How long have you been standing there?" she asked. "You might have at least cleared your throat or something."

Greta looked puzzled, as though the idea never occurred to her.

"I knew you'd look up eventually," she said, "and I wasn't in a hurry."

Annaliese shook her head. "Well, how can I help you?"

Greta closed the door and came to sit in the chair beside her desk.

"I'm assuming this is private?" Annaliese said.

"Yes, very," replied Greta. She cleared her throat nervously. "Can you hear us at night?" she asked in a low voice. "I mean, I try to keep quiet but sometimes I forget and…." her voice trailed off.

Annaliese laughed. "Yes, and I'll just bet you can hear us too."

Greta grinned. The upstairs at the store was one big room they had divided into three separate spaces using spare bookcases. Sound proofing wasn't included.

"The other night we were asleep, and it woke us up. Got us going too," said Annaliese. "From what we heard it affected you the same way. No wonder Jed looked so tired the next morning."

"What can we do about it?" asked Greta. "I just get so excited sometimes I can't help it."

"Sounds like restraint is out of the question, so I guess we'll just have to live with it," answered Annaliese. "We do need to realize they have to work the next day, poor boys." They were both giggling like schoolgirls by then.

Greta's face suddenly changed. "I need to talk about something else; something that frightens me."

"What is it?" asked Annaliese. "Are you worried about childbirth?"

"No." She was quiet for a long moment. "I know about having a baby and I know you would take care of me. No, it's afterwards. I'd have a baby to care for. How could I care for a baby? What if I make a mistake and it dies because I can't see?" This last came out as a low moan.

Tears were running down Greta's usually calm, smiling face. There was fear and anguish there. Annaliese suddenly stood and pulled the girl to her into a long, tight embrace.

Because she was a nurse, Annaliese was used to acting when faced with problems, so she was momentarily stunned. She prolonged the hug because Greta seemed to need the closeness, but also to give her time to think about how to handle this one.

This was not an irrational fear. It couldn't be explained away, so helping her learn to control it would take a plan and this was not something she'd done before.

On the other hand, who else could Greta go to for help? No one else jumped to mind; indeed, she couldn't think of a single person the girl knew who could handle it better. So, it looked like it was up to her. After all she was a nurse, in the business of healing hurts. Surely this qualified as one.

She held Greta at arm's length. "Are you pregnant?" she asked. Greta shook her head.

"Well then, we've got at least nine months to come up with ideas on how to solve the problem. As smart as we all are, we should be able to do it."

They were both quiet for a minute.

"Do you mind if I talk to Johnny about it? He's pretty smart about this kind of thing." Annaliese said and pulled her into another hug.

With her head on Annaliese's shoulder Greta said, "I don't mind. I need to tell Jed too. He should know." She paused for a long moment. "I'm so afraid of losing him."

Because she needed to think, Annaliese didn't say anything right away. Finally, she kissed the girl on the forehead and said, "I won't tell you not to worry about it, because it's too big a thing. But let your friends help you. That's what friends are for.

"So, here's the first idea from a friend. We have the names and addresses of a number of book dealers. I believe if there's a problem in life someone, probably a woman, has written a book about it. So, I'm going to write to all of our dealers and set them looking for anything they can find on being a blind parent."

She smiled at Greta. Then, realizing the girl couldn't see the smile, reached out and touched one of the tears on her face.

"We'll find the answers."

Chapter Eighteen

Johnny was standing with Jed, watching Lemuel. His partner was sitting in a wing chair by the big bay window in the reading room holding an open book and reading something to a young couple. His smile was a little weary, but it was easy to see he enjoyed what he was doing.

Still watching, he said to Jed, "He looks tired, but I think the idea is a success." After a few minutes, the couple got up and brought the book to the counter. When they left, he was there to hold the door and invite them back.

While Jed began the closing routine, Johnny dropped into a chair across from Lemuel and said, "Well, it looks like you stayed busy all night. Got to meet a lot of people from the looks of things. How do you feel?"

Lemuel gave him a wan smile. "For the first time since I got here, I felt like I accomplished something. I'm glad we did this. How'd we do tonight?"

Johnny stood. "I'll let you know in a few minutes after I count the till. So, why don't we get you into bed. I'll count the cash and then we can sit and talk about the day."

Lemuel was nodding when Johnny came into his room half an hour later. He was about to leave quietly when Lemuel opened his eyes. "I'm ready to talk if you are."

"You look kind of tuckered out," Johnny said with a smile.

"No, I'm fine," replied Lemuel but his face disagreed.

"It was a good day for selling books," said Johnny. "We took in $116.38 from nine to six. Then I emptied the drawer and we took in another $52.00 in the three hours of the Open House. We sold forty-two volumes, and the rest was from soft backs, magazines and newspapers."

He was quiet for a moment, then said, "It's the best day since we opened, and I think you're one reason it was so good."

"I don't see where you come up with that," protested Lemuel.

"At our first Open House many people picked up books and opened them and talked about them to us, but they didn't buy them. Tonight, they did."

He let that hang in the air for a moment then said, "I believe the reason is there was someone to talk with about them, to answer questions. One thing about most books, you have to read them to find out what's between the covers. With you here they don't. They bring the book to you and you can tell them about it, get them interested in it, and give them a reason to spend the money."

Lemuel looked at him steadily for a moment. "Do you really believe that?" he asked.

"Yes, I do, and if you'll keep doing it every other week, we will make this business work. And we'll make this place an important place in this city. People will tell their friends and more will come because you are here to help them do what they come here to do; learn."

After Johnny wished his partner good night and came out into the store, he found Greta and Jed waiting for him.

"It sounds like you've got him convinced," said Jed. "Maybe, if he can handle it, we can put him in the chair for another night, say Thursday again, and find another reason to advertise and draw more people."

"In Kansas City there were local authors who came to speak and lecturers who traveled around speaking for money or trying to sell their books," said Greta. "I'm sure we could find ways to bring people in. If he feels like it, he can help us sell lots of books."

"Well," said Annaliese who had joined them. "I think it's the best medicine for his recovery. He needs to feel useful, and this gave him a chance to feel that way for the first time since he was shot."

Johnny stood stroking his newly grown goatee for a moment

and finally said, "I think I'll try to find some other event to draw people in so he can sell the books for us. But for now, let's go up to bed. And can you two be quiet tonight?" he said to Jed and Greta. "I'm tired and need to get some rest."

As they all trooped up the stairs, Annaliese whispered, "I don't believe it" in his ear.

She was right.

The next morning, he was up early, and after a talk with Lemuel about where to find information on local authors, he and Jinx were standing at the door of the public library when it opened for business.

His conversation with the head librarian yielded some good ideas and he came back with his head full of ways to draw people into The BookSeller, and not just on Thursday nights.

Wash enjoyed watching Woman walk around the little cottage in the morning doing things. The fact she was usually in one state of undress or another made him enjoy it even more. Now she put her arm around his shoulder and sat in his lap. She gave him a long, searching look and kissed him, her tongue pushing insistently against his smiling lips.

"No," he said, emphatically and pushed her away. "I've got things to do and places to go. I don't have time for that."

She pouted. "What? Where?"

He frowned. "Give me a minute and I'll think of something." He held her at arm's length. She was grinning at him. "Don't you ever get tired?"

"No, not when you're around," she said, running her tongue over her lips. "Should I?"

He looked at her for a moment. "I reckon not, but don't forget I'm an old man and I need my rest."

"Speaking of rest," he continued, "you got up last night and left the house." It was not a question. "I laid here for several hours wondering where you were but fell asleep before you got back."

She looked at him with a mischievous grin. "What do you want to know?"

"I'd like to know why and where you went."

She cocked her head and looked at him with a mischievous

smile. "Now why would I tell you that?" She sat looking at him with the question on her face.

He knew her well enough to know she wasn't going to tell him, so he put it in the back of his mind, knowing he would eventually find out, just on her terms and not his.

Her clothes were draped over the other chair, and she began to put them on, slowly and deliberately. "You don't look tired."

"I'm not, really, but I'm supposed to meet Johnny and Lemuel this morning. They want to talk about things, and I'd like to be there." He stood and stretched. "You'll be here tonight, so you'll just have to wait"

"Madame and I are taking the boat over to Sausalito today and we may stay over there for a couple of days. She hasn't decided."

"Hmm," he said. "I'd like to go along. I've never been over there. What time are you planning on leaving?"

"She didn't say, but I don't think it matters. She has a nice place over there so sometimes she goes and stays for a while. As far as I know she doesn't need to be there for anything today. She's looking at some property tomorrow but later. Of course, with her you never know."

"Think she'll mind if I come along?"

"Nope, don't think so." She looked at him speculatively. "How do you feel about making love on a boat?"

The bay was choppy, and according to the boat pilot, there was a strong swell coming in from the ocean, so they decided to route the trip around Alcatraz Island and Angel Island and approach Sausalito from the east.

"It will make a smoother and much safer trip," said the pilot. Wash, who got a little queasy on boats, was glad Madame took his advice.

They were bundled up. Though it was high summer, the wind coming in off the ocean was biting, and it seemed to find its way through his coat. Having grown up and lived over half his life in the steaming heat of the South Carolina lowlands, he had never gotten comfortable with the weather on the bay.

Madame and Woman retreated to the protection of the cabin, but he stayed on deck with the crew looking at the stunning panorama of the bay. The weather had been cool and rainy in recent days, and he had noticed a pall of smoke over the city as people burned more coal and wood because of the wet chill.

Today the brisk wind had blown it all away and it was easy to pick out houses on the south shore. From this angle he could see the military prison on Alcatraz Island. Closer to hand, he could clearly see hitching posts standing in front of what looked like army barracks on Angel Island more than two miles distant.

The pilot lent him the boat's binoculars, and when Madame went into a tea shop to warm up, he and Woman wandered along the shore looking at the view.

He stopped and took Woman in his arms. "Looking at something like this," he gestured around the horizon with his arm, "makes me feel something deep down inside me. Like the first time I saw the Tetons or the lake in the crater." He led her to a rock, and they sat.

"As much as you mean to me, one day I'll leave because of that feeling. It's why I love to roam the country. I like to see new places and things. I don't think I'll ever get enough of that feeling."

She snuggled against him. "I know," she said.

Later that night she came to him with that special smile while he was sitting on the porch and held out her hand. "Would you like to join us?"

As was his habit, he took a little time to answer. He kissed her on the lips and whispered, "You go ahead. You can tell me about it when you get back."

She looked at him for a moment, then kissed him and left with a grin on her face. At the door she stopped and said, "That should be fun. When I get back, I mean."

Chapter Nineteen

For some reason Johnny woke up early and couldn't get back to sleep. His wife was snoring gently beside him, so he took Jinx on his chest and lay beside her thinking.

Things were going wonderfully with the store. Every day for the last two weeks they had equaled or bettered the previous day's income. Lemuel was getting around with a cane, and in addition to being their 'oracle', he was working with Greta on ordering and had begun to help Johnny with the books.

They decided the best way for each of them to know what was going on with the money was to alternate months in doing the sums. The last day of the month, one would finish the figures, share the month's totals with the other, and hand over the books until the end of the month. Tomorrow he would hand over the books to Lemuel and be relieved of a tedious chore for the next thirty days.

The four of them, Johnny, Jed, Lemuel and Greta, sat weekly in a meeting before the store opened to trade ideas about new ways to attract business and it was paying off at the till.

It was paying off in another way, too. More and more business leaders, city fathers and prominent men and their wives were becoming regular faces in the store. Fletcher Knobloch was in several times a week, and one or other of the Li family was in the place every time he turned around.

He and Annaliese made the topic of resistance to city hall a regular thing before sleep most nights. Their patrons, who were becoming more than acquaintances, were teaching them about the city and the undercurrents running through it. Every time he handed a payment to O'Donnell's collector he seethed, and those were the nights they talked about it a lot.

Madame and Woman were fixtures on open house nights. Madame had furnished a sitting area among the overstock shelves in the back room so they could have a place to visit with the staff or read when the reading room was full, which lately was most of the time.

Madame had given him something to think about earlier. Just before closing she took him into the reading room and when they were alone, suggested if they were interested in expanding the store, she would buy the building to the west. They would divide the construction costs to make it into what they wanted it to be. The buildings were only a few feet apart so joining them wouldn't be difficult.

In return she would receive ten percent share of the partnership. She would retain ownership of the new building and receive a reasonable rent for it. Wash had learned from Woman Madame did this kind of thing occasionally with businesses she felt were good for the city. She invited Lemuel and Johnny to come to the Mansion the following evening to discuss the idea. He hadn't mentioned it to Lemuel yet because he wanted to think about it and discuss it with Annaliese.

Beside him, his wife turned over and looked at him with one eye open. "What in the world are you doing? What time is it?" When he told her, she collapsed onto the pillow with an exasperated grunt and turned her back on him.

That was something else to think about. Annaliese had been accepted to the Medical School and would begin classes in the New Year. Besides being gone during the day, she would be studying at night and would no longer be the extra pair of hands they were beginning to need more and more in the store. He would like to bring Jason in to replace her. Their friend had been working for them in the evenings while he worked days at the livery stable down the street.

He must have finally dropped off to sleep again, because Jinx woke him with a tap on the nose as usual. The nights were cold now, so they kept the fire in the stove banked, and first thing he stoked it up and added coal before grabbing Jinx and climbing back under the covers till the room warmed up.

"What do you think about the offer Madame made me?" he asked while Annaliese was washing her face.

"Hmm?" she murmured and shook her head. "To tell the truth, I was half asleep. I remember something about it. Tell me again."

After he explained it to her, she looked puzzled. "What in the world brought that up?"

"Wash and I were talking about something along those lines the other night. He probably said something to Woman about it and she mentioned it to Madame," replied Johnny. "I'm going to talk to Lemuel about it and we'll probably go over there after we close this evening."

"What do you think about it?" she asked.

"It looks good at first glance, but I'll need Lemuel to pass on it. He knows a lot more about this kind of thing than I do. And I'd like to talk to Wash about it before we make up our minds."

"I'd be amazed if you didn't," she said.

Lemuel and Johnny were sitting in Lemuel's room, which had also become the office. Johnny had just finished telling him about Madame's offer.

Lemuel repositioned himself in the chair. He looked around the room and scratched his beard. "We sure could use the space. What do you think?" he asked Johnny. "Is she someone you'd want as a partner?"

"I don't think she'd be involved in the business at all. From what Wash tells me she does this kind of thing with businesses she thinks are good for the city. Ones she feels make it a better place."

"I'm glad she sees us that way," Lemuel said, smiling, "but it's something we need to think about. I assume tonight we will thrash out the details and we'll have a few days to make up our minds?"

"Then we need to get started thinking," said Johnny. "We need to decide how we feel about it and we're supposed to be there shortly after six." He stood. "Wash and I are going to take a walk. You think about it and when we get back, we'll talk."

It was clear blue above, but a brisk chill wind was blowing in their faces as they walked toward the water. Johnny wondered if he'd ever get used to the weather in the city. Sometimes it seemed to be colder in July than it was in November.

"Let's walk down to the Bay," said Johnny. "I want to know what you think about this idea."

As usual, Wash took his time. When he finally spoke, what he said took Johnny by surprise.

"I think she's a good person to have on your side in a fight."

Johnny walked on for a few steps then stopped and turned to face his friend. "What fight?" he asked. "What are you talking about?"

Wash turned and resumed walking. When Johnny caught up with him, Wash asked, "Why do you think the Li's can get away with living and running a business on Chestnut?"

The question hung in the air. Johnny stood looking at Wash and finally he nodded his head. "She owns the building."

Wash nodded and resumed walking. They walked in silence the rest of the way to the bay. In a small grove of wind battered pines, they sat on a log. Whitecaps were marching past and they could feel spray in the air.

Wash drew a mark in the sand beneath his feet.

"One, you'll get space, both for living and for growing the store. Two, you'll get a sympathetic landlady. Three, you'll always have money behind you if and when you need it. Four, you'll have one of the most respected, powerful people in the city in bed with you, so to speak," he finished with a smile.

"Johnny, I think having her as a partner would be like having a warm blanket on a cold night; you'd likely sleep better."

There were four marks in the sand. Wash handed Johnny the stick.

"Your turn."

Johnny shook his head and handed the stick back. Wash threw it into the water. "I've seen your face when the man comes to collect every month," he said. "I know you well enough to know one day you'll decide to do something about it. That's what fight."

Lemuel was waiting for them when they got back. "Well? What do you think?" he asked.

"I think we'd be fools if we don't," replied Johnny and told him about Wash's marks in the sand.

Lemuel grinned. "I'll give you one more mark, he said. "She sure ain't hard to look at."

Chapter Twenty

Annaliese was working at her desk when she heard Greta clear her throat. She looked up and saw a worried look on the girl's face.

"That's what you said to do, wasn't it? I don't want to interrupt you if you're busy."

"I'm never busy when you need to talk." She stood, took Greta by the hand, and led her to one of the chairs beside the barrel in the back room, then took the one on the other side. She opened a book lying there and began to read.

"'Blind Parents? Why Not?' That's the title of a book I just got from Kansas City. And there are two magazine articles too. How does that strike you?"

Greta was sitting silent with her mouth wide in astonishment. "Really?" she cried. "They finally sent one?" She was bouncing in the chair and clapping her hands.

"Yes, finally, so here's what we'll do," said Annaliese. "I'm going to read a chapter tonight, and then I'll read it to you tomorrow, and we'll talk about it. Then we'll see what we do next."

"Oh, thank you, Anna, I don't know how to thank you."

"You just did, twice," Annaliese said, laughing. "Now, go tell Jed and we'll start tomorrow. You're gonna be a good Mama to some handsome little boy or sweet little girl. Wait and see."

She stood, hugged the girl, then watched her go to tell her husband what she was going to learn.

Johnny had never seen a house like this one.

Standing on the front porch he could see for miles, and he couldn't imagine what it would look like at night. Maybe he'd find out tonight. He had no idea what to expect in meeting with Madame or how long it would take.

Wash stood beside him and said, "Wow! Some view."

Johnny looked at him in surprise. "Haven't you seen it before?"

"No," he grinned." Every time I've been here, she brings me in the back way, through the kitchen."

Lemuel had immediately gone to the swing and eased onto it with a groan. Johnny hadn't counted, but he thought there must be more than a dozen steps leading up to the landing, and his partner was still recovering.

Johnny grasped the heavy knocker, let it fall and the door was opened almost immediately by a man who looked like a butler. Another fellow took their coats, and the butler led them through a half dozen rooms, each larger than the whole upstairs at the store.

Everywhere he looked there was something to see - art, ceramics, ferns. But the things that fascinated him the most were the ceilings. They were ornate, pressed metal and so high they made him feel short. The draperies went from floor to ceiling and looked heavy enough to smother a man.

Woman was sitting in a wing chair on one side of a large fireplace when they entered the room. She turned, smiled, and came forward to take Lemuel's arm and help him to a chair at the long table in the center of the room. A door opened on the far wall of the room and Madame came in.

She immediately went to Lemuel, took his hand and said, "How are you feeling?" When he nodded, she looked around at a girl who was bringing a tray of glasses and a pitcher. "Put it here Carlotta," she said, and seated herself at the head of the table.

A man had followed her into the room and Johnny saw it was Nathan Jones, the attorney he had met in the store.

"Call me Nate," he said when he shook hands. "I'm representing Mrs. Grimes." He grinned. "Actually, I just carry the papers," he whispered from behind his hand.

Over the next hour they discussed the terms of the offer and asked any questions they had about it. Johnny was fascinated by Madame's behavior. He was used to the friendly good humor seeming to bubble out of her when they talked at the store. Now she was all business. No smiles, concentration on details, and a face reflecting relaxed confidence. For some reason he felt these were just two of the many sides to this fascinating woman.

"Are there any more questions or discussion?" she asked, looking around the table.

Johnny lifted a finger. "Yes," he said. "There is an aspect of the BookSeller you may not be aware of, and it might have a bearing on whether you decide to join us in a partnership."

"From the first day we heard about the extortion game they play here we've talked about finding others who want to resist this city hall gang. If we find a group we believe has a good chance of success, we will likely join it. I wouldn't want you to get caught up in a problem you might not want to be involved in."

There was silence in the room for a moment. Then Woman chuckled. "Told you," she said to Madame, who was smiling for the first time since the meeting began.

"I was wondering if you were going to bring that up," said Madame.

"Well, it wouldn't be very fair not to tell you and then drag you into a fight you didn't want." Johnny said.

"Oh, we want it," Madame murmured. "That's not even up for debate. What we've been trying to do is to figure out how to go about it.

"When I came here in '46 there were more goats than people. During the gold rush it just exploded. Eighteen months after gold was discovered we became a state with 50,000 people, most of them in and around this city. It was rough, and there were crooks on every corner for a few years.

"Finally, it began to smooth out, and over the years it's become something special. I believe, in time, it will become one of the great cities of the world, but not until we make some changes at City Hall."

She looked at Johnny. "The reason I made you this offer was because we believe you and your friends can be a big help to us. We want to accomplish the same thing, change the way the city's run. But we need to come up with a plan and we think you can help us. Your bookstore is becoming a center for people to meet and talk, and we can help decide what they talk about. Besides, you and your friends bring a lot of firepower to the game if we should happen to need it."

Johnny looked at Wash.

Wash shook his head. "I haven't said a word to them about it," he protested, "but it's not hard to figure out, Johnny. All you have to do is to take a look at your face when the collector comes around."

"Woman keeps her ear to the ground for me," said Madame, "and she figured it out a few weeks ago, hence the offer."

"So, do you have any plans on how to go about putting together a group to fight these people?" asked Lemuel. "It seems like you'd have to be organized pretty well to have any chance of success. Is there an organization now or is it just beginning?"

"We've some ideas on how to put it together, but right now your guess is as good as ours on the best way to go about it," said Madame. "What we'd like to do is have you people at The BookSeller come up with some ideas for organization and bring them to me. You know, San Francisco has a history with vigilantes. The people of the city might just need a spark, and we can sweep that bunch right out of there."

Lemuel stood. "Back to the original offer. I'm assuming Mr. Jones will have an agreement for us to sign before long?" When Nate nodded, he continued. "Why don't Johnny and I talk it over and when you come to Open House next week, we can slip into the back room and see what we've come up with, both on the offer and the other." He picked up his hat and cane and said, "I believe this idea will be beneficial to all of us, but I need to get in bed. My hip is killing me."

While Johnny and Wash stood on the porch looking at all the lights of the city below and across the bay, and watching Lemuel being helped into the carriage, Johnny said, "It sounds like Woman is a scout of sorts for her." When Wash nodded, he went on. "You know, that might be a good job for you, keeping your eyes open and your ear to the ground. We'll need information and with you two working at it, we might have all we need in a short time. Let's sit down tomorrow and think about the best way to go about it."

Wash was quiet for a minute. "I think Woman and I need to talk. I'll see you in the morning." So saying, he turned Master toward Woman's cottage and rode off into the dark.

Woman was already there. When they were seated across from

each other with cups of tea close to hand, he said, "So you're her eyes and ears. That's where you went the other night." She nodded and sat waiting for him to go on. "So, what do you do when you go out?"

"Like you said, I'm her eyes and ears. The things I find out I pass along to her, and she keeps her finger on what's happening in this city of 200,000. Of course, she has other sources. She takes it all in, thinks about it, and makes decisions about the future. She feels it's her city, and since she's got all this money, she tries to make it better when she can."

"You didn't answer my question."

"And I'm not going to. If you want to know what I do, you'll have to go out with me and find out."

They sat in silence for a minute while he thought.

"Johnny wants me to move around town and bring him information. What's the best way for me to do that?"

She smiled and stretched her arms over her head. "You need to go with me a couple of times just to watch and listen. This is my town, and I can show you a lot, introduce you to people. Then we'll usually go separately.

"We'll need to talk and plan. It's not just hit and miss, you know. We need to decide what we want to know and figure out how to get it. I know you're used to working alone, but this time each of us will need to know what the other is doing whenever we can."

They sat and looked at each other again for a long minute, then she said, "We can talk more about it tomorrow. Now, would you like to watch me wash up for bed?"

He couldn't imagine saying no.

When Johnny went upstairs after getting Lemuel into bed, Annaliese was reading. Her dark red hair was brushed and hanging around her shoulders. She looked altogether desirable, but he could tell she was immersed in something, so he stoked the stove, got into bed with Jinx and lay petting him until she was finished.

When she closed the book and reached to turn down the gas, he said, "Don't turn it off."

"Why not?" she asked.

"Because I want to watch you get undressed."

"What makes you think I won't just sleep in my gown?"

He just smiled. Actually, it was more of a smirk.

She gave him a stern look, "You, sir, are nothing but a dirty minded little boy." But she didn't turn out the light.

Afterward they talked.

"What were you reading?" he asked.

"It's the book on blind parenting I got from Kansas City," she replied. "I'm going to read the first chapter to Greta in the morning and we're going to talk about it. We're hoping it will teach us enough to make her feel better about her handling the responsibilities of parenting."

"I can see why she'd be frightened," he said. "I can't imagine how you'd care for a baby if you can't see. Of course, knowing her and what she does around here, nothing will surprise me."

"Tell me about the meeting," she said.

She snuggled against him and settled to listen. He told her about all things said and the discussion about the effort to resist.

"She wants us to get together and come up with some ideas. When they come to the open house next week, we'll all sneak into the back room and talk about it," said Johnny.

"Lemuel and I will sit and mull it over, and we'll begin to think about what we want to do with the place next door. I get the feeling she's not the kind to let grass grow under her feet."

Annaliese was already asleep, so he turned over and joined her.

Chapter Twenty-One

"I don't go out much in the daytime," said Woman. They turned into a livery stable near the area around City Hall and left their mounts with a young fellow Woman who apparently knew well because she just nodded at him. When they crossed the street, they stopped to stand looking up at the impressive building two blocks away.

San Francisco's City Hall was finished in 1870 and was larger and more impressive than most state capitol buildings; indeed, it was taller than the U.S. capitol dome in Washington. It sprawled across three city blocks and was surrounded by shops, stores and saloons in all directions.

It was evening and the streets were busy. Not so many wagons at this time, but a lot of carriages and horses. People moved along the sidewalks to various restaurants and shops still open.

"During the day," she said, "they do the business of the city and the county in there, but at night, out here" she swept her arm around, "are the things we want to see and hear. So, let's take a walk."

"I've been in many places like these. What do you do here?" he asked. "Most of those places don't allow women to even come in the door."

"Most of the time they're not even sure I'm a woman," she said, not smiling, "though not many have the courage to try to find out."

"I'll bet," he muttered.

"Thing to remember, we're looking for information. Try to mark all men we know work for the Hall. I know many of them and I'll point them out to you," she said. "One of the things we need to know is how many men Sunny Jim has on his payroll. You hear people say 'a hundred toughs' but I don't think so. Not even close to. Probably about twenty-five or thirty at the most. That's important. When we know that we can judge how many we'll need when we confront them.

"I think they have some people they know they can recruit from the Barbary Coast if he needs extras, but I don't think they'd be with him in a pinch."

"What about the law?" he asked. "Can we count on them for support?"

"I'd say no, generally," she answered. "There are good people among the coppers, but we need to make sure they're with us before we tell them anything. I know a couple of good ones, but most of them aren't to be trusted. They'd go right to the Boss with anything they find out."

"The Boss has certain men he counts on and sees as leaders. We need to know as much as we can about them and what they're up to. You've already seen one of them. Hershel Grieve was there the night you all broke up their try at lynching Jimmy Li. Barry Presgraves is another. They are the Boss's right and left hands, and one's as bad as the other."

"Hershel's the most dangerous because he's smart. Most of the others are just dumb toughs he gets drunk enough and they do what he wants them to do."

"Was it always this bad?" he asked. "Don't people get tired of all this corruption and looting?"

"A couple of times, back before the War, vigilantes got together. They hanged a couple of Sidney Ducks and ran the rest back to Australia, and it was good for a while. Then about 1856 another bunch of vigilantes got going and cleaned out City Hall, but it always seems to come back. The bunch you ran into when Lemuel got shot was probably some who've been run out of somewhere else and now, they're here.

"The good people don't want to take the time to govern so they let others do it, and when they get tired of watching, the bad ones sneak in again. Right now, the bad ones are running things and the good people are getting upset again. Probably a couple more hangings and things will get better for a while.

"It's funny; some of the businessmen who support Smiling Jim and make money because of it will switch over to our side if they think we can win. They're mostly opportunists who can play by the rules or not. It depends on who's on top."

He followed her into a saloon with a sign reading 'Paddy's Bucket O' Blood' over the entrance.

Johnny and Lemuel were drinking their morning coffee in Lemuel's room the next morning when Wash came in. He poured himself a cup and joined them around the stove.

"Morning Wash. Lemuel and I have been talking about the expansion into next door, so you didn't miss anything." Johnny gathered some papers to make a space for Wash's cup and said, "So how was your first night on the town?"

Washed nodded and replied, "I learned some stuff and found out how much I have to learn."

He stirred his coffee for a moment. "Got to see a couple of his noncoms." He looked at Johnny. "You met one of them, Hershel Grieve, up the street that night."

"Ah yes, the man in the shadows," said Johnny. "You know, I've thought about him more than once since. He had a look about him."

"He's no gun hand, but from what Woman says, most of the Boss's mischief goes through Grieves and a fellow named Barry Presgraves. They give the orders to the plug-uglies. Sometimes they go along, sometimes not. I guess it depends on the job."

Johnny laced his fingers behind his head and stretched his back. "We need to lay out a plan for how we're going to do this." He paused for a moment. "I don't know what to call it."

He looked at the two of them and asked, "Exactly what are we trying to accomplish here?"

He let them think while he got up and poured another cup of coffee. He spoke to Lemuel. "You know, if we make a commitment to join this group - hell, it looks like we'll be working to found the group - we could be risking everything we've worked for and lose it all. Some people might get hurt and it could be Greta or Annaliese."

Lemuel sat quiet for a minute. "These men are taking from us by threat of violence. If we can change that we should try," he finally said.

Johnny sat waiting for him to go on, but he sat mute. He turned to Wash. "It seems like you've made up your mind. Tell me what you think about us getting into this and what we stand to gain if we do."

After a minute Wash said, "Johnny, I need to think about this. I'll be here tonight and then we can talk. So why don't you two fellows go back to talking about what you're going to do with the place next door, and I'll go do some things. When I see you tonight, I'll let you know what I think."

When he was gone, Lemuel said, "I'm glad he's on our side. He'd make a bad enemy."

"I've thought that more than once," said Johnny.

When Wash left, he didn't take Master but instead walked slowly down to the water north of the store. He sat down on the log where he had drawn the marks for Johnny; there was no sign of them left in the sand.

The new things he had learned at the meeting with Madame were floating around in his head and he needed to find some kind of order for them if he was going to answer Johnny's question.

Night-time San Francisco with Woman was an eye opener. While she went into various bars and saloons, he would slip in, trying to avoid notice and sit or stand by the wall near the door to watch and listen.

They had set up a signal so when she wanted him to take notice of someone, she would lift her hat and settle it back on her head. That way he began to see the people they'd be facing if they got into this scrap over control of the city. He'd been around this type of men for years and could see some of this bunch were dangerous, even vicious, and picking a fight with them wasn't something to be done lightly.

So, what were the benefits of joining a group dedicated to overthrowing the current city government, and why did he want to get involved in it anyway? If Johnny and Lemuel decided to lead them into it, he, Wash, would follow. But why?

He remembered once when Woman asked him why he stayed with Johnny and his friends. "Because I can trust them," he had answered. But was it the only reason? If he followed them into this, he would be risking his life, and yet he had no dog in the fight. If they won, how would he benefit? If they lost what would he lose?

With all this running through his mind, he suddenly smiled. He knew he would stand by his friends because that's what he did and always had done. But why Johnny? What was there about him that drew Wash to his side and kept him there?

Wash long ago had decided the answer lay on a plantation back in South Carolina where he once had a son. When the old master died, the slaves were sold off and Wash was taken away from his wife and son to be sold at a slave auction in New Orleans. When he came back to the plantation with Sherman's army in 1864, they were gone, and the manor house had been gutted by fire. He never found out where they had gone, or even if they were still alive.

Johnny was the kind of man he would have wanted his son to be. Now he figured to give Johnny what he would have given his own son, the benefit of his experience to help him through a difficulty. As a father he could do no less.

Johnny and Lemuel and Annaliese were waiting for him in Lemuel's office.

"So, what do you think?" asked Johnny.

"OK, you asked me two questions. First, do we want to get in it? I think everyone in this room has already decided to get into it." Wash paused and looked at each of them. "Am I right?"

They all nodded.

"The second question wasn't the right question. The only thing we would gain is better government and a sense we'd done what was right."

He stopped again and let them think. "The question should have been 'What do we have to lose?'" Again, a pause. "I know each one of you can answer that question for yourself, so I won't get into it except to say I'll be in it with you."

"Just knowing that makes me feel better," said Johnny.

"Since it's settled, let's see if we can come up with ideas about how to do it," said Lemuel. "We can't plan until we know more about them. How many men? What other resources do they have? Who are their leaders and what kind of men are they? This is the kind of information you and Woman are trying to put together, isn't it?"

When Wash nodded, he continued. "What we want to do is organize and think of ways to do it so they won't know anything until we're strong enough and don't care if they know."

"Why don't we think about it and bring some suggestions to talk about when next we meet," said Annaliese. "I assume it will be tomorrow night."

"Needless to say, it's got to be kept quiet, at least for a while, so make sure a customer doesn't overhear." Lemuel laid a finger on his lips.

"You didn't say much tonight," said Annaliese when they were lying in bed. "A penny for your thoughts."

Johnny grinned at her. "Give me the penny and I'll talk."

She patted her legs. "Sorry, don't have any on me. Can we take it out in trade?"

He kissed her and held her for a while, rubbing her hair, stroking her the way he did Jinx every morning.

"I want to make sure you understand we could lose everything if we try this and don't come out on top. These people will likely fight hard and dirty to keep from losing what they have. I don't think there will be a slaughter or anything close to it, but for them killing is just another way to get their point across. A murder or two is not out of the question. People you love could die."

"And we might be forced to kill also, think of that. Could you do it if you had to? If you have a problem with it, this might not be the best thing to get involved in, because once you're in, getting out of it won't be easy."

She lay quiet for a while, and he thought she'd gone to sleep. "Johnny," she finally said, "I realize what it could cost but if we want to keep thinking of ourselves as good people then it's something we must try."

Chapter Twenty-Two

September 1885

Dear Johnny and all,

First thing, Rebecca is pregnant, and the doctor says it's due in the spring, probably in March sometime. She wants to come out there before the snow gets bad, so we will be leaving here in the next few days, but we won't be coming straight there. The last letter from my brother says my father is worse and if I want to see him, I should come soon. We will go home, stay for a few days, and then head to San Francisco. Because it's going to be late with the snow and all, we probably won't be able to come through Salt Lake, so Sarah's going to meet us in Tucson. From there to Los Angeles and then up the coast. Trains sure make it faster.

Bill wasn't too happy with me when I told him, but he understood. Family's family, so what are you going to do but try to be there when you're needed? I don't think he really needs me. I'm just a showpiece of sorts.

There are some here who really carry the show. There's a little girl who's a sharpshooter. I say girl but she's as old as Rebecca. She's really small and she's the darndest thing I've ever seen with a rifle. She never misses.

In one of her shots, she looks in a mirror and fires over her shoulder, and she never misses. They call her Annie Oakley but that's just a made-up name. Her name's Phoebe Anne and she and

Rebecca have become good friends. She's nice, but I wouldn't want her hunting me, that's for sure.

Sitting Bull, the Sioux chief who was one of the Indian leaders at the Little Bighorn, has joined the show. I met him, but he doesn't talk much. People just want to see him I reckon. He saw Phoebe Anne shoot one time somewhere and called her 'Little Sure Shot', so that's what they call her on all the posters they put up for the show.

Just a guess, but I think we'll probably be there sometime in late October or early November. How's Jinx? I miss the little fellow. I loved to watch him and Brutus play.

Your friend, Handy.

Chapter Twenty-Three

Annaliese looked down at the piece of paper in her hand, then looked up at the pole where the street sign should have been. Since the sign was missing, she spoke to a stranger walking down the street. "Could you help me? I'm looking for Lovejoy Street."

"Yes Ma'am," he replied. "That's it, right there. Looks like someone took the sign. What are you looking for? Maybe I can help."

"There's supposed to be a toy shop near here, but I'm new to the city and still learning my way around," she said.

"That would be Geppetto's Toy Shop." He pointed. "It's down Lovejoy on the next corner."

He tipped his hat and walked away, and in a minute, she was tying Dolly to a hitching post in front of a small store with a large window full of toys of all sorts and sizes. A bell tinkled above the door when she entered, and she stood bemused by what she saw.

Above the counter was an ornate sign: Giuseppe Lazzeri, Toy Maker. There were toys everywhere, in cases along a counter, on shelves in the front window, displayed on the wall behind the counter, even hanging from the ceiling. There were so many rocking horses and wagons on the floor, there was hardly room to turn around. From the back room someone called, "Uno momento," and a few seconds later a short, stocky, baldheaded man with a huge smile and a bushy black beard burst into the room.

"Welcome, welcome. How may I help you, Signora?" He had a strong accent, Italian, she thought.

"Yes, I'm looking for a doll," she said, "for a special purpose."

He half turned and indicated several dolls on shelves behind the counter. They were beautifully dressed and delicately painted but not what she wanted at all.

"I need one the size and about the weight of a one to two-month-old baby," she said, holding her hands about a foot and half apart.

"For a special purpose?" he asked.

"I have a young friend who's blind and is recently married and I want to help her learn how to care for a baby, if and when she has one."

He stood stroking his beard with a thoughtful expression on his face. "I have nothing of what you want, Signora, but I can make it for you."

"Make it?" she asked, "You could make it here?" When he nodded vigorously, she continued. "How long will it take?"

He pursed his lips and appeared to be in deep thought for a moment. "It would be three, four days."

"What would it cost?"

"I need to think," he said, "Uno momento," he said and disappeared into the back room. She stepped forward and could see him opening cupboards and drawers.

When he returned, he smiled and said, "It would be three dollars fifty cents, I think."

She looked at him for a moment and then nodded. "All right, when should I return?"

"No Signora, I will bring it to you. Where do you live."

She told him about The BookSeller, and he nodded vigorously. "I have heard of it. I want to visit with my son. He is teaching me how to read English. I love books. In the old country I read a book about a toy maker and that's why my store is called Geppetto's. Of course, my son is not Pinocchio," he said and laughed.

"Pinocchio?" she looked a question at him.

"I will bring the book when I bring the doll and show it to you. Then you will know of Pinocchio."

"So, you made all these toys in your shop?" she asked.

He smiled. "Many of them," and led her through the crowded room to a spacious workshop in the rear where he showed her examples of his craft.

Later when she was guiding the buggy through the crowded streets of downtown, it dawned on her she'd never come out of a store feeling so good, smiling so much. The man's good humor and enthusiasm were infectious.

When she came into the back room at The BookSeller, Johnny and Lemuel were sitting round the barrel waiting for her.

"Madame's agent is supposed to meet us next door so we can look around, take some measurements and maybe get some ideas about what we want to do with it," said Johnny. "Did you forget?"

"Yes, I did," she replied. "When is he supposed to be here?"

"He's a little late," began Johnny but the bell over the door announced his arrival.

It was Nate, Madame's lawyer. The agent had an emergency and couldn't make it, so he came instead.

For the next hour they inspected rooms, opened closets, measured things and did all the things people do when they plan to occupy a new place.

"When can we get to work in here?" Lemuel asked.

"Tomorrow night Mrs. Grimes wants me here with the papers," Nate said. "After we sign them, I will get the contractor in to talk with you. Then you can make plans and start working whenever you want."

While Lemuel and Annaliese were speculating about inside plumbing and its cost, Johnny took Nate aside.

"Since you were at the meeting the other night and heard everything, I'm assuming you are in the inner circle on things regarding our future confrontation with the powers that be."

Nate nodded, "She and I and others have talked about it for some time but now that you and your friends are in town, she and Woman feel it's time to get to work on plans and take the actions necessary to make them happen."

"Lemuel and I have been talking and we have some ideas, but we need a lot more information. Things like, how much of a plan you've got in place, who else knows about it and is committed to making it happen."

Nate shook his head. "Such information will come from Mrs. Grimes and Woman, so I'm sure you'll get some answers the next time you talk."

Lemuel and Annaliese rejoined them. They said goodbye to the lawyer and returned to the store.

Lemuel started to close the door to his room. "Did you tell her about Handy's letter?"

Annaliese looked at him sharply.

"I was going to tell you when we got in bed, if you can behave yourself," said Johnny, careful to stay out of reach.

"What did he say? Are they coming anytime soon?" she asked.

He said goodnight to Lemuel and herded her up the steps.

While they were undressing and washing each other, they talked about having three more people fall on them just as all this was happening.

"Do Greta and Jed know?" she asked.

"Yes, Lemuel told them this afternoon."

She looked thoughtful. "I wonder how Greta will feel about it. Having Sarah here, I mean."

"Have you two talked about it at all?"

"No, we've had other things to talk about and it's never come up."

"She's always liked Sarah, hasn't she?"

She was turning down the covers. While she crawled onto the bed, she rolled her eyes and looked at him with one of those 'men don't understand' looks on her face.

"That was before. No new bride wants her mother-in-law in residence six weeks after she's married the only son."

She pulled the blankets up and he immediately pulled them off.

"Johnny! It's cold in here."

"I want to see."

She assumed a look of resignation. "All right but turn down the gas and look while you're under the covers. I'm cold."

Under the covers, he couldn't see too well, so he began to kiss instead and before long she wasn't cold anymore and threw off the covers so they wouldn't get in the way.

The next morning Greta was waiting when she came downstairs.

"Did you get the doll?" she asked.

"No. He didn't have what I wanted but he's going to make it.

He makes them right in his shop," said Annaliese. "He said it would take two or three days, and he'll bring it here when it's ready." She took the girl's hand, led her into the backroom and closed the door. When they were seated, she asked, "Was there anything else you wanted to talk about?"

Greta sat still for a moment, puzzled. "You mean about Sarah coming to live?" She shook her head. "No, I'll be glad to have her here, although I wonder where they'll stay. Jed told me rent in the city is pretty high. He said there isn't any place around here close he knows of."

There was a knock, and Jed stuck his head in. "Did I hear someone speak my name?" he said and kissed his wife on the top of her head.

Greta took his hand. "We were just talking about Sarah coming and wondering where they'd stay."

He scratched his head, "Geez, maybe we got the building next door just in time."

Annaliese shook her head. "I think Johnny and Lemuel have plans for that place and they don't include them living there. Maybe for a few days, but they're planning to begin construction in the next little while. So, we'll have to look around and see what we can find close by."

Well, I just got a letter from Mama, so I guess it's official," said Jed. "Rebecca's gonna have a baby and they're all coming to California to live.

When she asked Johnny about it, he said, "We'll get Wash and Woman to look around for us. They can find something if anyone can."

Chapter Twenty-Four

The BookSeller was crowded, and when he was able to stop for a minute, Johnny couldn't help but get excited about the plans they were making for next door. It looked like whatever they were doing to drum up business was working. The open houses seemed to have become a favorite way to spend every other Thursday evening for some people, and he was rapidly learning the names and faces of the ones who usually attended them.

Jinx was the proprietor of the place. Lying on the counter where he could see everyone who came in, he got more than his share of attention, played with children while their parents looked at books, and with Brutus chasing him, delighted all with some of his acrobatics in escape.

Jason stopped beside him and said, "Just saw the funniest thing." When Johnny looked a question at him, he continued. "Brutus was walking between bookcases and Jinx was hiding in one. He jumped on Brutus and then took off into the back room with the dog right behind him. By the time I got there, Jinx was up on a shelf taking a bath and Brutus was growling at him like he wanted to commit murder."

"Yeh, he does that to me once in a while," said Johnny. "He does like to play. He's good for business, too. People ask for him all the time. I'm glad he and Brutus get along so well. It wouldn't do for anyone to try to hurt Jinx when he was around.

"Something I'd like to talk to you about," he continued. "Annaliese begins school first of the year and we'd like you to come on full time instead of three evenings a week."

"When?" Jason asked. "I'd like to give Mr. Green some notice, although the way business is, he wouldn't mind me leaving any time."

"Let's say the first of October," Johnny said. "We're getting busier and she's thinking about starting school, so she won't be much help between now and the first of the year. Lemuel and I have been talking and we're thinking we'd like you to learn the business if you're interested."

"I'd like that," said Jason. He gestured at Lemuel sitting in his chair talking to a couple. "Boy, the idea to sit him there to talk to the customers was great. He's selling some books for you."

"It was Jed's idea. The plan is for Lemuel, Greta and Jed to go back on the road selling books when he feels able to, and likely I'd be with them. If it works out, you'd be running the store. How does that strike you?"

"Seems like a step up from shoveling horse manure," he replied with a grin. "I think I'd like it fine."

When Jason went off to help someone find a book, Johnny walked over to Lemuel and spoke in a low tone. "You'll have to close up early so we can meet in the back."

Lemuel closed the book he was discussing with a customer and his wife, handed it to him and nodded at Johnny. "I'll be there shortly. Need to lie down for a bit first."

Madame was in her favorite chair talking to Wash when Johnny came into the back room. He took a seat and when Madame paused, he said, "Lemuel will be here in a few minutes. He just needed to lie down for a minute."

"Is he going to be able to take much part in what we're planning?" Madame asked. "He looks like he's got a way to go before he's really back on his feet."

"I don't think he'll let us keep him out. He wants to be right in the middle of it. He's a tough old bird."

"How old is he?" she asked.

"You know, I've never asked him," replied Johnny. "He rode with Sheridan and was on his headquarters staff. He told me once by the end of the war he was writing most of the orders for the Union

Cavalry. I think he was in his thirties when the War ended so he's probably about fifty-five."

As she came in the door Greta heard them and said, "Papa was born in 1830; he'll be fifty-six in February."

"He knows a lot about organization, strategy and tactics," said Johnny. "In addition to his experiences in the war, he's spent the last twenty years reading about it. I'm glad he's on our side."

Lemuel spoke first when everyone was seated. "Let's start at the beginning. What do we want to accomplish here?"

Everyone looked at Madame. Johnny noticed the same face she had on in the meeting the week before. "We want to get rid of the bad men running the city and stop the stealing and embezzling and the rest of the stuff they pull on us."

"Do we want to use the political system or use force to achieve it?" asked Lemuel.

It was quiet for a moment, then Wash spoke. "I think you'll need both. I don't believe we could win the election if we can't defend the voting places and the people who'll support us. We'll need to protect our homes and businesses too, for that matter."

Lemuel looked around. "Anyone disagree?"

When no one did, he went on. "I suggest tonight we begin to organize, and each agrees to do things we can discuss the next time we get together. Woman and Wash seem to already be working on gathering information. I'd say keep it up. If you find out anything you think we should know right away, come to Madame or me. "

"We also need education, so Johnny, I'd like you to go back to the library and get some histories of San Francisco we can use until we get some in stock. They might have back copies of newspapers, too. If not, go to the newspaper offices. Learn as much as you can about the Vigilantes in 1850 and 1856 and a little about how the city government is organized and when elections are held."

He looked at Madame. "I'm sure you know some people who could help us learn what we need to know about elections, when and how they are run. We'll need to know how things are when it's time to vote, and where all the polling places are.

"If we plan to unseat the current government, we might want to think about people we could put forward as candidates for the various offices." He looked around at them again. "There's also the matter of secrecy. Who do we trust and how do we communicate with them, so they'll be with us when we need them? Madame, I think that would be the best job for you. You and Woman know most of the important people in the city, the ones we need to stand with us if we're going to make this work."

When she nodded, he went on. "Never make a list of our main supporters. When we decide on someone, we can tell Greta. She'll remember it, so we won't have to write it down.

"I'll say one more thing, then I'll shut up and let someone else talk. No matter the best intentions we won't be able to keep this secret for long, so we better be ready, from right now, to defend ourselves and our property."

Everyone sat quiet for a minute, thinking about all he'd said. Finally, Madame broke the silence. "Well, Woman was right. You people will help us make the idea work."

Before she, Woman and Wash left, Nate brought out the papers for them to sign. "The contractor will be over to meet with you first thing Monday morning," he said. "He's worked with Madame for years and you can trust him to do good work."

Annaliese walked with Madame to the door and asked, "Do you know the toy shop on Lovejoy St.?"

"Oh yes, Giuseppe's son and his daughter-in-law work for me. I've known Tony since shortly after he arrived. The old fellow, his wife and Tony's wife only came over last year. Sometimes Carlotta brings their son to work. He's such a little dear. I love to have him running around the house. The five of them live above the shop, which I imagine is quite crowded, but they always seem so happy."

"Well Giuseppe's sure a happy fellow. I went in there today to buy a doll," she said. "He's going to make it and deliver it the day after tomorrow."

"What in the world do you want with a doll?" asked Madame.

"I'm going to use it to help Greta learn how to care for a baby in case she has one of her own."

"The more I see of her the more she amazes me," said Madame shaking her head.

"She amazes us all," agreed Annaliese.

Later, she was brushing her hair watching Johnny in the mirror. "You were awfully quiet tonight," she said. She noticed the more he was around Wash, the more he took his time answering serious questions.

"Pa always said you learn by listening not talking."

"Well, I guess that's true. So, what'd you learn tonight?"

"Lemuel's the one to lead this thing we're doing. He and Madame that is. He's got the experience, and she's got the influence. He knows how to organize things, and she knows most everyone in town on both sides of the street."

She turned down the gas and joined him in bed. "You don't look a bit sleepy," she said.

"I'm not, really," he said. "Got a lot to think about. Will you please come over here and distract me or something?"

So, she did.

Chapter Twenty-Five

Annaliese knocked on the door to Jed's and Greta's room. She was thinking about how to order the next hour, and when Greta opened the door, she could see the same on the girl's face.

"Are you ready to start?" she asked. Greta nodded and Jed got off the bed and pulled a third chair up to the stove where they all sat down.

"Jason's watching the store, and he'll call me if he needs help," said Jed. "I think it's important for me to learn these things with her as much as I can."

"I'm glad that's how you feel, Jed," said Annaliese. "What she needs is confidence, and you can help her with it, probably more than me."

For the next hour Annaliese read, and the others listened.

"Now, let's talk about it," she said when she finished. "The idea behind the first chapter of the book is to be organized. I know you, and I know how organized you are already, so we don't have to change much.

"One question is, where are you going to be living when you have the baby? From what Johnny has told me, the plans for next door include an upstairs apartment for us, which means you will have our room next door. Which room will you use for the baby, and will it also be the bedroom?"

She looked at Greta. "Have you thought about that?"

"Yes, we've talked about it." replied Greta. "There is no sense in moving the bedroom, and that's where I'd like to keep the baby's bed, right next to us when we're sleeping. On my side of the bed, of course."

"The doll will probably be here tomorrow. What we can do is set up everything you'll need for the baby in one place, and cover it with a cloth, so we won't have to set it up every time we practice."

Annaliese took up several sheets of paper and a lead pencil and continued. "We have some of what we'll need, but we need to make a list and get some more things. It would probably be good to go shopping with Rebecca when they get here. I'm sure Sarah will go along to help.

"After the first of the year, I should be in school, so you, Rebecca and Sarah will have to practice without me from then on. We'll talk to Rebecca when she gets here, and I'm sure you'll be able to help with her baby, which is exactly what you need to gain confidence in yourself."

Jed was sitting quietly, listening. "Where do we get all the things we'll need for a baby?" he asked. He reached out to take Greta's hand. "Where do we find out what we'll need?"

"Your mother could probably help you there since she's raised two of her own, and I helped a lot of babies into the world and took care of many newborns at the Doctor's. After the baby gets out of nappies we can learn together."

She held up a book. "Mrs. Keller has a list of things you'll need in here. There are several good department stores in the city, and I'll bet we can find a store just for baby's needs."

"I bet Mama would open one if need be. Then we'd get the stuff we need cheap," said Jed.

"Well, as many people as there are around here, I'm sure there's plenty of places with what we'll need," said Annaliese. "Let's just get what we need in the beginning and then go shopping with them when they get here. I know Sarah will want to go shopping with Rebecca, and we can keep them company."

She looked at Greta. "With you, me, Sarah and Rebecca we can get what we need, and Jed and Handy can come along to carry the packages."

Later that day, Annaliese stood looking up broad steps at a door she'd dreamed of passing through most of her life. The building looked like what she'd thought it would: a school. Red brick with three rows of windows, one above another, taking up half the block. As she climbed the steps, she could see letters edged in gold on glass above the lintel, The University of California School of Medicine, and below, Toland Hall.

She shifted the heavy book she was carrying to her left hand to open the door and was almost knocked down by a rush of men, mostly young men, coming out. Once inside, she oriented herself and found her way to the waiting room of Dr. Brown's office where she sat with four other women about her own age. They were all carrying the same book, a very large one, on the study of human anatomy.

She was just about to speak to the woman next to her when a nurse opened the door to the office. Each of the five women responded when her name was called, followed the nurse into a large room, and took a seat around a long table.

After a few minutes two women entered, and Annaliese recognized Dr. Wanzer and Dr. Brown who had visited her at the store. Each nodded to her in recognition and took a seat at the head of the table.

Dr. Wanzer spoke first. "Good afternoon," she began. "I'm Dr. Lucy Wanzer and this is Dr. Catherine Brown." She smiled and continued. "I'm glad to see you all brought the book, but we won't even be opening it today. The letter you received was a little deceptive. We want to talk to you about something else related to the beginning of school, so we had you bring the book to hide the real purpose of the meeting.

"The first week in January, you five will be the only women in the incoming class of a hundred and three members for the eighteen eighty-six school year," said Dr. Brown. She paused and let the words hang in the air.

"Dr. Wanzer and I attended here ten years ago. Since anatomy is one of the first classes you will attend, we wanted to prepare you for some of the problems you might face in the laboratory. Every year a certain number of students are winnowed out in anatomy. In the dissecting room, there are sights and smells simply too much for some students to deal with, though I'm proud to say none of these has ever been a woman.

"As if these issues weren't enough, this laboratory is also where some male students choose to harass women students with practical jokes and incidents designed to frighten and disgust. This type of thing might also happen in some of your other classes, and for that matter, anywhere in the building.

"One of our early colleagues", said Dr. Wanzer, "Dr. Elizabeth Follensbee, who was a year behind us at school, left in disgust and finished her schooling in Pennsylvania. She then returned and practiced here for several years before moving to Los Angeles for her health. She is still in practice there and has helped a number of our graduates get established in the Los Angeles area.

"One problem with this issue," she continued, "is that a few of the male professors here do not feel women belong in the profession, and they mostly look the other way when incidents such as these occur."

The future students looked at one another for a moment before Annaliese said, "I think we are all aware of that kind of thing. Exactly what recourse do we have in the event these things happen?"

"Unfortunately, very little," said Dr. Brown. "I don't recall any male student ever disciplined for this type of behavior. I'm afraid the only way is to smile and go on with your work."

Dr. Wanzer then asked each of the women to introduce herself and tell the rest a little of her history, and why she wanted to study medicine. Their names were Ginger, Margaret, Gertrude, the oldest, and Jessica, the youngest.

After they finished, she said, "If I were any of you, I would try to form study groups so you can help each other, when need be, and you should each try to make friends with some of the men you're going to be around over the next several years.

"One thing we discovered when we were in school is we all, men and women, have strong and weak points, and by working together everyone comes out ahead by the time it's over."

She asked for questions, answered them, congratulated each on their ambition, and offered to help in any way she could.

The five of them walked down the front steps together, and just as they were all getting ready to go their separate ways, Annaliese said, "We have a back room at The BookSeller where we can meet and study if anyone's interested."

Apparently, they were, and after a few minutes of consultation decided to meet there the following Sunday evening to get to know each other and plan how to go about getting through the next three years.

She was sitting on the bed absentmindedly brushing her hair when Johnny came in and flopped down beside her.

"What time is it?" she asked, looking around.

"Is that all you have to say to your hard-working husband at the end of a very long day?" he asked.

She put down her brush, took his face in her hands and kissed him. "There," she said. "Now, what time is it?"

"A little after midnight," he said looking at his pocket watch. "So, how was your day? Mine was long and interesting."

"Mine was pretty much the same," she answered. "Got Greta and Jed started on learning to care for a baby and met some of my classmates from school." She told him about the meeting and about her invitation to the other women to set up a study group at the store.

"We can study on nights when it's not too busy. You don't mind, do you?

He shook his head. "I think it's a great idea." He was quiet for a minute, thinking. "According to the contractor, we should have things ready next door by the first of November, and I'll bet we can find you some room over there, so it won't matter how busy it is."

"From what I can see," he continued, "Lemuel is moving forward against City Hall, but there's going to come a time when we have to confront those people. Then we'll really see where we stand. At least that seems to be what he's planning." Changing the subject he said, "What are the students you met today like?"

"I don't really know. It's one of the reasons I suggested they come here. We can get to know each other and make plans to study regularly."

He took her in his arms. "Are you excited?"

"Yes," she replied, "and nervous, although I sometimes wonder if those two things, down deep inside, don't feel the same."

Chapter Twenty-Six

Annaliese was perusing her anatomy book at the desk in the back room when Jason rapped on the door jam.

"Fellow out here to see you," he said.

She followed him into the store and smiled broadly when she saw Mr. Lazzeri standing at the counter with a package under his arm. Beside him was a young man who looked like his son and was holding a young copy of himself who looked to be about six years old.

"Buena sera, Signora," said Giuseppe with a grin showing all his teeth. "I have your doll." He handed it to her with a slight bow.

He turned to the young man and said, "This is my son, Antonio, and his son, Giuseppe, but we call him Geppetto."

"Welcome to The BookSeller." To the son she asked, "You work for Madame Grimes, don't you?"

"Yes ma'am," he answered, "and my wife, she works for her also."

"Please call me Annaliese. She told me about your family. I'm so glad you found our store."

The little boy took his grandfather's hand and said excitedly, "Come, Grandpa, let's look at all the books."

They stood and watched as Giuseppe took the little boy's hand and followed him to the bookshelves.

He lowered his voice and said, "Madame has told me of your

plans, and my father and I would like to help if we can."

"You'll have to talk to my husband, Johnny, about that. I'm not into their plans much." She looked at the toymaker again. Somehow, she couldn't see him involved in an insurrection but looks could be deceiving. Lemuel sure didn't look like the leader of one, but he seemed to be doing a great job.

Johnny came into the store looking at what looked like an invoice and spoke to Jason.

"I just checked this in. Can you file it for me when you go in the back?" He handed Jason the paper, then looked up at Annaliese and smiled.

"Hello there," he said cheerily. He kissed her on the cheek and looked inquiringly at Antonio.

She introduced him and told him her doll had been delivered.

"Yes," Johnny said, "Madame said I should talk to you and your father. Do you have some time now?"

"We have my son with us, but I think we can talk now."

Annaliese interjected, "I can watch him while yall talk. We have a small section with books for children. I'm sure he'd like to see them."

She and Geppetto were deep into a picture book of animals when the men returned. Giuseppe took a small book out of his pocket and handed it to her. "Here is Pinocchio, as I promised you. It's in Italian but my son or his wife can read it to you if you like. It is a very small book."

They all shook hands and when the toymaker and his family left, she joined Johnny in the back and looked a question at him. "So, what did you find out about the Lazzeris, father and son?"

"They can help us," he answered. "They have connections and influence with the Italians in the city, and the father marched with Garibaldi on Rome in 64' and fought with him in Sicily."

"Garibaldi?"

"He was a leader in the movement to unite Italy back in the 50's and 60's. Pa had some old newspapers, and I read about him. Seems he was a real hero, and Giuseppe was a scout for him. Antonio has been here for several years, but his father just arrived last year with Carlotta and little Geppetto. He brought many toys with him for the shop and has done well so far. They want very much to be Americans and will help us anyway they can."

"How can they help?"

"They can tell us who's safe to contact among a large group of citizens, maybe not quite like Mr. Li and the Chinese, but significant. Also, the old man was a scout in a fighting war for several years. He's like Lemuel. He knows things because he's been there."

"Do you know which of the servants Carlotta is? I don't recall her."

"No, I don't either, but I'll bet we will before long."

Annaliese had just finished arranging chairs around a small table when someone knocked on the door jamb. She looked up to see Ginger standing there.

"They told me up front you were back here," she said, smiling.

"Yes, come in and pick a seat; first come, first served," Annaliese replied. "Would you like some tea?"

Ginger smiled. "That would be nice, thank you."

By the time Annaliese had served her Margaret and Gertrude joined them and Jessica was removing her hat and hanging it on the hat rack.

When they were all seated Gertrude said, "This is the first time I've been in your store. It looks like a nice place to sit and read. You have so many books."

"We also have periodicals and newspapers. Which is why we put those chairs in the window, so people could sit and enjoy themselves," said Annaliese. "It was Greta's idea. Her father and mother owned a bookstore in Kansas City, and she's given us a lot of good suggestions from there."

"I met her the first time I was here," said Ginger. "She's an inspiring person."

"Greta is quite a tale," said Annaliese, "but before we get into talking about her, I thought we could introduce ourselves and get to know each other a little. It looks as though we're going to be together for a while if it all works out as expected."

They looked at each other and nodded, almost in unison.

"Since you're the hostess, why don't you start?" suggested Ginger.

For the next hour they shared their lives with each other. Ginger was from Tennessee and had come west with her family in 1870.

She was thirty-two, married with no children and she and her husband, Jasper, shared a home with her parents not far from the school. Jasper was an apprentice mortician, and their plans for the future involved moving to another town, once she finished school, where they both hoped to set up practice.

Margaret was from Carson City. She was a nurse who applied for a job at the clinic Annaliese and her father set up there earlier this year. She was twenty-eight and with her new husband, Charlie, lived with his parents where everyone called her Maggie. Her smile was constant and infectious.

Her ambition was to become a surgeon, as if being a doctor wasn't enough of a problem. Her heroine and idol was Dr. Mary Walker, and she believed in the right of women to wear comfortable and healthy clothes so would they please not be shocked if she wore pants sometimes. They all grinned and assured her they wouldn't be.

Gertrude was the oldest of the group at thirty-seven and like Annaliese spent years working with her father in his practice in San Francisco. Her family called her Tudie. She was not married and lived at home with her widowed mother and a sister.

Jessica, or Jess as she liked to be addressed among friends, was the youngest of the group at twenty-four and the only one who had been to college, attending two years at a women's college in Oswego, New York. Upon the death of her father, she and her brother decided to come west to attend medical school together.

She was small and quiet but seemed eager to be a part of the group. She was almost elven in appearance with a sharp nose and green eyes, almost oriental in their shape, and auburn hair probably as long as Annaliese's when she let it down.

She was not married and had no plans to be, at least not for the next few years. She lived with her brother in a small cottage only a few blocks from The BookSeller. He was also a member of the class beginning in January and would like to be a part of the group if they all agreed.

They did, and Annaliese asked if Johnny could also join them once in a while. "He's very well read and can usually contribute to any conversation." No one objected, so he was voted in.

After they left, she reviewed the notes she had taken. They agreed to two nights a week and felt it acceptable to increase the meetings as needed for any of them. They decided to rotate responsibility for refreshments. The meetings were to run for three hours, from six to nine PM Monday and Wednesday, but Annaliese pointed out the store was open and people sat reading at all times of the day, so if they wanted to come in anytime and study it was fine.

Annaliese also volunteered the men of the store to escort them home at night if need be. As the meeting broke up, it was easy to see they were all excited about this new thing in their lives, and she wouldn't be surprised if she saw any of them in the store any time.

Greta was leaning over at the counter with her hand on his side feeling Jinx purr. He was lying in his basket in the sun sleeping. She could hear him plainly, and the impulse to feel the rumble in his side was irresistible. When Jed pressed the front of his pants against her backside she gasped and then giggled.

"Stop it," she said, but felt the electric charge she felt whenever he touched her.

"You don't mean it," he whispered in her ear.

She agreed with him. She didn't mean it. Whenever she felt his body against hers, she felt excitement and it didn't really matter where or when. Nevertheless, she slapped his hand playfully. "This isn't a good time," she said. "What if someone should come in?"

"We'd hear the bell," he murmured into her ear. "It's slow. Let's close up and go upstairs. I haven't seen you in the sunshine yet and it's time."

"We can't do that," she said, exasperation plain in her voice. "Annaliese and her friends are in the back."

She giggled again. "You can't wait, huh? Well you'll just have to." She kissed him playfully and it turned into a long ardent embrace, in the middle of which the door to the back room opened and Annaliese led the ladies into the store.

"Don't mind them," she said. "They just got married."

Greta laughed with the rest, but she felt her face glowing.

When Annaliese came back from escorting her friends out, Jed said, "I'm sorry. It was my fault."

Annaliese snorted. "I hear what goes on over there at night and I know it was probably both of you." She stopped at the counter and surveyed them. "I guess it's to be expected, so we'll just have to put up with it for a while."

"How long will it last?" asked Greta.

Over her shoulder as she went toward the back room, Annaliese replied. "With you two it may take a while."

With the gaslights out, the moonlight coming in the window was bright. He could see her clearly where she lay on the bed and stood looking for a while.

"What are you doing?" she asked.

"Looking at you in the moonlight," Jed replied, "and you're beautiful."

When he entered her, she was almost frantic, and they made love for a long time. Afterward she lay awake, wondering why this time was so special. So far, they had learned much of each other's needs and desires, but it seemed somehow more this time. As she lay there beside her husband, the man she loved, it came to her she was pregnant.

She had no idea how she knew it, but she did. Her body felt different. She felt a surge of warmth when she realized it and then a stab of fear. She breathed deeply several times and slowly pushed the fear out of her mind.

Should she tell Jed? She had the urge to wake him up, but somehow, she wanted to talk to Annaliese first, to find out if it was possible, this thing she believed was true.

Annaliese sat staring at Greta, not quite sure what she just heard. "You think you got pregnant last night? Why do you think so?"

Greta took a moment to answer. "I just feel different, as though something changed inside me. I almost woke up Jed but wanted to talk to you first. Is it possible? Can I know that soon?"

Annaliese sat back in her chair. "Ordinarily I'd say no, but I've never known anyone like you. You seem to know yourself so well, down deep, so I guess it's possible."

"Do you think I should tell Jed?"

"I'd say not. It won't make any difference if he knows now or next month so let's not." She grinned. "The only way to know for sure is for you two to stop doing it for a month or so." She burst out laughing at the look of consternation on the girl's face. "I'm not suggesting it. I just wanted to see the look on your face when I said it."

"It's not going to hurt anything if we keep on, will it?" The look was akin to panic.

"No! No! It will have no effect at all, don't worry. But we might need to begin counting from today to see when. If you're right, it will be sometime in the middle of the summer. That means you'll have plenty of practice, and since Rebecca is due in the spring, you'll have plenty of time with a real baby before you have yours."

After Greta left, she sat for a moment thinking about the girl and things in general. She wondered if she should recommend both Rebecca and Greta see a doctor during pregnancy just to make sure everything was OK.

She had delivered many with The Doctor, but she had no real experience dealing with much of the time of actual pregnancy and she didn't want to fall victim to overconfidence. Both new mothers deserved better.

Chapter Twenty-Seven

Handy Josephson sat looking out the window of the train from Los Angeles to San Francisco. Though the reflection in the glass showed his wife and mother-in-law sleeping uncomfortably on the seats across the aisle, he didn't notice. He was staring out into the dark, thinking about seeing his friends in the morning and what it meant to him.

It was funny; it felt like a homecoming, but he'd never been to the city before. He and Rebecca had left from Sacramento, a hundred miles east of San Francisco, traveled all around the east, ending up in New York, then back to Minnesota to see his father, south to Tucson to get around the snow, to Los Angeles, then up the valley, probably ten thousand miles in all. He remembered how excited he had been on his first train ride but now, if he never took another, it would be fine with him.

He also thought about the last six months and how glad he was to be finished with that part of his life. Getting a chance to join the Wild West Show had been exciting and he'd never regret the time spent, but it wasn't for him, and he knew his wife felt the same.

Part of the reason for the long roundabout was their trip to see his father. Unfortunately, his father passed away before they arrived. They stayed for the funeral and found the passes through the Sierras were closed, hence the long roundabout trip south that would end in the morning.

Born on a farm in Minnesota to Swedish immigrants, he grew up the youngest of five, surrounded by relatives of one sort or another. There was never anything on the farm that prepared him for the life of a showman. Bill Cody hired him because of the way he looked, so he thought he'd give it a try. Rebecca's pregnancy had given them an excuse to leave the show, and he was glad.

They had saved most of their pay, and his family purchased his share of the farm, so they were well fixed and could take their time deciding about the future.

He looked across the aisle at the woman in his life. Even in the dim light of the lowered lamps he could see how beautiful she was. And she was going to have a baby.

He couldn't quite see himself as a father, but he guessed he would do alright. He tried to imagine a towheaded little boy and grinned to himself. Or maybe a little girl with her mother's dark, lustrous hair and those marvelous warm brown eyes.

He was glad Sarah was along. She met them in Tucson and she and Rebecca hadn't stopped talking for two days. The train would be in San Francisco in a few hours, and their new life would begin. He would worry a lot less about Rebecca's pregnancy with Sarah and Annaliese on hand.

And Johnny. He was anxious to see his friend and the others. That's why he felt like he was coming home, because they were here.

Rebecca opened her eyes and smiled at him.

"How long?" she asked, mouthing the words. He held out his arms and she moved carefully to join him.

"About three more hours," he answered. She snuggled against him. She was showing just a bit and he put his hand over her tummy.

"How do you feel?"

"Shaken up. I'll be so glad to get off this train." She sat up and stretched.

"Just thinking the same thing."

"Annaliese said they were looking for a place for us, but it might be a problem."

He nodded at Sarah. "She said she's got a place with a friend for a while, but we may have to stay in a hotel or get a room somewhere, at least for a while. From what we know, they don't have much room at the store."

"Annaliese thought maybe we could sleep in the wagon for a while and then we'll see." She stood. "Let's get some fresh air."

He draped a cloak around her shoulders and followed her to the rear of the car. They stood on the swaying platform, arms around each other, watching the dark countryside rush by, a chill wind buffeting them.

"It's cold, but I needed to feel this," she said, burying her face in his chest. "Oh Handy, I'm so excited to be coming here, to be seeing all our friends. It will be funny to be around Jed. It's hard to believe he's married and all. Wouldn't it be wonderful if Greta got pregnant too and we could raise them together and help each other?"

After a moment she shook her head. "I can't imagine having a baby when you're blind. How will she take care of it?" She was quiet for a moment. "Well, if anyone can do it, she can. Annaliese wrote to me that she can remember where all the books in the store are and find any one she wants."

"She's amazing and I'm cold, so let's go inside," he said.

"You're such a big softy," she said, poking him in the chest.

"You're the one with the cloak on." He pulled her into an embrace and kissed her, then picked her up, and lowering his head, carried her into the warm interior of the car.

There was a crowd of people on the platform when Handy handed Sarah and Rebecca down the steps from the train. After all the hugging and kissing and shaking hands, they loaded everything into two wagons and climbed aboard.

"We've been invited to breakfast at Madame's, so we'll head up there and you can meet them. We can eat and then decide what we're going to do next, OK?" asked Annaliese. "Lemuel and Greta are already up there."

"I'm sure you'll explain everything, so I won't ask," said Sarah with a laugh. Everyone talked while Gray, Madame's butler, drove the wagon through the streets and up the hill to the Mansion.

While Gray and Johnny helped the women out of the wagon, Handy just stood and stared up at the big house with his mouth open.

"Never saw anything quite like this," he said in awe. "How many people live here?"

"From what I understand, one woman and a lot of servants," Johnny replied. "Woman lives in a cottage somewhere around here, but she spends most of her time with Madame."

"That sure is a strange name," said Handy.

Johnny chuckled. "Well, it fits. She's a strange person." He paused and then said, "So is Madame, for that matter. But they're both good friends."

About that time, Madame appeared at the top of the steps to greet them. "We'll talk about her later and many other things," Johnny said as they climbed the steps. "When you get on the porch, turn around and look."

The breeze had cleared away the smoke from morning fires and the bay was laid out before them, Alcatraz and Angel Island in the distance and beyond them, Sausalito on the far shore.

Everyone else was inside and still Handy looked. "I never saw anything like this before. What a way to start your day, walking out the front door to this."

Johnny laughed. "I don't think they use the front door much. Most of the time they go in and out the back door by the stables, although it's right pretty out there too. I suspect they just use the front door for first time visitors." He reached up and squeezed his friend's shoulder. "I sure am glad you're here. Lots going on and I need some help working it out."

Handy grinned at him, "Sounds like old times," he said, and followed Johnny into the house. It took a while to get to breakfast. All the ladies wanted to look around and Madame was glad to give them a tour, but finally they were all seated at a long table in a beautiful room. Servants were bringing food and drink, and everyone was talking to everyone else.

It didn't slow down when they were finished eating so Johnny caught Handy's eye. They slipped out the door into the hall where Wash joined them and led them to a porch. North, east and south the view was uninterrupted.

"Well," said Wash around his pipe. "It's been a while. You look good, Handy."

"It's sure good to see all of you," Handy said with a grin. "Now tell me how you got hooked up with this woman. I doubt if you just walked into town and it happened."

Johnny looked at Wash, who took a long puff on his pipe and began. "I knew Woman from when I was here before."

"I should have known," said Handy. "I swear Wash, I believe

you know someone everywhere."

"Well, since I was here last, she started working for Madame. When we came to town, Madame wanted to see what the bookstore was all about, so she had Woman bring her the night we opened, and it just grew from there."

"She's gone into business with us," said Johnny and explained how they were expanding into the building next door with her help.

Handy was already sitting open mouthed when Johnny dropped the bomb on him.

"You don't know it yet but you're walking into the middle of what could be a nasty fight."

Handy's mouth closed with a snap, and he looked sharply at his friend, then at Wash who nodded.

For the next hour they brought Handy up to date with what had happened since the night Lemuel presented his ideas in The BookSeller and assumed command of the effort to rid the city of Sunny Jim and his gang.

"So, she just up and suggested she help you with the business?" Handy asked.

"Wash told me she does that. When she sees a new business she believes will make the city a better place, she helps it. And it's not just the money. She also helps by using her influence and connections in the city to protect us from problems with City Hall. There's a Chinese family near our place who run a business. She owns the building where they work and helps protect them from problems. You'll meet them. The Li family. "

Wash added, "It's the same thing with the people who work here in the house. They're old friends or people she's helped by giving them a job. Some of them are from other countries and she helps them get a foothold on life here."

"Woman got to know us and told Madame we could help her in her aim to rid the city of some of the crooks at City Hall."

Handy looked at Johnny. "So where do you two fit into this scheme to overthrow the government?"

"Wash works with Woman scouting the city at night and gathering information about the enemy, and I guess I'm sort of an adjutant to Lemuel. I help him by discussing plans, and once we decide on something, I try to get it done."

"How does Madame figure into all this?" asked Handy.

"She knows everyone in town we would like to have on our side and provides any funds we might need to carry out our ideas," answered Johnny.

"Here you are, we wondered where you'd got to." Annaliese and Rebecca were standing at the door. "Come back and join us. Madame has something she wants to talk about."

Everyone was gathered in the drawing room. Greta and Jed had gone to open the store, and as soon as Johnny, Handy and Wash were seated Madame began.

"I've just been getting to know these delightful newcomers and have heard of your problems with housing, so I've decided to offer a solution. I have much more room in this place than I can ever use, so I'd like to offer Sarah, Rebecca and Handy a part of my house to live in until things settle down and they decide what their futures are."

She paused for a moment and continued. "We can set up a couple of apartments so you'll have all the privacy you'd need, and the servants will be just as glad to have you here as I will. It gets lonely in this big place, and it would be nice to have someone to visit with besides Woman and the maids. So, what do you think?"

She was looking at Sarah when she asked this, and Sarah was so taken aback she sat quiet for a moment and then let out an "Ahhhh" and glanced at her daughter, who looked at Handy who said, "Whatever you two decide is fine with me."

"Tell you what," Madame said. "Several of us need to talk a bit, so we'll go into the billiard room and you two can talk about it." She nodded at Lemuel and Johnny, and they got up and followed her out of the room with Wash close behind. At the door Johnny motioned to Handy to join them.

"Woman," said Madame over her shoulder, "Why don't you sit with them in case they have any questions about the way we do things around here."

Chapter Twenty-Eight

When they were all seated and Wash had his pipe going, Madame opened the discussion.

"We're catching the seven o'clock ferry in the morning. What time do we meet the governor?"

"The wire said around five," answered Lemuel, "and we're meeting him at the Governor's Mansion which means we can have a drink and relax a bit." Since everyone was looking at him, he continued. "We were in the cavalry together and he stopped in the store a few times when he was on the way through Kansas City to a new station after the War. I guess I've known him for twenty years."

"Well good. It ought to mean we start a little ahead of the game," said Madame. "How are you going to approach the whole thing?"

"Well, we need to decide what we'd like him to do or say when the news of what we're up to gets to Sacramento." He paused for a minute to let them think about that and continued. "I've been thinking about it, and think we could ask him to make a statement that it's not something for the state to get involved in."

"I've met him, but I don't really know him. I think he knows who I am," said Madame. "I don't get much into state politics, but he seems like a reasonable fellow."

"He and I were the only two Democrats at headquarters for a while back in Virginia in 1864," said Lemuel, "and we talked about politics enough for me to know he's in the middle on most things. I was always surprised Little Phil put up with me all those years. He was a Black Republican."

"Little Phil?" asked Handy.

"That's what we called Sheridan when he wasn't around. He wasn't very big, but he didn't like being reminded of it. Since he was a Major General, it was best to stay on his good side."

"So, you're not going to ask him to come in on our side," said Handy. "How do you know he won't come in on theirs?"

"I don't really, but we're doing something that needs to be done, and if we succeed it will be a good thing for the state, so I think he'll go along with it. Remember this is the biggest city in the state. He would probably like to have it governed well." He looked around the room at each of them. "If he did come in on their side it would create problems we'd have trouble handling."

"You mean the Militia," said Madame.

"Yes, but I don't think it would come to that. George is a reasonable man and he generally does what he thinks is right even though it's gotten him in trouble a time or two over the years. One thing to remember, when California became a state almost all the people lived and worked in San Francisco or at the diggings on and around the American River.

"Did you ever notice how big city hall is? It's just in the last ten years or so the state has come to exert any control over the city. In Sacramento, they're used to San Francisco handling its own problems and going its own way. Since that's been the case, I think we can count on them to keep on doing it that way."

"What's next after the governor?" asked Johnny.

Madame answered. "Mayor Bartlett. We need to find out where he stands, but I know him pretty well. He'll either stay out of it or join us."

"I'd prefer the former," said Lemuel. "My mama used to say, 'too many cooks spoil the broth'."

"Something I'd like to discuss," said Wash. When Lemuel looked at him, he went on. "I think it would be best if I'm not seen with the rest of you for a while. I'll be out and around, and they'll probably just see me as some old nigger hanging around and I'd like to keep it that way. I plan to wear the dark suit and just watch and listen in the night. If I find out anything I need to tell you, I can meet you here."

"Makes sense," said Lemuel.

It made sense to Johnny too. He and Handy looked at one another, remembering Wash coming out of the desert night, almost invisible in the dark. The thought of him moving around in the dark in it, Bowie knife out, always made Johnny shiver a little.

When they filed back into the drawing room the ladies were all smiling.

"We accept your invitation on one condition," said Sarah. "When you get tired of the arrangement, you must throw us out."

Madame reached for the bell, and when Gray appeared gave instructions to unload the wagon. Then she led them to the section of the house where they'd be staying, and the ladies began to talk and plan.

Johnny's friend Jim Steyer was on the ferry's bridge the next morning and waved as they filed up the gangway. It was just dawn when they found seats in the cabin of the ferry and settled in for the trip across the bay.

"They hold the train until the ferry gets in, so we should be in Sacramento by about eleven," said Madame. All the men looked a little rough around the edges from the early hour, but she and Carlotta, her maid, looked fresh as daisies. Madame was dressed to impress and had a feather in her hat that made her appear almost as tall as Johnny.

"Where's Woman?" asked Johnny. "For some reason I expected her to come along."

"She and Wash were out and around last night, so I reckon they're in bed," said Madame. "That's one reason she likes to live out of the Mansion. She's out at night a lot. She's like an alley cat, that woman," and she laughed.

Handy stood and said to Johnny, "Let's go outside. This is my first ride on a boat like this and I'd like to look around."

They found their way to the stern and sat watching the water churn away behind them for a while. "So, tell me about what's happening and where are we as far as being organized?"

"You'll meet some of the others involved Thursday night," said Johnny. "We got a hundred or so people in the guard and probably another hundred we can call on if need be. But the core of the resistance is Lemuel and Madame. She has the influence and money and he's the planner and leader."

"You know," said Handy, "when I met you back in Nebraska, I could see you were going to make my life interesting. I've been here one day, and you've got me in the middle of a war and I'm on the way to meet the governor." He shook his head and chuckled. "So how do I fit into this?"

"I like to talk to you about things because you always give me a different point of view. Since some of the things we're going to be doing over the next little while could be important, I want that point of view." He looked at his friend. "Besides, I always feel better when you and Wash are beside me."

Madame had arranged a sitting room for them at a hotel where they had lunch and waited until the appointed time.

After Madame's place, the Governor's Mansion was a bit of a letdown. A butler led them to the governor, and he greeted Lemuel with a warm smile and handshake, after which he greeted the others.

"I haven't seen you much since I moved in," he said to Madame. "You look beautiful as always."

She grinned at him. "Why thank you sir," she said. "I don't hear that back home too often. I guess I'm just an old shoe to everyone in San Francisco."

"I can't imagine," he said with a big smile. He offered them a drink and seated them around the fire.

"Well, Lemuel, how long's it been, almost ten years?"

"I think you came through Kansas City in '76, the year of the Centennial," replied Lemuel. "I remember we were surrounded by books on the Revolution in the store."

"Sorry to hear about Mary," said the Governor. After a pause he said, "You had a daughter, if I remember right."

"Greta. She's back in San Francisco minding the store."

"I heard about your problems. I heard you got shot up a bit. Looks like you're mending well, though. It all happened a little north of San Jose, didn't it?"

"Right, but we got to town OK, and with Johnny and Greta doing most of the work, The BookSeller's open and doing really well." He paused. "I hear you've had some problems yourself."

"You heard about the fire I take it." When Lemuel nodded, he continued. "Yes, we lost pretty much everything. The papers hurt the most. But we've still got the vineyards and some of the outbuildings and no one was hurt. The house was a total loss."

He shook his head and sighed deeply. "You know, when you take a job like this, people sometimes forget you can have your own problems. They want me to solve everything for them and don't think about me having problems of my own that need solving."

He sat back in the chair and crossed his legs. "So, what can I do for you?"

For the next half hour Lemuel and Madame explained the issues in the city and how they proposed to deal with them.

"We're supposed to talk to the mayor this week, and what we do from there will depend on what he says. And of course, what you say," Lemuel added.

Stoneman looked around the circle at them and asked, "So, what is it you want from me?"

"We'd like a commitment that you would stay out of it. Back in the fifties there were some vigilantes in San Francisco, and it got out of hand. We're trying to avoid that kind of thing.

"We propose to hold special elections to replace the city councilors. There are three of them that are corrupt, and they are bleeding the city treasury, and each is extorting businesses in their bailiwicks."

Stoneman sat quiet for a minute considering. "You know the men you oppose have some people here abouts in their pockets?"

"We're aware of that and we will just have to wait and see what cards they play. We plan to force the resignation of all the members of the Board and then hold special elections to replace them. If we approach this right, we hope to avoid violence."

"If not, we are prepared to deal with it if necessary. But it's not up to us. We won't go looking for it, however we will be organized for defense." He paused and let a quiet settle over the room. "On the other hand, if the need arises and we must defend ourselves, afterwards we will go on the offensive. I believe the vigilantes hanged some fellows last time."

On the train back to the ferry, they all retired to the lounge car so Lemuel and Wash could smoke their pipes and the others could have a beer while they talked. It was unusual, if not unheard of, for a woman to sit in the lounge, but Madame was unusual, and no one objected.

"Back in Kansas I never had occasion to talk to any politicians, so I don't know much about them. Do you think he'll keep his word?" asked Johnny.

Lemuel puffed on his pipe and considered the question. "I've never known him as a politician. As a comrade and a friend, I always trusted him. I guess we'll have to wait and see if he's the same man.

"But he knows me, and I think he understands we'll do what's necessary to win. Politicians like to be on the winning side. Of course, I don't see him as a politician. He strikes me as a good man who's being used by politicians. I guess we'll see."

Chapter Twenty-Nine

Wash sat on the front porch of Woman's cottage smoking his pipe and watching the dawn light grow. She was asleep and by all rights he should be too, but there were things that needed thinking about, and he could never sleep when he needed to think. The previous week he had been out in his dark suit several times, and each time he heard things and saw people together that made him feel something was going on, something Johnny and Lemuel should know about.

But the more he thought, the more he couldn't put the pieces together. He needed more information to see the puzzle whole, and though he was tired, he felt the need to go again tonight to watch and listen some more to find the pieces he needed.

If that was the case, he should sleep. Inside he went to where Woman kept a bottle of brandy and poured a small drink. As a rule, he didn't like whiskey, but for some reason brandy oft-times made him sleepy and it helped now.

It was coming early dark when he awoke. She was gone but that wasn't unusual these days. They each had different things to do and different people to see. Right now, they had to take their time together as they found it.

He sat on the porch in the winter chill and watched the lights of the city come on through the fog for a while to see if she'd return. Fog was more frequent this time of year, near the bay.

He changed into his dark suit, saddled Master and rode slowly down the hill to a livery stable where he left the mule and walked several blocks to gain the vantage point he wanted. Then he settled down to wait.

Herschel Grieve paused and looked over the batwing doors into the loud, smoky interior of the Bucket O' Blood saloon. After a moment he entered and walked the length of the long bar to a table where three men sat drinking and talking.

When they saw him, two of the men greeted him and got up and left, leaving him alone with Barry Presgraves. The two men didn't really like each other so this was not a social visit, but since they both worked for the same man, they needed to be civil and talk when necessary. Tonight, it was necessary.

Five minutes after he arrived, Grieve left, crossed the street to a building with a front porch, and sat in a rocking chair. Five minutes later Barry joined him, and they sat quiet for a moment.

"What's on his mind?" asked Presgraves.

"He thinks it's time to make a move against them, soon," replied Grieve. He paused and then continued. "I thought we should have done it a month ago, but he felt it would blow itself out, so we waited. Now it will be more dangerous."

"Are we going to hit the bookstore?" asked Barry.

"That's what he wanted to do but I talked him out of it. Those boys have a lot of firepower and they'll probably be ready for it. We could get shot up or get into a gunfight we can't handle. No, we need to hit and run, somewhere they don't expect. Then we just fade away."

"Where then?"

Grieve ignored the question. "Did you know most of them stopped paying the gaff this week? It must mean they think they are strong enough to get away with it, which means they could be waiting for us to do something."

"What do you want from me?"

"I want twenty-five men ready with some torches the night after tomorrow. We'll meet down on the waterfront and go from there."

"Torches?"

"Yes, say a half dozen and enough chains, rocks and clubs to do some damage to a few buildings and probably muss up a few people."

"What time?"

"I'll give you the details tomorrow night. Make sure you pick men who won't be too drunk to do the job," said Herschel, and he stood and moved off toward the saloon. After a minute or two Presgraves followed.

In the alley between the two buildings, Wash moved quietly in the shadows along one of them to the rear and melted away into the dark.

Chapter Thirty

Johnny was surprised there wasn't more noise from the gang of men walking in a loose formation behind him. Then he remembered Lemuel's insistence each of the men be a veteran. His Pa had told him of night marches trying to catch the Rebs by surprise and likely many of these men had been there a time or two. Off to both sides behind buildings on both sides he heard and saw enough to realize the men Mr. Li had provided were moving in the alleys parallel to the main street.

Everyone had been told off. The ranks lined up in the street in front of the Bucket o' Blood Saloon, lit half a dozen torches and stood silent waiting to be noticed. Within a few minutes the door and both windows in the front of the place were full of men looking out. When all the men inside were crowded to the front looking out at the street, Johnny and Will Smith, shotguns in hand, entered the back door, positioned themselves on either side of it, and Lemuel stepped into the room between them and cleared his throat loudly.

The men at the doors and windows turned and gaped at the small, slight man leaning on a cane smiling at them.

"Which of you gentlemen are Mr. Grieve and Mr. Presgraves?" he asked genially.

Herschel Grieve growled, "Who the hell are you?"

"My name is Lemuel Waters and suppose we agree to hold this conversation in a civilized manner, shall we?"

Grieve looked at Johnny who was standing with the ten-gage pointed at no one and everyone. "Is this your partner, Mr. Bookseller?"

Johnny nodded. Lemuel continued. "We had some information you intended to pay us a visit, so we thought we'd come by and talk to save you the trouble."

"Where did you hear that?" asked Grieve.

"Now, why would you think I'd tell you that?" Lemuel answered with a smile.

"The men you see outside are but a tithe of our strength," he continued. "We can muster over a thousand guns, and most are men who have used guns before. I wanted to point a few things out to you so we don't have any future problems."

He knew he was not only speaking to the two men, now back at their table, but to the entire room. Many, if not all the men they had on the payroll, were listening raptly.

"First, we intend to call a special election for the Supervisors' seats and the mayor's office in the first week of the New Year. We have candidates to fill these positions, and we will support them as necessary to ensure a free and fair election. Which means there will be armed men at every polling place in the city, and they will act if provoked."

"Second, we are organized to defend our businesses and homes from any attempts to damage them or harm the people therein." He paused, and his gaze swept around the room.

"We need you to convey this message with our greeting to Councilmen O'Hanlon, R. Henderson and M. Henderson. We wish to let them know, while we will not seek a confrontation with you, we will strike back strongly at any provocation."

"What makes you think you can just choose to hold an election?" asked Grieve.

"All of the seats will be vacant due to the resignation of the present officeholders and must be filled. This house cleaning includes any minions they have lurking in city hall or anywhere in the city, for that matter," said Lemuel. "Unless, of course, they win the election."

"What if they don't want to resign?" asked Presgraves.

"Then we will show them the door." Lemuel had stopped smiling.

"Now, I will take my leave." He nodded and turned to go but paused and swept his gaze around the room. "I don't know if you gentlemen are up on your local history, but the two times before when citizens took matters into their own hands there were several hangings. Remember, a mob has no conscience." He stood for a moment and let that hang in the air, then touched his hat and departed.

Johnny and Will came behind him, covering the withdrawal. Will looked at Johnny. "You reckon any of them know what 'a tithe' is?"

"I bet Grieve does, but the rest of them? Probably not."

Johnny and Will sat looking at Lemuel, waiting for him to speak. He looked out the bay window of the store for a full minute before he sighed and said, "OK, we've touched gloves with them. They know things we hope will lead them where we want them to go."

Will shifted in his seat and said, "I would guess we'd better be alert until we find out what their next move is. Do you agree?"

Lemuel nodded. "So, Wash and Woman and the information they give us becomes even more important."

"When will we see Wash again?" asked Johnny.

"He'll likely be here in the morning. Usually comes by before he goes to bed." He stood and leaned on his cane. "Which is where I need to be. Tomorrow we will get together and talk about what Wash brings in?" He looked a question at them, and they both nodded.

Johnny walked Will to the door.

"Do you reckon he'll make it through this whole thing? He looks pretty beat tonight," said Will.

"You know, every night I think that, and every morning he's up before me raring to go," answered Johnny. "I remember when I first met him, I thought a strong breeze would blow him over. Fooled the hell out of me. He's a stubborn cuss. I think he'll make it."

"See you in the morning," said Will and left.

Johnny stood watching his breath take form in the cold night air, thinking. The fog was thick, and it changed the way noise sounded.

When Wash first brought them the information about the

projected raid on their forces, he wanted to lay an ambush and strike their enemies down.

Lemuel decided to take a different tack. He felt they were strong enough to issue a warning and then let them make the first move. If they struck out, we would strike back hard. But, if violence could be avoided and the change they wanted effected peacefully, so much the better. Many of the men with them had families and there was no sense in risking lives if a way could be found around it. They weren't out to punish anyone, just take their city back.

Chapter Thirty-One

"Ouch!" Annaliese looked up from the book she was leafing through to see Rebecca sucking her finger.

"That's three times already," said Rebecca. She looked at Greta standing beside her. "How many times did you stick yourself the first time?" she asked. The doll was laying, half diapered on the table in front of her.

"None," answered Annaliese. She held up a small volume that looked well used. "We worked out a system using advice we got from this book."

"I think I need to read the book," said Rebecca and they all laughed.

"Good idea," said Annaliese. "We've been working on this for a couple of weeks, and it will be a good thing for Greta to review what she's learned so far. So going over it again with you will help her too. Right now, we're working on smells and how she can use her nose to help her know where the baby is all the time.

"Let's sit and I'll tell you how we have organized it." Annaliese indicated the chairs by the bed.

"I'll take it home and read it tonight if you don't need it," said Rebecca as she sat on the bed. The room was so cramped with furniture there was only room for two chairs. "What have you learned so far?"

"Rather than go over it all now, we'll help you learn the same things over the next couple of weeks. We usually get together twice a week, and she practices in between. It might be a good idea for you to get another doll from Giuseppe, so you could practice at home."

"What do you mean, smells?" asked Rebecca.

"She needs to choose a fragrance she will recognize and use it for nothing else, so whenever she smells it, she knows where the baby is. When it begins crawling, and then walking, it will help her stay oriented to where it is. We will also put a small bell on the ankle so we can hear when it moves."

"Can we call the baby something besides 'it'?" said Greta. "It sounds so impersonal."

They sat considering the idea for a minute.

"Do you want it to be a boy or a girl?" asked Rebecca. "Sometimes I feel one way and sometimes the other."

It had been two weeks since Greta revealed to Annaliese, she believed she was pregnant, and it was still just between the two of them. Now she decided to let Rebecca in on the secret.

"I feel the same way, most of the time," Greta replied, "but let's say 'her' for now. Anything but 'it'." She took a deep breath. "I've believed I've been pregnant for two weeks now. I don't know how, but I just know."

Rebecca looked at Annaliese with a question on her face.

Annaliese shrugged "She felt it after lovemaking one night. Normally I'd say it was a wish more than anything, but with her I don't know. She seems to see inside herself in ways the rest of us don't." She looked at Greta. "Still feel it, Greta?" she asked.

"More than ever. I'm sure."

Annaliese stood and said, "I'm supposed to meet Maggie in a few minutes so if you want to sit here and talk, I will see you later."

When she came down the stairs, Maggie was sitting in the reading room engrossed in a book. She was also wearing bloomers which had been a fad about the time she was born but wasn't so much anymore. She smiled up at Annaliese and they soon departed for a planned buggy ride along the shore of the bay out to Fort Point.

There was a stiff breeze coming in from the ocean, so they decided instead to shelter in the loom of the hill under the Presidio, enjoy the view and talk.

Maggie was new to the city, so for a while Annaliese pointed out the features they could see around them.

"Tell me about this idol of yours. Her name is Mary Walker?" Annaliese asked.

"Dr. Mary Walker," Maggie corrected her. "She's really an amazing woman. My mother went to the school her family started in Oswego, New York, and though she had left by then, mama was always fascinated by her family's ideas on how women should be looked at in this country.

"Mama's no reformer but she talked about her and her ideas while my sisters and I were growing up, and I made an effort to find out all about her I could. The more I found out the more interested I became. I met her once and we talked for hours. I subscribed to the magazine she wrote for and tried to find everything she ever wrote.

"Dr. Walker became a surgeon in 1855 and volunteered during the war to work with the Union Army. She served all through the war, was captured and imprisoned as a spy by the Rebels, was exchanged and eventually given the Medal of Honor by President Johnson.

"She is a progressive who has written about women's suffrage, temperance and reforms in women's clothing. Her ideas about changes in women's clothes are based on health, comfort and sanitation. She believes things like corsets and tightlacing are detrimental to a woman's health by constricting the body in such a way as to cause damage and displacement of vital organs.

"She also believes they restrict movement and force women to live up to men's ideas of what they should look like. And finally, she believes the long skirts and heavy underclothing women wear trap dirt and water and are unsanitary.

"She's been arrested several times for wearing men's clothes, but she always says, "she doesn't wear men's clothes, she wears her clothes."

She grinned when she said this and watched Annaliese's face for a reaction.

"We moved to Carson City because my father was offered a position as an editor for one of the papers. I applied for a job as a nurse at the clinic you started, but you needed a Mormon.

"I met Charlie there and we married after he promised to help me get into medical school and to do his best to understand the demands the profession would make on me."

"So, do you wear pants because she does or because you believe what she teaches?" asked Annaliese.

Maggie grinned, "Because I believe she's right. I believe I should be as comfortable as I can and should wear clothes that make what I'm trying to do as easy as possible."

"Do you believe in women voting and participating in politics?"

"Not so much," replied Maggie, "and temperance is not something I worry about, either." She winked at Annaliese. "One fight at a time, is what I say."

"How do Charlie and his family feel about your reform ideas?"

"He's fine with it and so are his two sisters and his mother. Papa on the other hand is not happy about them, so we don't talk about it much when he's around. I think the first time one of his girls wears a pair of pants he'll probably fall over in a dead faint."

They were both silent for a minute, thinking.

"Do you worry it will be a problem in school?"

"I talked about it with Charlie, and he says I should be able to wear what I feel is appropriate for whatever I'm doing. I don't believe the women teachers will object but I may have a problem with some of the men."

After a moment she continued. "I read somewhere you don't just fight the fights you can win; you fight the ones that need fighting. I also read in Dr. Walker's magazine where an anatomy professor said women who have regularly worn corsets and other support garments are not suitable as cadavers because their internal organs are misshapen and displaced." She looked at Annaliese and raised her chin a little. "This is a fight that needs fighting."

"Well, I'll stand with you," said Annaliese, "and from what I've seen of the other ladies, likely they will too. From what I know of women doctors they have to be willing to push against barriers or they wouldn't be trying to be doctors in the first place."

They laughed and Maggie asked, "How long have you been married?"

"Two months."

"So. I'm sure you had the 'talk about being a doctor' with him."

"Johnny and I have decided to support each other and yet try to live the lives we can. With me in school for the next three years, I don't expect him to just hang around so we can be together whenever I can arrange it.

"We've agreed to make it work so we both need to live our lives and when we can do it together, we will. If he wants to take off with his friends for a few months, that's OK. I believe he loves me enough that he'll always come back."

"I heard you were a nurse for your father for a long time," said Maggie.

"Yes, seventeen years. That's where I met Johnny. He was thrown from a horse and the Doctor and I put him back together. He was in the hospital for about two and a half months and after a month I knew I loved him. I was just surprised he loved me too."

"That's very romantic," said Maggie with a laugh. Annaliese noticed she laughed a lot.

"What kind of work does Charlie do?"

"Charlie is a bank clerk, and they don't know he's a rebel at heart. They'll probably fire him if they find out."

"Probably. There aren't very many progressive bankers. They tend to be conservative, although back in Salt Lake all you needed to get a loan at the bank was one of the leading Saints vouching for you."

On the way back to the store, Maggie asked, "How do you think the people in the store will react to me wearing pants or pantaloons?"

"They won't care. We have a regular customer who's a woman. She wears trousers every day and no one says a thing. Of course, that's not surprising; she wears a Bowie knife with a foot-long blade behind her belt."

She laughed when Maggie gaped at her. "You'll meet her if you become a regular at the store. She comes in a lot with a friend."

Chapter Thirty-Two

It was getting dark over the city. Wash was sitting in Madame's easy chair, in a bathrobe, watching lights wink on below him and thinking he better get dressed and get going. In the dusk he could see the two women lying asleep in Madame's big bed. They had spent the afternoon doing things they enjoyed doing to each other and now he had work to do, though it looked like Woman was taking the night off.

After he finished dressing, he covered them with a blanket even as he admired the curves he enjoyed looking at. As he was turning away, Woman grabbed his wrist and pulled him back for a kiss.

"What if I want some more?" she whispered.

He grinned. "I got work to do, woman. Go back to sleep or wake her up."

She appeared to think for a moment and then fell back on the pillow and closed her eyes.

Exiting through the kitchen, he nodded to Carlotta and the cook and outside took Master's reins from the stable man and mounted for the short ride into the city, wondering as he rode if he'd ever get used to things like cooks, butlers or stable men.

He left the mule at a stable, walked the twenty blocks or so to the saloon nearest city hall and positioned himself in the shadows so he could see who came and went.

He was only there a short time when Herschel Grieve came

through the batwings, walked briskly across the street and sat down in the rocker on the porch where Wash had seen him before. Within a few minutes Presgraves joined him.

Even with the noise from the saloon, Wash could hear them clearly where he stood in the shadows.

"What's going on? Did you talk to him today?" asked Presgraves.

"We had a long talk but really didn't come to any conclusions. I'm supposed to see him again in the morning. We're going to meet with the others and decide what's best going forward." They rocked in silence for a while.

"Did he say anything about what he wanted to do? The boys are asking me what will happen next. A few have already skipped town. Said we didn't pay them enough to hang for it.

"He didn't say much, just listened mostly," said Grieve. "Tell you the truth I got the feeling he doesn't like the odds. He's going to think on it and let us know what he decides."

Presgraves stood, "If he takes too long to decide anything we probably won't have enough men left to pour piss out of a boot. The numbers scare them, and everyone knows the history of the vigilantes. They figure people are getting tired of being fleeced and now they're organized, it could be dangerous. Probably cost more to keep the ones who stay on the job too."

"I'd say they got a point." A match flared and Wash could see Grieve's face while he lit a cigar.

"It seems this Waters fellow is an old Army friend of the Governor. Could cause us problems in Sacramento. I'll meet you tomorrow night and let you know where we stand," said Grieve. He stood and stepped off the porch. "Try to keep them happy for another day," he said as he disappeared into the shadows.

Grieve was usually in bed by ten in the morning but this morning he needed to meet with Jim and his two cohorts on the Board. He had stayed up for the meeting and was tired. He hoped it wouldn't last too long.

By the time he got to the office on the fourth floor he was a little winded. The first time he rode in an elevator he realized it was not something he liked so whenever he came to talk to Jim, he usually took his time climbing the stairs. Today, however, he was a little late, so he hurried.

Jim's big corner office was down the hall, and he usually smiled a little at how small and insignificant the office door was; no name, no number and it was locked. When you went to see Sunny Jim, you needed to know where you were going and be expected.

Jim's other office for constituents and city business was downstairs, but it was small and a little dingy. "No sense in showing them what we do with their money," he always said.

Grieve knocked and was admitted. The windows wrapped around the corner and let in plenty of light the way Jim liked it. He took a seat at the long table and nodded to the men sitting there.

Jim was looking out the window at something, and after a minute he went to his desk, made a note on a sheet of paper, and then took his seat at the head of the table.

"Well gentlemen, it looks like it might be time to cash in our chips." He sat looking around at them for a long minute while the statement hung in the air.

"It's that bad?" asked Little Mick Henderson. He was sitting where he always sat, at Jim's right hand. Across the table was Big Bob Henderson, Mick's first cousin. The three of them were partners in crime. Grieve was the only one they allowed at these meetings and he usually just sat and listened. Afterwards he would talk to Jim alone and get his orders for what they wanted done. It was his job to see it got done.

Big Bob was tall, over six feet and husky with large hands and broad shoulders. He joined Jim as a bully boy when he was a kid working his way up the ladder until now, as President of the Board, he was rich and powerful, as were they all. Little Mick was small, barely topping five feet, and had come to San Francisco with Bob. They grew up together in the Bald Knob country of southern Missouri and came west in the 1860's to avoid the war.

"Do you know what a 'tithe' is?" asked Jim.

Though Grieve knew, he also knew the question wasn't for him, so he waited to see if either of the men answered. They didn't.

"It means a tenth of something." He let that sink in for a moment. "There were a hundred men in the street the other night. If that's a tithe it means they've got a thousand guns. Probably getting more every day. How many can we muster? Fifteen, maybe twenty."

"Most of those men were in the Army and they know their way

around a fight. Besides, I hear they got an in with someone in Chinatown, not to mention the Governor, which makes them more dangerous. And they have a cause; they're throwing the rascals out. All we got is a bunch of pug-uglies who are drunk more often than they're sober."

He got up and walked to the window again. "Do either of you think we can handle a fight like that?"

"I guess not," said Little Mick," but it goes against the grain to just give up."

"From what I gather, if we go peacefully, we can probably take some of what we have with us," said Jim, "but if we hit out at them, they'll hit back hard. Then all bets are off, and we could lose everything, not to mention the possibility of a bullet or of dancing on air."

Bob drummed his fingers on the table. "How long do you reckon we'll have to pack up and go?" he asked. "There's a lot of things we'll have to leave behind. No matter what you say, I don't believe they'll let us get away with much. Maybe the less trouble we give them the better. It would be nice to get out of this with a whole skin."

They looked at Grieve. He looked at Jim, and when the latter nodded, he said, "They plan to hold elections right after the first of the year, so probably any time before. Personally, I think it would be wise to fold your tents and go, the sooner the better, and keep the swag to what you can carry. The longer you hang around the more chances they'll lose patience with us. We've made some enemies and we shouldn't feel surprised if some want to get even."

They all looked at Jim and he nodded his head and said, "I'm planning to resign and leave in a few days, maybe sooner. You guys do what you think is best, but don't drag your feet. A mistake in judgment could be fatal." He pushed back his chair, a signal the meeting was over, and within a minute he and Grieve were alone.

"So, what are you going to do?" Jim asked as he lit a cigar.

"Well to tell you the truth, it's come on kind of sudden and I haven't thought much about it yet," Grieve replied. "I'm pretty well fixed so I may hang around for a while and see what happens. It will be interesting to see how they go about keeping things running. I doubt they've much experience in running a city, especially one this big."

"I wonder who they'll get to run for office?" said Jim. "Of course, they'll have Bartlett, and the Mayor does know a lot about how things work, and Tim knows a bit about it too. Some of our people will have to leave but there will still be a good number left to keep things going."

Grieve stood and held out his hand. "It's been interesting, working with you and the others, but I think if I'm going to stay around here I'll have to figure out another way to make a living."

Jim walked to his desk, took out a bundle of greenbacks tied with a string and handed it to Grieve.

"Here's what I figure I owe you." He shook Grieve's hand and walked him to the door. "Remember a few years ago we hired a guy to come in to do a job for us? What was his name?"

Grieve's brow knotted for a moment, "Unusual name. Gerhard Schweder."

"That's the one."

Grieve looked a question at him.

Jim smiled. "There's such a thing as revenge," he said as he closed the door.

Chapter Thirty-Three

Johnny was sitting in Lemuel's office playing with Jinx when Lemuel came in and sat at his desk to read the mail.

Suddenly he sat back in the chair and said, "I'll be damned."

Johnny looked up and responded with a grin, "Likely, but not for a while, I hope."

Lemuel handed him several folded sheets of paper. He laid two of them on the desk and unfolded the first one. It was a resignation letter from Sunny Jim O'Hanlon. The other two were the same thing from the other two Supervisors. He looked up at Lemuel and his partner burst out laughing.

"What so funny?" asked Johnny.

"The look on your face, although it's probably the same one I've got on mine."

"Do you think these are real?" asked Johnny. He stood and closed the door.

"Well, it makes sense. Jim's not stupid even if the rest of them are. He knows the numbers are against him, but I didn't think it would happen this quick."

Lemuel shook his head. "This puts us in the position where suddenly we have to run the city. We need to get up to Madame's right away and let her know about this and find out what needs to be done next. We might need to find out about putting in a telephone line if we keep doing this kind of thing."

"We also should put someone to watch the three of them so they don't sneak out of town with the loot. Why don't you and Jed ride out to Will's and have him get some people to watch them? By the time you get back, I'll be ready to go."

He stood and faced Johnny. "This is sort of an emergency situation regarding the running of the city, but I want you to understand something. I want no part of things from here on out. This is out of my bailiwick. Madame's got some candidates picked out and we're supposed to meet them at her place in the morning. Once we decide how to hand it to them, I'm back to being a bookseller."

"Agreed," said Johnny. "Me too."

Johnny was back inside an hour and they were soon on their way to the Mansion in the buggy.

"Where's Annaliese this morning?"

"She and a couple of her study partner friends are shopping for clothes and things for school; smocks and aprons and such." Johnny guided the horse to the back side of the Mansion and they entered through the kitchen.

Gray led them upstairs. A knock on the door and they were led in to where Madame was reading the paper over the remains of her breakfast. She was in her dressing gown but no one was embarrassed so they sat and got down to business.

She looked up from reading the resignations with surprise on her face. "Ahh, now what do we do?" she asked.

"That's why we busted in before you got dressed. What do we do now?" Lemuel answered with a question.

She sat quietly for a long minute. "I guess we need to get Mayor Bartlett and the remaining Supervisors up here right away. They'll be able to help get us through this."

"What will we do about the election?" asked Johnny.

"That's the kind of thing they can help us with," said Lemuel.

"Tim Reston has been on the board for a few years, so he and the Mayor know pretty much how things work and who does what," Madame said. "I don't really know the other Supervisor. He was just elected last year but he seems pretty straight." Madame rang the bell and by the time Gray appeared a note was ready for him to carry to City Hall.

Then she stood and said, "Gentlemen, I'm going to get dressed to meet our guests. Why don't you see if Sarah and Handy want to join us when they arrive? The more points of view we have the better."

"Do you think they'll be here that quickly?" asked Johnny.

She smiled at him from the door. "Of course," she said. "Given what's going on at present, they won't be surprised to get the message. And there's also the fact it's from me."

Johnny wanted Handy involved, so they asked Madame's maid to fetch him. By the time Madame was back Handy and Sarah were listening to Lemuel's explanation, and they were just as shocked.

"We're still getting settled in," said Sarah, "but I must say this is much more interesting than moving furniture. Doesn't this take you by surprise?"

"Surely it does," said Lemuel. "Johnny and I got into this to get them out of office. Suddenly they're out and we want to see what we need to do to get the whole thing in the hands of officeholders so we can get out of it. We want to sell books, not run for office."

"Would you like something to drink?" asked Madame. "I'm going to have some coffee."

They were all soon drinking coffee and talking about the remarkable situation they found themselves in.

"I would imagine there's a certain amount of inertial motion in something like a city government," said Lemuel, "so most of the everyday work of the city will go on without any real problem, at least for a while."

Handy raised a finger. "What's inertial motion?"

"It means it will keep running because it's been running even if we don't do anything," answered Johnny.

"It seems like the first thing we need to do is get people in the offices," said Lemuel. "The mayor can probably appoint someone to serve until we can get an election organized."

"Sounds reasonable. I mean they'd have to appoint someone if there was a death or resignation. Just have to do it three times now instead of once," said Madame. "I'm sure Wash knows how to handle it."

"It sure sounds funny to hear that," said Handy. "I mean, I've been thinking all along Wash is Wash, and now it turns out he's the mayor too."

They all laughed. "Who are these fellows we're supposed to see in the morning?" he continued.

"They're the men we've lined up to run for the vacancies," said Madame. "I've known a couple of them for a few years, and they all seem like solid people we can trust."

"Jonas Burke came out here to work for the Central Pacific in 1868 and he's been here ever since. He started a hauling business and now has a fleet of wagons working all up and down the peninsula. His wife died a few years ago and he's gotten into the city's affairs since then, usually in opposition to Sunny Jim and his gang.

"Robert Rasmussen is almost a newcomer. I think he came out here in the late 70's from Boston with another fellow to open a general store. In addition, he runs a newspaper. He's fairly new to the city's politics but he generally has a good reputation.

"The last one I don't know at all. He was recommended by Jonas. I think he's in the shipping business and has a couple of warehouses on the docks somewhere."

Just as she finished, the door opened and Gray announced the Mayor and Tim Reston, one of the sitting Supervisors. The other member of the Board was across the bay and wouldn't be back for a few days.

"Well, won't he be in for a surprise when he gets back," said Madame and laughed.

She introduced everyone and they all sat while the Mayor read the resignations. He finished, handed them to Reston, took a deep breath and leaned back in his chair. He was a big man with a paunch and his breathing was audible even in the big room.

"This is what we wanted but I didn't expect it this quick," he said.

"It does take us all by surprise," said Madame. "When we talked to you about our plans and the people we wanted to propose for the seats, we were thinking about an election six or seven weeks from now after a time of tussle with Sunny Jim and his friends," said Madame. "They've pulled the rug out from under us with these." She held up the papers. "We need to get people in place to move things forward and keep the city from grinding to a halt."

She paused and nodded at Lemuel.

"Lemuel has been our leader up to now and I know for a fact he has no desire to get involved in city government nor does Johnny over there. One of the things we need to decide is how we can best use him and his people to cover our flanks till we get things back on an even keel. I don't think Jim and the rest of them will double cross us, but it would be smart to have our friends around for a while just in case."

"How many men can you muster?" asked Reston, "And how fast?"

Lemuel rubbed his chin for a minute. "I think I could have a hundred men at city hall in a couple of hours."

"How do we go about getting our candidates in office officially, and what do we do about the election?" asked Madame.

"I can appoint them to the positions, and we can set up a special election for a few weeks down the road," said the mayor. "Give people a little time to get used to the idea and see if they want someone else in the job."

"No more like Sunny Jim and his crew," said Reston. "We don't want to have to do this all over again in a year."

"Can I make a suggestion?" asked Lemuel. "Let's stick to the schedule we set up. Let's schedule the election like we planned, after the first of the year. My men will cover the polls so there's no shenanigans. This will give the people of the city some time to think about things and give our candidates some time to let everyone know what kind of government they plan to have. Also, they'll have a little time to see if they like the job. Temporary appointments can keep things going for that long, can't they?"

The two men sat and thought. Within a minute they were both nodding. "When can we meet with the candidates?" asked the mayor. "If we can find them in the morning, let's put the idea to them and see where we stand."

"They will be here in the morning for a meeting. We already arranged it to get the process started. I told them about ten o'clock," said Madame. She looked at Lemuel. "In the meantime, can you get some men to cover the doors at city hall so no one takes anything we don't want them to take?"

"We did that as soon as we got these things," said Lemuel. He waved the resignations. "And we have men watching their houses. If they get away with anything, they'll have to be pretty slick."

After the visitors left, they sat and talked about the meeting next morning and what they needed to find out going forward. It was decided Johnny would draw up an agenda of sorts, and he and Lemuel would come early to let Madame look it over before the meeting.

Handy wanted to come back to the store with them to talk so he joined them, and Sarah went back to moving furniture. Fortunately, there were servants to help.

Chapter Thirty-Four

Annaliese came downstairs to quite a racket, which was unusual for the bookstore. The carpenters and workmen next door had forgotten to close the door between the old and new buildings and the sawing, hammering and other construction noise was unusually loud.

Since Lemuel and Johnny had gotten involved in the militia, some of the work around the store had fallen to her, and among other things she was keeping an eye on the workmen and their progress next door. She actually enjoyed watching the place take shape and had taken suggestions from some of the workmen. It was on their advice they decided to electrify the new addition, and this morning they were hanging the new chandelier and mounting the wall fixtures.

They had decided to make the main room a sitting and reading room, as Jed called it. The shelves and books would be arranged around the perimeter and the center would be furnished to create a quiet, pleasant place where people could sit and read or look through books they were interested in.

A bay window had been added, similar to the one in the store. Lemuel would sit there with people who wanted to talk to him about books. Two other downstairs rooms had been fitted with bookshelves, desks and small writing tables. The kitchen and dining room/meeting room stretched across the rear of the house, but they hadn't begun that work yet.

She picked her way through the cluttered room and ascended the stairs to what would be their new apartment. The east facing windows had all been replaced and enlarged to increase light, and in the living room two men were preparing to hang the new wallpaper she picked out.

She was thinking about how she wanted to furnish the bedroom when she heard her name called. When she got back into the store, Maggie and Jessica were waiting for her.

"We're a little early," said Maggie, "so if you're not ready, we'll just look around."

"I was just going to fix some coffee and sit in the back for a while. Why don't you join me? What time are we supposed to be there?"

"We can go anytime," replied Maggie. "Tudie works with her sister, and she said they'll be there all day. They have three girls who work the sewing machines so they can probably have what we decide we want ready before too long."

When they were all seated around the stove, Maggie said, "I'd really like to hear about you working with your father. You said you did it for sixteen years?"

"Actually, a little more," replied Annaliese. "I began when I was ten and I left just before I turned twenty-eight."

"In the beginning I just ran errands, but I asked, and he began to show me things, and it just grew from there. He has a large collection of medical books of one kind or another and he encouraged me to read as much as I wanted, so I did."

"Did he go to a medical school?" asked Jessica.

"He is a Mormon, and the church sent him to Germany to school a few years before the war. He finished and came back to Salt Lake City to practice among the Saints. Of course, he treated anyone who needed it as well as church members. When the War came along, he joined the Union Army and served as a surgeon and doctor until Appomattox.

"We talked a lot about his time during the War. He always said that's where he learned to be a doctor. I remember one time he told me the first time he used a scalpel on a man he didn't have anyone watching him because they were all too busy. He had to learn for himself as he went along.

"He once told me by the time the War was over, he'd seen the inside of almost all the human body because bullets hit them everywhere and it was his job to go in and dig 'em out or fix what they went through.

"He was also a regimental sanitation officer, and he learned about disease and how people became sick and why. He always said, 'if you know how to keep men healthy in the army then it's just a short step to helping a town or city stay healthy.'

"He learned about the germ theory in Germany, and it opened his eyes to how disease spreads and how poor sanitation can kill more effectively than bullets sometimes. You know, more soldiers died from disease during the War than from battle wounds.

"So, he practiced and learned surgery by cutting people up?" asked Maggie, eyes wide with amazement. "I can't imagine."

"He told me about a time he was a surgeon at Fredericksburg during the battles around there. He did nothing but cut off men's arms and legs for a day and a night. He came outside the hospital tent to stretch and sit for a while, and over the hill came another line of wagons full of men wounded at Chancellorsville and needing their arms or legs cut off."

"Why were there so many arms and legs amputated?" asked Jess.

"From what he told me, a new bullet was invented by a Frenchman in the 1830's. When the bullet struck a large bone, it fragmented. Between the pieces of lead and pieces of bone and cloth in the wound, the patients would likely have bled to death if they tried to get all the fragments out, or they would have missed some and the patient would have died from gangrene. They couldn't take the time to learn how to repair the wound, so they cut off arms and legs to save lives.

"He said you learned or went crazy trying. A lot of doctors he knew in the army were drunk much of the time when they weren't actually on duty, and sometimes even when they were.

"He always said there was so much waste and sorrow in the War, but that's where he learned to be a doctor and it was true of many who lived through it. Medical practice was so much different after the war because of what they'd been through - what they'd learned," she paused, "and the mistakes they'd made."

"I worked as a nurse for a doctor in Carson City and I thought

I'd seen some things, but nothing like that," said Maggie. "Did you do any surgery with him?"

"No." Annaliese smiled. "I got plenty of practice with cuts and scrapes, bullet wounds, and broken bones. I dug bullets out of people and sewed them up, but he didn't practice as a surgeon. He used to call himself a 'country doctor'.

"He took pretty much whatever walked in the door. By the time I was twenty-two, I would go out on calls by myself if he were doing something and couldn't make it. The people of Salt Lake were used to seeing me in a wagon or buggy going somewhere in the middle of the night, in all weather. They accepted me because, when you need a doctor, I suppose I was better than nothing."

"What do you all want to study?" asked Jessica. "It seems like most women go into mother and baby practice or work with children. I think I'm inclined to the latter."

"I want to be a surgeon," said Maggie, "but from what I understand, I'll probably have to make the choice as to what kind when I'm a little farther along in my studies. Besides, I might change my mind. Charlie think's I'm good at that."

They looked at Annaliese. "I think I'd like to go along the same lines as the Doctor," she said. She laughed when they looked puzzled. "That's what I call my father. We always took whatever came in the door, and at this point, that's what I want to aim for. I think they call it general practice."

She stood and said, "If we're going to get to Tudie's before lunchtime we'd better get going."

The Ladies Fashion Dress Shop was downtown, and while Annaliese was tying up Dolly out front, Jess and Maggie were staring around at the area. They were newcomers to the city and there was always something new to look at.

The bell above the door announced their arrival and Tudie looked up from where she was writing in a ledger and smiled broadly at them. She led them into a large room in the rear of the store where three sewing machines were being pedaled at a steady pace. Tudie's sister, Nelly, was measuring out some material but put it aside and invited them into another room where they hung their coats and hats and sat around a large table.

For the next hour they talked about what they would need for the labs and classrooms at school and Nelly took notes. Maggie immediately began questioning Nelly about whether she would make pants for her. When Nelly and the rest heard her reasons why she believed pants made the most sense for some of the things they would have to do, they all seemed to accept the idea.

"How many times has something on the floor or ground gotten on your dress early in the day and you were forced to wear it the rest of the day or go home and change it? I think it would be foolish to wear floor length dresses and skirts in rooms where blood and God knows what else is lying around on the floor."

They all seemed to agree, though Tudie, the oldest among them, wasn't sure she could step across the line the way the others seemed to be ready to.

"What would the men think of us if we all came to school in pants," she said. "They'd think we were trollops."

"Trollops don't go to medical school," said Maggie, and Jess chimed in. "We don't tell them what they can wear. Why should we care what they say?"

"What will Charlie say about pants?" asked Annaliese.

"He won't care. I believe he'll think they'll be easier to get off when the time comes," said Maggie with a laugh. Tudie looked scandalized for a moment and then joined the rest of them laughing.

"I'll have to think about it for a while," said Tudie. "Of course, I don't have a husband to worry about, but my mother won't know what to think."

"I can't imagine Johnny objecting much," said Annaliese. "He says I'm old enough to decide what's right or wrong and he's always been fine with that.

"We have a lot to decide before we begin classes," she continued. "Do we want to create a separate problem when we may have so many others to deal with?"

"What do we have to decide?" asked Jess.

"Just as an example, when we're in class, do we all sit together to support each other or spread out in the class among the men? How much do we trust our fellow students? And, indeed, our male professors, knowing some of them don't have our best interests at heart and would sabotage us the first chance they got?"

She sat quiet for a moment and let them think. "Will we reach a point where we don't have to be on the defensive and can take their behavior at face value? In other words, do we assume they'll eventually grow up?"

They talked about it while Nelly and Tudie made measurements and took notes about what they wanted, and finally, when they ready to leave, Jess said, "We'll have to tell Ginger about everything we've talked about. She had to go somewhere with her mother-in-law."

"She's coming by in the morning for coffee if any of you want to join us," said Annaliese.

Chapter Thirty-Five

When Annaliese came downstairs later that evening the door to Lemuel's room was closed, so she wandered through the store greeting customers and talking to friends. Walking around like this, it was unusual when she didn't see someone she recognized and talked with in the past. It looked as though the store was becoming what she hoped when they opened, a community center of sorts, where all kinds of people came together in friendship and a quest for new things to think about.

She was leaning on the counter petting Jinx when Johnny came in from the backroom looking thoughtful.

She kissed him on the nose and said, "Hi there fellow. What're you thinking about that's making you look so puzzled?"

He looked at her for a moment as though he was surprised to see her and then said, "Well, I'll tell you what, it's sure not what I was expecting to be thinking about when I got up this morning."

It was her turn to look puzzled. "You'll never guess what has happened today," he said.

She knew he'd tell her, so she waited.

"The three bad apples on the Board, Sunny Jim and his bunch, have all resigned." He paused and watched her mouth fall open. "For the last two hours I've been puzzling over what we need to talk about with the fellows we're supposed to meet with in the morning. You know, the ones we picked to run for the seats when they were open."

He grinned at her open-mouthed surprise and went on. "Well, now they're open and it's like trying to make bricks without straw. Suddenly, half the people who have been running the city are gone and we have candidates who don't even know where their offices are, much less how to do the jobs they're running for. Since I know absolutely nothing about running a city of 200,000 people, how am I supposed to know what to say to them?"

She laughed at him, and Jed and Greta, who were standing behind the counter joined in. "Well, it's a surprise, I know, but it's got to be better than being in the middle of a shooting war, which is what you were worrying about when you got up this morning," she said. He couldn't argue with her.

They all began the closing routine and afterwards walked upstairs together. At the top she said to Jed and Greta, "The workers next door tell me we should be in the new place within about two weeks."

Greta clapped her hands. "Oh, that's so nice. We've been talking about how we'll use the extra space and what kind of furniture we want to get."

When Annaliese and Johnny were alone, she said, "We'll have to do some shopping too, you know, for new furniture and such."

He murmured, "Uh huh," and she could tell he wasn't listening. When they were dressed for bed, which usually meant not much, she asked, 'How would you feel about me wearing pants to school for certain classes?" Suddenly he was listening.

He came up behind her where she sat brushing her hair and murmured into it, "They'd be easier to get off, wouldn't they?"

She turned and looked at him, "That's the same thing Maggie said Charlie would say. Do all you young men walk around all day thinking about how to undress women?"

"Probably," he answered, and they both laughed.

"Seriously, you remember I told you about Maggie's ideas about women's clothing?" When he nodded, she went on. "There are some classes where wearing a long dress or skirt simply wouldn't be sanitary. I'm liable to come home from anatomy class with God knows what on the hem and bottom of my dress and petticoat. We're also thinking about leaving a pair of shoes at the laboratory, so we won't have to wear them home.

"Anyway, I ordered some pants today, and some smocks and

aprons to use in laboratory classes, like anatomy and chemistry. We may have a problem or two with some of the teachers, men and women, but we've decided to stand our ground about it, and the sanitary argument is hard to argue with."

"Would you wear them to class or just put them on when need be?" he asked.

"We haven't talked about that, but knowing Maggie, probably the former."

"Sounds like you'd need to practice putting them on and taking them off. Best do that at night after work. Then I can help."

She looked at him, a slow smile growing on her face. "So I assume you have no objections?"

He pulled her to her feet and kissed her. "Whether you wear pants or nothing, I'll still love you." After a moment, he whispered, "But I do like nothing much better."

Which was pretty much how she felt.

Sarah answered the door, and Carlotta handed her a note inviting her to join Madame for breakfast. She accepted, and within ten minutes was knocking on the door to Madame's suite. Though the servants seemed to keep the entire house spotless, Madame used only the three-room suite on the second floor, a dressing room, a sitting room and her bedroom. The servants all lived on either the third floor or in the basement, and the rest of the house seemed to be for show when a visitor came to call.

During breakfast they chatted about this and that, but after the dishes were cleared away and each had a cup of coffee before them, Sarah asked the question she had been dying to ask.

"Annaliese tells me you've been out here since 1846, two years and some before the gold rush got going," she said, and when Madame nodded, she continued. "I'd love to know more about it and what it was like from the beginning if you don't mind talking about it."

Madame smiled at her. "Sarah, I have what is known as a 'checkered past'. Some of my tales are not for mixed company."

"I have a similar past, though not quite so checkered, from what I've heard. I'll tell you mine if you tell me yours," she said with a grin. "I have noticed many of your servants don't seem to have much to do and seem more like friends than retainers."

"True," answered Madame. "Actually, everyone here is here because sometime in my past they have helped me, or I could see they needed help. Not all of my friends from the old days live here. I have a number who live in the city, and they come by from time to time and keep me apprised of what passes in town."

She took a sip of coffee and seemed to think for a minute.

"You probably haven't met old Jose yet. He's the stableman, but when I first came here, he gave me a place to sleep and kept me from starving. I married young to an Irish ne'er-do-well who was always proud his grandfather was one of Ireland's 'wild geese' who came to America to help fight the English King during the Revolution.

"He was 23 and so handsome and charming I cut myself off from my family to marry him. I followed him to New Orleans and then to Vera Cruz, Mexico where he joined the Mexican Army."

She paused and looked back over the years. "He was so handsome in his uniform. He was sent to The Presidio of San Francisco and because he was an officer, he was allowed to take me with him. Unfortunately, he caught a fever when he'd only been here a week and died shortly thereafter, leaving me alone and penniless in a foreign country.

"The town was named Yerba Buena in those days. Jose was a young farmer and also my first customer. Since I had no other way to make a living, I made one on my back. He gave me a place to sleep and let me use a small shack out back of his house for my customers, a crib as it were."

She poured another cup for them both, took a sip and continued. "There wasn't much business in those days. Hell, the town only had about 300 souls in it. Once in a while a ship would come to port and I'd stay busy. But it was mostly soldiers from the Presidio, and since they didn't get paid very often, not many of them.

"All in all, it was a decent life and I realized it could have been much worse. Then they struck gold and suddenly the world turned upside down.

"Within a year there were 10,000 men in town from all over the world, and not many women. I was busy all the time and some of the men would give you a little extra, sometimes more than a little. Rather than waste what I made, I saved as much as I could and continued to live with Jose for several years. After the first year I quit working, except for special customers, and ran the house instead.

"Sarah, you would not believe what some men would do for a woman's company in those days. One fellow gave me a hundred dollars in gold just to sit beside him while he played cards in one of the saloons for a night. Nothing else, just keep him company.

"The first year there wasn't much crime. Everyone felt they could make more money from prospecting I guess, so they didn't bother to steal. I remember a man who came here to start a store, and he left all his merchandise in a pile on a vacant lot while he went somewhere for a couple of days. When he got back it was all still there. Unfortunately, that didn't last too long.

"The Sidney Ducks came to town late in 1849. They were criminals from England who were sent out to Australia to the penal colonies, and somehow, they ended up here. For a couple of years they were pretty bad.

"They would start fires in town, and while everyone was fighting the fires, they would loot and steal everything not nailed down. What with the wind and lack of water, they damn near burned the town down several times.

"If you happened to get too near what they called 'Sidney Town' you were liable to wake up with your pockets empty, aboard a ship headed somewhere you'd never even heard of. Finally, in 1850 the locals formed a vigilance committee and hung a couple and ran the rest out of town.

"Things calmed down for a while, but within a few years it got bad again and another group of vigilantes had to do it all over again. By 1856 things had settled down, and I was doing really well. I had a big house, and before long I was the Madame in town and was considered wealthy.

"I met my husband in 1863. He was a big man in town who hung around with Stanford and Crocker and their friends, and yet he was as nice a fellow as you could imagine. By the time he asked me to marry him we were both pretty well off, and every year got more so. He died about five years ago and left me the wealthiest woman on the Pacific slope.

"I have no heirs and don't need much, so I help my old friends by giving them jobs and places to live, and in return they take care of me. I also try to do what I can to make this city as good as it can be, which is what got me into this thing with your friends. The town needs cleaning up again so here we are.

"Besides, with my background and work history, I'm not welcomed at too many social events in the city, so I might as well do something to keep busy."

She said this last with a wry smile and Sarah laughed. "I'd say it's their loss," she said.

"So, tell me about your history. How did you end up in San Francisco?"

"By following my children," replied Sarah. "Going back to before the war, I was kidnapped by raiding Indians, and for two years I was the second wife to the warrior who fathered Rebecca. He was killed in a raid by another tribe and during the fighting, I managed to escape.

"When I got back home, I found my father had died and my mother left town. With an Indian daughter, the women in town let me know I wasn't welcome. A childhood sweetheart offered marriage, and we put together a wagon and what we needed to join a train coming west.

"When we got to the fifth crossing of the Sweetwater River in Wyoming, the woman who ran the store there had a sick husband and needed help. We stayed and within a month they both died and we knew of no kin, so we settled down as storekeepers.

"About ten years ago, Jed, my husband went hunting and disappeared. My friends looked but we never found a trace of him or what happened.

"Over the years I made a lot of friends among the mountain men and the Mormons that came through and they looked out for us, so we did right well. One of those was Wash.

"The year after Jed disappeared, we first spent the winter in Salt Lake City, and it became a regular thing. We'd close up the store about mid-October and some friends would keep an eye on things for us through the winter.

"I became friends with Annaliese and her family about then and they invited us to stay with them until spring. We did alright at the store, and we loved living along the river, so every spring we'd go back and open up again.

"A couple of years ago Johnny and Handy came through with Wash. While they were there, Handy and Rebecca fell in love and got engaged. We were planning to wait until they returned from their trip for the wedding, but Johnny had an accident and ended up in Dr. Crawford's hospital, and Handy and Rebecca got impatient, so some Mormons bought me out and we moved to town.

"By that time Jed Jr. was fifteen and he wanted to go with Johnny and Wash when they left the following spring. After Handy and Rebecca left, rather than stay without them I made arrangements to sell out again, and here I am."

Madame looked at her for a moment. "Have you ever thought about getting married again?" she asked.

"I've thought about it but as long as the children were around I didn't, for one reason or another. You?"

Madame shook her head. "Mostly gold diggers too lazy to dig it out of the hills. I'm not interested in company just for the sake of company. Over the years I've had a few ship captains as companions. They come into town, and we jump in bed and it's great for a couple of weeks and then they're gone, which suits me fine. Besides, if I want companionship, I've got Woman. That's enough for me."

She stood up and stretched. "Well, I have several men coming to a meeting in about a half an hour, so I need to get dressed. If you'd like to stay and meet the mayor and several of the City Supervisors, you're perfectly welcome to."

"I think I will. Do you have a place where I can wait until you're ready?"

"Of course, right here," said Madame, and she rang the bell. When Carlotta answered, they left, leaving Sarah sitting with a cup of coffee thinking about what she just heard.

Chapter Thirty-Six

Dear Carlotta,

Your father-in-law recently gave me the book Pinocchio to read, and since it's in Italian, he suggested I get someone to read it to me. Would you like to do so? If you would, please let me know and we can arrange a time and place. Thank you,

Annaliese Fry

Johnny awoke to a light tap tap on the nose. He opened his eyes to Jinx lying on his chest, eyes closed, purring softly. This was the way most all his days began, and since there was no hurry, he lay thinking about the day before him.

Listening to the five members of the city government talk about what needed to be done since Sunny Jim and his gang were gone was interesting. The surprise and astonishment the resignations generated was soon channeled into pronouncements, suggestions, and questions, and eventually they had a plan of sorts to deal with the next few days. There seemed to be a general agreement not to look too far ahead but to take it one step at a time until they got where they needed to be.

An announcement about what happened and the steps being taken to get control of things until the election to replace the departing Supervisors was decided on and would be printed and distributed to the newspapers. A telegram would be sent to make sure the Governor was informed of the chain of events underway.

Each of the replacements went from the meeting to City Hall and met with the people in their respective departments to make sure everyone knew things were happening according to the rules.

He and Lemuel listened and learned but contributed little. In fact, they really didn't feel they needed to be there. In the end, they were asked to use their militia to keep an eye on the bad guys to see they didn't sneak out of town with too much loot, guard the courthouse in case of need and arrange for men to protect against violence at the polling places around the city on election day.

When they were sitting in Lemuel's office afterward, they congratulated each other on being able to accomplish much without getting too far into the morass they felt government of any kind represented. The problem there was that's how Sunny Jim got where he was. When good people don't pay attention, the bad guys get in and the whole process has to be repeated.

He would need to get hold of Will and arrange to cover the commitments about protecting things, but it looked as though they were mostly through with the reform movement in San Francisco and could put these things behind them.

The whole thing was like a rock in his shoe since they started it. Lying there thinking he realized how taunt his nerves had been now that they weren't so much anymore. He took a deep breath and smiled and petted Jinx for a while longer.

When he kissed his still sleeping wife good morning, she opened one eye and asked, "What are you doing up so early."

"I've got things to do which I hope will finish up this business with the militia. Go back to sleep and I'll see you when I get back."

She turned over and was asleep before he was out of the room.

He met Will at a coffee shop near City Hall and they were just climbing the steps to the big building when Herschel Grieve came out the front door and almost bumped into him.

"Mr. Grieve," Johnny said inclining his head.

"The Bookseller," replied Grieve, inclining his in return.

"Lemuel's The Bookseller. He's teaching me the business. My name's Johnny."

They looked at each other probably thinking the same question about the other.

"Well Johnny, you'll probably see me in your place sometime

soon."

"You'll be welcome and if I can help you let me know."

Grieve looked at him for a moment. "Don't assume this thing is over," he said. "I don't know it for sure, but I think Sunny Jim has other ideas."

Johnny looked puzzled. "Where are you in all this?" he asked. "Are you still working for Jim?"

"No, I'm not. I have found another less unsavory, let's say, way of earning my bread and cheese." He smiled somewhat ruefully. "I've become a reporter covering City Hall for the largest daily in the city."

"I'm impressed," said Johnny. "Why that?"

"I'm reasonably well-educated and a good writer. Also, I learned to type in college back in Michigan and I have a certain expertise in the topic I'm covering. Besides, the reporter had left town." He paused. "I'm not a bad person, you know," he said. "It was just a bad job. But that's all over and I'd like to get to know you from a different point of view."

Johnny grinned. "I'm usually in Mattie's place about ten most mornings. Stop by and we'll talk."

He watched Grieve go down the steps and at the bottom he turned, smiled and touched his hat before walking away.

"What was that about?" asked Will.

"I'm not quite sure," replied Johnny. "But I think it amounted to a warning."

The whole time they were in City Hall, checking with the Supervisors and spotting militia men around the place, Johnny was thinking about Herschel Grieve. First thing when he saw Wash, he was going to see what he could find out about the man from Woman and Madame.

Once before he became friends with a man who stole his horses so maybe this wasn't so farfetched after all.

"Good morning."

Annaliese looked up and smiled at Carlotta standing in the door to the back room.

"Please come in," she said, indicating a chair at the long table. "Can I get you something to drink? We keep coffee on the stove and hot water for tea."

"No, thank you," replied Carlotta. Her accent was noticeable and charming. "I have your message and wanted to tell you I can come anytime it's right for you. I showed Madame the letter you sent. She said she'd care for Geppetto while I read."

"How about tomorrow morning?" asked Annaliese. "I'm excited about it. Giuseppe told me a little and I'm anxious to hear it. Do you mind if I ask Greta to join us?"

"That would be fine, and Rebecca and Sarah asked if they could come too." When Annaliese nodded Carlotta stood and said, "I want to get back. I don't like to leave him with Madame too long. She lets him do what he wants. She spoils him."

Annaliese laughed. "Why am I not surprised?"

When Johnny walked in a little later with a thoughtful expression on his face she asked, "What are you thinking about with such a face?"

"What's wrong with my face? I thought you liked my face," he said pouting.

"I love your face, dear," and she kissed him on the nose. "Now what are you thinking about?"

When he told her about Herschel, she seemed puzzled too.

"Huh," she said. "Of course," she kissed him on the nose again. "You have a face like that because you can't imagine what it all means, nor can I."

Johnny grinned at her, which he did a lot. Something about her made him happy so he grinned a lot when she was around or when he thought of her. It was probably because he loved her.

"Well, I'll probably know pretty soon. I got the impression he would be in here before long. It seems like he's got something to say but doesn't quite know how to say it."

The next morning Johnny was carrying some books from the back for Greta and Jed to shelve when he saw Grieve talking to Jason at the counter.

"Well, you're just in time to join me for coffee at Mattie's," said Johnny, "but somehow I think you knew that."

Grieve smiled at him and acknowledged the invitation.

As they were walking the block to the café, Grieve said, "Since we seem to have changed our relationship, I'm Herschel and you're Johnny, OK?"

"Fine," answered Johnny. "You know, I've been thinking about you and trying to put my finger on just what's going on between us, so why don't you tell me so I can quit thinking about it?"

"OK," he agreed. "Let's get some coffee between us, then we'll talk."

Mattie was used to seeing him at about that time and coffee was at his favorite table when they walked in. When she saw Hershel, she got another cup, set it before him with a smile and retreated out of earshot.

"Since I've decided to make my home here, I feel we should be friends, or at the very least, cordial to each other," began Herschel, coffee cup in his hands. He took a drink. "The last time I saw Jim he asked me something, I think you need to know about."

Johnny looked at him and waited for him to go on. "A few years ago we had a problem with a…" he paused and then went on, "let's say a competitor.

"Jim asked me if I knew someone who might help us get him out of the middle of things. I remembered a name I'd heard in the area around the Mexican border, and I told him the name.

"When we parted for the last time, he asked me the fellow's name again. I told him, and the last thing he said to me was, 'there's such a thing as revenge.'"

With that hanging in the air they sat and looked at each other in silence for a long minute.

"I haven't seen him since and have no idea if he got in touch with the guy or even tried."

Johnny had learned from Wash the value of thinking before talking and now he sat and considered this for a minute.

"Is this man a gunman?" he asked when he finally spoke.

Herschel shook his head. "I don't think so, more of an assassin, I think." He paused, "Johnny, I know nothing about him. What I knew was from sitting around a campfire at night listening to men talk. He had an unusual name, and I remembered it."

"I told Jim when he asked the first time, and one day a while later, they found this competitor dead with a bullet through his brain. As far as I know, they've never found out who did it."

"I have no idea if he found the guy and hired him or if he got someone else to do it or even if he did it himself, although I don't think he'd do it. Not his style."

"What else did you hear about this killer?" asked Johnny. "What were they talking about that night around the campfire?"

"He was unusual in a number of ways. He dressed like a farmer in town to get his wagon fixed. Overalls, homespun shirt, brown boots, and a wide straw hat. They said he was methodical and efficient and very expensive. Been doing it for years and no one ever found him out. They also said he talked with a heavy German or Slavic accent."

They sat and looked into each other's eyes for a moment. Finally, Johnny broke the silence.

"A few days ago, I saw an enemy when I looked at you, someone I might have to look at over a gunsight one day. I guess I can't figure why you're going out of your way to tell me this."

Herschel played with his cup for a minute. "It's for a very simple and selfish reason," he said. "I enjoy intelligent conversation.

"The men I've been working with for the last few years all seemed to be resolutely stupid and the people at the paper aren't much better. You and Lemuel and your friends speak through the eyes of what you've read, and you've read a lot. If I'm going to live somewhere I have to have people to talk to keep me from being bored or I'll be miserable."

"When I worked for Jim, I made up the deficit by reading constantly, but that's not enough anymore. Besides, I can use the resources in The BookSeller to do my job better. When we go back to the store this morning, I'm going to look for some books on the history of the city and state so I can find out what's around me and learn enough to do the job better."

He signaled Mattie for more coffee while Johnny sat and digested what he'd heard.

"Can I trust you?" he finally asked with a smile playing around his lips.

"It's easy to say, 'yes' but I know only time will tell, so I guess we'll have to see how it works out."

"Are you going to tell me the man's name?" asked Johnny.

"Don't ask me how to spell it," replied Herschel. His name was Gerhard Schweder."

Chapter Thirty-Seven

The next morning when Annaliese came downstairs, she found Maggie and Jessica browsing the shelves with Greta.

"What are you two doing here?" she asked. She was pleased to see them but had the thing with Carlotta arranged for the morning and didn't remember planning anything with her study mates.

"We're going to walk down by the bay and thought maybe you'd like to join us," said Maggie.

"I'm sorry, I have something planned, but if you'd like to join us, you're welcome to and maybe we can walk after." She told them about the reading they were doing.

"Ginger will be here in a few minutes, and we can have coffee and talk about it."

They looked at each other and agreed it would be nice, and soon were all sitting in the back with Greta waiting and talking. Ginger joined them and they caught her up on what was happening with the pants and other things. She also decided to join them and listen to Carlotta.

Carlotta was on time and soon found herself surrounded by a willing audience larger than she had anticipated.

"I hope you will forgive my accent and help me if I cannot find the words," she said. "I have only been in this country a short time and I'm still learning."

Annaliese was the hostess, so she responded. "We'll help you all we can," she assured the young woman. "We're here to learn and enjoy a new book, not to criticize."

Carlotta began in a halting voice and was noticeably nervous, but it wasn't long before they were all enthralled by the story of a toymaker who makes a marionette that, with the help of a good fairy, becomes a mischievous little boy, one whose nose grows longer when he tells a lie. When she stopped for the day, they were impatient for more. The fact the story was read with an entertaining Italian accent made it even more enjoyable.

"I want to read it in three parts so I can practice at home before each time," she said, smiling shyly.

"Thank you so much," said Annaliese and she was echoed by everyone there. "I believe you've only been here for a year or so. How is it that you speak English so well?"

"After Tony left for America, his Papa and I practiced every day until we left to come here. We read all we could find and spoke it when we were alone in the house."

After she left, they decided to take the walk Maggie and Jess had planned. Maggie and Annaliese and Ginger were sitting waiting for the others to use the necessary when Maggie turned to Annaliese with a frown and said, "You know, every time I see Charlie's thing it's growing. Do you reckon he's been lying to me?"

Annaliese had just taken the last swallow of her coffee. She burst out laughing and sprayed it all over the table.

When she finally got her breath back and everyone stopped laughing, Annaliese said, "Maggie, please make sure I have nothing in my mouth when you say something like that. I could have choked to death."

Maggie apologized profusely even though there was a mischievous smile on her face.

Johnny was in the front talking to a customer when he heard the laughter in the back room. When the customer left, he came to see what all the hilarity was about and ran into a stone wall. No one would tell him a thing about what was so funny.

Later, after closing, he followed Annaliese up the steps still trying to pry it out of her.

"Johnny, some things are just between us girls. Men wouldn't really understand them, anyway."

He pouted for a while, but she ignored him, so he picked up Jinx and climbed into bed.

"What happened with Mr. Grieve?" she asked while she sat before the mirror and went through the ritual of brushing her long red hair a hundred strokes before bed.

He enjoyed watching, forgot all about pouting and told her. When he finished and she was sitting with her mouth open in horror, he said, "You know, I almost decided not to tell you."

"Why?"

"Because I knew you would worry about it, and since you couldn't do anything about it, I didn't see the point in upsetting you."

He pulled her to her feet and into a long embrace. Petting her hair, he whispered, "You know why I decided to tell you anyway?"

She pulled away from him and looked into his eyes.

"Because it's part of my life and I promised you we would always share everything."

"Have you told Lemuel?"

"No, and I probably won't."

She looked a question at him.

"For one reason, he's not my wife and I didn't promise to tell him everything. And like you, he couldn't do anything about it anyway. Didn't see the point. If somehow I find out more I probably will."

"What can you do about it?" she asked, her eyes wide.

"Nothing I can think of. I don't even know who the target would be. Me or Lemuel or both of us? I have no idea when or even if. I mean, he just asked Herschel a question. Maybe he couldn't find the fellow. Hell, maybe he didn't even try. It's not like I could ask Sunny Jim. As far as I know he's gone, and no one knows where, and besides, I doubt he'd tell me the truth anyway.

"What would I do, go looking for this Schweder, fellow? And even if I could find him, what could I do? I can't shoot him because I think he might be after me. I'm liable to get hung if I do. No, the only thing I can do is be alert, and like Wash says, 'say my prayers and keep my powder dry'."

After a minute she said, "I suppose you want me to tell you my secret now?"

"Well, it would be nice," he answered.

"I think there are certain things a husband just doesn't need to know," she said, "and this is one of them."

He rolled his eyes and collapsed backwards onto the bed, narrowly missing Jinx.

Next door, Jed and Greta were lying in bed after making love.

"Did I tell you? Annaliese, Rebecca, and Sarah want to take me shopping after they're finished next door. We'll need some things to get settled in once they move," she said. "I've never been shopping before and I'm nervous about it."

"Why nervous?" he asked.

"They're talking about going into a large department store and I won't know how to find my way around. Since I can't see anything, I don't see why it would be as enjoyable for me as it will for them."

"Just tell them you don't want to go."

"They'll be getting baby things too, and Annaliese thinks I should be along, you know, in case I need such things one day."

"When is Rebecca's baby due?" he asked. "Isn't it a little soon to be worried about getting those sorts of things?"

"It's due sometime in March, and I think it's just because it will be exciting picking things out. From the way they talk, it will be almost as exciting for Annaliese, and especially for Sarah, as for her."

She still hadn't told him about her belief she was pregnant. When she was sure, she would, and Annaliese said she would know for sure in a week or so.

He put his hand on her abdomen. "It's strange one day you may have a baby in there," he put his ear against her stomach and listened.

"It's growling," he said.

She pulled him up to her for a kiss. After a while it became more than a kiss. That was one of the great things about being fifteen and sixteen. You didn't have to wait long.

Chapter Thirty-Eight

When Johnny came downstairs the first morning the new addition was finished and ready to open for business, he stood at the bottom of the stairs for a minute just looking around. For the last two weeks he had watched it all come together and now it was what he envisioned, had hoped for.

The large bay window and enlarged windows elsewhere gave plenty of light, so the new electrics wouldn't have to be on until late in the day. Because they were waiting for shipments, not all the bookcases were filled, but everything was clean and shiny new. There were tables, chairs and private little spaces arranged strategically, and it looked like a nice place to spend some time doing just about anything, although he could picture Annaliese's reaction if he suggested what suddenly flashed into his mind.

He heard her on the steps behind him and turned to see her looking around just like he was.

"Excited?" she asked, and he nodded.

"Oh yes," he answered. "It looks just like I imagined it would, and I hope it will add to our business, not just additional room. We'll have to try to find some more reasons for people to want to come and spend time with us. Using this space effectively will be a big part of it."

"Well, I surely hope we can justify it, considering all the money we spent to make it this way," she said. "For our sake and for

Madame's. It cost more than I thought it would."

"She can afford it," he said and held out a hand to her. She took it and came down the stairs to where he was. A hug and a kiss to start the day and he followed her through the door to where Greta and Jed were putting up some new books.

Since they were doubling their stock, Johnny assumed responsibility for the inventory on the new side rather than putting more on Greta. When they finished shelving new shipments, they would have more than two thousand volumes, and he and Jed had designed an inventory system to back up her memory.

While Jed and Greta took care of the customers, the rest of them worked on getting ready for the open house scheduled to launch 'the new addition', which, after much consultation, they had decided to call it.

After his first shower in their new bathroom and a change of clothes, Johnny came down to an already busy scene and it looked like things were off to a great beginning.

Lemuel was in his seat, Brutus lying at his feet, circled by several customers. Jed and Greta were working at the counter and Jason and Rebecca were wandering in the new addition, greeting people and offering help to any who seemed to need it. To complete the picture, Jinx was lying on the counter, bright green eyes watching all who came and went and being petted and made over by his friends.

After scratching Jink's ears and getting a short bath in return, he wandered into the back room. Annaliese was talking to Madame and Woman while Handy and Wash sat listening. They all looked up and Madame patted the chair beside her, inviting him to join without interrupting the conversation.

Annaliese was telling them how much she liked the new addition, especially the electric lights, although they were so bright she was planning to put shades of one kind or another on them. Johnny liked the gas lighting in the store better. It was more muted, and he felt it produced a proper atmosphere for a bookstore.

When Annaliese finished, he asked Wash, "Have you found out anything new about Herschel yet?"

Wash shook his head. "The man doesn't seem to have any friends. No one we've talked to knew much about him so they couldn't tell us much, other than he always seems to be in a sour mood."

Madame was listening and put in, "That's probably why he had no friends. To have friends it helps to be friendly."

"You know, the time we talked over coffee, he told me the people he worked with were, how did he put it?" Johnny scratched his head. "Resolutely stupid, that was it. He said he was starved for intelligent conversation."

"I'd say he can get it around here," said Madame. "I think that's the main reason people come to the place."

"Well, whatever the reason they're sure here tonight," said Annaliese. She glanced out the door and stood. "So, I better get out there and help."

She left, and Johnny said to Wash, "I don't know quite how to take him. He seems honest and straight-forward." He shook his head. "I can't seem to get past the night with Jimmy Li. Would he have let them hang Jimmy? That would have put him forever outside the line but talking to him I just don't know how much to trust him."

"Why should you have to trust him at all?" asked Handy. "He isn't part of your life, so why worry about it?"

"Well, it seems like he is, really," replied Johnny. They all looked a question at him. "I haven't told anyone except Annaliese, but he told me something strange the other day and I have the feeling he's going to be here, meaning in the BookSeller, quite frequently."

They waited for him to go on. He looked at each of them and then repeated what Herschel had told him.

"Do you believe him?" asked Madame after he'd finished.

"I've thought about it a lot over the last couple of weeks. I asked him if I could trust him."

"And he said?"

"Something along the lines of 'time will tell'".

"I wonder why he would tell you at all?" said Handy. "What's he stand to gain?"

"When I figure that out, I'll be able to quit worrying about it." He looked at Wash. "Have you ever heard anything about this fellow, Schweder?"

"It seems to me I have," said Wash, "but I can't pin it down. You said Herschel heard about him down near the border?"

Johnny nodded.

"You know it may have been a talk around the campfire, like

he said," continued Wash. "I've sat around a lot of campfires over the years and don't always remember everything I've heard. But it's like he said, it's a name you'd remember. I think I may have heard it before but maybe not."

Johnny stood and stretched. "I need to get out front and help. You all keep your ears open and if you hear anything about Herschel you think I should know, you know where I am."

Madame followed him to the front, and he showed her the new addition and explained how they intended to use the extra space. Since the workmen began on the new addition, she had avoided the place, limiting her visits at the store to the old side and the back room. When he mentioned this to Wash he said she didn't want us to think she was going to interfere just because she was putting up some money.

With that in mind, he said, "Any ideas you have about increasing our trade or making it better for our customers, please share them with us." He meant it. He felt good things when she was around, and he hoped she would continue to spend time there.

He suddenly grinned. And besides, Lemuel was right. She wasn't hard to look at.

When Madame wandered over to speak to Lemuel, Johnny helped a lady find a book and afterward stumbled on a scene that startled him. Annaliese was sitting in one of the alcoves talking to Herschel Grieve.

She looked up at him and smiled. "Hi. Since you two know each other, I don't have to bother introducing you." She stood and said, "I'm going to look for some customers to help." She nodded to each of them.

Herschel stood, nodded in response, and he and Johnny seated themselves while she disappeared.

"So, Johnny, looks like your new place is off to a good start."

"If the number of people is any indication, I'd say I agree, but the problem is how to get them to come back," said Johnny. "That's where the ideas come in. We've got some good idea people."

Herschel nodded and after a moment Johnny asked, "Tell me something. The night down at the livery stable, would you have let them hang Jimmy?"

Herschel looked at him, a slight smile playing around his lips.

"No. Jim wanted to rough him up a bit. He fought back and they were just drunk enough to get carried away. I was ready to call them off when you showed up and did it for me."

"Jim didn't like the Chinese?" Johnny asked.

"I don't think Jim liked or disliked many people. He just used them, usually to do his dirty work. The only one he really liked was himself. As far as Jimmy went, he didn't like them running a business outside of Chinatown, and especially didn't like them living outside of Chinatown, so he decided to send them a message."

"Woman said it might be something like that," said Johnny.

"Now there's someone I'd like to get to know," said Herschel. "She seems to be a fascinating creature."

"I'd be careful if I were you. I've heard she doesn't carry that Bowie for show. But you'll see her in here though she's usually in the back with Wash. She's not what you'd call a sociable person."

"Wash?"

"George Washington Moore, Wash to his friends. He's a friend of mine. Black fellow. We've been traveling together for a while."

"I understand he's been making inquiries about me lately," said Herschel with that smile again.

"He has at my request."

"Why?"

"Tell you the truth, you puzzle me. So I asked him and Woman to find out what they could about you."

"Learn anything?"

"Nothing I didn't know already."

"If you want to know something, ask. You already know more than most." He stood. "I'm going to look over your books on San Francisco and California."

As he walked away, he turned and said, "Your wife is somewhat older than you, is she not?"

"About ten years. She was my nurse after I'd had an accident back in Salt Lake City."

"That's a story I'd like to hear some time," he said, and disappeared between two bookshelves.

When Johnny came into the bedroom, Annaliese was brushing her hair, sitting on a new stool before a new mirror on a new dressing table with a new electric lamp nearby. He kissed her hair and sat down beside her on the bench.

"So how do you like your new home?" he asked.

"Oh, I like it, but I wish we hadn't gone out on such a limb to get it. She looked at him in the mirror. "Do you feel comfortable owing Madame so much?"

"If we keep having days like this one," he replied, "we won't have any trouble making it into a good investment for her. I really believe the additional space will pay for itself before long. From all I've seen and heard we've got something special going here and much sooner than we ever believed we would."

She started brushing her hair again. "Darn it, you made me lose count again. I'll start at fifty."

"Did I tell you where Handy has been the last couple of days?" asked Johnny. She ignored him and kept brushing. "He and Gray took a boat over to Sausalito. They want to look at a horse farm for sale over there."

"Gray? You mean Madame's butler?"

"Yes. They've gotten to be friends and have been talking about their futures and decided they might like to try raising horses. Handy believes it's a lot less work than farming crops, and he's looking for something he'd like to get into."

"I wonder what Rebecca will say about it?"

He had no answer to that.

"How's Pinocchio coming along?" he asked after a minute.

"She finished it yesterday." She turned to him. "It's a wonderful story for children. You know, I wonder if she could translate it into English. We could sell it at the store, couldn't we?" Before he could answer she continued. "She wants to be a teacher, and I think this might encourage her in that direction."

"You always like to help solve other people's problems, don't you?" asked Johnny.

"Isn't that what nurses do?" she answered, "and doctors too, for that matter."

"So how would she go about it? Do you know anything about that kind of thing?"

"No," she said, "but I do know some book distributors and I'll bet they could tell me."

"Let me know what you find out," he said.

When she finished her hundred strokes, he ran his hand over her hair and she turned toward him for a kiss, which soon became more than a kiss.

After, when they lay looking at nothing on the new ceiling, he said, "I guess this means we've christened our new place. I was going to suggest we did it downstairs. Some of those overstuffed chairs look inviting."

"Johnny, you have to stop thinking I'm eighteen. I'm not sure my back would take one of those chairs."

"Well, we could sneak downstairs and try it if you like."

"Let's make it tomorrow night, OK?"

"Now I'll have something to look forward to." He kissed her, took Jinx on his chest. "By the way what did you and Herschel talk about tonight?"

"He introduced himself and I did likewise, then you showed up. He seems like he's a nice enough fellow."

"I hope one day I'll figure him out."

"Maybe he's just what he seems and there's nothing to figure out."

"Maybe," said Johnny. He lay there beside her, feeling Jinx purr and drifted off to sleep.

Chapter Thirty-Nine

"Are you ready?" Annaliese asked. "They'll be here any minute."

Greta came from the back room buttoning up her coat. "Is it sunny today?"

"Not yet, but I think it will be before long. This kind of fog usually clears off around noon," replied Annaliese. "I want you to make sure to tell me if you need anything or if you need to sit for a few minutes. I know this will be different than anything you've done before, but we're all ready to help you or answer any questions you have."

"Thank you. I am a little nervous," said Greta. "Who all is going, did you say?"

"I know Rebecca and Sarah are, and Sarah said Madame might like to come too. I think we'll have a driver, and he'll wait for us, so if you want to come home, it won't be a problem."

Waiting outside they could hear the jangle of traces in the fog before they could see the surrey. It was longer than any Annaliese had seen, three seats and a space in the rear for luggage. She recognized the driver as Carlotta's husband, though she couldn't remember his name. When Madame introduced him as Tony, she remembered. He was the toymaker's son.

Soon they were riding through the city while Madame pointed out things of interest. Their first stop was at Helen's Mother and

Baby. Helen met them at the door and after introductions, began to show them around and talk about what they would need as new mothers.

"Have you told Jed yet?" asked Rebecca in a low voice. She was holding Greta's hand.

"I'm going to tell him tonight, when we go upstairs," answered Greta. She sighed and went on. "I don't know why I'm so nervous about it. We've talked about it happening and he seems to be as excited about the idea as I am."

"When are you going to see a doctor?" asked Madame.

"I'm going to see Dr. Brown at school to get an appointment this week," answered Annaliese. "Do you want me to make one for you too?" she asked Rebecca.

"Yes, I think so," said Rebecca. "Mama and I talked about it and since Greta will be going, it seems like a good idea for me too. The doctor will be a woman, won't she? When I went to one in Cincinnati to find out if I was pregnant, he was an old man, and I didn't feel comfortable about it at all."

"Dr. Brown is a woman and I'll be with you if you like," said Annaliese. "She's been doing this for a few years. Of course, she might have someone with her. She's a teacher and sometimes students might be with her to learn."

Helen interrupted them. "I know Dr. Brown well. She sometimes brings her students in here to show them what new mothers need. She's wonderful."

She led them around the store and seemed to realize she needed to describe the things she talked about for Greta's sake.

At first Greta was visibly nervous. It was the first time she'd been anywhere but the store in a long while, and away from those familiar and comfortable surroundings, she felt clumsy and hesitant. It didn't take her long to get beyond that. Rebecca held her hand lightly and guided her gently around the store, and the other women described things to her and explained their usage.

"I remember some of these things from the book we use," she said. "It's nice to be able to touch them and feel them and understand how they work. I'm sure glad you found the book and the magazine articles. I don't feel so lost about what I'll have to do now."

They purchased some things and talked to Helen about what else they might need, then left and walked the three blocks to The

City of Paris department store.

This was what Greta dreaded most. Entrance through a revolving door led them into an atrium with a soaring ceiling that immediately threw her into confusion. She could smell new fragrances, hear new sounds, and feel many people around her. It was all strange and frightening.

She squeezed Rebecca's hand and put the other one on Annaliese's arm to steady herself. This must be what vertigo was. She had heard the word before but now, with the dizziness and unsteadiness she understood what it meant.

"Do you want to sit down?" Annaliese's voice seemed to come from far away.

She took a deep breath and shook her head. "No," she said. "Just let me stand here a minute and get my bearings." Some more deep breaths and she gradually became calmer, then said, "Tell me what you see. Is the ceiling as high as it seems? Are there people all around me?"

She stood feeling the warmth of Rebecca's hand in hers, the space around and above her, taking it all in. Annaliese's descriptions and the sum of what she felt gradually brought her back to a reality she could cope with and she said, "I'm alright now. What are we going to do?"

"Why don't we eat lunch and then we can talk about what we want to do and how to go about it," suggested Madame.

They agreed and soon were seated somewhere else where the ceiling was high, and she could feel shafts of sunlight and air moving around her.

"Are you afraid of something?" asked Annaliese.

"Yes, but for the life of me, I couldn't tell you what," answered Greta.

"Much of what I've read about that kind of thing seems to be a man deciding it happens to women because of some silly reason or other, usually related to her female organs or functions," said Annaliese. "The Doctor believed it was an irrational fear, which makes the cause difficult to isolate. He called it anxiety. It seems to have different causes in different people, but he believed the root cause seemed to be fear of the unknown.

"Today you've suddenly been brought into a place new and strange, vastly different from the store where you spend most of your time, where you're familiar and comfortable."

She paused, took Greta's wrist and checked her pulse. "It's caused your heart to beat faster and made you short of breath, hasn't it?"

"Yes, and I felt dizzy and unsteady on my feet when we came in the store and I first felt the high ceiling."

Annaliese thought for a minute. "Remember when you were afraid of the idea of caring for a baby?" Greta nodded. "We wrote away for the book, and you learned, and you're not so afraid anymore. This is a new thing you're afraid of, so let's handle it the same way. Instead of being afraid and doing nothing, why not decide to learn about the thing you're afraid of, and maybe you won't be afraid of it so much."

After they all thought about that for a moment Madame said, "Sounds like good sense to me. And it looks like it's up to us to make it work, so whenever you're ready we'll start."

While they got things together to leave, Greta said to Annaliese, "Let's try furniture for the new room upstairs. Why don't you choose something you think I'll like? Tell me about it and I'll touch and feel it and decide what I think."

With that as a plan they descended to the furniture section on the first floor of the big store. Watching Greta run her hands over a headboard and dresser, a chair and table, feel sheets and pillow slips and inhale their scents, Annaliese was overwhelmed with a sense of joy and understanding. She felt tears on her cheeks, and beside her she saw the same tears on Rebecca's face. Madame and Sarah were standing, mouths open, shaking their heads in amazement.

"For some reason I don't think I'll ever look at sheets and pillow slips the same way again," Madame whispered to Sarah.

"Oh Jed," said Greta, voice trembling with excitement. "It was so much fun. After we had lunch and talked about it, we went through the store, and it was like a wonderland. There were all these things I had heard about from Papa when he read to me, and I could feel and taste and smell them."

Jed stood watching her, a smile on his face, happy with her excitement.

"I don't see you brought anything home," he said. "Did you buy anything?"

"Oh yes," she gushed, actually dancing around in a little circle. "It will all be delivered tomorrow morning. I can't wait till it gets here and we can have our home nice, the way we want it."

"Well, if it makes you happy then I'm excited too," he said. He swept her into an embrace, and as the kisses progressed, began to undress her.

With her assistance they were soon on the bed, and when she felt his body against hers, felt him inside her, she whispered next to his ear, "I'm pregnant. We're going to have a baby."

He stopped and was still for a long moment. "Is it all right to do this?" he asked.

"Oh, yes, please," she breathed in his ear, and they did.

Afterwards, when they lay holding hands in the dark, gazing at nothing, he asked, "Did you say, 'a baby'?"

Before she answered her fingers found his mouth and she felt his smile broaden into a grin when she said yes.

Chapter Forty

When she was up early, Woman had the habit of standing in the open door of the cottage in a thin nightgown that outlined her curves against the light. Unfortunately, Wash didn't get to enjoy seeing it as often as he would have liked. Their lives had changed much with the happenings at City Hall, among other things, and they slept different hours. Wash always liked to be up and around early, and though she sometimes grumbled, she usually joined him.

Now she walked behind where he sat with a cup of coffee and put her chin on the top of his head, pressed her breasts into his back.

"What ya thinkin about?" she asked, but she thought she knew. He had been here almost six months now and he was getting restless. The time he talked about that day in Sausalito had come, and he felt the need to seek the freedom he never seemed to get enough of.

The question was where did she fit in? Or did she want to fit in at all? She had been happy before he came, and she could probably be happy after he'd gone. Or could she? They had grown closer this time. He had moved deeper into her life, and she could sense the unease in him as he became aware of the permanence this place was beginning to represent. It seemed as though he wanted to go and also to stay, and she thought she knew the reason.

Sarah's arrival and residence at the Mansion had changed her relationship with Madame a little, and she felt her leaving would be accepted and understood. Madame and Sarah enjoyed each other's company, which was fine with her because it left her free to spend time with Wash. Besides, since the need for information was greatly reduced, her nightly forays into the dens of San Francisco were not as necessary as times past.

She knew she would always have a place with Madame and if she left for a while, the cottage would still be hers on her return. So, what would she do if he asked her to go along? To where? It didn't really matter. She'd never left San Francisco since she was orphaned here, so anywhere would be somewhere new and exciting.

Should she suggest it if he didn't? Somehow, she knew he would.

He pulled her around to sit on his lap and looked into her eyes for a minute. "I'm thinking about leaving for a while."

She tried to hide the smile she felt coming but with no success. "And you think I didn't know?"

"I'd like you to come with me." There it was, out in the open.

She looked at him and slowly nodded her head, saying nothing.

He grinned at her. "I'm assuming you mean yes?" There was a question in his voice. She kept nodding her head slowly and kissed him.

"I guess we're part of each other now," she said, "so yes, I'd like to go with you. Oh, by the way, where the hell are we going?"

He laughed. "You've heard me talk about Doc, the fellow I used to run around with up in Oregon?" When she nodded, he continued, "I got a letter from him last week. I'll let you read it, but he says nice things about a little town named San Diego down near the Mexican Border. Says the weather in the winter is like springtime up here. I could use a little of that. My South Carolina blood doesn't like the damp cold up here."

"I've heard that before," she said. "I can't imagine, but it sounds nice. When would you want to leave?"

"Why don't we plan on right after the first of the year? With Handy here now and Jason and Jed around, Johnny doesn't really need me, and they'll always be glad to see us when we come back.

"Do you want to get married?" he asked tentatively, not knowing what to expect.

She didn't even take time to think about it. "No," she said. "I've made it this far in life without a husband. I think I'd like to finish up the same way. Besides, if I get tired of you, I want to be able to get rid of you with no problems."

He grinned at her. "That's pretty much how I feel."

She embraced him, pulled his pelvis against her and muttered. "Let's go celebrate not getting married." When they broke the kiss, he said, "One reason's good as another." She led him to the bed, and they celebrated. There were even fireworks.

Later, lying in bed, she said "You've never told me much about your life."

"It's not something I usually talk about," he said after a minute.

"Because it was so bad?"

"I guess it was like most lives, some good but yeah, there was some bad. My father was sold away when I was a baby. It was a rice plantation in the low country of South Carolina, and the first thing I remember was going to the fields with my mother. When I was a boy, I hung around the blacksmith shop where they fixed things and the old fellow there took me in hand and taught me and when he died, I took over. It wasn't too bad."

He sat for a minute looking back. "I guess I was about twenty or so when the old master died. By then, I was newly married with a baby boy. When they settled the estate, we were sold off to different places. I went to a slave trader who took me to New Orleans. I never knew where they went. I was waiting to be sold at auction when the Yankees took the city and suddenly, I was free."

"I joined the army and was with them when they came back to the place in '64. No trace of my family. When the War ended, I was at loose ends for a while and then joined up again and came west with the Buffalo Soldiers."

"I've always wondered why they called them that," she said.

"It was the Indians. They said we had hair like the buffalo, so that's what they called us. I enjoyed my time with them, mostly. I went to new places and saw new things and finally decided I wanted to be free to roam around the mountains, so I took my discharge and spent ten years running around the Rockies and California with different groups of fellows. Ran into Johnny and Handy in Casper and you know the rest."

He looked at her in silence for a minute. "I never told anyone all of that before."

She kissed him and stretched out on the bed.

"You know all about me," she said. "My mother died and just about then, Daddy heard about the gold. He sold everything, left the memories behind, and we came to California. Been here ever since just waiting for someone to take me away." She kissed him and stroked his face. "And here you are. Sure took you long enough."

Johnny and Lemuel looked up when Wash knocked on the door jamb.

"Morning boys," he said and took his regular seat.

"So, with things as they are and no one trying to shoot us, what have you been up to?" asked Lemuel.

"Making plans and such," replied Wash.

"Sounds like you might be planning to leave us for a while," said Johnny. When Wash nodded, he continued. "Well, it's no surprise, really. I'll bet you've been thinking about it for a while."

"Just since we rousted those crooks out of City Hall. Hell, I've been here almost six months, and you know how I like to go places," replied Wash. "Aiming for San Diego to see how old Doc is getting along. We plan to go down there along the ocean and maybe come back up the east side of the Sierra Nevada to Carson City and cross back west at Tahoe."

"We?" asked Johnny. "Who all's going?

"Woman and me," answered Wash. "She's never been anywhere outside San Francisco and she's itching to go somewhere."

"Going to take the cars?" asked Lemuel.

"You know better than that," said Johnny with a grin. "He'd never leave Master. Where he goes, that mule goes. It's like me and Jinx.

"When are you leaving?" asked Lemuel.

"Talking like the first of the year. We'll pick a day when the weather's nice and take out. Figure to take a month or so to get there. How long we'll stay, we'll figure out when we get there." He looked at Johnny. "I'll be back. With you all here, it seems like I finally got a home to come back to."

"I'm glad," said Johnny. "We'll have to avoid trouble while you're gone, since you won't be around to pull us out."

"What did Madame say about you taking Woman away?" asked Lemuel. "Bet she wasn't happy about it."

"Woman's going to tell her this morning. With Sarah and Rebecca staying there she won't mind so much. Since she'll have someone to talk to and go places with."

Madame and Sarah were sitting over morning coffee when Woman walked into the sitting room.

She sat and listened to the ongoing conversation until Madame finally looked at her and asked, "Are you getting in the habit of rising early? What's caused that?" She raised her finger and looked at Sarah with a droll expression. "I know! It's that Wash fellow, isn't it?"

Woman grinned at the bantering tone. "I'd say that's a pretty good guess. He does like to greet the sun." They all laughed, and Sarah said, "I'm surprised he hasn't left yet. The only time he stays around anywhere very long is when the weather's bad."

"Funny you should mention it," said Woman. "He told me this morning he's thinking about leaving right after the first of the year." She looked at Sarah. "You know Doc, don't you?"

"Oh yes," Sarah responded with a smile. "He and Wash ran around together for a while. In fact, he rode into Salt Lake with them when Johnny was hurt. He ran into some fellows he knew and left with them. I think he went down south, near the border in California. He and Wash are good friends."

"Well, he wants to ride down there and spend some time." She paused and looked at Madame. "He wants me to go with him."

"Are you?" asked Madame.

"Yes, I am."

"Did he ask you to marry him?"

"Yes."

"What did you say?"

"I told him no."

"Why?"

Woman looked at her in silence for a moment and then said, "I don't really know."

Madame and Sarah were both smiling broadly.

"Well, I think you'll have fun, and when you come back maybe you can tell me," said Madame.

Chapter Forty-One

Just as Johnny came into the front of the store, the bell over the door jangled and Jimmy Li came in. He saw Johnny and came over to him with a frown on his face.

"I need to talk with you, if you have time."

"Always have time to talk to you, Jimmy," said Johnny. He led his friend to the office, closed the door and gestured him to a seat.

"How can I help you?"

Jimmy took a deep breath. "It's a difficult matter, and I must explain it to you, so you understand and do not become angry with me." Johnny could see him make up his mind and take the plunge.

"Three years ago, the Congress at Washington passed the Chinese Exclusion Act, and it has caused problems among my people. They have drawn more closely into Chinatown and become like a separate nation. They feel safer that way. My father believes this is not the way forward for us in America. He believes we must become a part of the whole instead of a different whole." He looked at Johnny as if to see how he was taking this.

"This is why he went to Madame Grimes and arranged for the business to begin here on this street. I came to live and work here when I was ten. I grew up much different than boys and men in Chinatown and I can feel the difference when I am around them. Sun Li, my sister, came to live with me and helped me at the restaurant and store when she was ten and also has grown up differently."

"My father's plan is working, and we have become more American, but now there is a problem, and I would ask you to help me to solve it."

By this time Johnny's face was knotted in a frown. He had no idea what kind of a problem Jimmy was talking about.

Jimmy went on. "Jason Redbird is your friend and works for you. He and my sister," he paused, seemingly searching for words, "want to be married and I need you to help me. My father wants us to be Americans, but I think he will believe this way is not good for my sister."

Johnny's face looked like someone had thrown cold water into it. He was so taken aback he was speechless for a moment until he realized Jimmy might misinterpret his silence and expression as one of disapproval.

"Let me make sure I got this straight. Jason and your sister want to get married, but you're worried how your father will take it, is that right?"

"Yes."

Johnny let out his breath in a whoosh. "Jimmy, I need to think about this for a bit. Tell you what. You haven't seen the new addition. Unless you're in a hurry, why don't you look around for a few minutes and give me a chance to sort this out? I'll come and get you when I've got a handle on it."

Jimmy was approaching the office door when Lemuel opened it and came in. Jimmy excused himself, and when he was gone and the door was closed behind him, Johnny said, "Boy am I glad you're here. Jimmy just handed me a knot I'm going to need some help to untie."

"Really? Tell me," said Lemuel and sat back in his chair.

By the time Johnny finished explaining Lemuel had a large grin on his face.

"What are you grinning about?" asked Johnny, a little irritated.

"Well, you've got to admit it's not like figuring out how to overthrow City Hall," said Lemuel with a chuckle. He was silent for a moment. "Have you talked to Jason about this?"

"No. I just heard about it myself."

"I'd say you need to talk to him and then we can get Jimmy back here and try to find an answer that doesn't create a diplomatic incident." He was still chuckling when Johnny went to find Jason.

He found Jason in the back room getting books for Greta to stock and brought him to the office, then found Jimmy, explained the situation and asked him to return later in the day so they could discuss it.

Back in the office, Johnny closed the door, leaned on it and looked at a puzzled Jason sitting, waiting for him to speak.

"Well, I guess the best way is to jump right in and see how it goes," he said. "Jason, are you and Sun Li planning to get married?"

Jason's mouth fell open at the question, and although it was difficult to tell, looked like he was blushing. "I just saw Jimmy in the store. Did he tell you that?"

"He doesn't know how to handle telling his father and he asked me if I could help him with the problem." He sat quietly, looking at his friend. The stoic Indian features didn't reveal much, so he waited for Jason to say something.

When he didn't, Johnny said, "Don't think I want to get involved in your love life, but Jimmy came to me about it and I'd like to help all of you work this out, if I can. If you don't want me sticking my nose in it, say so and I won't."

Again, Jason sat silent, obviously thinking about the situation and how to answer Johnny. "It began the night with Jimmy and the mob. She thinks I saved her brother's life. She started bringing me food, special things she prepared herself and we would sit and talk."

"I guess I love her, but I don't know how to go about this. We come from two different worlds and now we're both trying to escape one world and find our way into another. I don't know where not to step, if you know what I mean. I can't imagine talking to her father and yet the path ahead goes right through him." He shook his head and grinned ruefully. "Back with the tribe I just had to find a couple of horses as gifts for the father. This seems a lot more complicated."

"What little I know about it," said Johnny, "it does seem like each different group has its rituals around the idea of marriage and they always seem to be important to them, with things like tradition and honor mixed in."

Jason sat quiet for a moment. "I worry whenever I do something, it may be the wrong thing, and yet we both want to be in the same place: together. What we finally become will likely be different than what either of us came from."

Johnny shook his head. "Jason, it seems to me you've spent a lot more time thinking about this than I have. All I seem to bring to the table is a different point of view, which is useful sometimes.

"I would suggest this. First, we tell Jimmy he needs to discuss this with his father. Then we all need to get together and talk about where it goes from there."

"We? Meaning who?" asked Jason.

"Well, it seems to me we need to bring all the people who have something in the pot to the table to talk. Jimmy, Mr. Li, Sun Li and you. Lemuel and I will sort of moderate things. If we put it all on the table so everyone can look at it, maybe we can find a solution that one or two of us can't see."

Jason nodded and looked at Lemuel who had been sitting quietly letting them talk. Now he leaned forward and put his elbows on his knees. "Makes sense to me. I'll be there."

When Jason was gone Johnny sat back in his chair and observed, "Seems there's more to this business of selling books than I thought."

"This has nothing to do with selling books," said Lemuel. "It's just working with friends who need help getting round the curves."

Later that evening Johnny was standing looking out the bay window in the new addition when he heard Herschel's voice behind him.

"Not really much of a view from here," he said.

Johnny agreed. Pretty much all he could see were storefronts and houses on Scott Street, and a part of Chestnut around the corner.

He turned to face Herschel. "Can I help you find something?"

"No, I have what I came for. I just wanted to tell you something. In addition to my regular beat, the paper has me writing a column that runs every Sunday. Since I need all the readers I can get, I thought I'd stop and let you know. If you can spread the word around, I'd be grateful."

"Be glad to," replied Johnny. "What's the column about?"

"Good things happening in the city," Herschel answered with a grin. "Know of any?"

"Oh yeah, lots of things and some good people too. Sounds like it'd be fun."

Johnny invited him to sit and chat, and when they were seated in one of the quiet little corners of the new addition, Herschel said,

"You know, I never see you without that gun strapped on. Not what you'd expect for a bookseller. Why do you wear it all the time?"

Johnny smiled. He had been asked the question before and usually responded with a short comment to put people off but for some reason he didn't want to do that with this man.

"My Pa was a gunsmith and while I was growing up, he taught me to clean, care for and repair guns. When he had one to work on, he'd take me with him to test fire it." He paused, remembering how much he loved the time with his Pa. "As I got older, it became a contest of sorts to see which of us could shoot better.

"By the time I was sixteen I could beat him and still hit what I was aiming at. I still practice several times a week down by the bay. I carry it because I have since I was fourteen and wouldn't feel dressed without it." He pointed toward the window. "And, as one of Sunny Jim's henchmen once told me, the bad guys are just around the corner. Most of them don't like the looks of me with this on my hip."

"I spent enough time in the local saloons to swear to that," said Herschel. He peered at the canted holster on Johnny's left hip. "That's really an unusual piece. Can I look at it?"

Johnny gazed at him steadily for a moment, then removed the Colt from the holster, opened the loading gate and, rotating the cylinder, slowly let the bullets drop onto his palm. Then he handed Herschel the Colt, butt first.

"If you don't mind me asking, what did it cost you? Looks custom made," said Herschel as he examined the scrimshawed hand grips and intricate etching on the body and barrel.

Johnny gave a dry chuckle. "It almost cost me my life."

Herschel asked him a question.

"In the Spring of '83, I left Kansas to ride out here on the Pony Express Trail. A couple of men tried to rob me outside Marysville, Kansas. They were unsuccessful and ended walking back to town, barefoot in their long johns. I kept the horse and gun. I noticed it at the time, but I had the gun Pa gave me, so I wrapped it in an oilcloth and put it in my saddlebag.

"Handy joined up with me in Kearney, Nebraska and he had an old Remington that wasn't much good, so I gave it to him. When I was injured outside Salt Lake City, I lost my gun in the fall, so he bought a new one and gave me this one back."

"It seems this fellow who tried to rob me had something hidden in the saddle he wanted back, not to mention his horse and gun, so he followed us across the country to a showdown in Carson City."

"Since you and Handy are here, I'm assuming he's dead."

Johnny nodded slowly. "He and a fellow he hired to kill me."

"Really? What was the fellow's name?"

"Coe, Glenwood Coe."

Herschel's forehead knotted into a frown. "Tall, skinny guy?" When Johnny nodded, he continued, "I knew him. He was a gunnie when I was down along the border a few years ago. He was supposed to be pretty good."

Johnny smiled, almost grinned. "I had an edge."

The question look again. "Jinx," said Johnny. "He jumped up on the bar and knocked over a bottle. When Coe looked at him, I drew. Handy took one in the leg but both of them are dead."

"You mean the cat, Jinx?" Herschel said incredulously.

"Yeah, He's helped me out of a few scrapes over the last couple of years. Don't think I'd be here without my little buddy."

Herschel handed back the Colt and Johnny reloaded and holstered it.

"When do you practice?"

"Jed and I go down to the bay and shoot once a week, usually on Sunday morning, weather permitting, but I do practice drill a couple other mornings, usually in the stable out back."

"Do you mind if I watch sometime?"

"I don't mind. We usually go before breakfast. Sometimes Handy goes along."

"Once Jim was thinking about hitting your place, but I had heard rumors and I'd seen you and that ten-gage, so I talked him out of it."

"Of course, you didn't know about Wash then," said Johnny. "He's got a Sharps .50 and carries a Bowie that's even longer than Women's, and Jason's a dead shot with a Winchester."

He walked Herschel to the door and stood rubbing Jinx's head, wondering what there was about the man that fascinated him.

Chapter Forty-Two

Just before closing that night, Jimmy Li came in and Johnny took him into the office where Lemuel was doing the books for the week. After Johnny explained the plan they had decided on, Jimmy looked a little doubtful.

"You believe I should talk to my father before we all meet?"

"It doesn't seem fair to spring something like this on him for the first time with all of us sitting here watching. He needs to be able to think about it beforehand," answered Johnny, and Lemuel nodded in agreement.

"He will be very angry," said Jimmy, shaking his head. "I don't like to talk to him when he's angry."

Lemuel leaned back in his chair and stretched his bad leg. "Jimmy, if you explain it to him the way you talked to Johnny about it, he should see reason. It's the result of his idea and he needs to be given a chance to think it all out before we meet. He's an intelligent man and we should treat him that way."

"I will tell him tomorrow when he comes. When can we meet here to talk about it?"

"No sense in putting it off. Tomorrow night after we close?" said Johnny. "If, for some reason you can't make it then, we can make it some other time."

Considering the fact he was short, slight, and over seventy, it was amazing everyone involved with Jimmy's problem seemed to be very nervous about confronting Mr. Li with the idea his youngest daughter wanted to marry a half Cheyenne, half Kiowa Indian.

When they all assembled that night, Mr. Li didn't really seem upset. He greeted Johnny and Lemuel courteously, sat and calmly talked to Jason, asking him the same kind of questions any father might ask a prospective suitor for his daughter's hand.

"It is well you understand this is very unusual among Chinese families in America. In the past, the old ones have wanted to keep the Chinese people separate from the rest of America and the laws passed by the Congress have made it more so. I have never felt this was good for the future of our children and for this reason I have encouraged Jimmy and Sun Li to live apart from our family and the traditions we represent.

"When Jimmy came to me about this, I felt, much like my friends in Chinatown, that it was not a good thing. But now that I have thought about it, I must ask why. Tradition gives strength and structure and this is good. But growing and changing are needed to meet a different world with success. This is what I wanted, but thinking only of tradition, I opposed it. I do so no longer."

He inclined his head toward Jason and his daughter began to cry.

When Jason came to comfort her, Mr. Li spoke to him. "We are both outsiders in this world. Maybe we can help each other understand a little better what it is."

"So, you think Sun Li might want to join you in learning the book business?" Johnny was getting coffee ready while Jason and Jed were laying leather mats on the long table in the back room. The three of them had spent the previous hour demolishing sticks, branches, and a few bottles in a hail of gunfire in the waters of the bay, a few blocks from the store. Now the drill was to clean and oil their weapons before opening the store for the day. The mats were to protect the table from the oil and powder residue.

"She seems very excited about the idea," replied Jason, "although it's sometimes hard to tell. She's like an Indian; it's hard to read the emotions in her face, unless we're alone, that is." He smiled, "then it's not so hard."

Jed finished breaking down his Colt and was folding a swab he would push down the barrel to clean the grooves. Johnny had taught him well and he was diligent about maintaining his gun.

"Have you decided when you're getting married?" he asked.

"That seems like it will be a bit complicated," replied Jason. "Except for the people around the store, I have no one who will take notice if and when I get married. She, on the other hand, has relatives all around Chinatown, although I'm not sure they would come to our wedding if we invited them. Traditions again. So, we're trying to decide the best way to go about it and who we will get to perform the ceremony." He shook his head. "I decided it was best to let her make all the arrangements and just be there to say, 'I do.'"

"I think that's pretty much what happens most of the time in these situations," observed Johnny. "The women decide, and we stand where we're told and speak when spoken to."

"Sure is fun though," said Jeb, "especially when it's over."

"So, you like being married?" Johnny asked. "It sure sounds like it from all the noise we heard before we moved. It's nice to be able to get some sleep for a change."

"Ha," said Jed. "You all were making as much noise as we were." He paused with a grin on his face. "I didn't know what to expect in the beginning and she didn't either, but it sure was fun figuring it out together."

After Jason left to open the store Johnny said, "How does the idea of being a father sit with you?"

"Gosh, it hasn't really sunk in yet, I don't think," Jed answered, "but she's excited. I think she's still a little afraid. Annaliese has helped us get used to the idea with the books she's gotten for us. We've been practicing all the things we need to do to keep the baby safe. The girls all call it 'she', but I'm hoping for a boy, at least the first one. We can have a girl next time."

"Annaliese doesn't think we can have any children, so I guess I'll just have to watch. Maybe after she finishes school, we can find one or two who might need a home."

It was almost dark when Johnny emerged from the back room with books to restock the shelves. It had been busy, and at eight o'clock there was still a young man waiting to talk to Lemuel, and several other people browsing aimlessly. Stocking the lower shelves always made his back tired, so when he finished, he stepped out the front door to take a deep breath and stretch.

From the second story of a house down the street, he saw the muzzle flash of a rifle, heard glass break behind him and the thud of a bullet striking a body. Suddenly the Colt was in his hand and he triggered three shots at the window so fast there was but one rolling sound.

Back in the store he saw Jed lying face down in a pool of blood on the floor before Lemuel's chair while Lemuel tried to staunch the blood welling between his fingers from a bullet hole in his thigh.

Annaliese came rushing from the back, looked at the scene and turned to grab the black bag she kept on a table beside her desk. One look at the pool of blood running from beneath Jed's body and Johnny realized he was beyond help. No one could bleed that much, that quickly, and live. Jason knelt beside him and checked for a pulse. He looked at Johnny and shook his head. Behind him, Greta said, "I heard shots. Is everyone all right?"

"Greta, Jed and Lemuel have been shot," said Johnny, "I need you to stay back out of the way so Annaliese can work with Lemuel."

"Is Jed hurt?" she asked.

Johnny took a deep breath. "He's dead, Greta.

She straightened up, let out a long shuddering moan, turned and walked away. Suddenly she tripped and fell to her hands and knees. Even as he leapt up to help her, it struck him he had never seen her stumble before, ever.

Chapter Forty-Three

Whenever Herschel came into the store he and Johnny would usually sit and talk for a while in one of the little alcoves in the new addition and that's where he found Johnny the next morning sitting, elbows on knees, head in hands, staring at the floor. When Herschel walked in, he looked up, sat up and took a deep breath.

"Did you find anything?" he asked.

Herschel sat in the other chair. "I talked to the lady who owns the building. The room was one she rents out, but it was vacant. Had been for a while. The window was broken and there were three bullet holes in the wall. She figures you own her for the repairs, by the way. There were some blood stains on the floor by the window, and I found some more in the hall and on the steps."

"There was a lot of dust on the floor, and I could see footprints all over the place and where he knelt at the window. She doesn't live in the house and the only one at home at the time was an old railroad brakeman who's lost a foot and can't get around too good. He heard the shots and then someone coming down the steps, but by the time he got to the door the fellow was galloping away down the street."

"I found two women who heard the shots, looked out the window across the street and saw someone get on what looked like a mule and ride away. They both said he was holding a rag of some kind to the side of his head and they could see blood on his shirt." While he was talking, Johnny resumed staring at the floor but now he looked up again.

"Apparently at least one of your shots hit him," said Herschel. "The description I got was pretty much what I had heard. Dressed like a farmer, overalls, big straw hat."

Johnny sat quiet for a moment. "So, it might have been the fellow with the funny name you told me about," he said.

"I'd put money on it," said Herschel.

"Any idea where I might find him?"

"If I ever heard, I don't remember."

"Any idea where Sunny Jim is?"

"I've heard he's back east somewhere, but no one knows where."

Herschel ran his hand over his head. "You know, I was down near the border when I heard about him. Maybe it's where he hangs out. Johnny, I just don't recall anyone saying anything about where he was from, so that's just a guess, but if you run across someone with a fresh bullet scar on the right side of his face or maybe without an ear on that side, I'd say you'd be getting warm."

Johnny's eyes were red and puffy, and he didn't look like he slept much.

"How's your partner?" Herschel asked.

"She spent the night by his bed and was up and down all night with him. The bullet hit him just below where the other one hit and it tore things up pretty bad. He lost some blood, but she got it stopped and he's resting now. At this point she doesn't know if he'll be able to walk again. If he ever does, it may take a while, a long while."

Johnny looked at him for a while, thinking. "It looks like Lemuel was the target. It seems he spilled a cup of hot coffee and Jed leaned over him to help and took the bullet by accident." He was quiet for a while, staring out the window.

"I remember what Jim said to you. 'There's such a thing as revenge.' Well, he got his revenge. Greta's pregnant and she's a widow, and Lemuel's life is suddenly much, much different. He was happy and excited about the future. I doubt if he'll ever get that back. I'd say that's revenge enough."

"Well, I've got a column to write before tomorrow morning, so I better get going. If I find out anything else, I'll let you know." Herschel stood.

"What was his name again?" asked Johnny.

"Gerhard Schweder."

Annaliese looked up when the office door opened and smiled weakly when she saw Sarah and Rebecca standing there.

"Hi," she said. She stood and came out of the office, closing the door carefully behind her.

"How is he?" asked Sarah.

"The bullet hit him a couple of inches below where he was wounded before," Annaliese said.

"The bullet went through. I stopped the bleeding and got him in bed right after it happened. The shock has worn off and he's in a lot of pain. I don't want to give him too much laudanum, because it affects his breathing and could lead to pneumonia since he won't be up and around for a while." After a moment she murmured, "if ever."

"Have they found out anything about who fired the shot?" asked Rebecca. She closed her eyes and took a shuddering breath. "I still can't believe Jed is dead. Why would anyone want to shoot him?"

"How is Greta?" asked Sarah.

"I don't know," answered Annaliese. "I've been so busy with Lemuel I haven't been able to be with her at all. Johnny says she seems to be in another world. Just lies on the bed, saying nothing."

"I feel the same way," said Sarah. "It just seems so unbelievable. When his father disappeared, it was different. I waited for weeks, always hoping I would see him walk in the door. It was so gradual, but I finally accepted he was gone. This happened so suddenly it took my breath away. I feel like I'm living some horrible dream and he's not really gone at all."

"Is it possible the two of you can move in here for a while and help me until things get back on an even keel?"

"Of course," said Sarah. "Why don't I go back to the mansion and get some things we'll need, and we can stay as long as you need us."

"Is it OK if I go up and see her?" asked Rebecca.

"Please do," replied Annaliese. When Rebecca had disappeared up the steps, she motioned Sarah to the back room where they each took seats and sat looking at one another.

"I know this is difficult for you," Annaliese said. "I can't imagine what you feel, losing your son like this and such a special one at that. Johnny is in a daze. He and Jed were so close.”

“The problem is the rest of us need to keep on living,” said Sarah. “We have to deal with the problems around us even while we grieve for the loss. We can’t just stop. Lemuel needs care and since you’re focused on that, someone needs to help Greta come to grips with it, if anyone can. Is Johnny here?”

“I don’t know where he is. Herschel came in and they talked for a while. Then Johnny left; just walked out without saying anything to anybody.”

“That Herschel is one person I don’t think too much of,” said Sarah. “Given what he’s been, how can Johnny trust him?”

“I’m like you. I don’t trust him either, but Johnny seems to.”

“Sarah,” she continued. “I need to go to class tomorrow. If I’m going to keep up with the work, I need to be there. Can we set up a schedule, so someone is always here to care for Lemuel and be with Greta if she needs help?”

“We came down here today knowing you might need help. Let us know what needs to be done and we’ll do it. We’ll stay as long as you need us.”

“Will it be a problem with the baby?”

“Those girls at the Mansion love taking care of him. She nurses him and they take over, so I’d say no, it’s not a problem.”

Annaliese reached out to take her in a hug. When they parted, Jed’s mother had tears in her eyes. “I’m so sorry,” said Annaliese and could feel tears of her own coursing down her cheeks. They hugged again and stood for a long moment, part of each other.

Johnny had gone to the ocean. He was standing on a steep hill, almost a cliff, with Jinx on his shoulder, gazing down at a white sand beach running for miles to a distant headland jutting out into the Pacific Ocean.

He wasn’t seeing it at all. What with the mesmerizing sound of ocean waves breaking on the sand below him and the thoughts chasing each other around in his head, he was somewhere else, in another world.

In that world, Jed was still alive and everyone around him was happy and healthy and looking toward tomorrow; and suddenly there was a bullet, and they weren’t. When his thoughts reached that point, they went around again until finally, he stood up, and with Jinx leading the way, walked back to where he had tied Black under a tree out of the sun.

He picked the cat up and put him in the saddle. "Well, little Buddy, do I go after him and make sure he pays for what he did and never does this to someone else? Or do I stay here to help my wife and our friends get on with their lives?"

Jinx licked his hand but didn't answer.

With Lemuel injured again, he knew the whole idea of The BookSeller would die if he didn't step up. Since it opened, his wife and some of his friends had built their lives and futures around it and if he walked away now, dreams would die.

He mounted, turned the big black horse toward the store and rode back down the hill.

Book Two

Chapter Forty-Four

Dr. Catherine Brown removed the stethoscope from her ears and smiled at the young woman lying on the examination table before her.

"Greta, it sounds like you might have two babies in there," she said.

Greta's mouth opened but no sound came out. "Annaliese," she finally said, "did you hear that?"

"Yes Greta, I heard, but it will take me a while to get a hold of what it means," said Annaliese. She squeezed the hand she had been holding during the girl's examination. "It sounds like we'll need to change our lessons a little. Maybe I ought to keep a journal so we can write a book of our own one day."

Dr. Brown finished washing her hands and said, "It likely won't change anything about our plans, as far as the baby's birth, but it's good you know and can make arrangements to prepare if I'm right."

"How are your classes going?" she asked Annaliese.

"It's a lot of work but so far I'm managing to keep up," replied Annaliese. "The study group is wonderful. We not only help each other with schoolwork, but we've become good friends."

"Your friend Margaret is somewhat of a character, isn't she?" asked Dr. Brown with a twinkle in her eye.

"She is that," answered Annaliese with a laugh. "Never know what's going to come out of her mouth." She nodded her head toward the lavatory where Greta had gone and continued in a low voice. "She's not recovering from her husband's loss like I hoped she would. Is her grief and lethargy going to affect the baby?"

"It's hard to say," replied the doctor. "But she'll need all her wits about her if she really is going to have twins. I hope you can get her back to where she was. People have told me she was a remarkable young lady. She just seems to be so focused on what happened. We're lucky, we have medicine and schoolwork to keep us on track and moving forward. She needs to find something to help her move away from that event. Of course, I know it's easier said than done."

On the way home in the buggy, they were quiet, like they were so much of the time lately. She left Greta in her room above the store and came down to find Johnny in the office.

Greta's life wasn't the only one changed with Jed's death. The bullet that killed Jed exited his body and lodged in Lemuel's leg, so for the second time in six months, Johnny's partner was recovering from a gunshot wound in his right thigh and was not able to take part in the operation of the store or in much else, for that matter. Johnny was looking more harassed and tired as the days went by, but with classes, studies and working with Lemuel and Greta, she could do little to help.

Fortunately, Jason's marriage brought Sun Li into the store and the girl had stepped up and become Johnny's right hand when he needed it most. Her responsibilities in the Li family business taught her skills she could bring to bear on The BookSeller.

She had assumed the responsibility of keeping the books, taking on herself the one job Johnny hated most, as well as helping Jason in the front and learning with him all aspects of the trade necessary to keep the place humming.

And humming it was. Herschel Grieve wrote the first of his new columns about the store and how it was one of the good new things in the city. Between the extra publicity and an effective use of the new addition, they had seen steady growth over the past six months.

The continuing open house events had been expanded to include speakers and authors and the store had begun to champion certain civic improvements and work advocating for public education. Toward these goals, they invited county and city officials to speak which brought in even more business.

Annaliese walked into where Johnny was sitting and held out her arms.

"Need a hug?" he asked and when she nodded, he stood and embraced her, holding her tightly, close for a long time.

"Bad day?"

"It shouldn't have been. The doctor says she's doing fine and guess what?" He just looked at her. "It might be twins."

Over on the bed, Lemuel opened his eyes and said, "Twins?"

"Dr. Brown said she heard two heartbeats. She's been doing this for a long time. She sounded pretty sure."

"What did Greta say when she heard that?" asked Johnny.

"Johnny, that's what was so strange. She didn't say one word to me on the way home. Nothing!"

He seated himself again and she sat in his lap and put her head on his shoulder.

"It's been six months and she's no better," she almost moaned. "I don't know what to do. It won't be long, and she'll have two babies to care for, but she doesn't seem to care about anything." When she raised her head there were tears on her cheeks.

"Do either of you have any ideas?"

Johnny shook his head.

"Lemuel, she's your daughter," said Annaliese. "How do you think I should go about bringing her back into life? She's somewhere else right now and unless we do something she may never come back."

After a moment the old man shook his head. The bullet had struck his leg just below the old wound and the damage was extensive. Recovery had been slow. Between the wound and Jed's death, he too seemed to have lost something.

"Maybe talking to her about her responsibility to her children might break through to her," he finally said. "I don't know. I feel kind of in another world myself since this." He gestured toward his leg. "I might not be the best one to talk to about how to get through to her."

Annaliese stood up suddenly. "Well, I remember what a wonderful person she was before and I'm not going to stop trying to get her back."

Later when they were alone and Johnny was watching her brush her hair he said, "Here's what I suggest. Go up to the mansion tomorrow and talk to Madame, Sarah, and Rebecca about this. Tell them where things are and where you want them to be. Maybe they can help you come up with a way to reach her."

She stopped brushing her hair and stared at him in the mirror. Slowly she nodded. "That's a good idea." She finished and turned to face him. "I think you should take me to bed and help me get this off my mind so I can sleep."

"I thought you'd never ask," he said.

Usually, Jinx woke Johnny up early and she slept in, but the next morning she was up before him, dressed and ready to go out just as day was breaking. She stopped at Mattie's for coffee and to put some thoughts on paper. When she felt the people at the mansion would be up and moving around, she got out the buggy and was soon on her way.

The women in the kitchen told her the ladies were lingering over breakfast in Madame's sitting room and there she found them, reading and discussing local papers and drinking morning coffee.

"Sorry to barge in like this, but I need some help solving a problem that concerns us all," she began.

"I bet I can guess what the problem is," said Sarah. "Just last night, we were talking about how Greta was not back in this world yet."

"Yes, that's the problem and I can't let it go any further without a solution. Since you've been talking about it, it means you've been thinking about it?" She looked a question at Sarah. "Any ideas. I'm about at my wits end."

She told them about the new developments and went on. "As far as I know, she hasn't even told her father, and she hasn't spoken to me since we got back from Dr. Brown's office yesterday afternoon. She's in another world and if we don't bring her back to this one soon, we may lose her altogether."

Rebecca shook her head. "She doesn't even take an interest in Bobby." She gestured toward a small crib where the baby was asleep. "We planned for her to be with me and practice, but we only did it once and she didn't seem to care when we did."

They were all quiet for a minute thinking, then Annaliese said, "Johnny and I were talking about it last night and he said the darndest thing."

They all sat waiting for her to go on. "He said, 'someone needs to throw a bucket of cold water in her face.'"

Rebecca laughed but Sarah looked thoughtful and after a moment Madame said, "He's saying you might need to shock her to make her see what she's doing to herself and to everyone else." She too, looked thoughtful and finally said, "You know, I think he might be right. It's possible, even probable, that she can't see what she's doing and needs something to clear her vision. I know that sounds funny when we're talking about someone who's blind, but in her mind's eye she can't see what is or will be because she's so focused on what was."

That night she was brushing her hair before the mirror and Johnny was dozing with Jinx on his chest, when she suddenly stopped and laid down the brush. She sat on the bed and shook him gently.

"Thank you," she said and kissed him. He was still half asleep and looked at her for a moment, puzzled.

"You're welcome, I guess," he said and went back to sleep.

Chapter Forty-Five

Handy Josephson stood leaning on the entrance gate of his newly purchased horse farm looking out at Mt. Tamalpais as the first rays of sunrise began their slow climb up the mountain's eastern slopes. He had climbed to the top with Gray the week before and he was amazed at the view of the Pacific Ocean, San Francisco Bay and the Sierra Nevada beyond. It was hard for him to believe the ocean was only twenty miles away and yet it would take him hours to get there from where he was standing. For a fellow from the flat lands of Minnesota it seemed strange to have so much of the world looking down on him.

He was waiting for Johnny and his partner Gray. They were due this morning, and since he had been working at the farm by himself for the last couple of weeks, he'd be glad of the company. Handy was a gregarious creature who loved being married and surrounded by people to talk to. He wanted to have his beautiful wife lying beside him at night and wanted to see his newborn son.

The arrangement he had made with Gray involved each of them working turnabout for two weeks and then two weeks in San Francisco. They figured another month and they could have the farm ready for the two of them to be able to work it effectively and live in it comfortably. Once it was ready, he and Rebecca would move into the main farmhouse and Gray would have the cottage on the crest of a ridge about two miles east, overlooking Richardson's Bay.

The rising sun disappeared into a cloud bank, and he felt the first drops of the drizzling rain typical in this part of the world. He retreated to the front porch of the main house and sat in a rocking chair to wait for his friends.

Johnny was coming to see the place for the first time and join him on the ride back to the ferry in Sausalito and across the Narrows to San Francisco. He missed his wife and was anxious to get to know little Bobby, his new baby boy. They were staying at Madame's mansion with Grandma Sarah, as he loved to call her when teasing.

He would be glad to see Jinx too, who would be riding with Johnny, either on his shoulder or on the saddle before him. Jinx was a part of Johnny in the same way Annaliese was, and he knew there was a little good-natured jealousy between Johnny's cat and his wife. Both the cat and the wife knew they were important to him, and each had enough sense not to force Johnny to choose between them.

He met Johnny and Jinx two years before while visiting his Uncle Joe in Kearney, Nebraska and joined them in riding the Pony Express Trail to Sacramento. Traveling almost two thousand miles together had cemented a bond between them important to both and when Wash joined them in Casper, Wyoming they formed a team.

Though he'd never been there before, arriving with Rebecca and Sarah in San Francisco from the east was like coming home because Johnny and Jinx were here.

It was raining harder by the time Johnny and Gray rode into the yard, tied their horses at the rail and climbed onto the porch, shaking water from their slickers like two dogs.

"You fellows look like a couple of drowned rats," he said, grinning at them. Jinx jumped into Handy's lap to say hello and he noticed the cat was completely dry.

"He's been riding under my slicker since we left the ferry. You know how he hates to get wet."

They joined Handy sitting on the porch, and for a while they talked about the farm and the plans they had for it while Jinx explored the house. After a while, Gray excused himself and left to ride to his cottage to change clothes and settle in for his two-week stint.

"I think he and I are going to get along fine," said Handy. "He didn't have quite enough to put up for his share, so Madame made up the difference. He's a hard worker and he's bright and he's excited about the plans we've worked out so far."

"How did you guys get into this idea?" Johnny asked.

"Madame knew the family who owned the place, and they wanted to sell. Gray and I would sit in the kitchen and talk of a morning, and when the idea came up, we just grabbed a hold of it, and here we are. I didn't want to get into farming crops, so this seemed like a good alternative."

"Have you ever met Maxine?" Handy asked. When Johnny shook his head, he continued. "She's one of the maids at the mansion. She and Gray are making plans to get married and live in the cottage." He pointed to a small house on a ridge a couple of miles distant. "It's a little rough right now. It's been empty for a year or so, but it sits on the side of a hill above Richardson's Bay and the view is something special. We hope to have both the ladies up here by the end of next month."

"How's everything in the City?" asked Handy after a while.

"The store is going great guns," he replied. "Best week so far last week and it seems to be getting better all the time. Annaliese is so tied up with school and studying she's not much help around the store these days but fortunately Sun Li has picked up the slack. She did most of the bookwork for Jimmy at the restaurant and store so between her and Jason, they're able to keep things running smoothly and it leaves me free to do the ordering and such. I think Jason caught a good one when he got her.

"We've hired a new boy, a young fellow named Roy Carver, who helps a lot with lifting and carrying and runs errands while he's learning how things work. He's been a big help. Also, one of the girls in the study group helps out in the evenings a couple times a week. Have you ever met Jessica?"

"Yes, I think so. She's the real little one, right?"

"Handy, everyone's real little to you," Johnny said.

"Funny thing," said Handy. "I hired a boy here last week too. He was just hanging around. He loves horses so I gave him a job cleaning out the stables. Next thing I know he's grooming them and yesterday, he asked if he could exercise them."

Handy pointed to the barn and Johnny saw the boy pushing a wheelbarrow out the door. He looked up at the sky and then set it down and disappeared back inside.

"I think he's one of those sagebrush orphans you see around a lot these days. Says his ma's dead and he don't know where his pa is. I figure we can use the help, and he seems smart enough to learn whatever we decide to teach him.

"Besides, it will give him a place to live. Got a funny name, Bitsy. When I asked how he got it, he said he was the smallest in the family and they called him 'Little Bit' and after a while they just made it Bitsy. I call him Bits."

They sat quiet for a while. "Hear anything from Wash lately?"

"Yes, we got a note. Didn't say much, but that's Wash. They were in Los Angeles and were planning to ride down to San Diego and then maybe into Mexico for a bit."

"How's Lemuel doing?"

"I don't know, Handy." Johnny shook his head. "Annaliese says he's not pulling out of it like he did the last time. And Greta seems to be off in her own world since Jed was killed. Annaliese is pulling out her hair trying to figure out how to get her back to being Greta again." He shook his head again. "No luck so far."

"Oh, by the way, it looks like she's going to have twins."

"Twins!" exclaimed Handy. "Oh, wow! Wouldn't that be something?"

"You can see why Annaliese wants to get her back again. She was afraid about taking care of one baby; now she needs to learn how to handle two, and Annaliese says she'll never do it the shape she's in right now."

After he finished his inspection of the house, Jinx came out on the porch and Handy picked him up, put him on his shoulder and said, "Let me show you around the place."

For the next hour Handy showed his friend the farm and talked continuously about their plans and ideas for the future. He also met Bits and looked at the dozen horses the two men had to begin their venture.

When they were back on the porch eating lunch, Johnny asked, "Handy, I'd like to leave Black up here. I know I can count on you all to take good care of him."

Handy was a little taken aback by this, and Johnny explained further. "I can't ride him as much as he needs to stay in good health. He would be well cared for up here and yet available whenever I need him. There's one catch though. I want you to charge me the going rate for his stable fees. I'll find someplace else for him if you don't."

Handy looked at him for a long moment, then smiled. "I understand," he said. "He'll have the best stall in the house, and if you let me know when you're coming up, I'll meet you at the ferry with him saddled and ready."

"Did you ever meet Jim Steyer?" asked Johnny. When Handy shook his head, Johnny continued, "I met him when I first came out here. He was the first mate on the Alameda ferry and now he's the captain on the Sausalito ferry. The first time he saw Black, he asked if I'd ever raced him. When I saw him today, he brought it up again."

He waited for Handy to say something and when he didn't, went on, "What would you think about getting him ready to run in some races in the City?"

"Johnny, I don't know anything about racing horses. You'd need to find someone who knows what he's doing."

"I thought about that, and I think I can get Jim to help me find someone to help us learn about it." He nodded at the barn. "Bits might make a good jockey. Looks like he's small enough, and from what you say he loves horses. We could all learn together."

Handy sat thinking for a while. "Let's do some work on this idea while I'm in town this time. Although I'd never thought about it before, it does sound like a good thing for a horse farm to get tied in with. Let's talk to Gray about it before we leave and see what he says."

"You're not going to leave Black this trip, are you?" asked Handy.

"No, once you get everything ready will be soon enough. I'll feel strange when I do leave him. We've been through a lot together and he and Jinx have gotten to be good buddies. We'll both miss him."

"I'll have a stall set up just for him whenever you're ready."

After a spare dinner, all three were sitting at the table when Johnny brought up the subject again. Like Handy, Gray thought it would be a good thing for a horse farm to get involved with, but also like Handy he knew nothing about it.

"Some of my old friends could probably help us find someone," he said. "Before I started to work for Madame I ran with some pretty shady characters and they talked about the track and some of the stuff that went on out there."

"How did you get connected with her, Madame I mean?" asked Johnny, "and how did you get the name Gray?"

"She was in a spot one day and I stepped up to help her," he replied. "It just worked out from there. She's quite a lady. Most of the people working at the mansion are there because of some connection or another with her past. She likes to be around people she trusts and figures she has the money so why not help her friends who need it? As long as we do our job, stay out of trouble and are there when she needs us, it works out.

"As far as the name, my surname is Grayson. Gray just comes from that."

"Who's the butler at the mansion when you're not there?" asked Handy.

"I've been teaching the job to Tony. Most of it is just common sense. You know his wife is Madame's personal maid, so they're a good pair." He turned to a decanter on a sideboard and poured himself a glass of dark red wine, looking a question at them both. When they refused, he took a sip and smiled at them. "Madame allows us to sample the wine cellar as long as we don't get carried away. I found a glass after dinner is the perfect end to a meal. This one comes from a vineyard a little north of here, up the Napa River north of the bay. Madame has some friends who own it."

The conversation was pleasant, but since they wanted to catch the early ferry back to the City the next morning, they turned in early.

In the morning, they watched as the ferry docked, loaded their horses and on the run home, talked to the captain.

"Talking to Handy last night we decided we're going to look for someone in the City who can help us learn about racing horses," said Johnny. "Know anyone who could help us?"

Jim grinned, "Funny you should ask. I have an old friend who lives out near the track. He keeps me up on things out there and he knows everyone who's anyone when it comes to racing around here. His name's Harry Reed. I'll talk to him in the next couple of days. Just have him come to the store?"

"That'd be best," said Johnny.

"I may come with him. I've never been there."

"I didn't think you had," said Johnny. "It would be best if you could make it in the evening. I'm always there after five or so."

When they mounted at the landing and waved to Jim, it dawned on Johnny they might have just started something new and important.

Chapter Forty-Six

By the time she finished her breakfast, Annaliese had finally worked out what she needed to do with Greta, and she put the plan into action immediately.

A short ride in the buggy and she was guiding Greta to a small open space in the woods. Below and a little way off she could see Fort Point and hear the ocean breaking on the rocks.

When they were seated on a blanket she spread on the grass, Greta said, "I've been here before."

"Yes, you have," answered Annaliese. "Twice from what I remember. This is where we talked about boys, about making love and how to take the next step with Jed."

She sat quiet and waited for Greta to speak.

"Jed and I made love here once," Greta said. There were tears streaming down her face. "Why did you bring me here?"

"So, you could learn to feel again," answered Annaliese.

They were quiet for a minute. The silent tears were now dripping onto the blanket.

"It was here you had a wonderful time with the man you loved. I wanted you to remember that because you need to learn to live with his loss.

"What happened to your life when Jed was killed is something which will always be with you. Always! It's like a great, huge rock and when you stand next to it you can think of nothing else; it blocks out the sun and fills up your senses. But every step you take away from it makes it smaller and smaller until, one day, like a mountain in the distance it will be just part of your life."

She sat quiet for a moment. "Right now, every time you think about him you feel grief and sorrow and pain. This is the man you loved and yet when you think about him you feel terrible. You need to remember the joy and happiness you had with him and realize the only thing that can take it away from you is you. Greta, you need to learn to feel again.

"Smile when you think about Jed. Remember how he loved you and how you loved him and be happy about it. Or continue to drown in sorrow and grief and never feel happiness again."

They sat silent for a while, listening to the waves and feeling the cooling breeze off the ocean.

"There's something else you need to think about. Your Papa's not doing well. Between the bullet in his leg, Jed's death and the loss of his daughter, he could die. You've been the center of his life since your mother died and now, he's lost you. We all have.

"When Jed died you went somewhere, and none of us can follow you to bring you back. We want the Greta back we know and love and if you think about it, I think maybe you want to be back, but you don't know how. All I can say is take one step at a time away from that rock toward us and then another and another and eventually you'll make it back. We're all here to help you."

When Greta reached out to her, Annaliese felt a great surge of relief and she folded the girl in her arms and held her close for a long time.

"I feel guilty if I don't think about him all the time," she said, crying into Annaliese's shoulder. "I know he wouldn't want that. It's so confusing, what I feel."

"It's all new to you. You've never lost the man you love before. Because you can't handle what you feel right now, I think maybe you decided not to feel at all."

They sat and held each other and cried together for a while. Finally, she pulled Greta to her feet and said, "what say we go back and start your life again?"

When they got back to the store, they hugged each other again, then Greta squeezed her hand and walked into the office where her father was sitting up in his bed looking out the window. "Papa, will you read to me today?" she said,

Annaliese sank down on the steps, covered her face with her hands and cried.

Because the five ladies of the study group had decided to sit together whenever they could arrange it, they were usually early to class so they could make sure to get seats they wanted. Today Annaliese led them to the front row because this was their first class in Human Anatomy, and they wanted to be able to see and hear everything.

She was nervous as well as excited. Working with the Doctor, she had seen most of what lay beneath the skin of a human body, but never in an organized fashion. After cleaning a wound or removing a bullet, the idea was to get the skin back together as soon as possible so healing could begin.

Now she was going to have someone to teach her and show her and answer her questions. In fact, she was a little worried about all the questions she would have and whether or not the instructors would be tolerant enough to answer them. She guessed that's where the study partners came in.

When the professor entered the room, the chatter around her ceased abruptly. She turned her head to see him and was surprised by his youthful appearance. All of their teachers to this point were older men, and he looked to be in his forties somewhere.

His desk was to one side of the room, and in the center was an open space with a long table, empty now, but she somehow felt it wouldn't stay that way. Below it was a tile floor with drains at either end of where the table stood. The room itself was like a small auditorium with chairs in tiers, well-spaced so there was a good view of the table from everywhere. Around the back of the room was a viewing area which was glassed in where people with an interest could watch without disturbing the class.

When he finally cleared his throat, he spoke in a deep, clear voice, seemingly articulating his works carefully. She would soon learn he always spoke that way.

"Welcome to your first lecture in the study of the anatomy of the human body. My name is Henry Rose. Before we go on, I notice we have several women in the class." He nodded at the group and continued. "In the recent past, a class like this would be male almost exclusively. I want to make sure the men in this class understand this is a serious class, and I hope you will take it thus. Practical jokes and harassment of women students will not be tolerated." He paused, looked around the room and smiled. "Do I make myself clear?"

Annaliese was startled by his direct approach. Most of her other teachers made it clear they didn't care one way or another about it. Indeed, most of them felt women were intruders in a profession that should be left to men. She looked around at her friends and almost laughed out loud at the look on Maggie's face. The girl was grinning from ear to ear.

The class was short that day, an introduction of sorts outlining expectations and goals, with ideas about how to gain the most from what he would teach them. As she was getting ready to leave, Mr. Rose handed her an envelope with her name written on it. When she looked up at him, he smiled at her and left the room.

She stood looking at the envelope for a moment, then opened it and unfolded the paper within. When she finished reading it there was a puzzled expression on her face. She handed it to Maggie, who read it and handed it to Jess.

"I wonder what that's about," she said.

"Well, if you go along to his office at one o'clock, I'll bet you'll find out," said Maggie. "You didn't wink at him or anything, did you?"

Annaliese snatched the note from her hand and hit her playfully on the head with it, then followed her friends out of the room.

Sitting through her next lecture was a waste of time. She kept thinking about why he could possibly want to see her.

At exactly one o'clock she knocked on his office door and entered when he responded.

He welcomed her with a smile, and after standing to shake hands, handed her what appeared to be several pages of a letter. She unfolded it, and after reading the first few lines, looked up at him.

"You know the Doctor?"

His smile broadened into a grin. "Yes, though I never called him that. He was Billy and I was Hank back then. We went to school together in Germany before the War," he said. "He found out I was teaching here after you were admitted, wrote me a letter, and we decided to surprise you."

She finished reading the letter. "Well, does this mean I'll pass the class?" she said with a grin.

He laughed. "From what your father wrote me, you shouldn't have any trouble. He said you started working with him when you were ten years old?"

"That's right, and I stayed with it until I left and got married last year. So, seventeen years all together."

"Dr. Brown tells me you and your husband have a rather unique bookstore here in town."

"Yes sir, it's on Chestnut Street and we'd love to have you visit us. You'll have to come to an open house sometime. They're every other Thursday. Of course, you can come any time."

"My wife and I will be there in the near future, I assure you. Have you heard from your father recently?"

"I had a letter from him last week and he didn't mention you at all."

"We decided to surprise you. My wife Beverly and I would like to have you and your husband over for dinner soon. Bev loves to meet young women who aspire to the practice of medicine."

When she got back to the store later in the day Sarah was standing at the counter talking to Sun Li.

She greeted Sun Li and asked Sarah, "How's Lemuel this afternoon?"

"He and Greta talked for a while, he took a nap and woke up as cheerful as could be. He's been a model patient. Rebecca is just back from the mansion and she's going to take over while I go down to Mattie's and have dinner. You want to go along?"

"Yes, I would like to. I want to tell you what that scamp, the Doctor, did."

Johnny joined them, and when they were seated at the table with coffee before them, she told them what had happened.

Johnny was grinning when he said, "Which we hope should help you pass the class."

She laughed. "That's the first thing I thought. But he seems to be open to questions, and besides, most teachers enjoy helping students who are interested. The Doctor used to tell me how his professors in Germany loved to sit after class and talk with their students over a beer in a local tavern. He said sometimes they would talk for hours, and he often learned more there than in the classroom.

"I must say he's a refreshing change from some of the old farts we've had so far."

"Old farts?" said Johnny. "You need to be careful about hanging around with Maggie. She's corrupting you." He winked at Sarah. "Although, I must say, I kind of like it."

Later Annaliese was sitting at the vanity brushing her hair when Johnny came up behind her and kissed her on the head.

"We don't make love as much as we used to," he murmured into her hair. "Don't you love me anymore?"

She turned and looked at him while she was still counting. "Ninety-nine, one hundred," she said. She rose, walked to the bed and opened her dressing gown to him. "Come here you poor, deprived little boy."

He clapped his hand together, cried, "Oh boy, oh boy," and bounced across the room into her arms. They were both laughing into a kiss, until things got serious and then they weren't laughing.

Johnny broke the connection. "How about if we try one of those chairs downstairs tonight," he whispered.

She looked at him doubtfully, then grinned. "Yes, let's." She took his hand, and they tiptoed down the stairs.

The chair had surely been made for just that kind of thing.

Chapter Forty-Seven

"Fire, air, earth and water." Professor Rose finished writing on the slate board behind him, turned, and swept his eyes around the classroom. "Can anyone tell me what those are?"

He smiled and pointed at Maggie, whose hand was in the air.

"It's what people used to believe everything was made of. I think a Greek philosopher named Empedocles wrote about it, back years before Christ was born."

"That's exactly right Miss....?" He looked at her inquiringly.

"Kramer," she said, "and it's *Mrs.* Maggie Kramer."

He grinned at her. "I'm sure I'll remember, *Mrs. Maggie Kramer.*"

He looked back at the rest of the class. "Actually, people have been cutting up dead bodies to see what's inside them long before that, but in the 17th century, two fellows, one named Robert Hook, and a Dutchman named Leeuwenhoek, used simple microscopes to see and identify cells. We have since learned those cells are the building blocks of all matter, including everything in the body.

"From that time till this, scientists, doctors and laymen have described and catalogued tremendous amounts of information about the human body and what's inside it, using their eyes and much better microscopes."

Again, he turned to the slate board behind him and wrote on it. 'What is inside the human body', then turned back to the class.

"That's what you'll be learning in this class." He paused and swept his glance around the classroom again. "But as we study these things, I want you to keep several things in mind. First, though we know what's there, we are still a long way from knowing how all these different things work. For instance, we know the heart pumps blood throughout the body, but we have no idea what makes it beat."

He tossed the chalk on the desk and brushed the dust off his hands.

"Second, though most of you come to this class determined to be medical doctors of one kind or another, I want you to remember you are also researchers, people who ask questions and seek answers. Researchers contribute much to the practice of medicine. It's because of them the next generation of doctors will be better doctors because they'll know more about what they're doing. So be a researcher. Be curious. When you have a question, look for an answer.

"And finally, being a doctor is only one way to put your medical education to good use. For our profession to move forward, we need people who dedicate themselves to finding out the things we don't know about the human body and how it works. In the future, anatomy, physiology and research will need some of you to help us find out what we need to know to be better doctors."

Later that afternoon, the study group sat in the back room at The BookSeller and talked about Mr. Rose and their first lecture in Anatomy.

"It's not what I expected," said Tudie. "He doesn't even sound like any of the other professors. It's almost like he's having fun when he's up there showing us things."

"I like his voice," said Jess. "He seems to want to make sure you hear and understand him. In some of the other classes I can't even hear what they're saying half the time."

"That's one of the reasons I like it when we get to sit up front," said Maggie, "and you can see better which in this class is important."

"Where did you learn about that Greek person you talked about?" asked Ginger. "No one else had any idea how to answer the question."

"My father loved to read the Greek philosophers. He learned Greek when he was young, and we talked about it a lot."

"Well, next class we go inside the body, so we better make sure we're ready," said Annaliese.

"Well, it will probably be old hat to you," replied Ginger. "I'm sure you've seen most of it at one time or another while you were working with your father."

"Not so much as you'd think," said Annaliese. "Most of the time we were inside, there was a lot of blood, and the idea was to fix what was injured and get out. The longer you were inside the more the patient would bleed. Eventually they run out of blood. You don't have a lot of time to look around.

"That's one thing about cutting into cadavers; there won't be much blood," she continued. "If the heart's not pumping, it doesn't bleed."

Tudie shivered a little. "I must admit I'm a little nervous about next time. I've never seen anything like it before."

"Me too," said Jess. She looked around and saw the same look on everyone's faces.

Greta knocked on the door jamb of the back room where Annaliese was setting up her study materials on the long table.

"Hi Greta," she said. "Come in and sit down. I've been wondering how things are going, but the last few days I've been so busy with school and studying I haven't had a chance to talk to you."

Greta sat across from her and sighed deeply. "Anna, I didn't have any idea how much I wouldn't remember. I keep bumping into things and tripping over things and I know it hasn't changed much around here. And the bookshelves seem so different now. I've decided not to even try to get back to where I was right away. I don't know where any of the books are now, and I'm just going to have to start at the beginning and try to learn what types of books are where if I'm going to be any help to anybody. I can't remember many of the things I knew before. It's going to take me a while to settle in again."

"It's not going to be easy for you, I imagine," said Annaliese, "but I believe you can learn what you need. You did it before. Maybe if you talk to your Papa about how you learned it before it will help you to learn it again."

She reached across the table and took the girl's hand. "How are you feeling?"

Greta was quiet for a moment. "It's hard sometimes. When I wake up in the morning it's the first thing I think about. That he's gone. But I try to remember what you said about the big rock. I think every day I've been able to take some steps, but it's not getting much smaller yet.

"It helps having Papa here. I try to talk to him about the things we did when we were traveling, and try to remember how happy we were then, and how I was able to learn and remember things. It's as though I have to force my mind to remember and then maybe I can figure out how to get back the things I need."

She sat quiet for a while. "I think about him at night before I go to bed, too. But when I think about him during the day, I try to close it out and sometimes I can. Of course, sometimes I can't. I miss him and love him, but I need him to help me be here in this life and not there with him. Does that make any sense?"

"Yes, I'd say it does," replied Annaliese. "But I can only help you so much because I haven't been through what you have. This is something you'll have to learn how to do by yourself. When you lose great happiness there is great sorrow, but I hope you may be learning how to move past it. I will help you all I can, we all will. It might just be something you have to do yourself, but remember, I'll always be ready to listen when you need to talk."

"One thing I try to do is to think about him dying like it's the big rock you talked about. That's what I want to walk away from. I want to take his love for me with me. I don't ever want to walk away from that."

Annaliese sat looking at her, slowly nodding her head.

Lemuel was up in his wheelchair by the window when she came into the office.

Instead of the wan, tired smile she was used to lately, this one looked happy, or close to it; and when he spoke, it sounded that way.

"She's got her foot on the path," he said. "I think she may be on the way back."

"Yes, it seems so, but we need to keep helping her to find what she thinks she's lost." Annaliese ran her fingers through her hair, pulled it back and tied it in a ribbon.

"She thinks she lost some of her memory," continued Annaliese, "as though it's not there anymore. I think it probably is, but she needs to get back confidence in herself." She shook her head.

"There's something else, though. She never smiles or laughs. She always has the same expression on her face."

"I agree," replied Lemuel. "She needs to think on new things rather than try to remember the old; find some things to look forward to. I'll try to help her focus on the changes which have happened while she's been away. When she realizes she can learn new things again, I think she'll be on the way back."

"Sun Li and Jason are patient with her, which is a long step toward it," said Annaliese.

"So, it looks like you might be coming back too," she continued. "We were worried about you just like we were about her, but your smile tells me you might be on your way back yourself."

He looked at her for a moment, then smiled again. "Perhaps. I believe the shot that killed Jed was meant for me, and truth be told, I have wished many times over the last six months it had found its intended mark. He was so young and full of promise, and the source of all my daughter's happiness. I am an old man and my usefulness the last little while has been nil."

He shook his head. "With Greta coming back to life, it seems as though I may have to myself." He smiled at her. "Whatever that means."

"It means a lot to all of us, I assure you. You are important to us, and you contribute much to the success of The BookSeller. I know how Johnny will feel when you're back in your chair selling books for us again, and I hope that's soon."

"I think it will be, probably this Thursday. With the wheelchair I can move around pretty good, and then we'll just have to see. For what it's worth, the Oracle is back."

Chapter Forty-Eight

When she opened her eyes, Woman was puzzled by what she saw. Then she smiled. It was a tent. Wash put it up because it was raining when they stopped the night before. This was the first time it had rained since they left San Francisco, so they hadn't needed it before now. They usually slept under the stars on a bed of boughs he pulled from the evergreen trees around them and put under a cover.

Like most mornings since they left Los Angeles, she could hear the ocean, sometimes close, sometimes distant, but she had grown used to it and could almost tell how far away it was by the sound.

She found him sitting on a rock looking out at the waves rushing toward him and at the ocean beyond. She sat on the ground beside him and felt his hand in her hair, stroking it gently. One of the things she loved about their time together was the silence between them. Neither was inclined to talk much but they knew each other well. Thoughts passed with touch and glance, smile and frown; it was enough, most times.

"Will we be there today?" she asked.

He nodded. "I think it might be 10 or 15 miles. If we get going, we should be there before noon."

Their trip so far had been anything but a straight line. Wash loved to see new places. Sometimes they would sit on a crest, gaze at the view, pass binoculars back and forth, and decide to stay there for a few days. Sometimes they took a trail because it looked interesting, or someone had told him of a lake he wanted to see.

Occasionally they would stop in a small mountain town or farm village and spend a day just looking, noticing what was there and what wasn't. She'd always remember a night when they made love by a small waterfall, and after lay listening to the sounds of water over rocks till they fell asleep. This trip was a first for her and she was trying to remember it all.

Wash's life had taught him to be self-sufficient. Most meals on the trail were simple, bread and bacon, beans and hardtack. He loved cheese, and a good meal for him was several slices on a toasted biscuit. There were enough places along the way where they could purchase vegetables and supplies, and once in a while, they would sit down in a restaurant, though not often. Sometimes there were problems when they did, and he didn't like that. She knew he wasn't afraid, but she had learned he liked to slide through life making as few ripples as possible.

Though neither carried a belt gun, both had Bowies, and several times display of them had been part of avoiding a problem. Though Wash had his Sharps, he hadn't fired it since they left. The country they passed through was becoming more settled, and the need for defense or food diminished accordingly.

They rode into San Diego just before noon, swung down at a general store/post office, and within a few minutes found out Doc lived out of town a few miles to the south.

Wash and Doc had run together up in Oregon with some other fellows for a while before Wash connected with Johnny and Handy in Wyoming. Doc popped up again on the trail to Salt Lake and left there with some friends to travel to San Diego. They were old compatriots, comfortable with one another, and both liked to see what was over the next hill and the one after that.

Wash paid a boy at the post office to take a note to Doc's place, and they walked out to look the town over.

San Diego was in the midst of a boom. The railroads both from north and east had met there the year before, and people were streaming in from everywhere to see if what they'd heard of the fabled California was true. Some were tourists but many came to stay, and the place smelled of fresh lumber and paint and resounded with the noise of hammer and saw. The clerk at the post office told them there were at least 10,000 in residence now with more coming every day.

With no answer to their note, they rode a little way south of town and bedded down in a small grove within hearing of the ocean.

"We haven't talked much about what we're planning to do here. Are we going to stay for a while or head back soon?" she said.

He grinned at her. "I've been waiting for you to ask me, but you don't really seem to care, do you?"

She shrugged and took his hand. "Other than a long boat trip when I was a girl, I've never been anywhere or seen anything. I'm just along for the ride." She kissed his hand. "It's been a fun ride and I'm having a good time. So, answer my question."

"I have kept you in the dark, haven't I? Well, until I talk to Doc I don't really know. If he can put us up and we can find some work to keep us from starving, we may stay for a while. If he's not around, we might work for a while to get some money together and then maybe I'd like to see Mexico. It's only a few miles south to the border, and I hear there's a city right there on the other side. We might take a look." He looked at her for a moment in silence, then kissed her gently. "I believe you're the right one for me. We get along and have fun together, don't we?"

She smiled at him, nodding slowly.

The next morning, following directions from the postmaster, they took the road south out of town, and after an hour, turned off onto a trail leading to a small cabin with a porch off the front in a clearing close to a stream they could hear chattering over stones.

Since no one appeared in their hail, they tied their mounts and looked around. The front door was not locked, so they found a place to lay their bedrolls down and moved in until someone told them to move out.

The next afternoon they were in the middle of a meal at the hotel dining room when Doc walked in, a large grin on his face.

"I thought I knew that scruffy mule out front," he said. "When'd you get in town?"

"Couple days ago," replied Wash. "We slept out at your place last night."

"I haven't been home yet." He nodded at Woman and doffed his hat.

Introductions were made and they talked of old times for a

while, then Doc asked, "So how's everything in San Francisco? I read about Jed in the paper."

"I'm surprised you heard about it down here."

"The hotel leaves old Morning Calls laying around the lobby. I stop in once in a while just to catch up. He was murdered, right?" when Wash nodded, he went on. "Did they ever find out why?"

"It seems it might have been an assassination. Lemuel was the target and Jed got in the way. Johnny got three shots off and blood sign shows he probably hit something."

"From what I remember about Johnny, that doesn't surprise me." He leaned back in his chair. "When I left you in Salt Lake there was talk of opening a bookstore, and I see in the paper they did. I also read about what a good place it was to visit."

"That's Herschel Grieve's column. He's a friend of Johnny's." Wash shook his head. "That's one friendship I'll never understand."

When Doc looked a question, he continued. "Herschel was one of the gang we broke up at city hall. He claims he's reformed. I'd need more proof. Johnny seems to trust him." He shook his head again.

Doc laughed. "Well, I got to be friends with him after I stole his horses. Maybe it's a character defect."

Doc turned to Woman. "You don't talk much."

She smiled at him. "No," she agreed, "I don't. Unless I've got something to say."

"Is this the first time you've traveled with him?" When she nodded, he said, "Fun, ain't it."

Woman was sitting on the cabin porch the next day when Wash rode up.

"Well, I found something," he said. He led Master into the stable behind the cabin and came up on the porch to sit beside her. "Just as I rode into town, I saw a 'help wanted' sign, so I stopped. I'm now employed by Sessions Plant Nursery and Orchard Supply. I help out around the place three or four days a week. More if she needs me."

Doc joined them. "I know Kate. Help her out once in a while myself. She's a fine lady. Came down here a couple years ago from up north somewhere. Seems she came into a little money when her husband died, so she came down here to start over."

"Well, it looks like I've replaced you. She's got a new contract with the city to provide trees for the city park, so I guess I'll be planting them, among other things." He turned to Woman. "She says she's going to need more help. If you're interested, you can go in with me when I start to work tomorrow."

It didn't take them long to realize they enjoyed the work. Wash had planted trees in another lifetime and remembered the satisfaction he felt when he saw them grow and thrive. Besides helping Wash occasionally, Woman worked with Kate in the store doing whatever was necessary, and they quickly became friends. Kate loved to get out among the trees and flowers, and it didn't take them long to learn she was never afraid to get her hands dirty and was always available to lend a hand if need be.

Woman's father had been a farmer in New South Wales, and she had fond memories of working with her brothers growing up. The job took them all over the city, and they found nice places to sit and have lunch and just talk or look around them. Though it was spring turning to summer, the weather was mild, and the tales they heard of winter weather sounded wonderful.

"Annaliese asked me to find out what it was like down here," said Wash one evening when they were sitting on the porch. "When she finishes school, they plan to leave the city and find a place, how did she put it?" he paused, "a place they can grow up with."

"Well, they'll sure need some more doctors before long if people keep showing up," said Doc. "And I reckon I'll need to get used to them since I seem to have settled down here."

"When will your friends be back?" asked Woman.

He shrugged. "Lord only knows. They might decide to take off to South America. They're like me and Wash used to be. Never happy in one place too long."

"Did you all build this place?" she asked.

"No, actually we found it empty, and since no one ever came to dispute it with us, we just stayed. It was a little rough when we got here but we put some work into it and it's nice enough now. I like it here, and I can pick up enough work to keep me in beans and bullets. I'm looking for someone to settle down with; you interested?"

"No thanks. I got one," she said and smiled at Wash who smiled back.

"Shucks," he said. "Actually, I'm sparkin' a widow who lives north of town. She's gone to Los Angeles for a week or so to visit her brother. When she comes back, I'll introduce her to you. In addition to being right pretty, she's well off."

The next afternoon Wash was loading a wagon behind the store when he looked up and saw Woman standing in the doorway, motioning to him. When he approached, she put her finger to her lips and drew him inside to where he could see into the store.

At the counter, a tall man wearing a large straw hat was making a purchase. When he turned to look at something, Wash saw an angry red scar extending from near his eye, across the right side of his face to the place where his ear would have been. There was only the top of it left and a gaping hole where the rest of it should have been.

He dropped the rake he was holding and stared, mouth open.

When he recovered from the shock, he crossed to the office where Kate was working with some invoices.

"Do you know that fellow?" he asked, pointing to the man who by now was getting into a wagon with several trees swathed in burlap standing in the back.

"Sure," she replied. "He's a regular customer. Owns an orange and lemon grove out in the valley. Why?"

"Do you know his name?"

"Yes, it's Ger Schweder. He was one of my first customers when I opened. I think his full name is Gerhard."

Chapter Forty-Nine

"The business of her life was to get her daughters married; its solace was visiting and news."

Lemuel closed the book and looked at his daughter. "I thought you might like to hear that one again since you liked Jane Austin so much the first time we read it."

Greta was sitting very straight in her chair with her head clocked a little to the left. She always sat thus every night when he read to her while they traveled West selling books out of the wagon.

"You never smile anymore," he said. "You know, if you don't use those muscles, you forget how."

He got a slight smile out of her. "When your mother died, I felt like I'd lost my whole world, and I'd never smile again. Then I built the wagon, and we started traveling, and I found new things to smile about, to laugh about. I can see you're trying to move forward. I'm glad to see you working again and figuring new ways to do things, the way you used to.

"But you need to bring joy back into your life, to smile and laugh like you once did, to take the pleasures life gives you. All the people around you are moving on with their lives. If you stand by Jed's grave the rest of your life you won't have much of a life. You deserve to move on to what's out there, waiting for you, to have new joys and, yes, new sorrows. That's life, Greta, and it's the only one you've got. You need to make the best of what you're given, like all the rest of us.

"When your mother died, for a long time, I think I was afraid to be happy. It was as though I was being disloyal to her if I laughed or smiled. Ask yourself if that's where you are. Are you afraid to be happy?"

She sat silent for a moment, seemingly frozen into her listening pose. "I don't know, Papa. Maybe I am. But how am I supposed to go about doing what you said, bring joy back into my life again?"

"Greta, I've seen you solve problems most people don't have. I know what you can do. You just need to remember how special you are to all of us and why."

"Annaliese told me to walk away from it and I'm trying," she said, "but it doesn't seem to be getting much smaller."

"I'd say you need to be patient." He paused, then said, "Do you enjoy helping Rebecca with the baby?" When she nodded, he asked, "How about working with Sun Li and Jason?"

"Yes, I do," she replied, "She's so nice, and I've always liked Jason, but so many of the things I do remind me of Jed, and it bothers me. I can't not think about him when I'm in the store. We were always there together."

"Can you think of something you did together that made you laugh at the time?"

She was quiet for a minute, remembering.

"One day he tried to talk me into locking up the store and sneaking upstairs. I kept slapping his hands away and he kept grabbing me." Her face broke into a smile, almost reluctantly. "Annaliese and her friends were in the back, and they came out and caught us kissing. I think I blushed for five minutes, but we kept laughing about it the rest of the day. Kissing too."

"How did it feel just now, when you smiled?" he asked.

She thought for a moment. "It felt strange," she said, and then, "it felt good."

"Maybe that's what you need to do. Every time you think about him, try to remember something he did to make you smile or laugh, or just feel good because he was there. The good times, Greta, remember the good times. Maybe you can get your face used to smiling again."

Sarah was on her way to join Madame for their morning coffee, where they read the papers and chatted about things, when Carlotta came around the corner.

She smiled shyly and handed Sarah a bundle wrapped in paper. "Would you give this to Mrs. Fry when next you go to the bookstore?"

"I will," replied Sarah. "What is it?"

"It is the story I read to you. You remember Pinocchio?"

"Yes, of course."

"She said I should write it in English. So I did."

"You mean you've translated the story into English?"

Carlotta nodded.

"How wonderful," said Sarah. "Did she say she was going to get it published?"

Carlotta nodded again. "She said she would ask someone how to go about it and find a printer."

"I'll make sure she gets it."

She was sipping her coffee and reading the story when Madame came in in her dressing gown.

"What's that?" she asked, and when Sarah told her she smiled. "She told me she was doing it. I hope Annaliese can get it printed and they can sell it in the bookstore."

"With all the connections they have in the business, they might be able to sell it everywhere," said Sarah. "It would be nice if she could make money from it. She's much too bright to be a maid for the rest of her life."

"Am I going to lose another maid?" asked Madame plaintively.

"You might just, although it will probably be a while before she sees any money from it, so you'll have plenty of time to find another."

"Maxine and Gray will be leaving next month. They're getting married and moving up to the farm at Mill Valley. If this keeps up I may have to learn to pour my own coffee." While they were laughing Carlotta came in with a coffee service and poured them each a fresh cup.

"Where's Rebecca this morning?"

"She'll be going down to the store. She and Handy are working with Greta to help her get ready for the babies." Sarah shook her head. "Whenever I think about her having twins, it astonishes me."

"Is she pulling out of the fog she was in?" asked Madame.

"Rebecca says she's trying but it's slow going. She seems to be making a determined effort to get past it, but she still cries a lot. She and Lemuel are reading again, which I think is a step in the right direction. That old fellow has a lot in his head, but he's had a couple of hard knocks since he's been here."

"Don't talk about him being old. He's younger than I am," said Madame with a pained expression on her face.

"That's right, I forget sometimes," said Sarah. "He sure does look a lot older than you."

They read the paper for a while. "I understand The Honorable Jonas Burke has made it a point to call several times recently," said Madame.

"Yes, he asked me to go to a birthday celebration he's having for one of his assistants at City Hall."

"Is he someone you see in your future?"

"Maybe. We enjoy each other's company and we're both alone. I haven't known him for long, but he seems like someone special."

They each went back to their paper.

"Do you miss having a man around?" asked Madame.

"You know, when I was at the store in the canyon I had the children, and there were always some of the mountain men around if I needed help with anything, so I never looked." She grinned. "Of course, on some of those cold winter nights when the children would crawl in bed with me, I used to think about having a man to cuddle up with. I never really loved Jed the way he loved me, but he was a wonderful man, and we had a good life together. I miss him."

"What about Rebecca's father?"

She smiled, remembering. "I was so scared when I first saw him, and when I was given to him as his second wife, but he was so tender and gentle with me I grew to love him. We had good times in bed. I do miss that once in a while."

Back to the papers again.

"Have you heard anything from Woman lately?"

"She's not much of a writer. I know they made it to San Diego and are working there and staying with an old friend of his, but that's about all."

"I imagine you miss her."

"Yes, I do, very much."

"I've always wondered about your friendship with her. She

seems like she's much more than just an employee." Sarah grinned. "Of course, we all wonder how much more."

Madame drank the last sip of her coffee, motioned for a refill and said to Carlotta, "Could you tell Bertha I won't be here for lunch?"

After the maid left, she looked at Sarah for a long moment and asked, "You want to know if we're lovers, is that it?"

"Well, I have been a little curious. It's easy to see she's more than a friend."

"Well, the answer is yes, we are." After another long silence, she asked, "Does that shock you?"

"No, and it doesn't surprise me either. Just the way you two are around each other, it's not hard to see there's something between you that's more than friendship."

"I still enjoy men but she's something special, something different. Most men I know are usually just looking to latch on to me for the money, and I don't need anything like that.

"Once in a while a ship's captain from the old days will make port and I will invite him in, knowing he will be leaving before long. She puts no demands on me and wants nothing from me but what I want to give her." She smiled. "And there's also what she wants to give me. That's important too."

"Yes, I imagine it is. When are they coming back?"

"I'll know when I see her. Like I said, she's not much for writing letters, and neither is Wash."

She stood. "I'm going downtown this morning, and I'm going to drop little Tony off at his Grandpa's store. What are you up to today?"

"Jonas is meeting me at the store. Nothing planned, just a meeting to look at books."

Madame's eyebrows went up and her mouth formed an 'O'. "Well good luck if you think it's what you need. I won't tell you to behave because at your age you don't have to."

Chapter Fifty

"So where did you meet this fellow we're going to see?" asked Johnny. He was riding Black. Jinx was in the saddle with him and he and Handy were riding alongside the buggy Jim Steyer and Herschel were riding in.

"Years ago, we started as crewmen together on the old Alameda ferry," said Jim, raising his voice so he could be heard. "We were just kids, but where I loved working on the water and stayed with it, he was crazy about horses. The second year we were there a fellow offered him a job as a groom and exercise boy on a horse farm and he was gone. We've been friends ever since and he hasn't changed much. He's still crazy about horses. Most summer days I'm off in the city, so I stop out to see him."

"So, he runs a horse farm?" asked Handy.

"I wouldn't really call it that," replied Jim. "He bought the place on time years ago and to pay it off he does a little of everything. He built an exercise track, and he trains horses for some of the racing crowd in the city. He pretty much organizes the races they have in the season. He stables some and owns a few of his own he runs now and again."

They came in sight of the place and Jim pointed out the stable which had a top floor in the middle of a long narrow building. If he had to describe it, Johnny would call it rickety. It looked like it might fall down in a windstorm, and he would be reluctant to climb the stairs leading to the second floor. Only the railing around a well-maintained exercise track was painted. Here was a man who's priorities were in order.

"He lives up there," Jim said, pointing. "He's never gotten married, but he has a couple who work for him. She cooks and does around the place, and her husband works with the stock and keeps the place up."

Johnny laughed. "Sounds like me growing up. Pa and I lived above the livery stable, and I was working with him since I can remember. Of course, he did most of the cooking and stuff. We never had a woman around."

At the gate, Jim handed the reins to Herschel, got out and opened it, then closed it again when they were through.

"Hey Jim," called a wiry little man from the door of the stable.

"Harry," Jim replied. "These are the folks I was telling you about and this is the horse."

"Whose cat?" Harry asked. "I could sure use him in the barn. Both mine run off."

He was very bow legged and looked as though he'd be more comfortable on a horse than walking.

Jinx took him at his word and disappeared into the ramshackle barn to begin his exploration while Harry began to walk around Black, eyes moving, noting everything, hands running over the big horse's hindquarters and his chest.

"He's sure big enough. Can he run?" he asked no one in particular.

"Harry, it's better manners to meet the people before you look at the horse," said Jim laughing.

When they were all introduced Johnny said, "I've never let him run all out. Never needed to."

"Where'd you get him?" asked Harry.

"That's a long tale. Let's just say I don't know much about his history. But I've got ownership papers; he's mine."

"I'd like to see him move. You want to take him around the track once to get him used to it? Don't run him yet. Just a lope will do it for now."

Johnny didn't know about Black, but he'd never been on a track before. The ground was smooth and firm, and the horse's hooves kicked up dust as he cantered around the big oval.

"It's a half mile," said Harry when he pulled up back at the stable. Again, he ran his hands over the chest and forelegs.

All this time, Herschel had been quiet, watching and listening. "I'm a reporter for the Morning Call," he said. "I'd like to take some notes if you don't mind."

"Fine," said Harry. "I like to be in the newspaper. Good for business." He turned to Johnny. "I'd like to see him run if you don't mind. Get him an easy start and let him out when you get to the pole." He pointed to a white pole about fifty yards up the track. "Don't want him to pull something before we get him in good shape."

Johnny never wore spurs, but at the pole he booted Black in the sides and the big horse responded. Within a few strides he was running at full speed, and it was like nothing Johnny had ever felt. Trees went by like telegraph poles on a train track and the wind took his breath away. His hat flew off halfway round the oval and the wind tore a couple of buttons off his shirt.

They flashed by the men standing at the stable, and since he seemed to be enjoying himself, Johnny let Black keep running. It seemed like the second time around they went faster, and by the time he was finally able to pull Black to a stop, they had gone fifty yards past the start line.

"That looked like fun," said Handy with a grin. "It doesn't look like he worked up much of a sweat."

"Well, I did," said Johnny. "It's funny, he did all the work, but I was out of breath at the end and sweating more than he was." He shook his head. "I never felt anything like that before. He was running so fast I had trouble breathing."

Harry and Jim were standing looking at a stopwatch the little man held in his hand.

Harry looked up at his friend and nodded. "Yep, he can run. I can't wait to see him on the track." He looked at Johnny. "Next time you bring him out let's meet over there and we'll put the clock on him and see how he does."

Jim Steyer wanted to ride Black, so on the way back Johnny drove the buggy with Jinx on the seat beside him. The cat was not usually friendly with most people, but he let Herschel pet him and seemed to be comfortable with the idea.

"So, this is the fellow who helped you out against Glenwood

Coe. I've seen you draw, Johnny, and I think you'd have beat him anyway."

"I took what edge I could get. That was the first gunfight I was ever in, and I hope the last."

"Changing the subject a little, where do you and Handy plan to go with this horse racing thing?"

"Truth be told, we haven't thought much about where it's headed. We're just getting started with the idea. As it unfolds, we'll think about the future. Of course, it all has to be run by Gray."

"Gray?"

"He's Handy's partner. He's a butler at the Mansion. They got to talking about it and decided to go together and buy the place. They're still getting it in shape so they can move up there permanently. It's up in Mill Valley. They take turns working up there. Each stays two weeks. Won't be long and you can come up and see it."

"What's the name of the place?"

"I don't think they've gotten around to naming yet. When we talked about it, Handy said they were waiting until the ladies came up to pick one."

They watched Jim and Handy in an impromptu race across a field just off the road. Johnny pulled the buggy to a stop and for the first time watched his big black horse from a different place. Black was running away from Handy's mount when they disappeared behind some trees. They sat for a moment before he started up again.

"You know," said Herschel, "it's funny, but the whole time I've known you I've never heard you or anyone around you say one word about horse racing."

"It's not something we've thought about much lately," Johnny said. "Lots of other things going on. I guess the idea came from Jim." He nodded toward where the Black was thundering back across a field parallel to the road. "This is the first time I've ever seen him run from this angle. He is beautiful, and what a stride. Just eats up the road.

"The first time I rode the Alameda Ferry Jim was the mate, and he and I were talking with Fletcher when they led Black down the ramp in San Francisco." Johnny laughed. "The look on his face, you'd have thought he was in love. I'd never thought about horse racing in my life, but he took one look at my horse and asked if he'd ever raced."

"Of course, with setting up the store and Lemuel getting shot up and all, I never even thought about it again until last week. I went up to the farm with Gray to look around and ride back with Handy. Now Jim's captain on the Sausalito run and it's the first thing he asked me when I saw him.

"On the ride from the ferry, Gray and I talked about it. I've pretty much decided to stable Black at the farm. I don't get a chance to ride him much and up there he'd get plenty of exercise and I know Handy would take good care of him. I brought it up to them at the dinner table and suddenly we were thinking about the fact that a horse farm and horse racing fit together right well, so here we are."

Jim pulled up alongside them, breathing hard and sweating while Black wanted to keep running. "Wow, ain't he something?"

"Do you think Harry would mind if Handy and I came out just to talk about what we're thinking about doing?"

"He'd love it. The man doesn't feel complete without some new horse to fool around with. Talk all you want but bring Black with you, and Jinx too for that matter."

"We're going to have to sit down and organize our thoughts on this before we do that, so when are you going to be in town next week?"

"Wednesday afternoon."

"OK, we'll try to have all our ducks in a row by then. I'm looking to get inside his head. He sure seems like a good person to have around with a venture like we're planning."

"I'd say yes to that. Do you mind if I ride him on to the store? I'll wait for you there."

Johnny waved his hand to send him off. When he turned to Herschel again his friend was still petting Jinx, which amazed him. "Do you always get along with cats so well?"

"Actually, he's the first one I've ever been around much. He seems like a good friend."

"He is that," agreed Johnny.

He was under the covers watching Annaliese brush her hair when she turned and said, "You haven't said five words all evening. What are you thinkin' about?"

"This thing with Handy and the farm. We have all the makings of a good thing, what with the horse farm and with this friend of Jim's. Harry Reed's his name and he's a gold mine of knowledge about horses, how to train and race them, and he's been living and breathing horses all his life. With his experience and with Handy, Gray and I working hard, we might make something special."

He had thrown the covers off and was walking around the room.

She didn't say anything for a moment, looking puzzled, then, "Since when have you been involved with Handy, Gray and the farm? It's the first time I've heard anything about it."

He grinned a little sheepishly. Well, I haven't brought it up to them. I wanted to talk to you about it. I still got some of what Pa left me and I was thinking about working out something so the three of us would be equal partners."

"How much would you have to put up?" she asked.

"That's something we'd have to work out between the three of us. I know Madame's lent Gray some money, but I don't know if she's a part of things, sort of like her deal with us, or if it's just a loan. I'm going to talk to Handy about all this tomorrow, depending on what you say about the idea."

She finished her hair and turned to him. "Johnny, it's your money and the store's doing fine, so I'd say do what you think is best."

He stopped before where she sat and pulled her to her feet.

"Now you've finished brushing it, I think we should mess up your hair, what do you think?"

She rolled her eyes at him and asked with an air of resignation. "Is this one of those wifely duty things?"

He nodded.

She kissed him. "All right, as long as it doesn't take more than two hours." They were laughing when they crawled in on the same side of the bed.

Chapter Fifty-One

Johnny was amazed at how much becoming a partner in the Mill Valley Horse Farm two months before had changed his life. Now, every Friday he and Jinx caught the early ferry to Sausalito, found Black saddled and waiting at the livery stable, and rode into the farmyard in time to have breakfast with his partners and their wives.

In the routine he had fallen into, he loved standing by the back railing of the ferry, Friday morning going over and Saturday evening coming home, looking out over the bay at the land in the distance and watching the water churn away from behind them.

The sights and sounds were almost hypnotizing. It gave him a chance to think about his life and how much it had changed since he'd worked out a deal for a quarter share in the farm. Madame's share was the same type of thing as her share in The BookSeller, money in, nose out. She had been up to visit one time. The men decided the resources she commanded at need made up for her lack of sweat at haying time.

Of course, other things in life were changing too. Annaliese was getting more and more into school and studying. Also, she was still helping Lemuel and Greta at need, so usually most of the time they spent together was at night when she was brushing her hair and they talked before bedtime.

Lemuel was improving steadily. He was sitting in his chair every other Thursday evening selling books and had assumed his share of the administrative work of the store again. Greta's improvement had been his curative, and he was eager and involved in The BookSeller again, though still confined to a wheelchair.

Greta was nearly there, her tummy swollen to the point where she needed assistance with getting out of a chair. She was also coming back to a semblance of what she was before. She had been working hard to reacclimate herself and adjust to the changes in the store.

She had also been faithfully and diligently working with Rebecca and Sarah planning how to care for her new children. Ideas suggested in things they read had to be adjusted to the fact there would be two instead of one. Since they were traveling without a map, these adaptations were usually the product of discussion and agreement. Though she was making progress, Annaliese said she still appeared nervous at times.

Jason and Sun Li did most of the work up front in the store and she had taken the hated bookwork off their hands, giving he and Lemuel time to deal with tracking the inventory, ordering the books and promoting the store.

Harry usually got to the farm about noon on Friday, and for several hours they would talk about racing and horses. Then Bitsy would put Black through a workout Harry designed to prepare him for his first race. The sessions were as much training for the jockey as for the horse.

At five feet tall and maybe 110 pounds, Bits was ideal size for a jockey, and his work around the farm had given him the wiry strength in his hands and arms necessary to handle a horse the size of Black. The jockey and the horse learned fast, and together, impressed the old trainer who soon pronounced them ready for the track.

Today when he came, he would bring a date for the next race and which horses would be running. This would raise the level of excitement around the farm considerably.

Gray and Johnny were sitting on the porch watching Bits and Handy wash some of the horses when Harry drove into the yard.

"How about next Sunday afternoon?" he said with a grin. "Supposed to be five other horses running and it will give us a chance to see how he does in a crowd."

Handy joined them, and they sat for a while digesting the idea while Harry dragged up a chair and sat so he could see their faces.

"You know, ever since the first time I saw him run, I've had the idea he's been on a track before. Just something about the way he behaved, moved. I remembered what you told me about how you got him, so I wrote to a friend in New Orleans to see if he could find any history on him."

"It seems I was right. His owner, that Rene Paul fellow you were involved with, ran him quite a bit down there under the name of Satan. According to my friend he won a lot more than he lost. Might be why he wanted him back so bad."

Johnny sat quiet for a while digesting this. Finally, he asked, "will this help him when we put him on the track next week?"

"Oh yeah," said Harry, enthusiastically. "One of the problems you have with a young'un is getting him used to running with other horses. It's one thing to put him on the track by himself with a stopwatch and quite another when he's in a pack with all the noise and commotion from five or six horses running around him."

"So, what are you telling us?" asked Gray. "He's more likely to win because he's been there before?"

"It definitely lowers the odds on him. I'm going to put fifty bucks on his nose next Sunday. If he runs the way we've seen him run, he should win going away."

"What kind of odds?" asked Gray.

"Well, it's hard to say. Because this is the first time he's run, you might get three or four to one, maybe more. I know most of the dicers around here, and for a new horse they'll just look him over and make a guess. Are any of you interested in some?"

Gray shook his head. "No cash to spare right now. Maxine wouldn't like it if I took the money for food and bet it on a horse. Ask me another time."

Harry looked a question at Johnny and Handy.

"I'll match yours," said Handy.

"Fifty it is," said Harry, and looked at Johnny.

"Let me talk to Annaliese. We always make money decisions together."

Harry scratched his head. "I heard about a straight stretch of road north of here a ways, so when I left here last week, I rode up there and measured out a half mile. Unless you have other plans, let's take Black up there and see how he does today. We've cropped his mane and bobbed his tail, and Bits will be an easier carry for him than Johnny was, so we should get a good idea of what he can do over the distance.

"We'll need to get Bits dressed. I brought some things that should fit him. The idea is to make sure there's no drag from things catching the wind. I'd like to see what his time is today, and if you bring him down on Saturday afternoon, we can run him around the track and get him used to it a little. He can stay at my place and be ready for Saturday."

They left shortly with Rebecca and Maxine riding in the wagon with Harry, and after a quarter of an hour or so were at the stretch of road he had spoken of. It ran under a tunnel of overarching trees, and the road beneath them was in deep shade. Johnny was at the start to help Bits get mounted and ready. Handy, Gray and the ladies were near the middle of the road watching from among the trees while Harry was at the other end, stopwatch in hand.

Johnny drew the Colt, and when he was sure all was ready, pulled the trigger skyward. Black's hindquarters shifted marvelously. He bolted and was running at full speed after a couple of strides. The thunder of hooves on the road was loud under the trees and Johnny was enthralled watching the big black horse's tremendous strides eating up the distance. In less than a minute it was over. Everyone met at the finish and watched fascinated as Bits finally pulled Black to a halt a hundred yards down the road, then turned and rode him back to where they were waiting.

Johnny ran his hand over the horse's chest and neck and found no sweat, nor was he breathing hard. Among other things, Harry taught him to look at a horse differently, at his chest, his hind quarters, and to observe how he moved when he had a rider up and when he didn't.

He didn't like the cropped mane or bobbed tail. One of the things he loved about watching Black run was the beauty of his mane and tail streaming in the wind. He looked like a beautiful work of art. But he knew it made it easier for Black to run a race with the alterations because the jockey could see better, and since all the racers had their tails bobbed, they were not flying in the face of someone running close behind.

"The track is a mile, so he'll have to run twice this distance on Saturday," said Harry. He helped Bits from the saddle. "He did this one in forty-six and a half. Multiply it and you get about a minute and a half for the mile. If he's got other horses pushing him, he'll probably do better."

"What did it feel like up there when he was running like that?" Handy asked the jockey.

"Like he could run forever," answered Bits, a grin spread across his face. "Do you really think he'll run faster in the race?"

"That's what the man says, and I think he knows what he's talking about," answered Johnny.

Later that day Johnny finished the weekly bookwork and was heating a shoe in the forge they had installed in a small outbuilding next to the barn when Harry walked in.

"I'm leaving," he said. "Want to get some things done in town before I go home. We should have all the arrangements finished by Wednesday, so we'll know who's going to be running. Then we can make some plans and tell Bits how we want him to ride it. We'll want to put racing shoes on him, but we can do that Sunday at the track. They have a smithy there."

Johnny grinned at him. "Until I met you, I thought it was just horses running around a track. I learn more about this game every time I talk to you."

Harry sat down on a bale of hay, took off his hat and ran his hand over his bald pate. "You boys have a good thing going here. Plenty of room to spread out, good grass and water. Of course, there's more to raising horses than racing, but it's a good way to let people know you're here and what you can do. It wouldn't surprise me if you got some new business out of the race."

"You think so?"

"Oh yeah, it's great advertising and there should be a good crowd. Usually is when we have a race."

"Handy thinks we'll probably have the exercise track finished by next month sometime. We'll have it at a measured half mile with rails and good ground. Then we can exercise the horses right here and save a trip up the road. We should also be finished with most of the fencing on this end of the farm before long. That will make it look better to customers coming to look us over."

Gray and Maxine had gone home, and they could see the light in Bits' room in the barn when the three of them came out on the porch after dinner.

"I hope you fellows don't starve while I'm gone next week," said Rebecca.

"I expect Maxine will make sure we're fed. We can cook, you know," said Handy.

She snorted. "Beans and bacon isn't cooking."

"You're taking the baby when you go?" asked Johnny.

"Of course. You three would have him on a horse within a week if I don't. The girls at the mansion always help me take care of him. Sarah, Annaliese and I will be taking turns staying with Greta until she feels safe."

"So you think it will happen this week?" he asked.

"Annaliese seems to think so, and I want to be on hand just in case. Greta's been working hard at the lessons, but I know she'll be nervous when they first come home."

"I can't imagine how she'll handle it," said Johnny, "but I've seen her do some amazing things, so nothing will really surprise me."

"Well, she seems to be back to being Greta again, so I guess we'll see," said Rebecca.

Chapter Fifty-Two

Annaliese set up a place to study in a corner of the apartment. Though she had a lamp on her desk, when lit it made the room warm and stuffy. She preferred to study there on long summer evenings in light coming in the corner windows, with a cooling breeze off the bay. Two evenings a week she moved everything downstairs into the back room to join her study partners, but she enjoyed studying alone evenings in the quiet upstairs, so it was worth carting all her books and equipment up and down the steps each time.

She had just opened her book when someone knocked on the door, and after a moment she heard Greta.

"Annaliese, I think it's time. I think my water just broke. It feels like it anyway." There was strain in her voice, and a little fear.

Annaliese guided her to the edge of the bed and sat her down.

"I'm going to make some arrangements. I'll be right back." True to her word, she quickly returned. "Roy is taking a message to Sarah and Jason is hitching up Dolly. Then he's going to ride over to Dr. Brown's office and tell them we're on the way."

Greta's abdomen was large enough she needed help standing.

"Let's get you a wrap and then we'll be off. I'm going to drive very slowly so it won't bounce you so much." They decided weeks before to risk the ride across town to a clinic equipped for the birth, rather than try to birth the babies at the store.

Normally Johnny would drive them, but he was at Handy's farm overnight, so it was up to Annaliese to drive and support the expectant mother. When they arrived at the clinic, Sarah and Madame were already there and they waited in the Doctor's office until Annaliese came out and joined them.

"Her water's broken and she's just beginning to have pains, but there's no telling how long it will be. Everything's ready so all we can do is wait."

"Is the doctor here?" asked Madame.

"She's in a meeting at school right now," Annaliese replied, "but one of her partners is back there with Greta. They keep someone here most of the time just in case things like this happen. She's seen Greta before and doesn't see any problems. So we wait." She smiled at Sarah. "I'm sure you remember the process."

Sarah shook her head. "An Indian woman delivered Rebecca and I don't remember too much about it." Poor Jed helped me when little Jed was born. There was no one else. He was scared to death, but between the two of us we got it done." She smiled. "He was so scared he wouldn't come near me for a while. Of course that didn't last too long."

They talked for a while and then Madame stood and said, "I'm going to take Tony and head back. I'll be here in the morning, early."

Annaliese set up a cot for Sarah in a room usually reserved for expectant fathers and went back in to hold Greta's hand and talk to her.

"Rebecca told me it was uncomfortable, but she didn't say anything about having trouble catching my breath," said Greta, puffing a little after one spasm of pain.

The doctor came in with Dr. Brown. They examined her and decreed it would probably be the next morning.

"The pains are becoming regular, and everything seems to be as we planned," said Dr. Brown. "Harriet will be here in the front and I'll be sleeping in my office if things start coming sooner than we expect." She patted Greta's hand and smiled at her. "You're doing fine, and with all the help we have around here, you should become a mother sometime tomorrow without a problem."

Not so. Within an hour labor pains began to come more quickly, and the doctor delivered the first baby, a boy, after another hour, the second, a girl, shortly after.

Though she was confident Greta would be fine, it was a great relief when her bleeding stopped, and Annaliese and the doctor were able to put the babies in their mother's arms for the first time.

Over the last several months, Greta's face had become more animated and reflective of the world around her, and during the birth process she displayed the same reactions Annaliese had seen in most of the women she helped go through childbirth. It seemed as though the muscles around her mouth needed to learn again to show what was in her mind and heart and giving birth seemed to have worked them almost back to normal.

Now, holding her son and daughter for the first time, she looked the same as any new mother Annaliese had ever seen.

"Can you hold him for a minute?" she asked Annaliese. I want to feel her face."

Annaliese could feel her eyes beginning to tear as she watched Greta's hand gently find the shape of her daughter's eyes, nose and mouth, feel the fuzz on her head, shape of her ears, and lower her nose to breathe the scent of new life. After a minute she said, "Now him." She handed Annaliese her daughter and then came to know her son in the same intimate way.

"Have you thought about names?"

"I've thought about it. I want to talk to Papa about it and see what he thinks."

"Well, since you and the babies seem to be doing fine, I'm going to wake Sarah, take her home, and come back to the store and let everyone know you and they," she nodded at the babies, "are doing fine."

Instead of returning to the mansion, Sarah decided to spend the night at the store and return with Annaliese in the morning. Everyone gathered around to hear the news, and then Anneliese and Sarah retreated to the office with Lemuel.

"So, you're a grandfather," said Sarah, "and I'm a grandmother again. That's three this year. I think we need to slow things down a bit."

"And you say they're all fine?" asked Lemuel.

"Were when we left," replied Annaliese, "and the doctor and a nurse will be with them all night, so I think they're well cared for. She needs rest, but she should be home with your grandson and granddaughter within a week. Of course, you can go with us in the morning."

"She said she wanted to talk to you about names," she continued. "Have you all talked about it yet?"

"Some. I know she wants to name one after Mary if one's a girl. When we talked about a boy, she sort of talked around naming one after Jed, but never really said one way or the other."

The next morning Sun Li joined them, and the ladies sat in the lobby of the clinic and watched Lemuel quietly open the door and slip into his daughter's room to see his grandchildren for the first time. After a few minutes they joined them. Greta was awake and smiling.

Annaliese wondered if Greta could feel her father's happiness. She knew this was a special moment for him.

"Tell me how they look, Papa. What color are their eyes? Can you tell? Is everything as it should be? The nurse told me they seem normal and healthy, though they're a little small."

"I would think they would be," he said. "There wasn't much room to grow with two of them in there. As far as I can see, they have different colored eyes, but it's hard to tell. He has more hair and looks a little bigger."

"I've been thinking about names, and I like Mary and Lemuel. Is that alright with you?"

"Yes, it's wonderful." He was quiet for a moment. "Every time I look at her, I'll think of your mother, but why Lemuel? Why not Jed?"

He could see tears forming and tracking her cheeks. "No, I'll never forget Jed; what he was to me. But being reminded of him all day, every day, wouldn't be good. I'd have trouble moving away from what happened, and I need to move away." She was quiet for a minute, then lay her hand on her chest. "He'll always be here, but not so much here," and she touched her forehead.

"Let's let her get some rest," said Dr. Brown, sweeping into the room and feeling Greta's wrist, then her forehead. "She needs to get her strength back, and it will take a day or two. Think I can get you to eat and drink something?" she asked Greta.

Greta nodded. "I think so. Let's try it and see how it feels."

Annaliese turned at the door. Greta was sitting up in bed, her head cocked so her right ear was aimed at her children. Somehow Annaliese knew it would be.

Chapter Fifty-Three

She found him at his favorite place to sit of an evening; on a large flat stone, gazing out toward the ocean, listening to the waves breaking on the rocks below.

"I know you like to think about something for a while," said Woman, "but it's been a week, so do you want to talk about it yet?"

She sat on the ground beside him and felt his hand on her hair, stroking it for a moment before he answered.

"I'm still trying to figure out what to do, how to go about dealing with this." Wash sat quiet and the time stretched out a bit before he went on. "I'm pretty sure it's him, but the problem is, what do I do when I find out for sure it is?"

"What are the choices?" she asked.

"I guess that depends on what I think Johnny will do if I tell him."

"I'd say he'll want to give him the same thing Jed and Lemuel got - a bullet," she said.

"I'd say that's likely, but I don't know for sure. Johnny's hard to figure sometimes. I'd say it would be his first idea. But what then? He can't just go gunning for him. He doesn't know if it's the right guy.

"And if it is the right guy, what then? How do we prove it to the law? And if we do, he'd still have to go through court and be convicted. That's always a tricky thing. A good lawyer and he walks away. And he knows who put the finger on him. If he is the guy, it could mean a bullet for Johnny someday down the road when he's not looking."

They sat quiet for a while. "Do I want to tell Johnny if I think it might turn his life upside down? Revenge can be a powerful burden in someone's life. Johnny is like a son to me. Do I really want to hand him that burden to carry? If he goes after the man who killed his friend, it's not like it is in some places. Even if he's right, he could end up at the end of a rope.

"From another way, do I want to do nothing? Walk away and let him do the same thing again and again to someone else and destroy other lives like he did Greta's and Lemuel's?"

He took off his hat and ran his hand through his thick white hair and rubbed his head for a while. "I've killed men before, but usually when I thought they might be trying to harm me or rob me. I'd have to watch him and track him and make sure it was him. Let's say I find out it is him, then what do I do?"

She looked back into his eyes, almost invisible in the light of the setting moon.

"Let me know what you decide, and if you want to go after him, I'll be right there with you."

Again, he ran his hand over her hair, stood and pulled her to her feet.

"I know," he said. He kissed her gently on the forehead and led her back to the cabin.

Later, getting ready for bed, she said. "There were a lot of questions tonight but no answers. Have you decided anything yet?"

After a moment he answered. "I think for now I'll try to learn as much as I can about his habits and what he's about."

"Sounds like some night work to me," she said. "Don't forget, you've got a job. If you're up all hours of the night, it could be a problem."

"I found out we do deliveries for him, and I've already got the OK from Kate to start driving the wagon for deliveries. I'll learn my way around town, and I can have a reason to go to his place and look around once in a while, maybe talk to some of his help. If someone goes away for periods and no one knows why, people notice. I want to prove he's the one. When I know that, then I can decide what to do about it."

"That's reasonable. Can you do something for me, though? Tell me what you find out as you find it out and how you come to think about it. I'd kind of like to know what's going on as it happens instead of having you spring it on me all at once."

He looked at her, a slow smile spreading across his face. "You want me to change the way I do things for you, is that it?"

She nodded.

"That's not the way I am," he said, still smiling.

She nodded again.

"If I do, you might believe I'm in love with you or something."

She nodded again.

He kissed her and began to slowly unbutton her shirt. "And you don't want to get married?"

She shook her head.

"What say we celebrate not getting married again?"

She nodded and began to unbutton his shirt.

"So, you really believe it's him?" Woman asked. Wash nodded his head. It was several evenings later. He was sitting on the stone again and she was leaning back against his legs for him to stroke her hair.

"You're getting to be like a cat. I'm surprised you aren't purring,"

She pushed her head against his hand and purred. He chuckled.

"Yes, I'm pretty sure. Let's think about what we know. His people tell me he goes away, sometimes for long periods, with no explanation. One of them told me he heard rifle fire from a gully on the farm and found him shooting at a target with a special kind of rifle. I've heard him talk at the office, and he has an accent and I think it's German. He rides a mule when he goes away. When he came back the last time, he had a bandage on the right side of his face, and we've seen the scar. Also, it was just after Jed was shot."

He paused, still rubbing her hair. "I'd say he's the one. What do you think?"

"It surely looks that way," she answered.

They sat quiet, listening to the ocean in the distance, watching the sudden white as the waves broke on the beach below them.

"So, now what do you do about it?" she asked.

"I've decided not to tell Johnny I found him until things are resolved one way or another. I don't want to kill him, although it would be easy enough to get into his house one night."

"On the other hand, I don't want him to continue killing people and getting paid for it. I need to figure out a way to force him to change the way he makes his living and punish him for the murder he's done. Not just Jed, but all the others. We can't let him keep on getting paid for killing people he doesn't even know."

"Any ideas on how?"

"I'm still trying to puzzle that one out, but I promise you'll be the first to know when I figure it out."

There was a light on in the cabin and Doc was lighting his pipe with a brand taken from the stove when they walked in.

"You two been out tomcatting around again?" he asked.

"Just sitting watching the ocean," said Wash. "I like to check before I go to bed to make sure it's still there. Where've you been the last couple of days?"

Doc seated himself at the table. "Remember the widow lady I told you about? She's up the coast a little ways, visiting some friends. I caught the train up and we spent time together."

"Sounds like it's getting serious," said Wash. "You all talking about marriage?"

"She brought it up this time, so we might be."

"What would you do with this place? From what you've said, you'd be moving in with her?"

"Hadn't thought about it, to tell you the truth. Why, you want it?"

"Any idea when this might happen?"

"She sounds like she's getting impatient. Getting tired of having to sneak around when we want to be together."

Wash looked at Woman. She nodded and he said, "What would you want for it?"

"Hell, it was empty when we found it and we just moved in. Spent some time and money fixing it up a bit. I'd say check the land office, and if no one's filed on it you can have it. Of course, if she changes her mind and throws me out, I may have to move back in." This last he said with a grin.

"You'd be welcome," said Wash, and just like that they owned a house.

Skeet Will

The best thing about the cabin was where it was. A small stream ran within fifty yards of the front door and had gradually carved a small canyon on its way to a cliff above the beach where it dropped twenty feet onto the sand and wandered out to the ocean.

It was no more than a hundred yards from the flat stone where Wash liked to sit of an evening and listen to the ocean. A little farther along someone had shaped steps in the cliff leading down to the beach.

The cabin was set in a small clearing and rough built of logs cut, barked, chinked with mud and joined by notches at the corners. Over the years, most of the stumps from building the place had been pulled and the area leveled so there was enough room for a small stable and outhouse behind. A large, well-built fireplace centered along the back wall provided a place to cook and heat when needed, though the weather was nice most of the time.

Inside, the big room was centered around the fireplace with small rooms added on either end almost as an afterthought. There were openings for windows, but except for one, they were boarded up or covered with oiled paper. The floors were puncheon throughout and not well joined, which allowed various insects and small critters from below to visit on a regular basis. There was a half loft above the big room and one of the small ones. All in all, it was a place to sleep warm and dry but not a whole lot else.

Looking it over as an owner rather than a visitor, Wash had one thought in mind. He surely could use Lemuel to help put it in shape. On the other hand, his friend was a long way off and probably not really able to do the heavy work it was going to take to make this place comfortable.

His visit to the courthouse the next day was frustrating, but after traipsing from one office to another he finally found someone willing to help and came home to Woman that night with a lot to talk about.

Chapter Fifty-Four

Sun Li Redbird. Every time she thought of her new name she smiled, because it was unusual, almost unique, but also because she was very much in love with her husband and her new life.

She had come to live and work with her brother at their father's business down the street when she was ten years old. Though she lived and worked outside of Chinatown, which was unusual, she was still immersed in Chinese culture and most of the people she saw in a day's time were Chinese sailors or friends and relatives from Chinatown.

Shortly after her eighteenth birthday Jason began working at the livery stable across the street. He would come into the restaurant for lunch or dinner occasionally, and she would speak to him shyly when she served him.

From the first she was fascinated by the long dark hair, braided in two strands that fell below his shoulders. All her life she had been around men with pigtails, but his were different, as was the dark reddish tinge of his skin and stoic expression that changed so dramatically when, once in a while, he smiled at her.

Looking back, she realized she was smitten from the time he helped free her brother from the mob that seemed determined to hang him. From then on she took every opportunity to talk to him and learn about his life, present and past.

The day her father gave his permission for them to marry was the happiest of her life, and from the first, she was determined to be as useful as she could at the store. Since she had been there, she had applied herself to learn the business and made an effort to anticipate where she could help the most.

She finished the day's bookwork and was putting the ledgers away when Greta came into the office carrying a baby wrapped in a pink blanket.

"Good morning, Sun Li," she said. Right behind her came Rebecca pushing a carriage and carrying Bobby, her three-month-old son.

"Hello Sun Li," said Rebecca. "Is it alright if we have the babies in here while Greta's working? I'll be keeping an eye on them, and she'll come in and feed them later."

"No, that's wonderful," Sun Li replied. "I have not seen them much and I will like them here."

Greta went to the closet, pulled out another carriage and placed her daughter in it. Then she turned and took Lemuel from Rebecca and, using her knee against the carriage to feel where it was lowered her son into it. Rebecca made no move to help her.

They chatted for a minute, then Greta left to join Jason at the front and Rebecca sat in Lemuel's chair.

Sun Li felt a great urge to reach out in assistance to the blind girl with two babies, but when she stirred in her chair, Rebecca shook her head slightly. After Greta closed the door behind her she asked Rebecca, "How does she know things? She knew it was me sitting here when she came in. She knew where to put the children down in the carriages. How?"

Rebecca smiled. "You know, that's the question I've been asking since the first day I met her. You knew we were working with her to help her learn how to do the things she'd need to do when they were born, didn't you?"

Sun Li nodded. "Yes, Jason told me."

"She has an amazing memory. She thought she'd lost it over the tragedy with Jed, but it's coming back to her. She could tell it was you because of the way you smell."

Sun Li was taken aback. "How I smell?"

"We all smell a little different. Remember when we saw her holding the twins for the first time? She felt them all over and then smelled them. I didn't know it then, but it was like she looked at them, created something in her head that recognized them and always would.

"As far as the carriage, that's one of the things we learned from the books Annaliese got for her. Her knee was touching the carriage, and that's how she knew. She put a doll the size and weight of her babies into those carriages many, many times. She remembers."

They sat quiet for a minute, each thinking.

"You know," she continued, "I learned right along with her when she practiced those things. I remember the first time I tried to put a diaper on the doll. I stuck myself with the pin. She never does because of the way she does it. She taught me how to do it. I'm a whole lot better at taking care of Bobby because of what I learned watching her learn."

"Last week we all sat down and talked, all being me, Greta, Mother and Annaliese, and put together a rotation so one of us is with her most of the time. But we're not to help her unless she asks and we try not to talk to her too much. That way she can gain confidence and yet know one of us is there if she has a problem. There'll come a time when she doesn't need us. I have absolutely no doubt about that."

Many of the Chinese women who came to California in the 1850's were from the same villages, and more than a few were related, so Sun Li had many cousins on her mother's side. She was used to family members all around her. When she came to live with Jimmy, she still spent time with her female cousins. She knew the whites around her didn't like or understand the clannish nature of Chinese in America, so she was a little afraid of what it would be like working at The BookSeller.

She soon saw these people were different than she'd grown up believing they would be. Though there was little family connection between them, they treated each other like family. She was attracted to that and began to do things which would move her toward becoming a part of it. The one thing they seemed to have in common was The BookSeller.

"Hi Sarah," said Sun Li. "Can I ask you something?" Sarah had just come in to relieve her daughter.

"Sure. What can I do for you?"

"I hope I can do something for you. Could I join with your

group to help Greta get used to the babies?"

Sarah smiled. "That would be a big help to Annaliese. She does most of it at night. If you could help her in the evenings, it would be wonderful."

"When she returns, I will ask her when she needs help the most." Sun Li turned to leave and heard Sarah's "Thank you, so much" from behind her. She walked out of the room feeling warm inside.

Watching daybreak come to the city and the bay in the distance was a nice way to begin a day, thought Sarah. Russian Hill was above the fog this morning, and she could see the tops of some hills in the city and Sausalito and beyond, across the bay.

Madame came in behind her and took her accustomed chair on the other side of the window.

"So, tell me, how are things progressing with the Honorable Jonas Burke?" asked Madame with a mischievous smile.

"With all the gossip you gather, I doubt I can tell you much you don't already know."

"Has he tried to sleep with you yet?"

Sarah grinned. "Now why would I tell you?"

"Because I asked you and because you know I won't share the answer with a living soul."

Sarah laughed. "Well, we kissed last night for the first time and his hand did wander a little, but so far, no more."

"Are you thinking about a future with him?"

"It would be easy to, but I'd have to give it some thought. After Jed disappeared, I ran a store in the wilderness of South Pass for years and then had one in Salt Lake for a while before I came here. I don't know if I can be the wife he would want. I haven't needed a man in my life for a long time, and I can't see myself accepting the idea of having a lord and master who controls everything I have."

She took a sip of the coffee the maid put in front of her. "We'll need an understanding before I'd marry him, so I guess one evening soon, I'll have to let him know what to expect and see if he's still interested."

"I must admit the idea of a man in my bed again does make me feel a little strange," she went on. "I must say, I did have some interesting thoughts after I turned out the light last night."

"Even if you can't take the step into matrimony," said Madame, "at your age you don't need anyone's permission to sleep with someone. Just have to want to, that's all."

They sat quiet for a long minute, then Sarah said, "I don't think it will be too long before Greta will be able to handle the children by herself, which will give me more time to spend with Jonas and maybe work things out.

"From what I've heard," said Madame, "she's an amazing person. I know she had trouble coming back from Jed's death, but she seems to be out of that fog and coming back to what she was before."

"Yes, I think that's so," said Sarah. "The three of us just look over her shoulder, but she's learned so much on top of what she remembers. She feels confident now she can be a good mother and keep them safe. Sun Li has joined the rotation, and with her sharing the load we'll make it OK."

"How much longer before she's on her own?"

"I'd say maybe two weeks, maybe more. We're all going to get together and talk about it, and I think it won't be long and she'll be able to handle it by herself."

"Sun Li's a good addition to the store. I've known her since she came to live with her brother at the business. She's bright as a new penny. Johnny tells me she's always asking for more to do, and whatever she does, she does it well."

"Jason got a good one there, that's for sure. Where are you off to?" she asked when Madame stood up.

"I need to do some business with Nate. Some stuff I need to sign."

"Well, I won't be here when you get back. I told Rebecca I'd go to the Emporium to pick out some new clothes with Sun Li. She wants things she thinks will be more appropriate for work."

"She's really becoming a part of the group you have at the store, isn't she?"

"Yes, because she wants to be a part of it. She came to me and asked to help out with Greta, and she's constantly doing things to help Lemuel and Johnny. She and Rebecca do things together all the time."

"Well, I'm glad to see it. Her father wants her to become a bridge between Chinatown and the rest of us and she's perfect for the job. You mark my words; she's going to become important in our city."

"I think I'm going to need to talk to Mister Nate Jones sometime soon," said Sarah. "Can you ask him for an appointment and let me know when?"

Chapter Fifty-Five

The package was wrapped in brown paper and was from one of their main book distributors, who usually communicated with deliveries. She cut the string and tore the paper off to find something that made her smile. The English translation of Pinocchio by Carlo Collodi and below, translated by Carlotta Lazzeri.

The note enclosed read:

Dear Mrs. Fry, I am sending you this by regular post so I can let you know I read the story and found it so charming, I have decided to send some copies to several of my better customers with a special recommendation they display it in their section of children's books. The young lady who translated it will be due payments for every copy sold. I believe the book will sell well and I will forward payments due to Mrs. Lazzeri in care of The BookSeller. Please give her my congratulations and tell her we welcome the opportunity to publish any future translations she does.
Yours truly, Mattheu Crowder.

Johnny was working at his desk across the room, and he looked up at her whoop of joy.

"Look at this," she said, waving the letter at him and poking him in the stomach with the book. She held it up in front of his nose, then took it up front and showed everyone at the counter. When she came back, she noticed a small tan envelope lying on the floor by her desk.

Johnny heard her utter a grunt and when he turned to see, she was sitting back in her chair holding a small piece of paper, tapping it on the edge of the desk and staring at it.

He got up and kissed her on the top of her head. "What's that?" he asked.

"It's an invitation to dinner with Dr. Rose and his wife." She glanced at the note again. "Next Wednesday evening at 7:00 PM."

"You don't have to look like someone just died." He looked over her shoulder. "RSVP? What's that mean?"

"It means, please let them know if we'll be there."

"Well, will we?"

"Of course. He's my anatomy teacher. He mentioned he and his wife wanted us to come to dinner, but I thought he was just being nice. He said his wife loves to talk to budding women doctors."

Rather than deal with the problems in the growing city, the Roses bought an old mansion near San Mateo, south of the city, and with her father helping, had been upgrading it for several years.

It took better than two hours to get to the place, but it was worth the trip. The house was a Victorian but had been deserted for several years due to a family legal squabble and was beginning to fall into disrepair when the problem was finally settled with their purchase of it.

Dr. Rose had a local practice and drove to the city twice a week to teach. With the slow pace of his practice, he was able to work with his carpenter father-in-law to remodel the house and to make it a marvelous place for the doctor and his wife to live, with a separate apartment for the father-in-law.

They were shown to a screened-in porch looking out on a paddock where several beautiful horses were grazing near a fence no more than thirty feet from the porch.

"This time of year, we like to sit out here and watch the horses." He nodded to where two horses were looking curiously at the four humans who were looking back.

Horses and houses dominated the conversation until they were shown into the dining room for a nice dinner and more talk about horses and horse farming. Dr. Rose had never run a horse at the local track but was grooming several while trying to decide if he really wanted to commit to the time and expense involved in racing.

When dinner was finished, Bev announced, "Hank likes to smoke some dreadful cigars after dinner, so we usually go our separate ways for a while." She looked at Annaliese and continued. "If you'd like to join me, we have a nice library where we can sit, have a sherry and chat, while they fill up good air with smelly smoke."

They left together, and Johnny and Hank went back out on the porch overlooking the paddock, now bright under a full moon.

"I've learned some about you and your place of business," said Dr. Rose." Do you mind if I ask you some questions?"

"Not at all." Johnny accepted a cigar but put it in his pocket. "I'll take this back to Lemuel if you don't mind. I don't smoke.

"Something I wanted to tell you before we start talking," he continued. "I have a friend who never answers a serious question right away. I've seen him sit thinking over a question for a good long minute before he answers. It's a habit I've picked up from him, so when I take a little time to answer a question, you'll understand why."

Hank grinned. "By the way, call me Hank. So, why did you decide to come to California? I understand you're from Kansas and you traveled out here with a cat?" When Johnny nodded, he continued. "The next time you come, bring him with you. Bev has been after me to find her a nice kitten to raise as a house cat. She'd love to meet him."

Johnny wrinkled his forehead. "Dreams. That's where it began. My Pa was the first Pony Express Rider back in 1860. He waited for the mail on the Missouri side of the river, took the ferry across and rode the first forty-five-mile leg of the first Pony trip across the country.

"When my Uncle Bill would come to visit, I'd listen while he and Pa talked about those days and of their adventures. I grew up dreaming about it. When Pa died in the Spring of 1884, I put Jinx on a horse and we left Kansas for Sacramento, riding the Pony Express Trail all the way, and here I am. In Emigration Canyon, outside of Salt Lake City, my horse shied at a rattler, fell off the side of a hill and banged me up pretty bad."

He took a sip of the tea a servant had set on the table beside him. "I woke up in the hospital with Annaliese and her father taking care of me. Over the next two months, Annaliese and I fell in love, and we later married."

Hank blew a cloud of smoke toward the ceiling, where a nice breeze took it away. "She looks like she's quite a bit older than you?"

"Ten years."

"Cause you any problems?"

Johnny smiled, "She is a little hard to keep up with sometimes."

Hank burst out laughing. "Lucky man.

"She's going to be a good doctor one day," he said. "She is a hard worker, and she seems to be the leader of the study gang she's in. I think before it's over she'll make us all proud."

"That wouldn't surprise me at all," said Johnny.

"It seems like The BookSeller is fast becoming a landmark in the City. How long have you been open?"

"Coming up on a year," answered Johnny. "You should come to one of our open houses. You and Lemuel would enjoy talking."

"Lemuel?"

"Lemuel is my partner in the store."

"Oh yes, I remember his name. Wasn't he the leader of the people who ran Sunny Jim and his gang out of town?"

Johnny nodded. "He and Madame." When Hank looked a question, Johnny continued. "Mrs. Hannah Grimes. I believe she's one of your patrons."

"I'd say she is. She's the one who gave the money for the new anatomy lab they got me out here to run." He paused, then asked, "Why do you call her Madame?"

When Johnny recounted her past, Hank roared with laughter.

"I met her and have seen her several times at events to raise money," he said, "but I never knew that. She sure doesn't look the part."

"She's a friend and she put up some money so we could open the new addition," said Johnny. "As far as looking the part, I think she's able to look any part she needs to. She's an interesting woman."

"I think I need to get to know her better."

"It's worth the effort."

They sat silent while Hank blew some more smoke at the

ceiling.

"Sometime," said Johnny, "I'd like you to put on your teacher's hat and talk to me about what it takes to be a teacher in college. It's something I've thought about a lot but don't know what it takes to qualify."

"I'll be glad to help you as much as I can. What would you like to teach? You'll need to decide what field you'd like to get into and then find a school with such a program. Different schools have different requirements, so you need to decide which ones fit your aims and contact them for admission requirements. In most cases you'll probably find a school that will teach what they require to be a lecturer.

"And now, before we rejoin the ladies, can you tell me why you carry the gun all the time?"

Johnny smiled and took his time answering. "I learned to shoot back in Kansas. My Pa was a gunsmith, and he taught me how to use a gun. Three times during my trip out here that gun saved my life. I read somewhere about talismans, and I guess that's what it is for me. A talisman. I feel comfortable and safe with it on my hip. And it's where I can get to it in a hurry if I need it."

In the library Annaliese was drinking as little sherry as she could get away with and talking about medical school.

"What's your favorite class so far?" Bev asked.

"I like most of them, but anatomy is my favorite, naturally. Working with the Doctor, I sewed up a lot of wounds and fixed what I could when someone's skin was broken but never really knew a lot about what I was seeing. These classes give me the opportunity to study and learn what's where.

"Before I was just trying to get the body sewn up so it could begin healing. Now I'm learning in an organized manner, and with my experience I feel it's all coming together at the right place and at the right time."

"Have you had problems with the men in your classes?"

"There's been some of that stuff but most of us are working much too hard to waste time on such things. The ladies in my study group are like most women who go to medical school. They're smart and hardworking and usually ready to push back against such nonsense."

"Hank tells me there's one lady in the class who's a bit of a character."

"Oh yeah, Maggie. She's liable to say or do anything to anybody. When it gets too hectic, she always comes up with a way to make us laugh."

"Do you still work at the bookstore?"

"I help out some, but I'm usually too busy doing other things. In addition to school, I've had to help Johnny's partner recover from a gunshot wound. Also, I've been helping his daughter recover from the murder of her husband and learn how to care for her new twins."

"Yes, Doctor Brown told me about her. She's blind, isn't she?"

"That's right, so with all that going on I don't have much time at the store."

"So, tell me, why do you want to become a doctor?"

Annaliese sat and thought about that for a moment, then shrugged and said, "I started working with the Doctor when I was ten. As I grew older, it was just expected that I would become a doctor."

"Lots of people don't do what's expected of them. As they get older, they change their minds. So why did you decide to continue on this path?"

Again, she thought for a while. "I love the Doctor and loved working with him all those years. I guess I felt this is what he wanted for me, and I wanted to live up to that goal." She paused for a moment. "But now I want to do it because I'm fascinated by what I'm learning, and I love finding the answers to questions I've had for years. More and more I'm thinking about what your husband said about needing researchers and how they can help change the nature of medical practice.

"It's not what I signed up for, but as a doctor I can help a limited number of people. As a researcher I might solve mysteries which could help mankind. At this point, I still hope to practice but would very much like to be near a large university where I can take part in medical research too, like Dr. Rose."

"Don't call him that. Call him Hank. Everyone else does. Don't want his head to get too big for his hat."

Annaliese grinned. "I don't know how that would work in class. He might object."

"Yes, you're probably right." She looked up at her husband

leading Johnny into the room. "Well, gentlemen, glad you could finally join us."

Annaliese was brushing her hair and Johnny was sponging the dust off.

"Hank said they'd probably come down to the open house this week," said Johnny, "and he wants to go out to the track with me Sunday for the race. I'd say we may get to know them pretty well."

"I like them both," said Annaliese. "She's nice and they seem to be well suited for each other."

He leaned over her and kissed her on the shoulder and nibbled on her ear "Like us, you mean?" he said and began to count the freckles on her cheek with his tongue.

She put the brush down, turned to face him and he pulled her to her feet and into an ardent embrace.

After a minute she pulled away and looked at him, "Do you think you'll get tired of me when I get old?"

"I doubt it. You see I'll be getting old right along with you. Besides, I've heard if you make love a lot it keeps you from getting old." He kissed her again and whispered in her ear. "I'm just trying my best to keep you young."

One reason is as good as another.

Chapter Fifty-Six

Johnny woke up early the morning of the race. On mornings like this, he enjoyed lying in bed next to his sleeping wife thinking about the day ahead with Jinx purring on his chest or nestled in the hollow of his arm.

Except for the dinner earlier in the week, the last week of his life was almost entirely about the race that afternoon. The newness and unknowns about the whole thing made him a little nervous. Harry felt Black was ready, and from what he'd found out, Black had been on a track before, so he'd probably be able to handle the race; but Johnny was still nervous.

He would put special shoes on Black before the horse was led out to the start, and then things were out of his hands. Bits exercised Black every day for the last two weeks, and Harry worked with them using many of the things he'd learned in a lifetime of working with horses and racing. They had a plan for how to run the race, but once it started, the plan would likely go out the window. It was up to the horse and jockey to handle whatever came along.

Harry and Jim told them how rough it could be running in the middle of five or six horses, all running at full speed, each jockey determined to be the first over the finish line. There was so much beyond anyone's control or foresight that could affect things in the minute and a half or so it would take them to cover the mile around the track.

The jockeys all used whips, and most of them were older than Bits and got paid for winning. Harry told stories of the whips being used on things other than their own horses; things like the rumps of horses ahead of them or beside them, and occasionally at the heads of those coming from behind.

There were also the faces of other jockeys. A whip across the face could blind someone, and a jockey who lost his seat in the middle of the pounding herd was usually either buried or crippled for life. The only rule once the horses started running was to get to the finish ahead of everyone else.

As usual, while Johnny and Handy tied their horses in front of Mattie's, Jinx was already through the front door and in the kitchen, charming Mattie out of some extra breakfast. Considering how much he ate it was amazing how slim and agile he still was. Jim and Harry were already drinking coffee and Herschel and Jimmy Li came in right after Johnny sat down.

Soon they were all talking about the race and the chances of Black winning, but Johnny sat quiet, staring out the front window at the growing daylight.

"So, what do you think, Johnny?" asked Herschel.

Johnny gave him a blank look. "About what?"

"About putting a bet on Black today."

"Oh," he said, coming back to the present. "Annaliese and I talked about it, and as usual, she said 'it's your money Johnny.'"

Harry looked across the table, a question on his face. "Are you really sure about this, Johnny? Do you want him to run today?"

Johnny sat quiet thinking for a moment. "Well, we've come this far and today's the day we've been aiming toward so I'd say yes. But at this point, I admit I'm a little nervous about the whole idea."

"Me too," said Handy. "Got butterflies flying around in my gut."

"I've been in this business for a lot of years, and I still feel it when I've got a horse in the race," said Harry. "I think when you reach the point where you don't, you should probably quit."

He took off his hat and rubbed his eyes. "Of course, I sometimes wonder if it's just because I'm excited. Look at all we've done to get him ready over the last month, and it will all be over in less than two minutes after the start. Of course, that two minutes can get pretty exciting, which is probably why I still do it after all these years."

"There's one thing that bothers me about it," said Johnny. "There are going to be six horses out there today and only one can win. I'm not so much worried about losing as I am what some of them might do to win. Bits is a kid, and that horse means something to me. The idea we might have bitten off more than we can chew is definitely on my mind."

"Do you want to call it off?" asked Harry.

"No. We won't really know what it's like until we're on the other side, so let's get the day started and we'll see how it ends."

There were more people than he expected to see at the rail that afternoon. He saw Hank Rose and Bev sitting in a small grandstand a little farther down the rail and waved to them. He and Handy found a place beside Herschel and watched as Harry led Black, with Bits in the saddle, to the starting line. At times like these, he liked his wife beside him, but she and her partners were studying hard for an exam. He always felt better when she was around. Of course, Handy was a good second best.

"Jim tells me the track is in good shape," said Herschel. "If Black runs like Harry says he can, he should run away from this bunch." He paused and looked at Johnny. "You're having bad feelings about this aren't you?"

"Does it show? I guess it does if you asked the question. I'll just be glad when it's over. I may not be cut out for this."

From his place on the other side of Herschel, Jim leaned out and said, "There are times when I've stood here that were the longest minute and a half I've ever felt."

"I can believe it." said Handy. "I've been nervous about it since I woke up this morning."

Johnny looked at Herschel. "You know, you always have the same calm expression on your face. Does anything bother you?"

"Not something like this," Herschel replied. "I get nervous about some things. I remember a night when seeing a little fellow leaning on a cane made me downright fluttery.

"Did you ever decide whether to put some money on the race?" he continued after a moment.

Johnny shook his head. "For some reason it didn't seem like the right thing to do." He shrugged. "I don't know, it just seemed like tempting fate. It looks like I'm the only one, except for Gray."

"Nope," said Handy. "He slipped me ten when I left the ranch."

"By the way, we decided 'horse ranch' sounded better than 'horse farm'."

"Don't I get a vote?

"You did. I was your proxy. You lost, two to one."

Jim called their attention to the starting line and they watched as the horses, some moving restlessly, waited for the gun. When it went off Black bolted, but so did several of the others, and he was just hitting his stride at the first pole, running behind three veteran horses who had gotten a length or two on him off the line.

Johnny could see Bits trying to bring him up into the pack when suddenly the horse veered away and fell off the pace. He recovered and began to stretch out again but was several lengths behind at the halfway pole.

Then he was running them down, and at three quarters had passed all except two who were fighting for the lead. Johnny and his friends were yelling themselves hoarse but didn't seem to notice. Black was even with the leaders in the home stretch when they saw the middle jockey's hand lash out and his whip caught Bits across the mouth.

At that instant, Black accelerated and surged ahead, crossing the line in the lead by several lengths.

It took Bits a hundred yards or so to pull the horse to a stop. Then he turned him and rode back to where Johnny and his friends stood along the rail. As he approached, they could see blood across his mouth and watched him run his hand over the side of his face and come away bloody.

Johnny vaulted the rail and helped the boy down. Harry came running up, threw a blanket over the horse, and took Black's reins. Johnny and Bits followed him back to the stall. Walking behind, Johnny could see a welt on the horse's flank where it looked like he had been struck or run into something. It hadn't been there before the race.

Harry removed Black's blanket and was rubbing him down while Johnny was examining the mark on the horse's side. When Harry's hands got to the welt, Black moved away from him, snorting.

He looked up at Johnny and said, "Don't lose your temper.

These things happen, and nothing you do is going to change that."

Johnny ran his hand up and down the canted holster and shook his head. "Next time you see him tell him how lucky he is."

Bits was sitting on a hay bale submitting to Harry's ministrations when Jim, Handy and Herschel walked up, smiling because they were a little richer.

"Whoa," said Handy when he saw Bits' face. He reached out and turned the boy's head to examine his cut.

"Well, it's clean and it's not bleeding anymore. I don't think it's deep enough to need stitches," said Harry.

"Stitches!" said Bits a little louder than necessary. "I don't want no stitches."

"Let's get him back to the store; I want Annaliese to take a look at it," said Johnny. He led the horse and jockey out the gate without looking back.

Annaliese dumped the blood-tinged water into the sink and wrung out the towel. She turned to Bits and smiled. "Can I count on you to keep the bandage on for a while? Next Friday I'll be coming up to the farm when Johnny comes up and I'll see how it looks then."

"Ranch," said Handy. "It's a horse ranch."

"Ranch, then" she replied. To Bits she said, "Try to keep it as clean as you can. It may not leave a scar if we're lucky."

Later when she was sitting at the mirror brushing her hair, Johnny said. "Don't you know kids his age like to have a scar or two? It proves they're a man."

"What about all your scars?" she asked. "They don't prove anything. No one ever sees them but me."

"So far," he said and ducked. Wrestling at this time of night was fun.

By the time he had her pinned down on the bed, she changed her mind and kissed him.

"So, did you get it out of your system?"

"It sure gave me a lot to think about."

"Make up your mind?"

"I'm not the only one in the game. I'll need to talk to the rest of them before I decide."

"Johnny, remember he's your horse. The others might have opinions, but you're the one who has to choose whether to put him on the track again or not."

"You know, today when I saw what that guy had done to them, I almost lost my head. I don't like feeling that way when I've got the Colt on my hip. One day I might do something I regret."

"Johnny, there's no way to undo what comes out of the barrel of a gun. I hope you'll always keep that in mind. Now come here and I'll see if I can make you forget it for a while."

It was something she was good at.

Chapter Fifty-Seven

Sarah was a little early for her appointment and nervous about her first visit to a lawyer's office. Nate Jones was Madame's lawyer and as such she trusted him, but she never needed help with anything to do with the law before and had no idea about what to expect.

When Nate showed her into the office and seated her at his desk, she figured the best way to approach the problem was to tell him how things stood and let him lead her to a solution, if one existed.

"How can I help you Mrs. Travers?" Nate's nice smile showed large white teeth, and his hair and eyebrows were thick and dark. "First off, we have seen enough of each other at the mansion to be on a first name basis. So, Nate, please call me Sarah. Second, I'm thinking about getting married and I have questions about how it would affect any property I now own. I think I need a lawyer to tell me where I stand with the law."

"Let me think for a minute and make sure I understand exactly what you're asking me," said Nate.

Sarah nodded and he got up and began to walk around the room. Now that she noticed, there was a discernible path worn in the carpet.

He smiled at her. "I think better when I'm walking. It's a habit I picked up at law school." He made several circles of the room and then resumed his seat.

"Let's begin by describing, in a general sense, this property for me." When she had done so, he continued. "What you want from me is an opinion as to whether or not your husband would have any control of, or access to, your assets without your consent after you marry, correct?"

When she nodded, he said, "Do you plan to reside in California after you marry?"

"Why is that important?" she asked.

"To answer, I'll have to bore you with a little legal history. Beginning about 1840, some states began to write laws about married women owning property they brought into the marriage, and in some cases, having the right to keep any income they earned separate from the joint assets of the marriage. This wasn't necessarily to give a married woman more rights, but rather to protect her husband's estate and keep a new widow and her family from falling into poverty. Each law was a little different, and some states haven't passed any laws on the subject at all.

"Collectively these laws are known as the 'Married Women's Property Acts'. There is no federal law on the issue, only state.

"One strange aspect of these laws is non-married, that is single, women could always acquire and hold property in their names before they're married, but as soon as a woman married, everything went to her husband. What you want to do is by no means uncommon. More and more frequently women are seeking an agreement before marriage on that issue, especially in a second or third marriage."

"As far as I know, we would live in San Francisco."

"That's fortunate because California has a different law. Most of the other states take their legal system from English Common Law. However, California was a Mexican province until 1846 and when it became a state, it adopted the Spanish Legal Code instead."

He got up and took a thick book off one of the shelves behind his desk. He thumbed through it for a moment and then began to read.

"All property, both real and personal, of the wife, owned or claimed by her before marriage, and that acquired afterward by gift, devise, or descent, shall be her separate property; and laws shall be passed more clearly defining the rights of the wife in relation as well to her separate property, as to that held in common with her husband."

He closed the book with a snap and a little puff of dust rose in the air. He looked at her and said, "That's from the California Constitution of 1849. I would say if you continued to live in California, your property is secure to yourself. If you should change your place of residence there may be new problems to deal with depending on where you go." He drew a sheet of paper toward him and continued. "If it would make you feel more secure, I can draw up an agreement you and your intended could stipulate to."

Sarah relaxed, just realizing she had been tense since she walked in the door. "Sounds like it's exactly what I need."

He nodded and began to make a list. "If you can give me the particulars of your assets, I can do it today and bring it to you in the morning when I come to the Mansion. I have to bring some papers for Mrs. Grimes to sign."

She walked out of the office feeling twenty pounds lighter.

She was sitting at the mirror of her vanity, pinning up her hair and making sure everything was as it should be. Jonas was coming for his first visit in her part of the mansion, and she wanted to look her best. She felt she might be falling in love with him, though she couldn't recall being in love before, so she wasn't sure.

The closest she had come to love was with the Indian brave to whom she was given after she was captured in a raid on her father's Wisconsin farm. She was frightened of him in the beginning, but she gradually came to see he was a gentle, considerate, honorable man. Looking back, she could see love might have been happening between them when he was killed defending her in a raid by another tribe. She escaped into the forest with Rebecca.

Her future husband, Jed, was part of the hunting party she stumbled upon two nights later, and who returned her to her home. When she was shunned by the women of her home village for 'bringing her Indian bastard among them', he married her and they left together to travel west in a wagon train.

They stopped at a store in the Wyoming wilderness where they found the proprietor on his deathbed and his wife desperate for help. Within two weeks both had passed away, and with no known heirs, suddenly they were storekeepers.

She and Jed had been friends more than lovers, but they seemed to have the same ideas on how to live together and be happy. One day, several years later, Jed went hunting and disappeared. She never saw him again. At that time and place, it was not unusual. In the mountains of Wyoming in the 1870's, there were a hundred different ways to die, and many bodies were never found. Without a husband and with two children, she decided to stay where she was and run the store.

Between a garden, fishing in the Sweetwater, hunting and gathering, and the friendship of a few Mormons and some mountain men such as Wash, she managed to have a decent life and later, sold out and followed her children to Salt Lake City and then on to San Francisco.

Jonas Burke made her think about having a man in her life again. The kiss they had shared at the door the other night had led to interesting thoughts floating around in her head that night when she lay in bed and occasionally on days since.

He was coming tonight, and she expected him to talk of marriage. If he did, she would probably accept, but only after they discussed the legal paper laying on her vanity.

She really had no idea of what to expect for the rest of the evening, although she had hopes.

Jonas had the bright blue eyes and thick dark hair of an Irishman, and she felt her heart jump when she opened the door to his knock and saw him standing there. When he was inside and they were alone, she took his chin in her hand and kissed him lightly on the lips.

"That's for what I've been thinking the last couple days."

He grinned at her and took her in his arms, looked at her for a moment and then kissed her passionately. She responded and they were both a little breathless when they finally broke apart.

"My oh my!" he said. "What's got into you?"

She led him to the sofa that looked out over the city, and they sat looking at each other.

"I've been thinking about you a lot since you kissed me goodnight last time."

He looked at her steadily for a while and said, "You know I want to marry you, don't you?"

"I was hoping you'd ask because I've been thinking about it too. But we have to talk about some things first."

"What things?"

"I have a daughter and three grandchildren, and I have some property I would like to pass to them. If we decide to marry it won't be a traditional one. I've been alone for quite a while and have my own life, just like you have yours. We need to agree to make decisions together and realize each of us has things important to us that must be accepted by the other." She paused for a moment. "Kiss me again and then we can talk about it."

"If I kiss you again, we won't be talking for a while," he said, reaching for the top button on her blouse.

She stood, held out her hand and led him to the bedroom. There was moonlight coming in through the curtains and they enjoyed undressing each other and finding out what was there.

Running his hands over her body he muttered, "Ummm, you're Junoesque. I love that."

"What does it mean?"

He kissed her in the hollow of her throat. "It means you have nice, soft curves in all the right places," he murmured.

She led him to the bed and lay down invitingly. He accepted the invitation and soon they were making each other feel the way men and women do when they're in love.

When they had finished, she lay a little breathless, covered with a light sheen of perspiration, cool in the slight breeze coming in the window. She pulled the sheet over her breasts and stared up at the darkness, content. When he spoke, it startled her.

"I'm sorry it was so quick. It's been a while, and you excite me. Next time we'll take our time, and it will be better."

"Where did you learn a word like Junoesque?" she asked after a minute.

"Patricia and I used to read erotica to each other in bed. It was a word I picked up from one or another of the things we read about. I had to look it up to see what it meant."

"So, what does it mean?"

"It means a woman, not a girl."

"So, you like buxom women?"

Slowly he pulled the sheet off her and began to trace the shape of her breasts with his finger, stopping at the nipple and bending to kiss it. "Let me show you how much I like what you are."

"Oh yes," she said, a little breathless. "Please do."

He was right. It was much better the second time; and the third.

Every once in a great while a ground fog would settle over the city, leaving the hills above in the sunrise. The view was stunning, much like a cotton blanket shot through with pale pastel threads. Here and there hills could be seen, and an occasional church bell tower or steeple, but the city itself was just waking up out of sight below the fog.

Sarah pulled the bell, and when Carlotta appeared, asked her to invite Madame to have coffee and talk in Sarah's apartment while they enjoyed the special view.

Madame arrived soon but she had just settled herself in her chair when Carlotta came in with the coffee and a small book under her arm. She laid the tray on the table and when she finished serving, handed the book to Madame who read the cover and looked up with a smile.

"That's wonderful, Carlotta," she said. "How long did it take for you to do this?"

She handed it back to Carlotta who handed it to Sarah, who said, "Annaliese showed it to me when it came."

"Congratulations," said Madame.

"I tried to work on it a little every day and it took me two and a half months, and then it took almost as long before it came back."

"So, does this mean I'll be losing my maid?" asked Madame.

"Oh no, we love working here and it is something I can do when I have time. Annaliese thinks she can find me other books, and since I enjoyed it, I may try again."

When Carlotta closed the door behind her, Madame immediately said, "Well?"

Sarah grinned at her. "Well, what?"

Madame looked at her with a slow smile spreading across her face. "All right. I know he was here last night, and I know what time he left, and you look amazingly cheerful this morning. Do I have to go on or are you going to tell me?"

"Let's just say, I remembered a good reason for having a man around the house." She was trying without success to look demure and innocent.

They laughed together.

"So, did he ask?"

"Yes, he did, and I said yes, but I told him we need to talk. If either of us is going to be happy we're going to have to agree on what's the best way for it to work. I long ago outgrew the need for someone to support me, and there are certain aspects of my life that would interfere with a traditional marriage."

"Such as?"

"Rebecca and the grandchildren, for one thing. I need to think about it, and I need to talk to you and probably Annaliese before I can really say. And since there's no real hurry, I'm going to take my time before I make up my mind.

"Of course," she continued, "I remember what you said about not needing anyone's permission, so I don't plan on abstaining while I make up my mind."

Madame laughed, and Sarah continued. "Either I forgot how much fun it is or maybe I never knew, but I know now."

"I'm sure Mr. Burke will indulge your slightest wish," said Madame. "I will miss having you have coffee with me every morning."

"I have no idea how long it will be, but you'll be the first to know when we set a date.

"Have you ever heard the word 'Junoesque'?" Sarah asked.

"Oh yes, many times," replied Madame. "Men have been calling me that since I was a girl." She patted her backside. "I've always been a bit hefty."

"He told me he and his wife used to read erotica to each other in bed. He told me about some of it and it definitely seems to warm things up."

"Sounds like you might have caught a live one."

"Sure seemed like it last night."

Chapter Fifty-Eight

When Handy was growing up in Minnesota, his older brothers made sure to roll him out of bed every morning before the sun peeped over the horizon. He retained the habit and this morning, like most mornings, he was standing on the porch watching the sun come creeping over the mountains to the east, sipping a cup of hot coffee. Behind him Rebecca was getting ready for her every-other-week trip to the City.

Traveling with a year-old baby involved being organized and thorough, and after several months of it, Rebecca had things pretty well down pat. She carried only what she needed, mainly baby things, in a large carpet bag. Lately her life seemed to swing around two poles, one at the ranch and one at the mansion, so she kept clothing and other things she needed in both places.

Handy had realized early there was no way to keep a lively young mother happy isolated from her friends, also young mothers, for very long. Because most days he and Gray spent long hours working around the ranch, he decided to encourage her to travel to see her mother and her friends whenever she liked rather than watch her turn sour and unhappy from boredom and loneliness. Besides, it was so much fun when she got home.

They developed a ritual whenever she left for the City. He would sweep her into his arms, give her a passionate kiss, then carry her down the front steps, baby in a basket swinging from his arm and deposit them on the seat of the wagon where Bits was waiting to drive her to the ferry.

The railroad was building a spur which would pass less than a mile from the ranch, but it would be a month or so before it was completed. Until then the twelve-mile wagon ride to the ferry was something to be endured, not enjoyed, especially by Bobby.

Handy was watching them turn left onto the road south when a rider came through the open gate, hesitated a moment, saw Handy and rode up to the house. There was something about him that made Handy reach inside the front door, pick up the ten-gage shotgun standing there, and prop it against the porch rail close to hand.

"Can I help you, sir?" he asked when the man stopped in front of him. "If I've ever seen anyone riding the rough string it's this one," he thought.

"I'm looking for someone," the man answered. "I was told he lives around here. Name's Grayson, they call him Gray."

"He's my partner," said Handy. "Maybe I can help you."

"I'm his brother, Clement," he reached out to shake Handy's hand.

Handy looked at him with a smile. "Over the years I've decided never to shake hands with anyone. Gives them an edge on you." It wasn't really true. He just didn't want to shake the man's hand. "Does he know you're coming? He never mentioned it to me."

"No, I haven't seen him for a few years. I just wanted to stop by and say 'Howdy'."

"Well, see the road that runs alongside the white rail?" When the man turned in the saddle and nodded, Handy continued. "Take it around the exercise track till you come to a road off to the left. Take that till it ends, and you'll see his place."

Watching him ride away, Handy instinctively felt something was wrong. He watched through the binoculars he kept by the door until the man was out of sight. Nothing he saw made him feel any different.

Madame and Sarah had become close friends and Sarah's rooms at the mansion included space for the family. Handy was usually too busy to come with her, but Rebecca caught the same ferry twice a month and spent a week each time, dividing her time between the mansion and The BookSeller, between her mother and her friends.

She thought she'd ask her mother this time if her recurring presence in the City was the reason she and Jonas seemed to always be on the verge of getting married but never quite ready to step over the line.

There was no question how Sarah felt about her life at the mansion, and as much as she loved Jonas and the time they spent together, she seemed loath to walk away from the pleasant life she enjoyed with Madame and the people around her. Though they shared everything else, Rebecca felt, for the first time in her life, her Mama was keeping secrets from her.

Growing up at the wilderness store with only her mother and her brother Jed for company most times she had shared everything with her mother, at least until Handy came along. She guessed maybe Jonas was for Mama the same thing Handy was for her; that is, someone to share intimate secrets with. She felt a little strange when she thought of Mama in bed doing with Jonas what she and Handy did whenever they got the chance and one day it dawned on her that must be where the secrets came from.

When she walked into the kitchen at the Mansion, Rebecca was not surprised to see Carlotta sitting at the table, a book before her, writing on a thick pad with papers scattered around. Bertha, the cook, was putting a plate in front of Geppetto, and Jose, the stable man, was sitting smoking a pipe.

"Are you doing another book?" she asked Carlotta.

"Yes, I am. I asked the man in Kansas City, his name is Mr. Crowder, if he could recommend one and he did. I think this one will take much longer. It is a bigger book."

She looked over the girl's shoulder. "I'll bet the more of that you do the better your English will become."

"My teacher says the same thing," said Carlotta. "Already I speak better than Tony, and my handwriting is getting much better."

"What's the book?"

"It's called The Betrothed," Carlotta answered. "It's a novel about life in Italy in the old days. The author is Italian, but he lived in San Francisco for a while. Mr. Crowder wants me to translate some of his other writings when I'm through with this one. He's gotten the author's permission, so I won't make as much on each book, but I don't care about that. I do it to learn English better."

"It seems like you want to be more than a maid," said Rebecca.

Carlotta shook her head. "One day I would like to be a teacher, but we would never leave Madame if she wanted us to stay. She has been so good to us and everyone here is so nice. Everyone here is so good to Geppetto. It is like a big family. She has offered for me to go to school so I can be a teacher. She will pay, but I will wait to do that."

She figured Sarah would be in Madame's dressing room and she was right. As usual, they were drinking coffee, reading the papers and talking. Sarah smiled at her daughter and cooed at her grandson, kissing him on the forehead.

"Can you watch him for a while today?" Rebecca asked. "Greta, Sun Li and I are going to Helen's Mother and Baby to find some things for the twins, and then we're meeting Annaliese and Maggie at The City of Paris to have lunch and a walk around."

Carlotta had come in behind her and said, "We love to have him here. We will help with him and take care of him if you wish," she said to Sarah.

"Well, I guess it's alright to leave him for a while," said Sarah. "I'm going somewhere with Jonas, but the girls downstairs have so much fun taking care of him they really shouldn't be getting paid for it."

Madame laughed. "Children are spoiled in this house, as you well know. All the girls want to practice being mothers."

When Rebecca came into the store, Greta spoke to her first. "Good morning, Rebecca. I have several things to do before we can leave but it shouldn't take long."

"How did you know it was me?" Rebecca asked. "I put on some of mother's rose water to see if I could fool you."

"I could tell by the sounds you made coming in the back door," replied Greta, smiling, "and I knew you were coming.

Probably because she hadn't seen it much until recently, she noticed Greta's smile.

Greta went into the back room and Rebecca rolled her eyes at Sun Li and Jason.

"Can't fool that girl," said Jason, chuckling.

"So, what are we looking for today?" asked Sun Li.

"Greta wants to get some clothes for the twins. They are growing so fast, and I need to do the same for Bobby. I swear, that boy is going to be as big as his father."

They chatted for a while and then Rebecca asked Sun Li, "You weren't with us the last time Greta went into the department store, were you?"

"No, that was just before I came here, but I heard about it," replied Sun Li.

"It was a trip I'll never forget," said Rebecca." Just then Greta came out of the back room putting on her coat. "I'm ready when you are," she said.

Rebecca was driving. They all bundled up against the chill March wind coming off the bay and were glad to be seated in the department store dining room.

"I feel a breeze from somewhere," said Greta. "It's not cold so I know it's not an open window."

"There are three large electric fans in the high ceiling above us," said Sun Li. "They are moving the air around."

"I can feel the heat from the sun," said Greta. "How is that possible?"

"You're in a room with a glass ceiling so you feel the sun, but not the cold wind we felt outside," answered Rebecca. Do you remember being here before?"

"Yes, I do. It's not the kind of place you forget. I can smell the plants and some flowers, too."

They had just been served beverages when Annaliese and Maggie joined them.

For an hour the friends talked. They learned Sun Li was expecting, probably in early fall; that she and Jason were, with money from her father, looking for a house she hoped to bring the baby home to; that Maggie and Annaliese were over half way through medical school and were trying to decide how and where to begin their careers; that Rebecca was happy at the ranch and planning a gathering of her friends from the city at the Mill Valley Horse Ranch sometime in May; and that Greta was happy, enjoying being a mother and learning her way around the BookSeller again.

Annaliese listened and talked a little, but mostly she watched Greta. The girl of last year was now a young woman and her face reflected the pleasure of the moment in a way Annaliese had wondered if she'd ever find again.

The loss of Jed no longer overshadowed her life, and she was moving forward now, happy rather than standing miserably in one place. She thought Lemuel's resumption of reading to her every night had been an essential part of the emotional path Greta had taken away from the events that almost destroyed her.

When the others left, she and Maggie sat over coffee for a while.

"How's Charlie these days?" asked Annaliese. "With all the work we have to do right now he must be feeling neglected."

Maggie sighed deeply and shook her head. "He's not too happy with me," she said. "He feels I'm not giving him enough time in bed as well as everywhere else. He pouts when he's ready for bed and I'm still studying. It's not really fair. We sat and talked for hours about how hard it would be in school, and he said he would support me. Now it's getting tough and he's complaining. Grrrrr."

She looked at her friend. "How's Johnny doing with it?"

"The way we agreed to do it was we would each live our lives and when we could, we'd live them together. So far it's worked pretty good. What I try to do is whenever we are together to make it special. Johnny's only twenty and he's pretty frisky most times, so I try to be ready any night he's in the mood. I'm not an authority on it or anything, but I'd say the best way to keep him happy is to be ready whenever he is."

Maggie looked thoughtful and Annaliese continued. "Is there any time he feels better than the morning after?"

"No, probably not," answered Maggie.

"So, there you are. Besides, whether you're tired or not, it's fun once you get started, isn't it?"

"Yeah, I guess it is, though, sometimes it's hard to get started," answered Maggie.

"I guess you need to decide whether it's worth keeping him happy," said Annaliese, pushing her chair back and standing. "We're going to have to hurry back if we want to be there when the girls get there. I have to get everything set up, and I think Jessica's brother is coming with her today."

Chapter Fifty-Nine

Jim Steyer hailed Johnny as he walked up the gangplank to the ferry. "Come on up," he called, gesturing at the ladder which led to the bridge. "Got some hot coffee for you."

Johnny got there just in time to watch Jim and the crew maneuver the ferry away from the dock and head out for the other side of the Golden Gate. The view and the breeze were more significant up here and he stepped out on the wing to see it all.

"Aren't you a day early this week?" asked Jim.

"You mean it's not Friday?" asked Johnny. They both laughed.

"I got a wire from Handy saying he needed me early. It's nice the store's running so smoothly I can get away pretty much any time I want."

They were quiet for a moment, looking out over the bay to Alcatraz Island in the distance.

"I get the impression you're not going to run Black anymore."

Johnny nodded. "That's right," he said. "I love my horse and if someone laid open his flank with a whip again, I really don't know what I'd do." He paused and looked at Jim. "And I don't want to find out."

"Besides, Bits will have a scar across his face for the rest of his life from that ride and I don't want to be responsible for it maybe happening again."

"Does Bits want to race again?"

"Haven't asked him. Saw no reason to bring it up. If he wants to, that's fine but not on any horse of mine."

"How about your partners? Do they feel the same way?"

Johnny turned and put his back against the rail and said, "Don't get me wrong. If The Mill Valley Horse Ranch decides to raise, train and stable horses for racing, I'm fine with it. But not Black. Not my horse. He's a gentle, good-natured soul and I have no desire to see him change."

Handy was waiting on the dock in Sausalito and they were soon on their way to the ranch.

"Gray's got a visitor I didn't like the looks of and I haven't seen him for two days," said Handy. "The fellow said he was Gray's brother, but why would that keep Gray from coming over to let me know the situation?"

Johnny shook his head. "I can't think of a good reason, though Gray would have known you'd check on him so he might have done it just so you would."

"It don't seem right, but I didn't want to go out there without someone to cover my back," said Handy, "and you're the one I like to have back there when I need someone."

Since they didn't have much ready cash, Gray and Maxine spent time and elbow grease instead sprucing up the cottage. Gray was in the process of building two rooms on the back of the house for the family they hoped was coming.

Maxine was hanging clothes on a line behind the house when Johnny and Handy rode into the yard. They swung down and she met them at the front porch, gave them a meaningful look and nodded her head toward the front door.

Gray came out to greet them and it was easy to see he was nervous about something.

"You met my brother," he said to Handy. "He'll be bunking here for a while and may be hanging around the ranch."

Just then his brother came to the door and Handy saw he'd taken the chance to spruce up a bit and shave, but he still looked like someone who'd been riding the owl hoot trail.

"We just stopped by to see if you were alright," said Handy. "Haven't seen you for a couple of days and we were supposed to grade the exercise track this week."

"I haven't seen my brother for a while, so I thought I'd take a little time to catch up on things," said Gray, looking everywhere but at Johnny. Johnny, on the other hand, was looking at Clement Grayson, who was looking back.

"That's an unusual way to wear a gun," said Clement.

Johnny smiled. "I was injured a couple years ago. When I was learning how to use the left hand, I thought I'd try something new."

"So does it work?"

"It does," said Johnny, and left it at that.

As they rode away from the cottage, Handy said, "Something about him makes me nervous."

"Seemed to make Gray and Maxine nervous too," replied Johnny. They rode in silence for a while. "Did you notice his holster?" When Handy shook his head, Johnny continued. "The leather was shiny and worn smooth. It looks like he uses it a lot. I'll bet he cleans his gun more often than he takes a bath."

"That's a bet I wouldn't take," replied Handy.

The next morning while they were drinking morning coffee on the front porch, they saw Gray's wagon top the small rise in the distance and come down toward them. This was normal most every day, but today Maxine was with him, and his brother rode alongside the wagon. They stopped at the turnoff into the ranch yard, talked for a moment, and then Clement rode out of the gate and turned toward town.

"Good," said Johnny, standing and walking to the porch rail. "Now we can get some answers."

Gray parked the wagon by the barn and the couple joined them sitting on the porch.

"So, tell us what's going on," said Handy. "Things don't seem quite right."

Gray took off his hat and ran his fingers through his hair. "You're right there. He showed up here the other day and he seems to want to stay for a while. And he's going to meet another of my brothers and a friend at the ferry this morning, and he wants us to put them up too."

This hung in the air while they all sat and thought about it.

"I don't like it one bit," said Maxine, "but he's Gray's brother and I don't want to cause a family problem."

"You think he's on the dodge?" asked Johnny. "If his friends look anything like him, I'd say it's likely."

"I'd say it's likely too," said Gray. "One of the reasons I left home was because he and Zack, another brother, were bringing men I didn't like into the house. Don't know it for sure but I think they've been running outside the law for a while, at least that's what letters I get from my sister say. It's our older brother Zack he's supposed to meet today and another fellow from back home."

"So, what you're saying is he's bringing trouble into our lives whether we want it or not," said Handy. "Why didn't you do something about it?"

Gray shook his head, "From what I remember, he can be violent, and Maxine was there. Seemed best to wait till I could let you two know and we'd decide how to deal with it." He looked at Johnny. "What do you think we should do?"

As was his wont, Johnny took a while to answer. "It looks to me like we have a bully to deal with." He looked at the others and they nodded. "Pa taught me the best way to handle someone when they're pushing is to push back hard before they get set. Of course, the problem here is, they're family." He looked at Gray. "How would you feel if we confront him when he returns and simply tell him he and his friends aren't welcome?"

"I left home to get away from this kind of thing," replied Gray. "If that's what we need to do, I have no problem with it, family be damned."

"Well, the next step is to plan how we deal with it." He looked at Handy. "What do you think?"

"Johnny, I've never gotten in trouble following your lead. You decide."

"Gray?"

"I agree; you lead, and we'll back you."

"I can shoot a rifle," said Maxine. "This is my home, and I want to help."

Johnny stood up. "I'm going to take a walk for a few minutes and when I get back let's sit down over coffee and talk about it."

When he got back, they were all seated around the table, and he joined them.

"Gray, how likely are these men to strike out if we confront them?"

Gray took his time answering. "I haven't been around them for several years. I've heard tell of problems, but I don't know them well enough anymore to answer that. When they were younger, they did things without thinking, but then I guess we all did. Whether they've changed or not?" He held up his hands and looked at the ceiling.

"Johnny, it seems to me we need to act based on the threat," said Handy. "Like Wash says. 'Plan on what they could do rather than on what you think they'll do'."

Johnny nodded, "Yes. So, let's do this. I doubt if they'll stay in town too long so here's the plan. We'll send Bits to a spot on the road where he can see them coming and we'll set up to receive them.

"Handy, find Bits. Tell him to ride Black up to the crest of Maynard's Knob and when he sees them coming, get back here as quick as he can. Gray, in the loft with the Henry; Maxine, take a Winchester and cover the gate from the bedroom window upstairs. Take enough ammunition and some water in case this takes a while.

"Handy and I will be on either side of the gate and I'll talk to them when they get here. Handy will have the ten-gage. If anything happens wait 'til I fire. Understood?"

Everyone nodded and chairs scraped as they all stood up. Gray and Maxine kissed and hugged and followed Johnny out on the porch. As they came out the front door, Bits closed the gate behind him and rode away on Black.

After they had checked their positions, Gray and Maxine joined them on the porch.

"This is the first time I've ever sat and waited for something like this," said Gray. "Makes you a bit nervous, doesn't it?"

Johnny and Handy both chuckled. "Well, we've been through it twice before and it doesn't get any easier," said Handy.

They didn't have long to wait. Bits came pounding up the road about a quarter of an hour later and they all headed to their positions, Bits joining Gray in the loft, Winchester in hand.

Johnny and Handy were standing about ten feet apart inside the entrance gate when the three men rode up.

They were sitting their horses looking at a large 'No Trespassing' sign affixed to the gate when Johnny said, "Good morning gentlemen, how can we help you?" His pleasant greeting belied the huge ten-gage, double barreled shotgun Handy was holding pointed in their general direction. They could see both hammers were cocked.

"Does this sign mean we can't come in?" said Clement.

"Yes sir, it does," replied Johnny.

"And who are you?" said one of them, probably his older brother.

"My name is Johnny Fry and with my partners, Gray Grayson and Handy Josephson, I own this ranch. After talking it over, we have decided we do not want you and your friends on the place."

"Gray's our brother," said Clement, "and you're telling us he doesn't want us here?"

From the barn Gray's voice was loud enough to be heard clearly. "That's right Clement. I left home to get away from you and Zack and your friends, and I don't want the kind of trouble you bring. And, by the way, I'm holding a seventeen shot Henry rifle."

The brothers looked at each other. "I notice you're not holding a gun," said Zack.

"Need be, I can get it out pretty quick," replied Johnny.

"Hmm, might have to try that one day," said Clement, and he turned his horse and led the other two back down the road to Sausalito.

Chapter Sixty

Johnny occasionally varied his trips to the ranch by going into the general store in Sausalito for one reason or another. Today it was to see if they had the apples he ordered, and he wanted to get a can of sardines for Jinx, who was prowling around the store like he always did. Johnny liked to use the apples as treats for horses he thought were special. Black usually got more than his share.

He was hoisting the forty-pound bag on his shoulder when through the window he saw Gray's brothers coming across the street. At a glance he recognized the threat their presence represented and turned to the lady behind the counter.

"It looks as though there might be trouble when I go outside," he said. "It may be best if you go in back until we see what happens. Tell Virgil to stay back there too."

She looked at him with her mouth open for a moment, then looked out the window, and with a little cry, ducked through the door behind the counter.

From habit Johnny pulled the Colt and turned the cylinder. He already knew it was loaded. He holstered it and stepped through the door, Jinx following close behind.

They were spread out, waiting, hands hanging, ready. Johnny stopped on the edge of the boardwalk and said, "You look like you're the bull of the woods here," he said to Zack, "so I'll talk to you. I'm very good with this gun," he said, looking directly into the man's eyes. "If you touch your gun, I'll probably kill you."

Zack looked a little startled at this. His mouth dropped open and he stood for a moment, then shook his head. "What about him?" he nodded at his brother.

"What happens with him won't matter to you cause you'll be dead." Johnny stood looking at him, relaxed, easy on his feet. "Make your move or leave, I'm not real patient."

Across the street a man came out of the café, lifted a shotgun to port-arms, cocked both hammers, and called out, "I should let Johnny hang your hides on the wall, but it would mean a lot of paperwork for me. Now, you boys get on your horses right now and leave. Don't come back, ever."

The brothers stood frozen. The sheriff came up behind Clement, pushed the shotgun into his back.

"I'll bet you can feel both barrels, can't you?" he said, and stepped back several paces. They turned to look at him, and seeing the star on his vest, and the shotgun in his hands, turned away and began to walk slowly toward the livery stable, occasionally glancing over their shoulder at where Johnny was standing on the boardwalk.

"Thanks, Hern," said Johnny. He turned and reentered the store to get his apples and his cat, who had slipped back inside. He met the sheriff as he came out.

"What was that all about?" asked Sheriff Herndon.

"We had a problem with them at the ranch last week. They were looking for it and I was ready to give it to them when you stepped in."

"Well, it's probably for the best. The county really can't afford to bury 'em." He looked at Johnny for a moment and said, "Jim Steyer told me he'd seen you work with the Colt. I target shoot every once in a while. One time when you're in town why don't you go out with me. I never could get the hang of it with a six-gun. That's why I carry this thing." He lifted the shotgun. "It saves a lot of arguing."

Handy and Gray were at work in the barn when he rode into the yard, and Bits was exercising some horses. The first thing he did every week when he came up to the ranch was to do the bookwork. Then he blew the forge up and got to work shoeing horses and repairing any small metal work that needed doing.

A couple hours later the triangle rang for lunch and he met his partners and Bits at the kitchen table. Wendy, the new cook and housekeeper, set food before them and for a while there wasn't much conversation. On the porch after, while they let things settle, Johnny told them about meeting Gray's brothers.

"If Hern hadn't stepped in, there might have been gunplay." He looked at Gray. "How would you feel if I'd killed one or both of your brothers?"

Gray sat quiet for a moment. "Johnny, do what you have to do. I trust you not to go looking for it. If they bring it on themselves?" he shrugged. "I'll make sure they have nice gravestones."

They sat for a while, watching Bits pump water to wash some stock.

"Family's a funny thing," said Gray. "Where I come from, they have feuds where families fight for years over one thing or another. Family meant everything. If someone shoots your cousin you're supposed to shoot his cousin. It never made much sense to me. I left Missouri to get away from that kind of thinking.

"One of the things I liked about working for Madame was learning that family didn't have to be like that. Loyalty is fine and it's still a part of my life. But it's something you have to earn. I'm loyal to Madame and the people at the mansion because they deserve it, not because we came from the same womb."

"Do you think we'll be facing a gunfight whenever we see them?" asked Handy.

Gray shook his head. "I honestly couldn't tell you but from the way they acted today, I'd say be ready whenever they're around."

Annaliese was asleep when Johnny got home, so he shaded the light, undressed, and slipped under the covers. He thought for a moment about not telling her about the almost gunfight but then thought about his promise to her.

He kissed her on the ear. She opened one eye and saw him sitting on his knees beside her, looking at her expectantly. "I want to play," he said.

She closed the eye and asked sternly, "What makes you think it's OK to wake me up from a sound sleep for that?"

He sat thinking, then smiled. "Experience," he said. He looked like a puppy waiting on a treat.

By now she was smiling too, and when he kissed her again, she put her arms around him and drew him down to her.

Afterwards he whispered to her, "I know one day you'll tell me no, but I sure am glad that day hasn't come."

She giggled. "There are times," she said, "when I forget how much fun it is, but you're always good at reminding me."

He turned on the light and came to sit beside her on the bed. "Almost had a problem Friday when I got off the ferry in Sausalito. Remember Gray's brothers I told you about?" When she nodded, he continued. "They braced me outside Virgil's store. We were right on the edge of gunplay when the sheriff came up behind them and cocked his shotgun."

As he was saying this she had scrambled into a sitting position and was looking at him with her mouth open, eyes wide.

"Oh my God, Johnny. What did you do?

"I went on up to the ranch. What else could I do?" I wasn't about to go after them."

"Are they going to be staying around here?"

"Couldn't tell you."

"Does this mean if they see you in town you may have to fight them?"

"I'd say there's a good chance."

She sat quiet for a moment then said, "That's intolerable."

"I tend to agree, but what can I do? I can't hunt them down and shoot them. The law frowns on that kind of thing."

She shook her head. "Tell me again what happened with them up at the ranch last week."

"What it amounts to is, these men were going to bring trouble into our lives by forcing Gray to shelter them for a while. When Clement went to pick up his brother at the ferry, we faced them down at the gate when they came back." He chuckled. "Maxine was at a window upstairs with a Winchester. She said it was her home and she was going to fight for it if need be.

"Anyway, they left, and then I ran into them in town. Hern told them to leave and not come back, but who knows what they'll do. We'll all have to be on our toes for a while."

"Why does it always have to be with guns?" she asked. "Why do men feel the need to shoot other men? It wasn't like that in Salt Lake."

"Couldn't tell you, but if someone wants to shoot you, you

better be ready to shoot back or you might be dead. As far as Salt Lake goes, I remember reading about Porter Rockwell and Bill Hickman doing some shooting for Brigham a time or two."

"That's true," she said. "I forgot. I heard stories about them when I was growing up. Turn off the light and I'll try to go to sleep. Unless you're not through, that is."

He wasn't.

Chapter Sixty-one

Wash nailed the last shingle on the roof, hung the hammer on his belt, and sat on the edge of the roof to rest. Up this high he could hear the sound of the ocean, and it was something he never tired of. When he looked down, Woman was standing in the yard looking up at him.

"Hungry?" she asked. When he nodded, she continued. "I can put it on the table whenever you're ready."

"I'll wash at the pump and be in in a minute," he said, swinging his feet onto the ladder. She disappeared and he heard the rattle of dishes.

Though she didn't really like to cook, she didn't much like his cooking, so she had taken on the job shortly after they moved into the cabin.

Since Doc moved out, they had fallen into a routine, and most of their conversation in the evenings was at the rock where they could hear the ocean or when they sat in rocking chairs on the front porch after supper. Tonight, they were at the rock.

She was sitting on the grass, leaning back against his knees. He was petting her hair, and she was purring. Since he had seen Schweder during a delivery to The Grove that morning, they just naturally fell to talking about him.

"He's really a strange duck," said Wash, "but he's a first-class farmer. That's one of the nicest places I've ever seen."

"Do you reckon it's because he uses the money he makes with the gun to keep it up?" she asked. "Didn't you say he's expensive?"

"That's the rumor, although I couldn't swear to it. The fellows who work for him say he's fair and straight with them, a good boss and when a dirty job needs doing, he gets out there with 'em and does his share. He has more help than he really needs, so he can get the small things done most farmers don't bother with. Kate seems to think highly of him."

"Have you made up your mind what you're going to do and when and how?"

He sat quiet for a minute, still petting the top of her head.

"One of the things I loved about traveling around the mountains was the nights around a campfire." She was used to these digressions when he was explaining something, so she listened patiently. "Sometimes it would just be Doc and me and sometimes there would be two or three others. We'd talk and they were some good talks. Some of those boys were smart and had read a good bit. Most of the time I just listened and learned, but once in a while I could chip something into the pot.

"One time Doc and a couple others started talking about killing people; how we felt about it and such. It's an easy thing to justify when you're out there far from any law and you need to kill to protect you and yours, like you'd have to do with a catamount or a wolf. I've laid for someone I knew was after me and never felt a thing when I saw his body lying where he'd fallen with my bullet in him.

"But what about when you're in a town or city where there's law, or what about a time like we have here - where the law can't do anything until the crime's been done, or you know but can't prove something, so someone is getting away with murder, probably many times? Civilization is good in most ways, but it forces you to think about things you don't have to worry about out on the trail."

He was quiet for a while, and she sat listening to the ocean.

"It's cost me a lot of thinking, I tell you. I don't want to kill him, not because he doesn't deserve it, but because what it would make me if I did. Johnny and I talked about that one time, and he said he didn't want to become someone who killed without thinking or feeling regret. That's how I feel. I'm not out in the hills anymore so I can't keep acting like I am.

"Of course, I can't keep putting off doing something to stop him. He might disappear one day on a job, and I'd hate to think someone else died because I couldn't make up my mind.

"On the other hand, what if I'm wrong and he's not guilty? How much faith should I put in the evidence I have? Looking at the way he lives and how people think about him, he doesn't seem like the type who would stalk and kill another human being the way you take down an elk or deer. You know how many things point to his guilt; what do you think?"

She turned to him. The moon hadn't risen but he could see her faintly in the starlight. "I can't help you with this one," she said softly. "Once you decide what to do, I'll help you do it, but this is one you'll have to figure out yourself."

"There's an awful lot of things that point to him, so I've pretty much decided to do something. I can't brace him in a gunfight. I'm not a magician with a six gun like Johnny. I have come up with an idea though.

"It seems like one essential to being in his kind of work is the ability to sneak up on someone to do the job, then get away in a hurry. I wonder how well he could do that if I put a Sharp's .50 caliber slug through one of his knees?"

She was quiet for a moment, thinking. "I'd say it should put him out of action for quite a while if not permanently. Have you made any plans in that direction?"

"The last couple of times I've been out there I've looked around, and I think I've got a place picked out. It's along the road leading into town, about a mile from the farm. The fellows who work there tell me he drives the wagon into town every week at the same time, on Saturday morning.

"If it's true, I think that'd be a habit that'd put him in my sights. It's close enough to the farm someone would likely hear the shot and come to see what it was. They'd probably find him before he bleeds to death."

"Does anyone live with him? He's not married, is he?"

"No. He has a lady who lives with him. She seems to be a cook and housekeeper. From what I hear, she might also be a bed partner of sorts too."

"So, let's just say you get it done. What do we do afterwards?" she asked.

"I've been thinking about that too. The natural impulse would be to get out of town, but that would seem to draw attention to us and maybe give someone the idea we were running from something or other.

"I think maybe we ought to make sure we cover our tracks when we do the job, then sit tight for a while. I think business at the nursery might fall off a bit in winter, so we can probably take off for a couple of months and ride the cars back home before Christmas. We'd be gone for a while and come back in the spring when she needs us. That would be natural and not suspicious."

They sat quietly for a while. "When do you think it'd be best to do it?" she asked.

"I can't wait too long. He could get a wire, and if he leaves on a job I'd have to wait until he got back." He shook his head. "That would be hard to live with."

"Will you need my help, ya think?"

"I'm sure you'd be a help, but I need to figure out how and decide when. Then we can talk about it. This is a strange thing to be talking with your lady friend about especially at such a romantic place. Just curious - what do you think about the whole thing?" He was still petting her head.

She leaned back against him, took the hand not busy and squeezed it gently. "I believe you'll do the right thing," she said.

The next morning Woman approached Kate while she was working in the office.

"Got a minute?" she asked.

Kate looked up and smiled. "Of course. How can I help you?"

"You know San Francisco is home for us," said Woman, "so we'd like to plan to take off, say the first of December or so, and go up there for a while. We'd come back in early spring, so we'd be here when it starts getting busy."

"You two haven't been around here for a winter, have you?" asked Kate. "We don't really have much winter down here, so business is pretty steady year-round. On the other hand, I like having the two of you around. You do good work, and I can depend on you, so I think I can keep a spot open for you until you come back. We'll probably begin working on the parks project for the city again in early spring. Are you planning on moving down here for good anytime soon?"

"That's something we'll probably talk about while we're up there. We have a friend who's in medical school at the university there and she and her husband have talked about moving down here, or maybe Los Angeles, when she finishes. Might be next year about this time so when we come back we'll probably stay for a while, although with Wash you never know. He's a rambler."

That night they were sitting on the porch when suddenly he stopped rocking and sat still.

"Looking at you, I'd say you just made up your mind about something," she said. "Tell me."

He sat quiet for a long minute. "I 've decided to do it and I can't think of a reason not to do it right away. Let's make a plan and try to get it done in the next couple of days."

"Really? Tell me."

"Let me think a bit about it and then I'll lay it out for you." He got up and walked slowly out to his rock where he could sit and listen to the ocean and think.

Chapter Sixty-Two

Sarah was sitting in Madame's dressing room looking out over the city and the bay, seeing nothing.

"What ya thinking about with such a face?" asked Madame. "I'll bet it's about that Jonas fellow."

Sarah laughed. "I do seem to spend a lot of time thinking about him these days, don't I?"

"That's not too surprising, but why the face? You almost look like something hurts."

"I've been wrestling with a decision for the last several weeks and I'm no closer to an answer than when I started."

"Want to talk about it?"

"You know, when we go somewhere, we always go back to his place after. Then we have to get dressed and he has to bring me back home."

"Why?"

"For some reason I don't want to stay the night."

"Why not?"

"That's another problem; I don't know why not. No one I love cares one way or another about it, so why should I?" Sarah was quiet for a moment, then said, "I want you to tell me exactly how you feel about me continuing to live here."

Madame grinned at her. "You mean to tell me that's the reason you haven't gone on and gotten married?"

Sarah's smile was rueful. "No, that's not it exactly. I know we've become good friends and believe me I value that. But I've become the original visitor who won't go home, and I don't want to wear out my welcome, so we need to talk about it."

Madame laughed. "I never thought about it that way," she said. "I just know I like having you here and my people do too. It doesn't cost me anything and the girls would be here doing for me whether you were here or not. It's not like I need your rooms for anything. No one's ever used them for anything since I've been here. You're not inconveniencing me in the slightest."

They sat looking at one another for a long moment. "The people who live and work here have become like a family to me," said Madame, "something I've never had before. You and Rebecca, Bobby and Handy are part of that family now. You come and go as you wish, but I hope you'll always come back."

Sarah's eyes were suddenly blurry with unshed tears, and she had trouble getting her words out. "I'm glad," she said finally. "These mornings with you have become one of the best parts of my life.

"And that brings us to the other problem," she continued. "I love Jonas, but I don't want to leave the life I have here. I'm nervous about telling him because I love the time we spend together."

"And if he gives you a choice?"

"That's a problem. But thinking about it, I've come to realize if I choose to marry him because of an ultimatum, I might come to resent the fact he made me choose."

Madame stretched in her chair and chuckled. "I'd say you've contracted the same disease that infected me a few years ago."

Sarah stared at her, a question on her face.

"I call it 'independentitus'. You've become independent and you like it. After the old man died, I decided I never wanted to tie myself to a man again; let him make decisions for me. I found I liked not having to please anyone but myself.

"Occasionally someone will come along, and we spend good time in the bedroom and around, but I have to know they'll leave before long or I won't let them in the bed. That's why I tend toward sailors. I know they won't hang around but so long. Although with Woman around, it hasn't happened in a while."

Carlotta appeared with a pot of coffee and refilled their cups.

When she had gone, Sarah said, "It sounds like I might have a case of the same stuff, although I'm not much attracted to sailors."

"Have you talked to Jonas about it?"

"We've talked around it. We went over the property issue, and he had no problems with that. But I don't really want to move out of here. I mean, he's got a nice place and all, but I don't believe his kids, especially his daughter, think they need a new mother. Besides, with a daughter and three grandchildren, I have enough of my own to worry about. I don't really feel the need to take on anymore.

"He works a lot, and it keeps him busy at night with all the political stuff that goes with the job. It seems like he expects me to join him in that life and I'm not sure I want to, at least not to the same extent he's involved."

"It sounds to me like you've already made up your mind."

"I guess I have. The problem is how to tell him about it."

"I knew an author once who said the way to write anything was to put one word after another till you say what you want to. Over the years I've found it works pretty well for telling someone something you don't want to tell them."

"OK, but how do I begin?"

"I'd start by saying 'Jonas, I love you but'. And take it from there."

"You make it sound so simple."

"Well, when I've looked back on times I've had to do it, I've found it was usually easier than I thought it'd be."

Johnny looked up when the bell at the door tinkled and saw Herschel come in, shaking rain off his hat. It was a blustery day, and even though it was only a short walk from the store, it felt good to be sitting at the front window of Mattie's, out of the wet.

Johnny and Lemuel greeted their friend as he pulled out a chair and joined them.

"Well, did you find out anything?" Johnny asked.

"Good morning to you too," said Herschel, grinning at Lemuel and acknowledging Mattie as she put a cup of coffee before him. "Yes, I've spotted them. They're staying in a shack out behind The Miner's Hole." When Johnny looked a question at him, he continued. "It's a saloon in the Barberry. Pretty seedy place. When they've got money, which they do occasionally, they sit in there and drink. Other than that, they seem to roam around town looking for anything where they can make a dollar or two, including knocking people on the head if it's what the job requires.

"The bartender there's a friend. He tells me they talk about you and your partners sometimes, about how they plan to get even with you. They've been warned a couple of times about you, but they seem to be stupid enough or drunk enough it doesn't seem to sink in."

"Are these the ones you were telling me about?" asked Lemuel.

Johnny nodded. "It bothers me they're still around. It's like having a rattlesnake under the front porch. You can't relax while it's there."

"What can you do about them?" asked Lemuel.

"I'm not sure, but I can't just leave it alone hoping they'll go away. I guess I'm going to have to force a showdown."

"I'd make sure you talk to Brad Crystal before you do anything," said Herschel. "Tell him the situation and ask him where you stand if you decide to push things with them."

"Crystal?" Lemuel asked.

"He's the new chief of police," replied Herschel. "From what I know he'll likely come down on your side, seeing as how you're a substantial citizen and all, and they're just a couple of no account Bald Knobbers." He said this last with a wry smile.

"Is it just the two of them now? When they came to the ranch there were three."

"From what my friend said, the other fellow left when the money ran out."

Lemuel looked at Johnny. "Any ideas?"

Johnny shook his head. He looked at Herschel. "You wouldn't be interested in backing me up if I decide to brace them, would you?"

His friend held up both hands. "I'm just a newspaperman these days. A peaceful soul as it were. Don't even carry a gun."

"That's alright, I'll drop Handy a note. Take him a day or two to get down here, but that'll give me time to think about how to go about it."

They sat quiet for a bit, probably all thinking about the same thing.

Herschel asked about Lemuel's leg, and they talked about that for a while, Johnny listening out of the corner of his mind.

"Johnny?"

Johnny started. He was so deep in thought he had lost the conversation. "I'm sorry, what did you say?"

"I asked if you'd ever thought about getting the wagon in shape and making a trip with it," said Lemuel. "Maybe sell a few books. Between here and Los Angeles there are a lot of small towns and growing cities."

"Tell you the truth, I haven't. Guess I've had too many things going on. Are you sure you're up for something like that?"

Lemuel grasped his right leg and re-positioned it with a grimace. "Probably not right now but say next spring I might be. I think working toward something like that would be good for me."

"I can see it would." Johnny leaned back in the chair. "With what I've got to deal with right now I'll have to put off thinking about it for a bit but," he grinned, "it does sound like it'd be fun, and we might make a few dollars while we're at it. Besides, we might get to see Wash. I miss talking to the old fellow."

Lemuel was trying to get used to walking without a cane, so on the way back to the store they stopped to sit on a bench in front of Fletcher's store to let him catch his breath.

"Any ideas about how you'll handle those two?" asked Lemuel.

"I'm thinking the best way is to run them out of town, which if I brace them to do it, will probably lead to a gunfight, so it's probably not the best way after all. First thing I'm going to talk to Chief Crystal. I think Herschel's right. I need to let him know the what and why so then I can figure out the how."

It was one of those times when living up to his promise of sharing everything with Annaliese was hard to do. He waited until she'd finished brushing her hair and was getting ready to turn out the light.

"Sit beside me," he said, patting the bed.

She looked at him suspiciously, hands on her hips. "What did you do?"

He laughed and pulled her down to sit beside him.

"I decided to do something today, and as much as I don't want to, I've got to tell you about it."

Her eyes widened suddenly. "Does this have to do with those men?"

He nodded. "I found out they're in town, living in the Barberry Coast, and a bartender friend of Herschel heard them talking when they've been drunk. They seemed set on having it out, so I've decided I need to beat them to the punch."

"What are you going to do?"

"Talk to the law to see where I stand, then brace them and tell them to leave or fight."

"Not by yourself!"

"No, Handy will be down in a couple of days and he'll have the ten-gauge with him. That thing tends to breed caution in a man. Of course, so does Handy, for that matter."

Chapter Sixty-Three

Annaliese was standing in the door to the office when Johnny and Handy came into the store, stopped at the counter to speak to Jason, then came toward her.

"I talked to the chief," he told her in a low voice. "He said he understands the situation, but he's just learning the job and he's not sure where he stands, or if I go ahead with it, where I stand either, for that matter, which makes me a little nervous."

She turned and led the way to the office where Lemuel was sitting by the window reading. He looked up, assessed the situation, and asked, "Do you want me to leave?"

"Not necessary. You know about it already," said Johnny. He perched on the edge of the desk and Annaliese could feel his nervous energy. "The chief says he can't act until something's happened; can't 'act before the fact' is how he put it. Then he has to go on the evidence.

"Sure ain't like Kansas. Back there if someone threatened you and you called them out, no one gave a damn. Figured they got what they deserved."

"You've got a problem," said Lemuel. "Sounds like you need to talk about it, so I'll just listen."

Annaliese was almost tearful. "Johnny, why can't you just leave it alone?" she said. "Maybe they'll just leave and solve the problem."

Johnny smiled ruefully. "It's a little complicated but I think I can explain. OK, these are bad men, and if I wait, they'll have the advantage in a gunfight. They'll decide when and where, even where to stand to give them the best chance. They could even lay out in the dark or shoot from ambush.

"They come from a part of the country where wrongs are avenged and they feel Handy and I, and most especially their brother Gray, have wronged them. I believe they'll get drunk enough one night to try, and I think I'd be a fool to wait for them to make their move.

"And another thing. I'm spread out too much. They could hurt me at the store or at the ranch. They could hurt people and things I love at any one of a hundred places or times. I believe they'd do so without thinking anything about it other than the satisfaction of getting even.

"I won't wait and live to regret it." He had been looking at Annaliese when he said this and could see the tears running down her face. He reached out and touched one. "I'm sorry. It's something I have to do."

He stood, drew her into his arms and kissed her and said, "But don't forget, Handy will be with me and he'll have the ten-gauge. We've done this kind of thing before and come out alright, and besides, I'll take Jinx along for luck."

"When will you do it?" she almost whispered to him.

"No sense in waiting. Herschel's supposed to meet me here in a few minutes. Handy's already here so we'll just go and get it over with."

"Is Herschel going with you?" asked Lemuel.

"Only as an observer. We talked it over and he'll go in the saloon right before we do and pick a spot where he can see what happens. He plans to be a credible witness if the chief needs one. Also, I think he just wants to watch."

"He'll probably write about it in his column," said Annaliese, a little bitterly.

"No, I asked him if he would and he said no. He said he might write about it in his diary though." He chuckled. "I think I'd like to read it if he does."

"Me too," said Handy. "He seems to be a good writer.

Jason stuck his head in the door. "Herschel's here."

Johnny stood and pulled Annaliese into a hug. When he tried to disengage, she clung to him until he finally had to gently pull away from her.

"I'll come by here when it's over," he said and was gone.

Herschel looked over the batwing doors into The Miner's Hole. The brothers were sitting at a table near the back door to the left of the bar. The plan was for him to go inside, and if he didn't come out right away, things were in place. He pushed one door open, surveyed the saloon and walked to a vacant table near the wall.

He was seated, drink on the table before him, when Johnny pushed his way through the doors with Handy close behind, shotgun in his hands, Jinx riding on his shoulder. They stopped for a moment to let their eyes adjust to the dimly lit interior, then Handy moved to a spot near the door where he could survey the room. Jinx dropped to the floor and sat, eyes wide, watching Johnny walk along the bar to the table where the brothers were sitting.

They looked up and he immediately drew the Colt and fired. A bottle on the table between the two men exploded, showering them with glass and whiskey. Clement pushed back from the table so fast his chair tipped over and he sprawled on the floor. Men around them scattered, and then things were silent. Zack wiped his hand across his face and looked openmouthed at Johnny standing with his gun cocked, leveled at a spot between the two of them.

After Clement had struggled to his feet and righted the chair, Johnny holstered the gun and said, "I wanted to make sure I had your attention. Now, I hear you two have been threatening to come after me. If that's the case, I thought I'd save you the trouble."

He stood in silence for a moment, then said, "I'm here to let you know after today, if I see you two anywhere in the city, I'm going to assume bad things and start shooting. The best way for you to avoid that is to pack and leave. Right now!"

He turned slightly and facing Clement said, "I hear you're the gunny in the family so you're first. If you want to, we can finish this now. Your choice."

The man looked at him. Johnny could tell he'd been drinking and knew it made him more dangerous. Clement looked at his brother, nodded his head toward the back door, and turned toward it. Johnny took a quick step to the right, and when Clement quickly turned, gun coming up, he saw Johnny wasn't where he thought, and suddenly the barrel of Johnny's gun was blossoming fire.

Clement's bullet tore a hole in the floor, and he felt a numbing blow to his chest which knocked him into the wall behind him where, leaving a trail of blood, he slid slowly down to a seat on the floor and died.

Johnny pivoted quickly to his right, but Zack Grayson was standing, empty hands raised to shoulder height. He turned his head to look at Handy standing by the door, shotgun trained on him and cocked, then at his brother sprawled on the floor in a widening pool of blood.

"Are you going to kill me too?" he asked, his voice husky with emotion.

"Your call," replied Johnny. "I didn't want to kill him, but he seemed rather insistent about it. You know, I busted the bottle so you fellows could see what you were up against, but he'd had a few drinks, and it warped his judgement. How do you feel about it?"

"I just want to get my gear and go."

"Don't let me hold you up; but remember, you'll probably lead a much longer, happier life if you stay out of San Francisco in the future."

He holstered the Colt and watched the man exit the back door. Then he turned to the bartender and said, "If the chief wants to talk to me, I'll be at The BookSeller." He stopped where Jinx had jumped onto the bar, allowed him to hop on his shoulder, and with Handy backing out behind him, left through the front door.

Rebecca had come to the store with Handy, and she, Sarah and Greta were sitting with Annaliese when the sharp sound of a gunshot split the air. The Miner's Hole was not far from The BookSeller and the crashing shot jarred Annaliese's every nerve.

She leapt to her feet with a cry and stood looking out at the front door. At the table Sarah, Rebecca and Greta looked at her, all frozen, mouths open, not knowing what to do. When another shot sounded, she sat down again, bowed her head, closed her eyes and laid her hands on the table before her and cried.

Greta reached out and laid a hand on Annaliese's. Rebecca was holding her mother's hand tightly, mouth open in horror, and they were all frozen in position when the front door opened and Johnny,

Handy and Herschel came in with Jinx riding on Johnny's shoulder.

Annaliese didn't stir until Johnny put his hand under her chin, lifted her head and kissed her on the forehead. She opened her eyes, gave a little cry, leapt to her feet, and threw herself into his arms. They stood for a long while, locked together, her crying into his chest. Across the table the same thing was happening except Rebecca's feet were off the floor.

Finally, she raised her head. "Please, don't ever do this to me again. I heard those shots, and I thought you were dead. I thought I lost you."

"I'll do my best to avoid it in the future."

"Promise?"

"Promise."

When Johnny and Handy came out of the back room, Herschel was waiting with the chief and another fellow with a star on his vest he didn't recognize. Herschel introduced him as the county sheriff. Johnny led them into the new addition, to the place where he and Herschel regularly sat and talked. When all were seated the chief said, "The witnesses said you gave him every chance, and he tried anyway. Sounds like he was trying to catch you out."

Johnny nodded. "He turned toward the door to leave and then turned back and drew. I shot him once and turned to the other one. He decided he didn't want any part of it. He went to get his things and leave town."

"What was the original kerfuffle about?" the sheriff asked.

"My partners and I were enforcing a no trespassing sign on the gate at our ranch, and they wanted to come in anyway. We were armed and ready in case they started something, so they left.

"Couple days later I ran into them in Sausalito. We were ready to have a go when Hern came up behind them with a shotgun and they changed their minds."

"Herschel said you went looking for them," said the sheriff. "You're supposed to leave that sort of thing to us."

"A friend heard them talking about revenge and I decided not to wait. I gave them a chance. One of them took it. He's leaving town as we speak." Johnny motioned to the Chief. "I talked to him, and he said he couldn't do anything until something happened. I felt it was the only way I could protect me and mine, so I decided to make it happen rather than wait until they got drunk enough to try.

He could have left town. He chose not to."

"The two lawmen looked at each other. "I heard tell they were brothers of your partner up at the ranch. That right?" asked the sheriff.

When Johnny nodded, the sheriff looked at the chief. "I don't have any problem with it," said the chief. "In fact, I'd likely have done the same thing. You threaten a man, you got to expect this kind of thing."

"I guess that's so," said the sheriff. "We'll let it go this time, but another time let me know before you go after someone."

After the two men left, Johnny and Herschel sat quiet for a while, Johnny staring at the floor, Herschel waiting until he was ready to talk.

Finally, Johnny looked up and said, "I want to read it if you write about it in your diary."

Herschel chuckled. "Done. I'll let you know when." He paused for a moment then said, "Talk to me about it."

Johnny leaned back in his chair, laced his fingers on top of his head and stared at the ceiling for a long moment.

"Pa told me there are certain men that will walk over you if you let them. The choice is to let them or fight. I chose to fight, and I didn't see much sense in waiting for them to open the ball. As soon as you told me about their conversations, I realized what I had to do, so I did it. From the way things turned out I think there will be consequences, but the consequences of not doing it were not things I could let happen."

"How did it feel to walk in there, knowing what could happen?"

"I could see they'd been drinking, and I pegged Clement from the first time I met him. I knew he'd try. When he turned to go out the door I somehow knew he was trying to set me up. It wasn't even close. Fortunately, his brother had better sense.

"When something like that is over, you feel a letdown. I just killed a man. It's not something I like doing. I can't forget it and I have a feeling my wife won't forget it either."

Johnny looked down at the floor again, and after a moment at Herschel. "Got enough for your diary?"

"I'd say."

"At least I won't have any trouble with the law over it. Thanks for standing up for me."

"There were plenty of witnesses."

"You seem to know these lawmen pretty well."

"It's a part of the job. I spend time at both of their offices several times a week looking for news. You know this'll be all over town in a day or two."

"I kind of figured it would. The other times I left town afterwards, so it wasn't a problem. I guess I'll have to get used to it."

Handy walked into the room. "We just got a note from Madame. She's put out a buffet for everyone at the mansion so we're going to be leaving shortly. Herschel, you're welcome if you want to come."

"Is that her invitation or yours?"

"It's mine but it's still good."

"Thanks, I think I will. I hear she sets a good table."

Chapter Sixty-Four

While Johnny and his friends tended to meet at Mattie's for morning coffee and conversation, the ladies all felt lunch at The City of Paris dining room was more their style. At one time or other in the course of a week, they would meet, accidentally or by appointment, afternoons in the atrium of the big department store to enjoy lunch and conversation and look around afterwards.

On the day after the gunfight, Annaliese, Maggie, and Jess were just being seated when Hank and Bev Rose stopped at the table to say hello.

They accepted the invitation to join the group and talked about classes and studying for a while, though they could all see Annaliese was distracted.

"So, have you been thinking about it later, after you finish?" asked Bev. "How much longer do you have?"

She had been speaking to Annaliese, whose mind was elsewhere.

"Annaliese? Are you still with us?" Bev waved her hand in front of her friend.

"What? Oh, I'm sorry. My mind was taking a walk. What were you saying?"

"I ask why you looked so blank this morning."

Annaliese looked a little dazed. "I'm sorry." She looked around the table. "For some reason I thought everyone knew about it."

"About what?"

"Johnny was in a gunfight yesterday. He killed a man."

Shocked silence. Everyone's mouth fell open. "What?" asked Maggie. "Why didn't you tell us?"

"I thought everyone knew. In Salt Lake if you sneezed the whole town knew about it before you wiped your nose."

"It's not quite the same around here," said Hank.

"What happened?" asked Maggie.

Annaliese took a deep breath, told the story while everyone sat silent, almost holding their breath.

"Didn't the police get involved?" asked Bev when she finished.

"Johnny went to see the chief beforehand and he said his hands were tied until something actually happened. Johnny's friend was watching as a witness and Handy was backing him up. He and Handy fought with guns before, in Carson City and then another time in a place called Julesburg in Colorado, but I thought that kind of thing was behind him. Apparently not."

Everyone was quiet for a moment, then Hank spoke. "Just looking at the rig he wears, I'd think people would leave him alone."

"From what Handy said, Johnny gave them a chance and one of them wouldn't take it. The other one left town shortly after the fight."

"Sounds like one of them had some sense, anyway," said Maggie.

"You said Johnny went after them?" asked Hank.

"He told me he couldn't let them decide how to handle the fight. That way they'd have all the advantages."

"There's sense in that," said Hank. "If they jumped him, it might have been bad. Sounds like he took the initiative. When you have to fight, that's supposed to be the way. Everything I've read about war agrees."

"Maybe, but when you're waiting at home and you hear a gunshot. . ." she shook her head. "It was terrible. I don't know if I'll ever get over it."

Johnny wondered if she'd ever get over it too.

He was sitting in the small grove of trees by the bay thinking. The night before he felt he might have been lying next to a block of ice instead of his warm and exciting wife. All day at the store they had not spoken five words to each other. This was the first time anything had come between them, and try as he might, he could find no answers to the myriad questions churning his mind.

Jinx had gone prowling in the little wood for a while but was now curled up in his lap helping him think. When he examined the chain of thoughts that led to his decision to confront the two men, he could see no weak links. He felt he did what had to be done to protect his wife, their friends and their futures. To stand aside and allow their lives to be torn apart by what these men could do, might do, was not in his nature.

He didn't believe she thought he had decided wrongly, so why was she upset? Would it be best to ignore her behavior, hope things would go back to normal, or was there something he could do to bring her back to the way things were?

At just past his twentieth birthday and a complete novice with women, the whole thing was a mystery to him. If he chose to act and was wrong, would it destroy what they had rather than repair the breach that was suddenly there? That it might frightened him.

Suddenly he jumped to his feet, totally forgetting about the cat, who, though rudely awakened, naturally landed on his feet. Johnny picked him up and put him on his shoulder. "You're not helping much," he muttered and began to walk along the small beach.

He stopped when confronted by a small stream and stood staring across the Golden Gate at Sausalito and the hills behind it. He knew his problem had a solution; it must have. She was too much a part of him for them not to work it out. His heart ached when he thought of her brushing her hair, of reaching out and touching that glorious red mane. He had no idea how she would react to his touch and wasn't sure if he wanted to find out.

He turned away from the water and picked his way to a path that led along the shore. In the distance he could see the lights of Fort Point and began to walk rapidly toward it. The breeze was freshening and becoming chill, but he didn't notice. He noticed nothing but his thoughts. A tree had fallen across the path and as he climbed over it he was suddenly struck with an idea.

He needed someone to talk to about it but the one he usually talked to wasn't talking to him. That didn't mean he couldn't talk to her. If she answered they could talk. If she didn't, well what was the old saying? 'Nothing ventured, nothing gained'. It seemed to be a reasonable approach. As he walked back along the path, he began to plan carefully what he would say.

By the time he got back to the store he had worked out a plan and discussed it with Jinx, so he was ready. He was smiling wryly as he climbed the stairs, realizing he felt more nervous about talking to her than he did walking into the saloon to face the Grayson brothers.

When he entered the bedroom, she was sitting at the mirror brushing her hair and his knees suddenly felt weak.

He sat on the bed and watched her in silence for a minute, trying to find a way to say what he wanted to say. His carefully conceived plan disappeared the moment he saw her, so in default, he finally blurted, "Are you mad at me?"

She continued brushing her hair in silence for a moment then said, "Yes, I am." She turned to face him. "But I really have no right to be."

That confused him. He shook his head. "I don't understand."

"I don't know if I do either," she said, and began to brush her hair again. "Johnny, when I heard that shot, I almost fainted. I was so frightened." She stopped and shook her head. "I just wanted to close my eyes and disappear, run and hide, because of the way I felt. When you came into the room and touched me afterward, I wanted to hit you and hug you at the same time. I felt such a feeling of relief, but at the same time, I was also furious at you, I guess because of how afraid I was. I felt like my life was over. For the first time I really understood what Greta felt when Jed was killed."

Though he was new at romance, he was smart enough to sit in silence. When he was sure she was through, he stood, held out his hand and pulled her into a long, close embrace.

"If it will make you feel better you can hit me."

She leaned back and looked at him. Suddenly she doubled her fist and hit him hard on the chest two, three times and then leaned her face against where she struck him.

After a minute they separated and sat down on the bed.

"Ouch," he said. She kissed it and it felt better.

They sat for a minute looking into each other's eyes, then she moved back to the mirror and began to brush her hair again.

"So, you remember how many strokes you were at when you quit?" he asked, feeling strangely awkward.

"Yes," she answered, and he sat and watched her hair glisten in the light when the brush moved through it.

He came up behind her and leaned to kiss her on the top of her head. "You still love me?"

"Of course I do, Johnny," she answered. "That's why I was so afraid. I thought for a few minutes you were gone, and I knew my life would never be the same. I'm not sure it ever will. Yes, I still love you, but I think that kind of fear stirs things up inside you and when they settle down again, you're different. I think we may find out how different over the next little while, but different somehow."

She was right. That night lovemaking was different. She was there, but somehow, she wasn't. It was different but he couldn't say how.

Still the next morning things seemed a little more normal when they stood by the bed and began their day with a long hug and a kiss. After he released her, she stood looking into his eyes with the beginnings of tears in her's, and he was confused again.

Chapter Sixty-Five

"Come sit and talk with me," said Lemuel to his daughter. They were in the office, and he was sitting in his chair by the window. Greta had just put the babies down for their nap, so she sat with him in her listening pose as though he was going to read to her, though he hadn't done it in a while.

Since she became a mother her life revolved around her children, like all mothers, and he was sort of a presence on the edges of it, not the center like he was after Mary died. He was gradually working toward return to health from the gunshot wounds and now was able to help with the children when her duties in the store took her away.

"I don't know if you remember," he began, "but the original plan when we came here was, we would get this store up and running and then take the wagon back on the road to sell books and open other stores, maybe down south. Of course, since then things have happened and things have changed, but now Johnny and I are beginning to talk about maybe trying it in the spring."

She was a little taken aback. "Are you thinking I could go with you? But I couldn't with the babies. Maybe when they are older, but not by next spring."

"No, I wasn't thinking that. I think you should plan to stay here and help with the store, and we can get someone to help with the children while you're working."

She was startled into silence and sat for a minute trying to come to grips with what she was hearing. All her life she had known he was there; knew he would help her whatever her need. She knew he was talking again but she didn't hear him.

"I've never been without you," she said, interrupting him. "Since Mama died we've always been together."

"And we always will be. I'm not talking about me being gone for that long. The route I'm thinking of would take us about six weeks, maybe two months. With the cars running, we could be back pretty quick if need be."

"Aren't you happy here, Papa?"

"It's not that so much as I love to travel in the wagon and sell books. Besides, if we can get another store set up, say in Los Angeles or San Diego, it would be there when Annaliese finishes school. She has said she would like to look down there for a place to start her practice. If she does, we could have a place to live in the winter and be up here in the summer.

"But I have another motive for doing this. I'm getting old and I've had a rough time lately. I've sat looking out the window at people passing by and thought a lot about life." He smiled to himself. "And death," he murmured. "There'll come a time when I'm not around. This might help you get used to the idea a little at a time.

"Of course, there are a lot of ifs in the idea, the first of which is my leg and how much I improve by next spring.

"I told you this because we've always shared everything. You are the center of my life but I'm no longer the center of yours, and rightly so. With the children and the store, you have your life, but you must admit, I really don't have much to do around here. Something like this would be good for me right now. I need something to work toward, and I feel this will help me get back to some sense of normal.

"I don't want you to get upset over this. I love you and since your mother died, we've lived our lives together. With Jed and later the children, you have a new life now and this is a way I can have one too."

Sun Li knocked on the door jam and asked, "Did you remember I have a doctor's appointment?"

Greta came back to the present with a jerk.

"I'm sorry, I did forget. I'll be out in a minute. Papa, can you watch them for a while?"

He waved her toward the door and said. "I'll be a good Grandpapa; go along."

When he was alone, he checked on the twins and resumed his seat by the window. He wondered why he did things like waving her to the door since he knew she couldn't see him do it. He guessed it was because she was so competent at negotiating her life, he sometimes forgot she couldn't see.

It really was extraordinary how she was able to move around the store again doing her job, helping people find books and re-shelving and stocking the shelves. It was the same with the children. She seemed completely sure handed with them and he had long since stopped worrying about their safety or welfare. She had recovered marvelously from the loss of Jed, and she seemed to be able to be happy again.

Johnny sometimes talked about 'throwing a bucket of water in someone's face' meaning to shock them into paying attention. He guessed that was what he just did to his daughter. He had to tell her, and at the same time help her understand the value of the idea. It would give him the kind of adventure he remembered fondly and help her adapt to something inevitable that lay in her future.

He knew it shocked her when he brought it up, but they would talk about it and he would help her understand. She would learn like she always did and be ready for the challenge of his absence come spring. Of course, he would have many challenges himself making it all happen.

Lemuel was stirring sugar into his tea at Mattie's the next morning when Johnny and Herschel walked in.

"Morning boys," he said. "Pull up a chair."

He eyed Johnny. "You look a little frazzled."

Johnny shook his head. "My wife is mad at me, and she doesn't even know why. How am I supposed to handle that?"

Herschel looked at him with a smile. "Can't help you. Never got married because I never understood women. Still don't"

"You're not much good, are you?" asked Johnny, rolling his eyes at Lemuel.

"I am a man who understands his limits," said Herschel, still smiling. "Is this about the fight?"

"I think so. But since she doesn't know, it's kind of hard for me to figure out how to deal with it." Johnny shook his head again. "Once before something happened to me and I remember telling Jinx it was like someone dropped a large stone into a pond. This gunfight seems like the same kind of thing. Could be wrong, but I think the ripples might go out a long way."

"Shucks," said Lemuel. "I thought since the fight was over, we could talk about the trip with the wagon."

"Sounds like more fun than trying to make bricks without straw," said Johnny. "Knowing you, you've already got everything all planned out, so talk to me."

"Well, I told Greta about it yesterday."

"How'd that go?"

"She was surprised, but I think I got her started with the idea. She'll come around. If it's to happen, we need to do some planning."

"What ideas have you got so far?"

"There are a lot of aspects to it and they all hinge on what I'll be able to do. So, I guess we first need to decide exactly what I'll have to be able to do to hold up my end of the bargain. This evening I'll sit down and think about what it would require of me and see if you're willing to do whatever I can't do."

"Here I thought you could just throw some books in the wagon and go," said Herschel.

"No, I can see what he means," said Johnny. "We've done it before, but there were a lot more of us then. We'll have to decide how to do it with just the two of us."

"It's a shame Wash isn't here. This kind of thing is right up his alley," said Lemuel.

"They might be back by then. I haven't heard much from him lately and been wondering what he's up to. He may be back for the winter, at least. I don't know why I say 'he' when it ought to be 'them'. They sure are an odd couple."

I'll say," said Herschel. "She is one fascinating woman."

"Odd or not, I miss them, and I'll be glad to see them."

"It would be nice to have him around. It wouldn't feel right to make plans without him to help," said Lemuel.

Chapter Sixty-Six

At that moment, their friend was sitting in a tree with the Sharps resting on a branch before him, watching the road which ran from Schweder's farm into San Diego. Below him and a few yards to one side, Woman was sitting on her horse screened from the road by a thick stand of trees around the oak he was sitting in, firmly holding the reins of his mule. If all went as planned, their target would be along in the next few minutes. Wash wasn't happy about what he was about to do but was determined to do it anyway.

He thought about it and he and Woman talked about it for the last week, and the result was he was waiting to ambush a man, probably cripple him for life, all the while trying to justify it to himself and never really succeeding. In spite of his ambivalence, the evidence pointed to the fact that if he didn't pull the trigger, then someone else would die because the man in the wagon had been paid to kill him, and that disturbed him.

Suddenly he smelled dust and heard the approach of the wagon. The tree he had chosen was in some woods at the crest of a small hill where the road ran between trees on either side for fifty yards or so. He leveled the Sharps, steadied it on the branch, cocked it and waited until the wagon came into sight.

All of a sudden, he sat back, un-cocked the rifle and watched the wagon pass beneath him. There were two farm hands riding on the gate and a woman sitting next to Schweder in front. He held his breath until they were out of sight, then climbed out of the tree.

Woman could see him but couldn't see the road, so she had no idea what happened. The absence of the booming Sharps being fired told her he hadn't done it. Though she was curious about why, she knew he would tell her when he was ready, which wasn't until they were sitting on the front porch at home and he had his pipe in hand.

"There were three people in the wagon with him. Two of them were hired hands I met when I was delivering at the farm. The woman on the seat with him must be his hired woman. There were two arm baskets in the bed, so he was probably taking her to do marketing or something."

She sat silent when he paused because she knew he'd say more.

"It gives me a few more days to think about it, I reckon. I don't think I've ever felt so two-ways about something." He chuckled and shook his head. "Of course, I've never before planned to shoot a man I've never spoken a word to before."

"Do you think you'll change your mind?"

He looked at her for a while, pulling at his lower lip. "No, I don't think so. I don't want to hash it over again, but I know he's the one. He deserves not a whit of the worry it's causing me, but it ain't him I worry about. It's me.

"I've never told you this, but when I first met Johnny and Handy, some men were chasing them. They were pretty bad men and there were more of them than there were of us. We figured to whittle down the odds and laid for them. I shot a man out of the saddle and he never knew what hit him. Never done that before. I've been in fights where I've killed, but they were trying to kill me. These men were looking for a way, so I didn't feel bad about it.

"If I do this, or when I do this, he'll never know who or why. Here he was, minding his business on an ordinary day, when someone ambushed him and shot him in the knee. He might figure it out. No attempt at robbery. Just a bullet and he'll hear us riding away. He'll probably put two and two together. But he'll never know who.

"And it's not like he doesn't deserve it. He's done it for years to others and not just the ones he's killed. He's destroyed other lives even if he didn't kill them. Hell, he did it to people I love.

"When I shot the fellow before, I knew they were coming for us, so I was defending myself. Here I'm judge, jury and executioner and this is retribution, a whole different proposition."

He sat rocking and smoking his pipe for a while and she waited for him to go on.

"You know one thing I love about you," he said after a while, "is the way you let me say what's on my mind, let me think about something and don't talk till I'm finished. Then you say something." He put his hand over hers. "And it's usually worth listening to. So what do you think about all this?"

"I think I've never heard of anything quite like it," she replied. "Everything you've found out points to him as a killer for hire, but you can't prove it. On top of that, who would you prove it to? I don't know much about such things, but I can't believe a law man from San Francisco would listen to you and come down here to arrest him. If you took him into the sheriff here would he believe you, your word against a prosperous local farmer? Not likely.

"And besides, it's not just retribution. You want to stop him from ever doing it again. If he gets a bullet through the knee and can't do it again, that's justice, but it also keeps him from doing to someone else what he did to Jed, and Greta and Lemuel and God knows how many others. That's plenty enough justification for me."

He stood, pulled her to her feet and wrapped her in a warm hug. "You always make me feel better about myself."

Wash was coming to love San Diego. He traveled around the city and into the surrounding countryside delivering supplies and equipment to orchards and farms. He spent time planting trees and shrubs along streets in the city and in the new city park. He especially loved to tend the plants in the nursery, then plant them somewhere he could watch them flourish.

San Diego had a long history with Spain and Mexico but had only been a part of the United States since the end of the Mexican War in 1848. At statehood, the city was a village of less than five hundred people, mostly Mexican, and as late as the end of the Civil War, had a population of less than a thousand, by that time mostly whites with a few Mexican and Indians. Then came the railroads.

A truism in the west was when the railroads came, things changed and it was especially true in California. In the late 1880's after a number of false starts and several ownership battles between the Southern Pacific and the Atchison, Topeka and the Santa Fe, a local connection to a transcontinental line brought a real estate boom to San Diego. Between the influx of railroad labor and the efforts of several wealthy promoters, land values began a spectacular rise and suddenly people were flocking to the area.

By 1888, almost 17,000 people lived in and around an area known as New Town and developers began to build a large hotel on a spit of land that curved out around San Diego Bay in what became the town of Coronado.

About the same time the railroads developed refrigerated cars which allowed farmers growing the newly created Navel oranges to begin shipping them all over the country to a populace who bought them obsessively. This craving brought newfound wealth to the local orchard men and many of them used it to expand and improve their farms.

The grounds around the new Hotel Del Coronado were extensive and Wash's boss, Kate Sessions, had been selected to landscape the grounds. This took Wash out to the building site on a regular basis and the morning after the aborted plan, he was delivering a load of trees to the hotel building site when he recognized one of the workers as someone he had met at Schweder's farm.

"You're Manuel, aren't you?" he said to the fellow as they were unloading trees along a row of holes dug to receive them.

"Si," he replied. "I worked at Schweder's Farm until last week. I remember we talked out there." Wash helped him lower one of the trees into its hole. "I took this job because I'm getting married and wanted to live in town with my wife."

"Do you like it better?" asked Wash.

"It's a job," Manuel shrugged his shoulders and continued. "The pay's about the same but I'm closer to my family and the senorita soon to become my senora." He grinned. "I do miss the oranges. We could eat all we wanted, and I liked them very much."

He took the shovel and began to fill in the hole around the tree. Wash picked up a shovel and helped him.

When they had finished and were leaning on the shovels, Manuel said. "The capataz there is not such a good man, and when the boss goes away, he makes us work much harder. This is a much easier job"

"He's going away again?" Wash was suddenly very alert.

"He is shooting the rifle again and the senora told me he is preparing to leave."

"Did she say when?" asked Wash. When Manuel looked a question at him, he hurriedly went on. "My boss will want to know whether or not to make deliveries out there if he's not around."

His friend shrugged again. "Quien sabe? Who knows? I do not."

On the way back to the nursery Wash was so distracted he missed a turn and found himself on a dead-end street. He sat for a moment staring out at the bay, finally turned around and within a couple of minutes was tying the horse up in the nursery yard.

When he came into the store Woman was finishing up with a customer, so he waited, and when she was alone said, "I found out he's got another job and is leaving soon."

"Schweder?" she asked.

He nodded. "The train leaves early so we'll have to be at the tree early in the morning for the next few days until he leaves. It's that or someone else dies."

Normally, Gerhard Schweder began his day standing on the front porch, stretching prodigiously, and gazing out over his beloved orange and lemon trees. This morning, however, was different. First he carefully disassembled the rifle, wrapped all three pieces in a slightly oiled cloth, placed it on the bottom of a large carpet bag and covered it with a towel. Then he packed a few clothes and sundries on top of it and carried the bag downstairs to where the cook was putting his breakfast on the table.

He ate quickly, and without a word of goodbye, took a wide brimmed straw hat and old ragged coat from a stand by the door, and walked out onto the porch where one of the farm hands was waiting for him by the front steps in a buckboard wagon. When he was settled in the seat beside the driver, he nodded, the driver chirped to a pair of horses, and they headed for the gate leading to the road to San Diego.

About a mile farther on they came to a grove of trees atop a hill. He had just turned on the seat to lay his coat over his bag in the back when a rifle boomed from somewhere in the trees. The bullet smashed into his left knee, exited, and tore the cap from his right knee. He grasped at the driver, missed, fell backward onto the road and lay bleeding in the dust while the driver fought to control the startled horses.

When the hired man reached him, he was unconscious and the blood from the wounds pooled under his legs had begun to run away to a small ditch beside the road. Unable to lift him and frantic to get help, he tried to staunch the bleeding by wrapping each of his legs tightly with some clothes taken from the carpet bag and moved him off the road. Then he turned the wagon, whipped up the horses and raced back to the farm to get some help. As he was tightening the bandages over the wounded legs he thought he heard, in the distance, the sound of horses galloping away.

Chapter Sixty-Seven

A nice breeze lifted the curtains in his bedroom, so the half-moon gave just enough light for her to see him lying naked beside her, eyes closed, resting. The breeze felt good on her overheated skin and she closed her eyes and drifted off on a gentle wave of satisfaction. When she opened them, he was leaning on his elbow looking at her. In the dim light she could just see a smile on his lips. She reached up and touched them and his mouth widened into a grin.

"Hello there Sarah Travers. Did you know I want you in my bed forever?" he asked.

"Hmm," she answered. "Sounds like an illicit proposition."

"Of course, there are other reasons, but you know them all cause I've told you many times before." He kissed her on the end of her nose, then ran his tongue over it. "What do you say? Want to find a preacher this week?"

She looked at him so long he finally asked, "Did I say something wrong?"

"No, of course not," she answered, shaking her head. "I've wanted to tell you something for a while but can't seem to find the right time, so I'm going to jump right in. But first I want you to promise to listen to what I say, and we can talk after."

There was enough light for her to see he looked taken aback.

"Promise?" she asked.

"Sure," he said. He wiggled his way into a cross-legged position and settled down to listen.

"I love you and I know you love me. I always want you in my life, but I don't want to get married."

When he started to speak, she held up her finger. He settled back on the bed, and she went on.

"The only person I care about," she smiled at him, "other than you that is, is Rebecca. She loves me, and if she doesn't care I'm lying in bed with you, naked and unmarried, then I don't care what anyone else thinks.

"I can't imagine a more pleasant life than the one I have now. Living at the mansion with Madame is wonderful. It's comfortable and elegant and has every convenience I could imagine. There's room for my family when they're in town and the people there cater to my every whim. Not only that but she pays all the bills and wouldn't take money if I offered it to her.

"Every morning Carlotta brings me coffee when I ring, and I sit with Madame and talk and read the paper. Madame and I can sit there and talk or not talk as long as we damn well please because we don't have anything we have to do unless we want to.

"Jose in the stable will take me anywhere I want to go anytime, day or night, and would feel insulted if I tried to pay him." She paused. "And I also have this considerate, caring lover who makes me feel wonderful about being a woman whenever he's around." She leaned over and kissed him.

"So, what you're saying, in a most delightful manner, I might add," he said, grinning at her, "is you'd rather be my mistress than my wife."

"Well, I wouldn't have put it quite like that, but yes I guess I am."

"So, he has no objection?" asked Madame the next morning.

"No objection? Ha, I thought he was going to die laughing. He finally stopped and said it was the nicest thing any woman ever said to him and then started laughing again."

"Well, that scoundrel. So, he didn't really want to make an honest woman of you, after all. He thought you'd want to get married and that's why he asked."

"Pretty much."

"Seems to me I told you looking back on it, it wouldn't be as bad as you expected."

"That's for sure. I grabbed him and we started wrestling and next thing you know we were at it again. He is fun to have around and I'm glad I finally told him. The whole thing has been like a pebble in my shoe, and I am so glad to have it behind me."

"So, I guess this means you'll be hanging around awhile yet?" asked Madame.

"As long as you'll put up with me. Oh, and he said even though we're not getting married he still wants to go on a honeymoon. He likes honeymoons and says he's heard so much about Hawaii, he'd like for us to go for a month or so next spring. Do you know anything about Hawaii?"

"Oh yes, a couple of my sailors have talked about it. Sounds like absolute paradise. Would you wear a wedding ring? Just for the trip I mean."

Sarah shrugged, "These days I don't know if anyone cares. I don't. Next time I go to the bookstore I'll see if they have any books about Hawaii and if not, I'll get Sun Li to order one for me."

"Sun Li? Why not Johnny or Annaliese?"

"She and Jason pretty much run The BookSeller with Greta now. Annaliese is busy with school and Johnny is up at the ranch a lot. Lemuel still sits and talks to people about books every other Thursday, although he's talking about him and Johnny taking the wagon back on the road come spring, if he's able that is."

"They repaid me the money I put into the store so I'm just their landlord now, and a regular customer, of course. That place sure did change things when they came to town. It's funny, it seems to draw good people to it. Almost like it's a magnet or something."

She reached out and touched Sarah's hand. "I'm glad you finally got everything straightened out with Jonas. I like having you around and if you need any advice about the mistress thing, I can help. I've some experience with that sort of thing."

They grinned at each other.

Hearing Wendy in the kitchen awoke Rebecca. Early morning sunlight was coming in through the curtains and it looked like it was going to be a nice day. Across the room she could see Bobby sleeping with his butt in the air and his thumb in his mouth and she smiled.

Since there was a cook and housekeeper, now she could sleep late if she chose and Wendy took care of Bobby when he needed anything. Handy was usually up and gone before she was stirring these days, though some mornings she got up to have breakfast with him. This morning, she sat up to kiss him goodbye, stretched and decided it was the kind of day when forty winks seemed like a good idea.

Later, she just seated herself at the kitchen table when she saw Maxine coming to the screen door.

"Come on in," she said and reached for another cup. Since she married Gray, Maxine was a regular part of her life, usually coming for coffee when Gray came in to work. Besides just gabbing over coffee, they loved to talk about what they planned to do with their houses and gardens, about their husbands and Bobby, and what Rebecca had done while she was in town the previous week.

Sometimes they got so involved in their tete a tete they were still going when the men came in for lunch. Wendy poured her coffee and Maxine joined Rebecca at the kitchen table.

"Is Johnny coming up today?" she asked.

"Tomorrow, I think," replied Rebecca.

"Gray said he saw him in town yesterday and he said he might be here today. Something about needing to get away from the store for a while."

"Good. The pedal on my sewing machine needs fixing. He's really good at that kind of thing and Handy's usually too busy."

Maxine sat quiet for a minute, glancing through a paper Gray brought home from town. She finally folded it and placed it neatly on the table then she took a deep breath and said, "I think I might be pregnant."

Rebecca looked at her, mouth open. "Have you told Gray?"

"Not yet, but he can't be surprised the way he's been dragging me into the bedroom every chance he gets since we got married."

"Ha," said Rebecca. "This might slow him down a bit. It did Handy. He treated me like a china vase for a while after I told him. Well congratulations."

"I hear we finally have a doctor in Sausalito, so I guess I better stop and see him next time I'm in town."

"If I were you, I wouldn't wait. That's the kind of thing you don't wait for."

She grinned at her friend. "Any idea how Gray feels about it? Have you talked about it? I think I could have knocked Handy over with a feather when I told him. He just stood there with his mouth open for the longest time."

She was looking at Maxine, and instead of the smile she expected she could see something else, fear?

"Are you afraid?"

Maxine's answer was a tight-lipped nod, and tears welled up in her soft brown eyes. Rebecca looked at her in astonishment that quickly turned to compassion, and she pulled her friend into an embrace and held her tightly while she cried.

When the crying finally stopped, she led Maxine to a couch in the parlor and sat next to her.

"My mother died when my sister was born and I was there, in the next room. I was six years old. I'll never forget the screams, and the woman came out of the room with blood on her hands and all over her clothes." She buried her face in her hands and moaned as though there were more tears inside, but it hurt too much to let them out. "I want to have children, be a proper wife and mother, and I love Gray so much, but I'm afraid whenever I remember those screams."

Wendy came into the room and Rebecca sent her for a washcloth and they watched Maxine dry her eyes.

She let out a shaky breath. "I'm OK now but I don't want Gray to see me like this," she said. "I think I need to lie down for a few minutes."

Rebecca closed the bedroom door and retreated to the kitchen. When Bobby was born, she was in labor for several hours, and she remembered it vividly; but she made it through, and looked forward to more children, although maybe not necessarily to having them. Childbirth in the nineteenth century west could be a painful and debilitating ordeal for some women, and she could understand Maxine's reaction to the memories of her childhood and the loss of her mother.

Of course, mothers loved their children, as they should, but at the same time the dangers involved in birthing a child were evident in the high percentage of widowers in the population. There were men in the nineteenth century west who lost as many as three or four wives to the perils of childbirth. The frightening nature of the whole process made for generally mixed reactions in people who were made aware of impending motherhood, including and especially new fathers.

Rebecca was putting out plates of bread, meat and cheese for lunch when Maxine came into the kitchen a couple of hours later.

"Feeling better? "asked Rebecca. When Maxine nodded, she gestured to a chair and said, "First thing, just forget about the doctor in Sausalito. I'll get you an appointment with Dr. Brown. She delivered Bobby and the twins, and she's been delivering babies for ten years. She's one of Annaliese's teachers at the medical school and she's really nice. You'll love her."

"I've never been to a doctor before," said Maxine. "A doctor was with my mother when she died, and ever after Pa wouldn't have one in the house."

"Well, take my word for it, you'll like Dr. Brown."

By the time the men came in for lunch Maxine's eyes were clear again and she was her usual chipper self.

Chapter Sixty-Eight

They were all sitting on the porch talking after lunch when Johnny rode up with Jinx on the saddle in front of him.

"Can I get you something?" Wendy said when he walked up on the porch.

"Just coffee," he answered. I stopped at the new restaurant in Sausalito and had a bite." Jinx followed Wendy inside knowing she'd give him a treat.

Johnny took a seat, took a sip and said, "I thought I'd come up a day early this week. I still can't figure out what's going on with Annaliese. When I'm by myself and doing something around here I can usually relax and think better than when I'm surrounded by everyone at the store."

"There are some nice places around here to sit and solve problems," said Handy.

"It's funny, the best place for me to think is when I'm at the forge working," said Johnny.

Rebecca snorted. "I think that'd be the last place I'd go. All the heat and dust and noise. I'd go out on Cat's Paw and sit looking at the bay."

"Is that what you've decided to call it? asked Johnny. "How come?"

"Maxine thinks the ridge that runs out toward the bay looks like a cat's paw, so she picked it." replied Gray.

"So, she runs the show out there?" said Johnny with a grin.

"If I know what's good for me," replied Gray. He kissed his wife and smiled at her.

His wife was smiling too. "Why the forge?" she asked Johnny. "That'd be the last place I'd pick, too."

"It reminds me of Pa and when we'd work together at the forge back home. Sometimes we'd talk about things we'd read the night before. Sometimes we'd talk about guns and what we were working on, and sometimes we wouldn't talk at all. For hours. Just working together. It was good time." He was quiet for a moment. "Time to time I still talk to him out there and he still helps me work on knots I can't unravel."

Gray left to do something in the barn and the girls went inside leaving Handy and Johnny rocking on the porch.

"She's still upset about something, and you don't know what it is?" asked Handy.

"Oh, she's told me why she was mad at me but that doesn't tell me how to get past it; what to do to make it like it was before."

"Rebecca was scared and fussed a bit, but she hasn't said anymore about it since we got home,"

They sat quiet for a minute then Handy said, "Tell me what she said to you." When Johnny did, he sat thinking for a long minute.

"It sounds like she was terrified, especially when she heard the shots." When Johnny nodded, he continued. "That kind of fear can leave a mark on a person's mind and in their heart. My brother read me a story when I was a kid, and I've always remembered it. A man was so afraid he felt his knees turn to jelly and they wouldn't hold him up. It sounds like if she'd have been standing, she'd have fallen over."

"Yeh, that's pretty much what she told me. She made me promise never to do it again. I promised but how do you know what's going to happen? I didn't want it but that didn't keep it from happening. Things were done that pushed me into a corner and I didn't feel I had a choice. When you wear a gun things happen sometimes."

Handy sat quiet for a while, thinking, and Johnny had enough sense to sit and wait.

"Johnny, have you ever thought about not wearing the gun anymore?"

For two hours while he was working at the forge that afternoon the words 'not wearing your gun anymore?' kept running through his mind. To him getting dressed in the morning meant slinging the gun belt around his waist and settling the Colt into place on his hip. Except when he was in the hospital in Salt Lake City, he had worn the gun almost every waking minute since he left Junction City, Kansas over three years before. There were times it saved his life. Like he told Hank Rose, it felt like a talisman, and he knew he would feel vulnerable without it, not to mention decidedly undressed.

But was keeping it on his hip worth the loss of something he valued? Something that made him happy and he was desperate not to lose? Especially now when he was living in a city where there were laws and people to enforce them, did he really need it? Would taking it off solve his problem? Was it the balm that would heal what seemed to be an open wound between him and the woman he loved?

Although there was no guarantee he thought it was worth a try. It might not be *the* answer, but it could be *an* answer, one which might lead him to the answer he needed.

Annaliese was carrying her books and study materials downstairs when she saw Tudie and Maggie talking to Greta at the front counter.

"Hi," she called. "Think we can be ready by tomorrow?"

"Did you read it all?" asked Maggie. "I couldn't make heads or tails of some of it."

There was an exam the next day and the reading assignment was almost prohibitively long and involved.

"Maybe we can figure it out if we put our heads together," said Trudie.

"That's what a study group does," said Maggie. "We put our heads together and solve any problem. Forward into the breach, we band of sisters, and we will triumph."

Annaliese looked at her, jaw slack. "Where in the world do you come up with this stuff?"

"My father used to read Shakespeare to us as bedtime stories. I think that's from Henry the Fifth or something. One of those English kings anyway. It's the way they talked in those days." Maggie answered, grinning.

Jess had come in while they were talking. "Maggie, I don't

think I'd have made it through this year without you. You always make me laugh when things are darkest, like now with this exam tomorrow," she said.

Maggie put her arm around the shorter girl. "That's what study partners are for, isn't it? I'm on the bucking up brigade" she said.

"Where did you hear that?" asked Annaliese.

"I think I read it somewhere."

Annaliese led them into the study room, put her books down and went to the office to get another chair. She walked into the room, stopped, and stared. Hanging on the hat tree by the window was Johnny's gun belt. She managed to get to the chair before she collapsed, and suddenly tears were running down her cheeks and she began sobbing.

She was suddenly surrounded by her study mates. "What happened? Are you alright?"

For a moment she couldn't answer and finally she pointed at the holstered pistol. "That," she said.

They looked at it puzzled. "It's a gun," said Ginger. "It's Johnny's, isn't it? He always wears it."

"Yes, it's Johnny's and you wouldn't understand. I'm not sure I do either." She shook her head as though to clear it. "But we've got some studying to do so we better get started," and she led the way back to the study room.

That night she was brushing her hair when Johnny came in in a bathrobe, hair tousled and wet from the shower.

"We got to figure out a way to get more hot water in the shower." He was drying his hair, and she watched till he was through.

"Why did you take off your gun?"

He smiled at her. "Usually, I'd be like Wash and sit thinking about that one for a while, but I haven't thought of much else for the last few days so I'm ready to talk about it.

"I was talking to Handy about us and what it's been like lately, and I said, 'when you carry a gun such things happen sometimes.'" He let that hang in the air for a moment.

"And what did he say?" she asked.

"He said, 'Johnny, have you ever thought about not wearing your gun?'"

They looked at each other across a silence.

"Remind me to give him a kiss the next time I see him," she said, totally straight faced.

"I don't think I'd have done it right then, but I've had time to think about it, and I think it's time not only because of you but because of something else.

"It reminds me of Pa and my home, and for three years, since he died, it's been on my hip, and there were times when I needed it. I told Hank Rose it was like a talisman, something that had my luck in it. Maybe I feel it was like Pa, there to protect me when I need it. Whatever it is, I believe as long as I wear the gun, you'll be afraid of something like this happening again. I don't want you to have to feel like that ever again. So, it's hanging in the office, and I'd like a kiss."

She gave him a good one, fierce and lasting. "Thank you, Johnny, thank you, thank you." she said when they could breathe again. "You know if you didn't have Handy and Wash around you'd have a lot more problems with life."

"I also feel it's time for the boy in me to put away the things from boyhood. You've helped me become a man, a good one I hope, and I don't need to wear a gun to prove it."

She kissed him again and whispered, "take me to bed."

"Yes ma'am. Whatever you say ma'am!" He opened her robe. "My O' my, ain't you something."

"Will you hurry up," she said impatiently and let the robe drop to the floor.

There was a full moon that night and they really enjoyed it.

When he walked into the office the next morning Lemuel was waiting for him in his chair by the window.

"Pull up a chair, let's talk a bit."

Johnny did so, and when he was settled in Lemuel asked. "Why are you so chipper this morning?"

"I pulled a rabbit out of a hat last night but if I tell you anymore, my wife will leave me."

Lemuel laughed and held up his hands. "Mums the word. I talked to one of the doctors at the medical school yesterday. He's going to set me up with a program to help me get my strength back and get me back on my feet. He called it rehabilitation. He checked me out and feels I might just be ready for the trip next spring if I work at it."

"When do you start?"

"Right away. He wants me to come in ready to work the day after tomorrow. He and another fellow will see me three times a week for an hour each time at first and then see how it goes from there."

Johnny could see the excitement bubbling out of him. "Sounds like hard work. Are you up for it?"

"You bet I am."

"So, you're serious about taking a trip next spring?" asked Johnny. When Lemuel nodded, he continued. "Let's put together a list of what stock we want to take, and we can start getting it together. We'll need to look over the wagon and see what it needs, too."

"Why don't I go through it and make a list and then we can check off what we do," said Lemuel who was almost jumping out of his seat. "I may need you to stand by when I get in and out of the wagon for a while, but once I'm in I'll be alright. We'll need to keep records and such, but I'll take care of that."

Johnny laughed at the energy bursting out of him. "You look like you want to leave tomorrow."

"You betcha."

Chapter Sixty-Nine

The store was quiet at this time of the morning. Johnny was in the back room checking a new shipment when the back door opened and Wash came in, all teeth showing when he saw Johnny.

"Wash," Johnny exclaimed. "What are you doing here?"

"I was in the neighborhood, so I thought I'd stop by," said Wash, still grinning. As much as he was coming to love San Diego, the store felt like home.

"Somehow I knew I'd find you with a book in your hand," said Wash. "Is Lemuel in his room?"

Johnny nodded and started to speak but Wash put his finger to his lips. They stood in the doorway and watched Lemuel putting his room in order so he could begin his day. The back door opened behind them and Lemuel looked up and saw Wash in the doorway.

"Well look who's here," he exclaimed. He picked up his cane and began to limp across the room, but Wash met him halfway and they embraced and shook hands. "When did you get in town?"

"Last night. We came in on the cars late. I went to bed about midnight, and the ladies were still talking, so Woman's sleeping in, but you know me. Can't sleep when the sun's up."

Jason and Sun Li came in while they were talking, and after greeting Wash, began the routine to open the store.

"We got nothing to do that can't wait," said Johnny. "Let's go to Mattie's and have breakfast."

"Where's Annaliese and Greta?" asked Wash.

"Greta's upstairs with the children and I think I heard Annaliese leave earlier," replied Lemuel.

"She works in the lab with the specimens for Dr. Rose, her anatomy instructor," said Johnny, "so she's gone early a couple of times a week now."

The walk to Mattie's gave Wash a chance to gage how much Lemuel's gait had improved, and when they were seated, coffee before them, he said "You sure are in better shape than the last time I saw you. When I left here, I wasn't sure I'd see you again."

Lemuel grinned ruefully. "Truth be told, I wasn't either. But some things happened, and I got myself back together. The main thing was having something to work toward. This trip has given me back my life, given me something to be excited about, might even say given me a reason to live."

"You sure do look good, and I'm amazed at how well you get around with the cane."

"It's the doctors and the work they've got me doing. Every week I go to them they give me things to do that are supposed to get my muscles back to doing things instead of wasting away."

Johnny interrupted. "They aren't the ones who've done the work. None of it would have made any difference if you hadn't done the work."

It was a little hard to eat because they wanted to talk, but they managed. After, they moved to the porch and Wash and Lemuel, pipes in hand, talked about the trip.

"When are you planning on leaving?" asked Wash.

"We were thinking around April first," said Lemuel. "Everything's pretty much ready to go, so it's waiting on the weather."

"And my wife," said Johnny.

Wash looked surprised. "She's not going, is she?"

"No, but she graduates in June, and next week we're going to take the cars down to Los Angeles. She's supposed to talk to several people about joining a practice down there and she also is trying to get into a research position at the university. We're going to stay a week and when we get back we can make the final decision about when to go."

"So, it will be about a month?"

"I'd say," said Johnny, "although if it was up to him," he nodded at Lemuel, "we'd leave tomorrow."

"Well, I may go with you on the trip," said Wash. "We told our boss down there we'd be back in late spring. How long do you figure to be on the road?

"I'd say a month to six weeks," said Lemuel. "Of course, we'd probably be somewhere you could catch the cars if you needed to get back earlier.

"No need to tell you how glad we'll be to have you along. You reckon Woman will come along?"

"Don't know, she may stay here and catch the cars. We haven't talked much about it," said Wash.

"That doesn't surprise me since neither of you talk much," said Lemuel with a grin.

"She and Madame and Sarah were back at it this morning and I'll bet they'll still be talking when I get there," said Wash.

And they were. When Wash walked into the dressing room they were sitting around the bay window, drinking coffee, looking out at the city and talking.

"Won't you join us?" asked Madame.

"Don't think I will," answered Wash. "I want to go to the cottage and settle in."

"I'll go with you," said Woman jumping to her feet. "We just dropped everything last night and fell in bed."

"Well, welcome back," said Madame. "Same as always, come and go as you please."

"Have you decided whether to tell him?" She was looking at him. They were at the kitchen table in the cottage drinking coffee.

He looked at her in silence for a moment then slowly shook his head.

"Does that mean you aren't going to, or you haven't decided."

"Haven't decided," he said. "I can't see any reason to tell him except he has a right to know. But the question is what will he do if I tell him? I can't believe he'd go down there and shoot the man, but how will it affect him? It's over and I'm not sure it's needful to dig it up again."

"You want me to tell you what I think?" she asked.

He grinned at her. "As if I could stop you."

"I think if you don't tell him, you'll have it on your mind whenever you're around him. I think it means, deep down inside, you want to tell him."

"Ok, let's say I agree with you. What will he do if I tell him?"

"That's something you won't know until you do, but I think it'll bother you the rest of your life if you don't."

They sat in silence for a while drinking coffee, her looking at him, and him staring out the front window. Then he stood up, looked at her and said, "Well, I think you might be right, and I guess now is as good a time as any."

"I noticed you're not wearing your gun anymore. How come?" Wash was sitting in the back room at the store and Johnny was sitting across the table.

"Long story," replied Johnny. "Tell you what, let's take a walk like we used to. Down to the bay. This seems like it might be one of those 'down to the bay' kind of things."

By the time they were seated on the logs looking out at Alcatraz, Angel Island and Sausalito in the distance, Johnny had finished the story. "So, what do you think?"

Wash looked at him steadily for a moment. "How do you feel about it?"

Johnny grinned at him. "Don't you hate it when someone answers a question with a question?"

"I guess I do, but there's still the question. How do you feel about taking the Colt off?"

"I've thought about it a lot. The main thing is the way Annaliese feels about it. Without her I'm nothing. With her I'm everything. If it will make her happy, why not?"

"You haven't answered my question."

Johnny pressed his fingers to his temples and rubbed, eyes downcast. "When I think about it, sometimes I feel an empty feeling inside, in my gut, I mean." He looked up sharply at Wash. "You knew that didn't you?"

Wash looked at him steadily but didn't answer.

Johnny looked down again. "It was as much a part of me as my hand. When I walk in the office and see it hanging there, I feel it here." He gestured to his stomach.

He stood up suddenly, restless, wanting to walk and think.

Instead, he looked out across the bay and said to his friend, "Once I read a story about a knight in medieval times who was given a medal to wear around his neck to give him courage. He called it his fortune, and he always wore it. But he lost it, and for a long time after he was afraid.

"I told Hank Rose the Colt was like a talisman to me and now I've taken it off…" His voice trailed off and he looked at Wash. "I think what I feel is fear."

They sat quiet for a while, listening to the waves lapping on the beach.

"That kind of feeling can come from lots of things. Excitement, anger, sorrow," said Wash. "If memory serves me, you've killed three men with that gun, and each time you were defending yourself. Each time it was justified. That ever bother you?"

"No, it doesn't, never really has. I did what I had to do to stay alive or protect loved ones from harm."

"I noticed Handy hasn't worn a gun since he got here. Do you know anyone, besides lawmen, who go armed in the city?"

Johnny shook his head. "I guess maybe I carry it because I felt comfortable and safe with it on. What you're saying is while I'm in the city I can probably learn to feel comfortable without it."

"When we were in the wilderness without law, it was necessary. Here, not so much. I'd say you'll get accustomed to it not being there, especially since it seems to make Annaliese happy. Life's like that, sometimes we trade one thing for another and move on. I'd say you did right.

"Now, there's something I want to tell you. Hear me out and then we'll talk.

"I found Gerhard Schweder." He paused. "He's a farmer outside San Diego. I'm as sure as I can be that he's the one who shot Jed. I thought about it a lot and since I couldn't prove it to the law, I decided to do something to keep him from killing anyone else. So, he won't be plying his trade in the future."

"You killed him?"

"No. I crippled him. A Sharp's slug through his knees put him in a wheelchair. He'll probably never walk again and I'm pretty sure he'll never shoot someone from ambush again."

Johnny was quiet for a minute, staring out over the bay. "I'd have killed him."

"Maybe you would have. I thought about it but finally decided assassination wasn't something I wanted to carry around with me the rest of my life. I don't want you to either. It's over and hating him won't undo what he did. And that snake has his fangs pulled. Don't let it become a part of your life.

"If y'all move down there you may come across him. He's got a ways to go to get out of bed but if he lives, he'll probably still be a farmer down there. I'd like it if you just cancel that debt, go on with your life and let him go on with his, what's left of it."

"You talk as if you know him."

"I deliver supplies to his orchard. The people who work there talk to me. I've seen him sitting on his porch. He's one of our best customers at the store."

"Hmm," said Johnny. "If we do get down that way, I may look him up."

"Just don't mention my name. Shooting people in the knee is frowned upon thereabouts."

Chapter Seventy

Johnny put the two carpet bags on the seat facing him and settled in next to his wife. She was watching the countryside go by, but he could tell her mind was elsewhere.

"What're you thinking about?" he asked, "as if I didn't know."

She smiled at him. "About tomorrow and talking to Dr. Follensbee."

"That wasn't hard to figure. Tell me about her."

"She's a friend and former colleague of Dr. Brown. She was in the class with Dr. Wanzer and Dr. Brown at the medical school. She got disgusted with the way she was treated and left. She went back east, stayed with some family while she went to the University of Michigan for a while and then to somewhere in Pennsylvania to get her MD.

"She came back here after and went into practice, but the climate caused her health problems, so she moved to Los Angeles several years ago.

"She was one of the founders of the Children's Hospital here and was involved in starting the nursing school at Toland. She was the first woman doctor down there, and when they started a medical school, she joined the faculty and teaches pediatrics. Dr. Brown told me she is the first woman faculty member to teach at a medical school in California."

"So, what do you reckon you'll talk about?"

"She knows all the doctors in the area so she might know someone who's looking for a new doctor who would take me on to teach me what I need to know to practice on my own. Of course, working with the Doctor all those years helped me learn a lot of the business side of it and how to order supplies and care for equipment and things like that, so I won't be a burden to someone if they take me on."

"Are you still set on general practice?"

"I'll say yes for right now but let's see what happens over the next few days."

"So, tomorrow you'll be finding out about how you'll begin your life as a doctor, and where."

She nodded. "For the last three months I've written pages of questions about the things I want to know, but yesterday I sat down and cut it all down to ten questions. And the answers I get to those questions will have a lot to do with our future."

"Well, I'm just along for the ride, so let me know when you know," he said with a grin. "I'll be waiting anxiously." He paused and looked at her meaningfully. "I'm assuming all this will interfere with my love life."

"Of course not, *dear*," she said with a smile he was sure was sarcastic. "The meeting will probably just take one afternoon and then we have the rest of the week to do what we want."

"I'd like to take the cars down to San Diego," he said. "Wash told me how to find his place and I'd like to see it. I'd also like to see the place where Wash and Woman work. Their boss sounds like someone I'd like to meet. I think he said her name was Kate Sessions. We might be able to see Doc while we're here too. Wash told me how to find him and I wrote telling him we were coming."

He put his arm around her and she snuggled against him. "What else are we planning while we're here?" she asked. "I've never been on a vacation before."

He looked at her with a silly grin and glint in his eye.

"Oh Johnny, we do that at home all the time. Vacations are for doing things you don't do at home."

When he pouted, she rolled her eyes and said with an exasperated sigh, said. "All right, but we have to do other things too."

He smiled happily and agreed.

The first thing they saw when they got off the train was the mountains to the north and east. High, rugged mountains, snowcapped and rocky. To the west the city spread out and ran away to water they could glimpse in the distance.

When they left San Francisco there had still been a hint of winter in the air, but here it felt like early summer. The air was clear too, and it smelled better. Back home the constant smoke from coal fires mixed with frequent fog made it hard to see any distance at times, and the outhouses for a couple of hundred thousand people could be bad some days. Here the mountains almost jumped out at you, and they could see the crowding they took for granted at home wasn't the case here.

The town of the Queen of the Angels or El Pueblo de la Reina de Los Angeles in Spanish, began like most California towns as an adjunct to a mission and had originally grown outward from the mission in an organized fashion according to a plan King Phillip II of Spain laid down in 1573 in the Law of the Indies. Power in this plan flowed from the mission out to the surrounding area.

When the Mexican War transferred California to the United States, the arriving Anglos preferred to live on the outskirts where there was room to spread out and the power went with them. It was almost like the city was several different towns spread in and around the hills and valleys.

When gold was discovered in 1848 on the American River and created the boom in San Francisco, the village of Los Angeles boasted a population of about 2600, mostly farmers and stockmen of varying ethnicities. Even after the Civil War it was still a small town with less than 5000 people and its main industry was selling beef and produce to the miners up north.

Then came the railroads, specifically the Santa Fe from the east and suddenly there were people everywhere. When Johnny and Annaliese arrived in the Spring of 1887 and stood looking at the city spread out among the hills and valleys of the Los Angeles Basin, there were probably close to 50,000 people there with more coming every day.

Along with letters of introduction, Dr. Brown had given her the name of a hotel where they were shown to a room with unusual decor and comfort.

Annaliese turned off the lights when she came out of the

bathroom and was startled by the dark bedroom. When her eyes adjusted, she could see a candle flickering on a dresser near the door and could make out her husband lying on the bed with the coverings opened for her in invitation.

She stopped by the bed and let her gown drop to the floor.

"Why the candle?" she asked. "Don't you like electric lights?"

"Candle's more romantic, and this place makes me feel romantic."

She moved to join him, but he held up his hand.

"Just stand there so I can look at you in the candlelight. You know I like looking at you."

She felt his eyes on her and she liked it, liked how it made her feel. Right now, for the first time in days she wasn't thinking about her future, just the now, and she knew this would be special. And it was, first exciting, then passionate, then urgent and finally frantic.

"We need to go to a hotel more often," he whispered in her ear afterward when she was lying beside him taking deep satisfying breaths. He had opened the windows earlier and the night had come inside. It felt marvelous on her overheated body, and she felt as if she was glowing.

"The air feels so soft," she said, "so different from home."

"Maybe this will be home one day soon," he said. "So far I like it." He kissed her and she responded, putting her arms around his neck and pulling him down to her.

"Whoa," he sputtered. "I need to catch my breath. Give me a few minutes anyway."

She giggled. "What if I don't want to wait?"

"It could be that what you want is not possible right now, so let me touch you and stroke you for a while and let's talk a bit."

"Stroke me? You mean like you stroke your cat?

"He seems to like it," he said, grinning at her.

"I do too, but you have to be thinking about me, not him."

"Of course," he said with a straight face. "I must say it's nice when you're like this. I wonder why tonight's so special."

"For one thing, you're more excited than usual." She ran her finger over his lips. "Doing it at the same time, in the same place, almost the same days of the week, it becomes routine and maybe a little stale.

"Being here in a new place, new city, the air feels and smells different, the light and the noise and the bed squeaking are all different and exciting. I can feel it in you, and I know you can feel it in me."

She reached out for him. "Come here and let me excite you again." He did, and she did.

The next morning walking out of the hotel was like walking into a painting. Everything felt fresh and new, like someone stayed up all night making it just for them.

Johnny turned to her. "What if Jinx doesn't like it down here?"

She snorted. "He likes it wherever you are. Don't tell me you miss him."

When he grinned at her she swatted him with her handbag. "After last night, you're still thinking about that cat."

They ate at a small café and hailed a cab to take them to Dr. Follensbee's office. On the way she lost some of her euphoria and gained a fair amount of anxiety.

The University of Southern California College of Medicine would graduate its first class the following year, and its facilities were located in an aging former winery which definitely didn't look like anyone had stayed up all night making it just for them.

Inside they were directed to the doctor's office, introduced themselves and almost immediately were informed the Doctor had been called away for an emergency and they had no idea when she would return. If they would telephone in the morning they could make another appointment.

Ten minutes and they were back on the street with nothing planned for the day. The cab had disappeared, so they walked a few blocks and found another that took them to the hotel.

After coffee in the hotel restaurant, they decided to get their bags and take the cars to San Diego. They could spend the night, look around and come back the following day. When they got back, they would call and make another appointment. Then they would still have several more days in the city before they returned home.

Because of swamps and bogs south of Los Angeles, the tracks ran east/southeast inland for a stretch, and when they turned west again, they were treated to some of the same type of desert, red rock scenery they had seen crossing Utah and Nevada. They finally came down into a beautiful valley and in the distance could see a vast, beautiful harbor hemmed in by spits of land north and south.

Wash had given them directions, so they rented a buggy, and after getting lost a little, finally found the cabin. They could hear the ocean in the distance and sat for a minute taking in the scene.

"What a beautiful place to live," she said in wonder. "I'm surprised they would ever leave. Of course, the house isn't much but that could be fixed, in fact it looks like Wash has been working on it."

"I don't think we passed one house in the last five miles," said Johnny. "It feels so strange and quiet after having so many people around at home.

"Tell you what. Wash told me where the screw is for the padlock; what say we look inside and if there's a place to sleep, we'll just stay here overnight and spend tomorrow looking over the town. It's not very big so we should be able to look it over in one day."

She agreed and inside they found all they needed for a meal and a snug night. They settled in and were walking along a path toward the ocean when they came upon Wash and Woman's rock, though they didn't know it as such. Seated side by side they listened to the waves for a while.

"What a wonderful place to just sit and talk or think or daydream or even plan your life." There was a dream-like quality to her voice. "Maybe her emergency today was a sign." She looked at him. "Maybe we were meant to come to San Diego and sit on a rock by the ocean and fall in love with a place. Maybe San Diego is the place we're meant to be."

He looked a question at her.

"I feel good here. It feels soft and warm, like when you take a blanket off the clothesline on a sunny day and wrap yourself in it.

"We live in a big city back home. Big and noisy and dirty. When we got there, we had to fight to make it a decent place to live. Why not try a smaller place and be a part of helping it grow into what we want it to be instead?"

"You'd be a long way from any place where you could do research," he pointed out. "Are you still thinking about that?"

"From the looks of that school, I'd say it will be a while before they'll be doing much research there. And besides, I've got plenty of time if I want to try it later. Right now I think it might be best if I learn one job at a time, and for some reason this seems like a place

I could do it."

"Sounds like a good idea to me, and besides, we'd have Wash around, at least part of the time anyway."

They walked back to the house holding hands.

As she was unbuttoning his shirt between kisses she whispered. "And if we get bored living here, that hotel room is not far away."

After an early morning walk to the ocean the next day they left and were back in San Diego by mid-morning. Over breakfast at a small café near downtown they talked about how to begin what they needed to do to make the idea of the previous night into the future they wanted.

"I guess I'll need to find out about the doctors here. If there's a lot of them, I may have to go elsewhere."

"We can ask around and find a doctor's office without much trouble," said Johnny. He raised a finger at the proprietor and when he came to the table asked about a doctor.

"Are you sick?" the man asked, wiping his hands on an apron.

Annaliese answered, "No, I'm a doctor and I'm wondering if there was one I could talk to about coming here to live."

"With all the new people coming in we could probably use a few more doctors," he said. He looked at her with a frown wrinkling his forehead. "I never seen a woman doctor before."

"Well, you have now," Johnny said. "She finishes school this spring and we're looking for someplace to settle."

He took them outside and pointed. Fifty feet or so down and across the street they saw a sign 'James Bone, M.D.'. An older man opened the door to their knock, smiled and said, "Come in." When they were inside, he led them into his office and when everyone was seated asked. "How can I help you and which one can I help?"

Johnny pointed at his wife, and she said, "Dr. Bone, my name is Annaliese Fry and in June I will graduate from medical school in San Francisco. This is my husband Johnny, and we are thinking about settling here."

The Doctor looked a little startled and then smiled. "Well, not the kind of thing I hear too often. I was hoping for some grave problem that would require immediate surgery." He laughed and after a moment they joined him.

"I'd say you're coming at a good time, for you and especially for the community. The way we're growing we could definitely use a new physician or three or four. A whole train load of settlers came in last week. A hundred and fifteen people from New England somewhere."

"It seems like such a wonderful place," said Annaliese. "We live in San Francisco, but I believe we'll be down here by mid-summer."

The doctor took out his vest watch, glanced at it and said, "I have a lady coming in shortly, so I won't be able to talk much longer but I think you should talk to Dr. Place. He and his wife have been here about a year so he can give you an idea of what it's like to begin a practice around here. He's supposed to take my patients for a few days while I go out of town, so I know he's at home."

He scribbled something on a slip of paper. "Here's his address. He practices out of his home. His wife is a nurse, so she helps."

The last thing he said before he closed the door was, "If I were you, I'd look for a place now and buy if you can. Prices are going up right fast and by summer it could cost you a lot more."

Chapter Seventy-One

They found the house with no trouble. The doctor was at home and not busy, so they sat in the parlor and talked to Dr. Homer Place and his wife Genevieve.

"We've been here just a year next month and we love it," said Gen. "We've heard tales of bad storms and such, but so far the weather has been wonderful."

"When are you planning to move down?" asked Homer. He was a towhead and looked not much older than Johnny.

"I'll probably be here first, "said Johnny. "I'm in the book business and my partner and I will probably be down sometime in May. We sell books from town to town out of a wagon and want to open a store down here. We plan to leave up there in a week or so and take a couple of months for the trip."

"When I finish school, I'll meet him here and hopefully begin my practice," said Annaliese.

"You want to join my practice, is that it?" he asked, leaning back in his chair.

"I don't know," she answered. "Are you looking for a partner?"

He shook his head. "My brother is coming out here this summer and we plan to practice together." He rubbed his goatee and looked at her over his glasses. "We might work out a temporary arrangement until he gets here, but a better solution would be to talk to old Dr. Clark. He's been around since this place was a Mexican village. I'm not sure how much of a doctor he is but he stays pretty busy.

"He wants to move to Mexico City to be with his daughter. You might do better to talk to him. Maybe you could work out something. He might even sell you his practice, which would be a good way to begin. If not, it may take you a while to build one of your own. It did me, although we do all right now."

While they were thinking about that he said, "I have no objections to a woman doctor, but some people do." He shrugged. "You might do all right with mothers and children for a start. We have a couple of healers and midwives here, but they mostly work with the Mexicans over the hill."

"Do you know when this doctor is leaving?" she asked.

"It seems to me he said mid-September. He has an office in Old Town."

"Someone else said, 'Old Town.' Is it a separate place?" asked Johnny.

"No. From what I hear, the original settlement was around a hill and a mission a little to the east of us here. That's where the Mexicans and Indians lived before the war. By the way, when someone says 'the war' around here it's usually the Mexican War.

"When Anglos began moving in they settled around here instead. So that's Old Town and this is New Town, but it's all San Diego."

They talked for a while about setting up a practice and some of the problems he'd had in the beginning and then looked over his office and treatment area. Two of the rooms on the first floor were set up as patient rooms for people who needed care overnight.

"There isn't a hospital near here, is there?" Annaliese asked.

He shook his head. "No, the closest is Los Angeles. All the doctors around here have rooms like this, so I guess we've got the need but right now these are all we have."

"There is a lady who lives close who comes in at night when we have someone in one of these rooms," said Gen. "We've had several here for a week or more, so I'd say we need a hospital."

"So, you live upstairs?" asked Johnny.

"Yes. We've plenty of room and it saves us money. The other doctors have offices, although Dr. Clark lives above his office in an old building. Been there for years."

Someone knocked on the front door and shortly Gen ushered a lady in to see the doctor and then walked with them to the door.

"I guess the next stop is Dr. Clark's office," said Annaliese.

"Are you staying here?" asked Gen.

"Well, it looks like we are, but we have a friend in the area and we're staying at his place," said Johnny.

"The Horton House in New Town is nice. We eat there once in a while. They have a nice dining room."

She took Annaliese's hand. "I guess I'll be the first one to welcome you to town, so welcome, and call on us when you finish school, and we'll help you get settled in."

"The more I see of this place the more I like it," said Annaliese after Gen closed the door.

"Let's stop at the nursery and meet Wash's boss," suggested Johnny. "Then we can meet the doctor, have dinner at the hotel and go back to the cabin for the night."

A woman was helping someone load a burlap wrapped tree into a wagon at the nursery and on a guess Johnny asked. "Are you Kate Sessions?"

"The very same," the woman said with a smile. There was an independent, no-nonsense air about her.

"We're the Frys, Annaliese and Johnny. Wash told us to stop and see you," said Annaliese. She held out her hand, but Kate raised hers showing dirt on them.

"I won't shake hands but I'm glad to meet you. Wash has told me all about you two."

"Knowing Wash as I do, I kind of doubt that. He doesn't talk much," replied Annaliese.

"You're right there. Let's say I read between the lines. Let's see, you're going to medical school, and he sells books and you're thinking about moving down here when you finish."

"Sounds like he's told you something, anyway," said Johnny with a chuckle. "Yes, we spent last night at his place and looking around we've decided this might be a good place to start a new life. He said you were a good person to talk to about the town."

"I know it pretty well. I've planted a lot of the trees and flowers around here, that's for sure, and I know most of the people too."

She was a pretty woman with a capable look about her, maybe forty, not big, not small. When she stood looking at them, they could see the dirt on her hands and a smear on her cheek and Johnny would have bet money it wasn't unusual for her.

"I like your friends. Woman is the kind of person you show something once and she's got it and Wash, well, I don't really know much about him, but I love having him around the place."

"That's pretty much the way I feel about him," said Johnny. "Things are better when he's around."

"I'd love to sit and talk with you but right now I'm shorthanded and I've got some things that need doing. How long are you in town?"

Annaliese said, "We need to stop in Los Angeles on the way home, so I'd say four days."

"Let's have dinner at the Horton House one night before you leave, and I'll tell you all about the place."

"That would be wonderful," said Annaliese. "We're going to try to see Dr. Clark this afternoon or tomorrow. Any night is fine with us.

"Last time we talked he said he was leaving. Is that what the talk is about?" When Annaliese nodded, she continued. "Why don't we make it tomorrow night then, say about seven."

They soon found their way to Dr. Clark's office. It was in a ramshackle two-story building surrounded by mostly aging Mexican architecture. Near the foot of a large hill, it was on a square with an old fountain in the middle, and across the square from a decaying mission.

Since there was no sign anywhere, they knocked tentatively on a door. The door opened and bushy white hair and eyebrows were the first things they noticed, and then a gruff, "How do."

The man left the door for them to close, walked to a desk, sat down and said, "Well?"

Annaliese, a little flustered, finally asked, "Are you Dr. Clark?"

"That's what the sign says." His brow knotted and he continued. "Oh, that's right. I took the damn sign down. I forgot." Despite his demeanor and his appearance, white shirt with sleeves rolled up and old carpet slippers on his feet, they could see a pair of blue eyes bright with alert intelligence.

"You don't look sick. Are you sure you're in the right place?"

Annaliese replied, "We talked to Dr. Place, and he told us you were leaving. So, we wanted to talk to you about buying your practice."

"You're a doctor?" The question sounded like he didn't believe what he was hearing.

"I graduate from Toland Medical School at the University in San Francisco this June and we're looking for a place for me to begin practice."

"Do you speak Spanish?"

"No, I don't.

"Well, you'd have trouble with most of my patients then. I didn't think anyone would want my practice, to tell you the truth, so I never thought about selling it." He sat back in his chair and rubbed his eyebrow, apparently thinking. "Tell me about yourself."

He sat without interrupting while she told of her education and experience.

"You say you worked with your father for how many years?" He clearly sounded skeptical.

"From the time I was ten until I left home at twenty-seven."

"And then this young fellow here swept you off your feet. Is that it?"

She tried to keep from smiling. "Actually, it was the other way round, but that's neither here nor there. The point is I have education and experience and now I want to put them to use."

He sat picking at his fingernails then looked up and said, "I've been here since before the War and I've never seen a woman doctor."

She smiled at him. "Time moves on, Dr. Clark. Now do you want to talk about selling the practice or not?"

"Don't get all huffy. I'll need to think about this a bit. I take it you're in town for a while?" When she nodded, he said, "Why don't you stop in tomorrow afternoon and we can talk for a while? That'll give me time to think it over."

When they were back on the street they looked at one another and laughed.

"What a strange man," Annaliese said.

"I don't know, when you consider how he lives and where he lives maybe not so strange. It seems he takes care of the ones other doctors don't want to, which would make him a pretty good man no matter how he looks."

"Considering how long he's been here he doesn't seem to have gotten rich," she said looking up at the rickety old building.

"After just our short visit I'd bet that's never been important to him."

"You're probably right. So now what do we do?"

"I would say we need to think about this at least as much as he does, so why don't we go back to the rock out from the cabin and sit and talk about it?" He raised a finger. "But let's take some food with us. It seems like we're going to be here longer than we thought so we need to fill up the larder a bit."

After a stop at a greengrocer on the way, she was quiet on the ride back out to the cabin. He could tell she was thinking, and he let her.

It was twilight by the time they were seated on the rock, and he said, "So tell me what you're thinking."

"I've been thinking about what Dr. Place said." She looked at him and he could see the set of her jaw. "Johnny, I don't want to be just a 'mother and baby' doctor, and if that's what his practice is then I'd rather start my own from scratch. If it's a general practice including that kind of thing, I'm fine with it, but I'll be a doctor not a midwife."

"What about the language thing? How much Spanish do you think you can learn in the three months before you finish school?"

"The question is how much Spanish do I need? If I find someone to teach me, we have books at the store I can use but with the work I already need to do before I finish, would I be stretching myself too thin?"

"That's for you to decide. I'll help you all I can, but I'll be leaving about a week after we get back, so I won't be around."

"I guess it all depends on what he tells us about his people tomorrow," she said. She nudged him playfully. "So, let's talk about something else." She kissed him.

"If you're suggesting what I think you are, the answer is yes, you can have me."

The next kiss was long and involved and while they were walking back to the cabin she whispered, "There does seem to be something about the ocean that gets me going."

He grinned at her. "That or patting you on the tummy with a damp washcloth."

She stopped, "Are you saying I'm easy?"

"Yes, and it's one of the things I love about you."

"Me too."

Later, afterward, she asked suddenly, "I wonder why he took the sign down?" but he was already asleep.

Chapter Seventy-Two

The hour before the store opened would usually find Sun Li doing the books for the previous day. She had just finished and was putting everything away when Jinx jumped on the desk with a good morning meow. He butted his head against her hand, and she scratched his ears and stroked his body from head to tail a few times.

"Good morning little kitty," she crooned. He lay down on the desk, looked up at her and in his eyes she could see 'where is he'?

Johnny told her this trip to Los Angeles would be the first time they had not been together since he was a kitten, and it was easy to see the cat missed his friend. He was sleeping in Johnny's room, on his bed and being fed just like always but she had noticed he wasn't purring, and she didn't remember him doing so since Johnny and Annaliese left.

He followed her into the store and assumed his position in the bed on the counter where he could see all who came and went. Brutus came trotting in from walking with Lemuel and Jinx joined him for breakfast in the back room. Within a few minutes everyone was there, and she unlocked the front door for the day.

Greta was downstairs so she knew Mrs. Keane was with the children. Her six-month-old son had recently joined the twins in the nursery upstairs and when Rebecca came down for a week, Bobby would be up there too.

Her life had been so different since Ross was born. Her cousins and sisters came into the store occasionally now with their mothers. She was no longer shunned in Chinatown. She never really had been, but when she first married and came to work at the store, no one came in except Jimmy. Even her father seemed a little reserved but recently she noticed changes. Now she was visiting them at home and really beginning to feel she had a foot in each of two different worlds.

It was something she and Jason talked about a lot. He had been through it when he came into the white world, and he helped her when the little hurts came thoughtlessly from both sides. She also noticed some of the regular customers who were cold and reserved when she first came to work at the store were becoming less and less so.

Roy pushed a rack full of new books in from the storeroom and he and Greta began to shelve them. Greta's unusual memory was returning, and she was constantly astonishing them with its accuracy, unerringly able to pick any book off the shelf in the old section of the store. Recently she began to work with the books in the new addition and believed she would have them all memorized in place in a few more weeks.

Hiring a day nurse to care for the children had helped both women adjust back into the store's routine after childbirth. Business at the store was still increasing and the crowds at every other Thursday open house had increased so steadily there were two part-time women who just came in to help on those nights.

Lemuel had increased his schedule to where he was sitting in his chair three nights a week now, and receipts those nights reflected it. Of course, lately the focus in the store had shifted to preparation for the departure of the wagon, which looked to be about ten days from leaving.

Greta was sitting in the back room with a cup of tea when Roy walked in and asked, "Mind if I join you?"

"Of course not," she answered. "Are there any more books to put on the shelves?"

"No," he answered. "We've finished until someone checks in the new shipment. I do need to read you the sales list, though."

They were quiet while he got some tea and joined her at the table.

"Can I ask you something?" she said.

"Sure," he answered. "Anything."

"We work together all the time and I'm getting to know you pretty well, but I don't know what you look like. Do you mind if I touch your face so I can feel how you look?"

He understood this was how she would 'see' him. "Sure," he said again. "Go ahead."

"What color is your hair? And your eyes?"

She rose and came around the table and he stood and moved toward her.

"My hair's brown and my eyes are. . ." he hesitated. "I guess my eyes are sort of greenish brown. I've never really looked at them closely."

She put her hands on his shoulders and ran them up to his ears and then began to move them gently across and around his head, feeling his nose, eyelids, mouth and chin, running her hands along his jaw then putting them on his cheeks and sliding them down around his neck.

When she finished, she leaned forward and sniffed his hair then resumed her seat.

"You're tall, aren't you?"

"Mama measured me and said I'm just six feet. I don't know how much I weigh. Never been on a scale."

"How old are you?"

"I'm sixteen. How old are you?"

She smiled at him. "Don't you know that's something you never ask a woman?"

"I'm sorry," he blurted.

"I'm just seventeen. I was fifteen when the twins were born."

She sat quiet for a while and he asked, "What are you thinking about?"

"I'm making your face in my mind so I'll remember it."

The back door opened, and Sarah and Madame came in with Wash trailing behind. After greeting them the three continued into the store.

"You knew who they were before they said hello, didn't you?

When she nodded, he asked, "How do you do that?"

She thought for a moment. "Little things. I know who they are but it's not one thing, it's a lot of little things. For one thing, not many people come in the back door so that narrows it down a bit, and they make different sounds when they come in. Everyone has a different smell too, and once I know it I don't have to think about it. I just know it. It's like you know two and two is four, but if you had to say how you know it, you'd have to think about it.

"I really like working with you," he said. "I learn a lot."

"I feel the same about you, Roy. We work well together."

He loved shelving books with her. Over the years on the road, she had listened to many, and she would tell him about them as they lined them up on the shelves. Books she didn't know they would sometimes try to guess what they were about by their titles, and they could get right silly about it. Occasionally they would try to smother their laughter so others wouldn't hear. He hadn't been there long enough to know how much they all loved to hear Greta laugh.

One thing he liked about being around her was that he could look at her without feeling embarrassed. With most girls, if they caught him looking, he would feel blood rush to his face, feel like he was glowing, and stutter if he tried to speak to them.

With her was the first time he was able to look at a girl long enough to see all there was to see. And he liked what he saw. She cared for her hair the way Annaliese did, washing it regularly and brushing it every night before bed. It was a beautiful honey gold and fell almost to her waist.

It had been a while before he could look at her eyes. They were a cloudy blue and for some reason their blank stare made him uncomfortable. Her cheeks were rosy almost as though she used rouge, though he knew she didn't. Her lips were full and though just seventeen, childbirth had given her a woman's body.

At first he thought she didn't know he was looking but later found out she probably did so he tried not to make it too obvious. He liked all he saw and wanted to tell her so.

He grew up around two older sisters who lived at home with their husbands and in the crowded house there was little privacy, so he was more aware of things than many boys his age. But knowledge and experience are very different things, so he was as bashful as anyone his age around someone he was attracted to.

And then there was his job. Even after a month he knew he loved The BookSeller and wanted to learn whatever anyone there wanted to teach him. The people of the store cast a protective shield around Greta, and early on he heard of Jed's death and how it affected her for so long. Everyone there was very careful not to leave anything out of place so she could move around with confidence. It didn't take him long to learn to be as careful as they were, and he was constantly watching to make sure she was safe.

The whole thing was becoming a problem for him because he wanted to tell her how he felt and see where it led. She was in his dreams at night and his thoughts most days, but the idea he might lose his position if he spoke out bothered him.

He didn't know she was coming to feel the same way about him.

Besides the great feelings of loss she felt when Jed had been killed, she gradually came to believe she would never find someone else and was fated to have only her children for company as she grew old. Now she wasn't so sure.

Roy was her age, and the more they worked together the more she began to feel an attraction to him. He seemed to enjoy the children and there were things about him that reminded her of Jed. His consideration for her and the laughter they sometimes shared triggered memories of what she had lost.

She needed to talk to Annaliese and get some advice about how to move toward what she was feeling, which might be a chance she didn't want to let pass untaken.

Sun Li heard them talking and laughing together and purposely left them alone. Whatever was happening between them, she felt it was good and didn't want to interfere even a little. Since she had been at the store, she had come to understand what a unique and fascinating person Greta was.

When Rebecca was in town the three of them spent time doing all the things young mothers like to do together, both with their children and without them. A nice thing about having Mrs. Keane around was they were able to have lunch and shop without having to hurry home.

Since she had grown up at the store with Jimmy, away from her family and Chinatown, she hadn't any close friends her own age. She loved the time she spent with her new friends and never failed to be astonished at how Greta managed to care for the twins when sometimes it was all she could do to care for one.

Sun Li was very bright and working at the store had planted seeds in a fertile ground. She tried to read for two hours a day and thankfully Jason didn't complain about all the time she spent with her nose in a book. She read different things, but her interest gradually settled on learning California history and especially the history and political landscape of the city.

It was just after she returned to work after the baby was born that Lemuel and Annaliese began inviting speakers for evening talks once a week. Though there were a variety of topics she always stayed to listen when it related to the city.

Occasionally, when downtown on an errand, she would stop at city hall or the library and see what she could find out about a chosen topic. Sometimes she would be told to leave, and she always went, but a few days later she was back at another department, asking questions and always learning.

She talked to Johnny and Lemuel about the fight to cleanse the city of corruption, and, on Johnny's advice, approached Herschel as a source on all things city related. He not only had a history with the dark side of local politics, but as a reporter, it was his job to know the inside of every office in city hall. He became accustomed to her posing questions whenever he came into the store and several times met her at city hall to introduce her to someone who could answer her questions.

When Jason asked her why this fascination, she had to think for a while before she could answer him.

"I'm not really sure," she finally said. "I know I will never be allowed to become a part of the system. The law shuts me out and I have no way to change that. But I know there are those among the whites who see the injustice of it, so one day it might not be so. I have learned that knowledge is power, so if I learn enough I may help give my power to one who wants to change the law, to make whites live up to what they say they believe."

"Herschel?"

"He helps me because his friend wants him to. I'm sure Johnny hasn't told him to help me. He does it because he's Johnny's friend and I work here."

She put her arms around him, and he embraced her too.

"I have a good life because I married you, Jason, and The BookSeller is part of that." She lifted her lips to him, and he kissed her. "Thank you," she said.

Chapter Seventy-Three

When Dr. Clark answered her knock the next afternoon, she noticed he was smiling. She and Johnny had barely settled into their chairs when he began a monologue.

"Let's do this. I'll talk for a while and when I'm through, you can ask questions. Agreed?" They nodded. "I want to make sure you are under no illusions about what you're taking on here. When I came here it was a small village of Mexicans and Indians. I was the only doctor within two hundred miles or more, not to mention the only white man. When someone knocked on my door, they were my patient. Right now, my practice is the sons and daughters and even grandchildren of those people who first knocked on my door. I've brought many of them into the world, watched them grow up and buried more of them than I like to remember. When I leave here there will be sorrow, on both sides.

"But I have decided to leave, no matter the reasons. They don't matter to you." He shifted in his seat and locked his gaze on her eyes "If you take on this practice the majority of your patients will be Mexican, the great majority. It would be helpful if you spoke the language, but I didn't when I first got here so I guess you'll make out.

"They are good people. They love their families and work hard every day to give them food and clothing and take care of them. If you treat them, there will be Anglos who will not come to you because of it." He paused, let a silence pass, and looking into her eyes again said, "How do you feel about that?"

Meeting his gaze she said, "My father is a doctor. He's a Mormon. He opens clinics all over the west for Mormons. These clinics never turn away a patient in need. I have worked with him as his nurse and assistant since I was ten years old." She smiled at him. "Does that answer your question?"

His mouth twisted into half a smile. "I know your father, at least I know who he is. William Crawford. I have read of his work with those clinics." He looked at her speculatively. "So you're telling me you're your father's daughter." Now the smile was whole. "Put me in my place, didn't you?" He laughed and sat forward on his chair. "So, you think you'll become rich and famous, do you? Because outside of this small town no one will know your name."

"My husband will and my father and my friends. That's enough for me."

"As patients, my people are like most, I guess. They work hard, eat a very poor diet and it affects their health. Like all people, some live a long time and some die at birth.

"A good portion of my fees are paid in kind, so you'll always eat pretty well." He patted his stomach. "Do you have any questions?"

"When are you leaving?"

"It looks like early September. My daughter is marrying a wealthy Mexican. There are some, you know. His father has secured him a diplomatic post, and I've been appointed physician for the mission, so I will travel with them."

"Sounds fascinating," said Johnny

"I must admit I'm looking forward to it," said the doctor.

"Of course, one question we haven't dealt with," said Annaliese. "How much do you want for the practice?"

The penetrating stare again. "Will you take care of my people?"

Again, she met his gaze and nodded slowly. "Every day," she said.

"Let's make it a dollar and a handshake, then." When her mouth fell open in astonishment he added. "He's very rich and I won't want for anything. Besides, to tell you the truth, I'm not sure it's worth much more. These people don't have much money, but they have fed me well over the years."

"Are you sure?"

"And besides, I've saved most of what I've made since I've been here. Not many places to spend money around here anyway. A woman cooks for me, and another cleans the house and office, and they won't take any money for it. The people here even gave me a horse and wagon, and they take care of the horse."

He turned to Johnny. "So, what will you do while she's doctoring?"

"Sell books", Johnny said, beaming. "My partner and I will be selling books out of a wagon and traveling here from San Francisco. When we get here, we plan to open a bookstore."

"Is this a new thing for you?"

"No," answered Annaliese. "We have a successful store back home that's been open several years. And before that his partner sold books all the way from Kansas City to Salt Lake."

"Darn, just when I'm leaving."

"We hope to be open the first part of June, so you'll have time to visit us," said Johnny.

"I'm sure I'll be a regular customer." He turned back to Annaliese. "When will you be here?"

"I finish school the first week in June, so as of now, the first week in June. Will you be able to work with me for a little while to introduce me to the community?"

He nodded. "Certainly. I was hoping it would be like that."

"If I may change the subject a bit," said Johnny, "I can't imagine how you came here back then. Will you tell us how you got here and when?"

Dr. Clark laughed and ran his fingers through his long white hair.

"I haven't thought about that for a while." He laced his fingers on top of his head, leaned back in his chair and looked out across the years.

"Left New Bedford on a whaler in the spring of '41. Got round the Horn OK but a storm caught us just south of here and we were dismasted and sank. I came ashore floating on my sea trunk, half drowned. When I came to I found myself thousands of miles from anywhere with nothing and no way to make a living.

I was a loblolly boy on the ship…" He looked at Johnny. "Bet you don't know what that is, do you?"

Johnny looked at him and grinned. "It's the assistant to the ship's surgeon, isn't it?"

"That's right. Well, on this voyage the doctor was a drunk. But when he was sober, he taught me how to do things so he could lay about and drink, so I had a fair bit of experience with sickness and injury. When the ship was sinking, I made sure I had my sea chest from the cabin and when it went down, I floated to shore on it. Fortunately, there were some medical books in it he'd given me to read." He pointed at three books on a shelf above his head. They looked water stained and well used.

"A fellow found me on the beach and took me to his house. He dried me out, fed me and let me sleep in his bed. After a while I set myself up as a doctor. Wasn't anybody around to tell me I couldn't, and besides they needed someone.

He smiled at them. "So here I am forty-five years later, physician to the Embassy of Mexico in London, England."

"Are you married?" asked Annaliese.

"No, never have been. I call her my daughter, but she and her brother were left orphaned years ago and I took them in until I could find someone to take 'em. Never did. So now I'm off to London with her. Life takes some funny turns, doesn't it?"

The next morning, they met Kate Sessions at her place and using a plat map of the city, she helped them pick out a lot in town for a house. They made a payment to secure it, and they were residents of San Diego.

At dinner with her that night, she brought a map, showed them the town and talked about her vision for it as a horticulturist. She was excited about the contract with the city to plant a hundred trees a year in City Park. She sent away for trees from all over the world and drew up a plan for their placement looking toward the future of the park. She and Wash planted two of them last summer and she said he watched over them like they were his children.

They boarded the train the next day, and after a hurried change in Los Angeles where they dropped off a letter at the medical school for Dr. Follansbee, were soon on their way home.

"Did you enjoy your vacation?" she asked Johnny when they were seated and his arm was around her again.

"I think we should have spent one last night in that hotel," he said.

"It will be here when we come back," she said. "Let's talk about the decisions we made while we were here."

He moved to the seat facing her. "I want to look at you when we're talking about this."

"OK. The two most important things are deciding to move to San Diego instead, and Dr. Clark's practice. What do you think about Dr. Clark?"

"I think it will let you begin your life as a doctor on a good note. It sounds like it will be like one of the Doctor's clinics with Mexicans instead of Mormons. You will be helping people who need your help and be there to help anyone else who comes to the door.

"As far as the money goes, we've enough coming in to make ends meet, so the money doesn't matter to me if it doesn't matter to you. Besides, I believe the store will help you get to know the people of the city and they'll come to you as a doctor because of what you are as a person."

She looked at him for a moment, then leaned forward and kissed him. "That's just what I needed to hear, my love."

"How do you think we should arrange the living quarters?" she asked. "Do we live over my office or over the store or do we get a house away from both?"

He looked a question at her. "Hadn't thought about it," he said. "I just figured we'd set up over the store like always."

"I've been thinking, and I believe we should probably leave the office where it is for a while. Changing doctors will be disrupting enough for the patients without moving the office at the same time."

"And the lot we bought today?"

"I've thought about that too. Do your plans for the store include the type of things we do at home to drum up business?"

"Yes, it makes sense. If they work in one place they should work in another."

"Not necessarily. Lots more people in San Francisco. You may have to rethink things about the people you're selling to and what kind of people they are."

"All right, tell me what you're talking about."

"There are more Mexicans here than back home and I doubt if the people down here are as educated either. You might want to look at the population and see what you think they'd like instead of assuming you'll sell the same books here you do back home.

"As far as the lot goes, I think maybe we should build the house to be the store, build it to a plan of what we want it to be. Let's say a store with an apartment upstairs for us. We can always move later and expand the store if we need to."

"That makes sense." He looked at her suspiciously. "How'd you get so smart, anyway?"

She looked at him with wide eyed innocence. "It's all because of you, dear."

"I knew that," He resumed his seat beside her, and she lifted his arm and put it around her shoulders.

"Are you happy about what we've done?" he asked.

"Really happy."

"Me too."

Chapter Seventy-Four

The first thing Johnny did when they walked into the store late that afternoon was pick up Jinx and love him. The rumbling purr was audible.

"That's the first time I've heard him purr since you left," said Sun Li. After all the greetings were done, Lemuel and Wash took Johnny, cat on his shoulders, for a walk down to the bay. Walking in the sand was hard for Lemuel so Wash laid some boards across it and they sat on the logs and talked.

"We decided on San Diego and stayed at the cabin while we were there. Had dinner with Kate one night and talked and talked. Put a payment on a lot in town the next day. Annaliese has agreed to take the practice of a doctor who's leaving in September. She'll be on the job as soon as she gets there. That will give him a chance to introduce her to his patients and help her get on her feet before she's by herself.

"Kate showed us a couple of maps of the city, and we saw those two trees you planted in the park, Wash. The park doesn't look like much now, but that lady has plans and I wouldn't bet against her."

"I like working for Kate. So does Woman."

"She sure likes having you two around, and she's anxious for you to get back. We told her you'd likely be coming back with us, and she was fine with the idea. She thinks if we move down there, she'll have you two regularly."

"So why San Diego, not Los Angeles? I thought it was settled. She wanted to work there," asked Lemuel.

"We were sitting on a big flat rock toward the ocean out from the cabin talking the first night we were there and she just up and changed her mind."

"I know that rock," said Wash with a chuckle. "Don't surprise me a bit. It's a good place to sit and think and decide things."

"What do you think about moving down there instead of Los Angeles?" asked Lemuel.

"Well, you boys know I'm just the tail on her kite. We made a deal back in Salt Lake and that's the way it is. I ain't about to try to change the rules at this stage of the game. If she told me we were moving next door to hell, I'd bring along the ice water."

"I knew that," said Wash with a grin. "I'm glad Johnny. I like the town, and with the cabin and all, I think I may have found a place to call home."

"So, when do you want to plan to leave?" asked Lemuel. "Did you get to look over any of the towns in the valley?"

"Yes, I did. Wow, that's flat country. Of course, plenty of mountains on both flanks out in the distance but man, some of those farms are big. Crops as far as you can see, sometimes on both sides of the tracks.

"It reminds me of coming out of Salt Lake except that's just for a few miles. This valley runs all the way down the state, almost to Los Angeles. Looking at it and knowing we're going to be selling books in some of those towns was interesting."

"When we went through western Kansas it was wonderful," said Lemuel. "We'd come into a town, and in most of them, it was an event. We didn't get to see much of the towns, but we met a lot of people, had a lot of nice meals where we sat and talked and got to know a little about their lives. There were times on that trip I felt like a farmer myself; selling those books was like planting seeds in plowed ground."

"This time of year, we shouldn't have problems with the skeeters," said Wash. "Not so many low places once you get out of the delta. I haven't been south in the valley much. We traveled within sight of the ocean for much of the trip last time."

"Is Woman coming with us?" asked Johnny.

"No. She's going to wait a few weeks and catch the cars."

"I noticed you brought that old mule with you."

"He goes where I go."

Johnny reached down to pet the cat who was settled in his lap. "I know what you mean. This trip's the longest I've been away from this one since he was born. He probably won't let me out of his sight for the next week."

"What more do we need to do before we're ready to leave?

"Load the food, water, ammunition and fodder for the horses and that's it, "answered Lemuel. "Won't need much for them. We'll be passing through plenty of places to buy it." He paused for a moment. "Are you going to wear the Colt on the road or just take the Henry?"

"I think both, but I'm not looking forward to telling her."

"She'll understand. She knows what it can be like out there," said Wash. "I'll have the Sharps and Lemuel will have his twelve gauge. So, we'll have plenty of firepower."

"You going to bring the ten gage?" asked Lemuel.

"No, Handy's got it by the door up at the ranch. I'll just leave it there. It fits him better than it does me, anyway."

"What are you going to do about the ranch?" asked Lemuel.

"I'm still thinking about that. I love going up there and working, but when we move down south, I don't think it would be fair to them if I kept my share. We'll work something out, I'm sure."

Annaliese looked up at the knock and saw Greta standing in the doorway.

"Can we talk?" said the girl. Annaliese smiled. It was a habit to call Greta a girl. No question she was a woman now, a mother and a necessary and important part of the store. She had grown a lot in the last year and even looked the part.

"Any time," she said. When Greta was seated, she continued, "What's on your mind?"

Greta sat for a moment, apparently ordering her thoughts.

"After Jed was killed, I thought I'd lost any chance I'd ever have of leading a normal life, that I'd be alone with the children for the rest of my life. The last little while has made me think that may not be so."

Annaliese sat back in her chair not sure what she was hearing.

"Roy and I work together a lot and we're good friends. We're almost the same age and I think over the last month or so we've become more than friends."

Annaliese didn't know what to say so she sat quiet so Greta would continue.

"I think he likes me. If I can figure out how to let him know it's alright with me, maybe something can come of it. The problem is I don't know how to do it."

Because it was so out of the blue, Annaliese was dumbfounded.

"Uh, Greta, you've taken me completely by surprise here. I need to think about this and see what I come up with."

"It's taken me by surprise too. I know you've a lot to think about right now with school and all, but if I let this chance go by, I may not have it again."

"Greta, I'll think about it and maybe talk to Johnny about it, but I believe in the end it's going to be up to you. You're going to have to work up the courage to tell him how you feel or at least ask him how he feels."

"If you could think about it and tell me tomorrow if you have any ideas, then if you feel it's best just to talk to him, I'll do it."

"How did you and Jed solve this problem?"

Greta smiled faintly. "Johnny told him he should write a letter and read it to me. One night when we were coming from Sacramento he did, and I asked if he wanted to kiss me." She was really smiling now. "He said 'yes, but I don't know how'".

Annaliese could picture the scene, and she smiled too. "Do you want me to tell Johnny to have him write you a letter?" They both laughed.

"No, that's the kind of thing he'd have to figure out for himself. He's not as shy as Jed was but I think he doesn't want to say the wrong thing and cause a problem at the store."

When she left, Annaliese just stared out the window for a minute trying to get her thoughts organized. She had so much to do what with school and planning the move, and Johnny leaving, and now she needed to learn as much Spanish as she could before they moved south. She needed to find someone to help her learn it, too. She shook her head and sighed.

But Greta was right at the top of the list of important people in her life. Her happiness was important to Annaliese. She was used to helping people solve their problems. Greta and Lemuel were family now, and when family asked for help with a problem, you gave it if you could.

She was halfway out of her chair when an idea struck her. She sank back and was sitting thinking when Johnny and Jinx came in a few minutes later.

"What ya thinking about with such a face?" he asked. "I'll bet it's me."

"Oh, of course," she said in a sarcastic tone. "What could I *possibly* be thinking about besides you? No, Greta just came in with a problem and I think I've figured out a way to help her."

"Tell me."

"She wants to find out if Roy likes her enough to make it romantic. I'm going to suggest she and I write him a letter and give it to him."

"That's funny. I suggested Jed do that back in Salt Lake when he wanted to tell her the same thing."

"I know. That's where I got the idea."

"When did all this come about?"

"Greta just came in to talk to me. She says they're becoming more than friends but she doesn't know how to take it any further."

His eyes widened and he scratched his chin. "Sounds as good a way as any," he said after a minute. "Any idea how he feels?"

"Not a clue, but I think it's a good idea, so I'll talk to her in the morning and maybe we can do it right away. That'll get it off her mind and off mine too. I don't need anything more to think about right now."

That's how he felt. In addition to planning for the trip, he and Lemuel had to sit down with Jason and Sun Li and chart the future of The BookSeller.

The idea of the store had been the center of their lives since they left Salt Lake three years before. Now they were leaving it to strike out on a new adventure. He wanted Jason and Sun Li to have a future here and wanted to see what they felt was fair. He knew Lemuel felt the same, but they all needed to sit down and put together a plan for the store's future everyone would be happy with before they left.

He also needed to talk to Handy and Gray about the ranch. His trip this week would be his last, and he would ride back to the city on his big black horse. He knew he could just tell them what he wanted to do, and they would accept it, but he wanted to see how they felt about it too. They had been fair to him when he became a partner, and he wanted to be fair too. Besides, they might have some ideas he hadn't thought of, and he always liked to hear what Handy had to say.

He was excited to be going back on the road with Black. Over the last little while he left most of the job of exercising the big black horse to Bits, but he would be glad to have him around all the time again.

He was mulling all this over in his head the next morning when Herschel came in the door at Mattie's and sat down with a cup of coffee.

"So, when are you leaving?" Herschel asked.

"We've decided on a week from Friday," said Lemuel

"How many books are you taking?"

"Around five hundred. We have no idea how business will be, but most of the farm towns in the valley don't have bookstores, so we feel pretty good about our prospects. If we run short we can send a note back here and Jason can put some on a train for us."

"Did you find a place down there?" he asked, speaking to Johnny.

"We decided on San Diego," said Johnny and told him about the trip.

"So, it will be San Diego, not Los Angeles?"

"That's what she wants. The arrangement we made when we married was that she'd finish school, decide where she wanted to practice, we'd move there, and I'd open a new store. We saw one other bookstore in town. The plan was to use the same ideas we used to build up business here down there. But Annaliese pointed out it was a different town with different people so we may have to change things a little."

"Are you going to rent or buy?"

"Annaliese suggested we build the store we wanted rather than take what we could find. That will take some time, but we can sell out of the wagon until we get things set up the way we want.

"The practice she's taking over has living space upstairs, so after Dr. Clark leaves, we might live there while we're building." He nodded at his partner. "Lemuel will be content living in the wagon and Wash and Woman have a cabin south of town where we can spread our blankets if need be."

"Sounds like you got it all set up."

"Well, there are a lot of details we'll need to smooth out, but yes, we have a good place to start."

"We'll miss you around here."

"Oh, we'll be back. Too many things pulling us back here to stay away too long. With Greta and the twins here, Lemuel won't stay away, and I'm sure Woman will be back to see her friends at the Mansion, as will we, although Annaliese might find it hard to get away. The practice she's buying could keep her pretty busy for a while. I'll sure be back occasionally anyway.

"I'll probably drop down to see you before long just to see how you're doing."

Johnny stood and tossed a bill on the table. "We're going to work out our route today and finish buttoning up the wagon. Then it will just be putting perishables aboard and we'll be ready."

"I'll see you before you leave, I'm sure," said Herschel. When they separated Johnny watched as his friend walked away, marveling again at how far the two of them had come from where they had begun.

Chapter Seventy-Five

Lemuel and Greta were sitting at Mattie's when Johnny walked in with Jason and Sun Li. After they all finished eating and were sitting over coffee, Lemuel said, "We're leaving soon, and I just wanted to talk a bit about the store and how it will be when we're gone."

He nodded at Johnny. "We both believe you all will treat it like it's yours and look after our interest in the management of it. We got Nate Jones to draw up some papers for you to sign. These will make the two of you joint owners of one third of The BookSeller as of the date of our departure. Of course, you'll both continue to draw your pay for management of the store, plus you will have one third of the profit calculated by Nate in the annual statement of profit."

He paused. "The reason we've decided to do this is because we believe you would operate the store the way we would want whether or not we did this. In other words, we trust you and want to reward you for it. Is this acceptable to you?"

Jason and San Li looked at one another, clasped hands and smiled.

"Thank you. It is good of you to do this. We will do our best to live up to it," said Jason.

Sun Li nodded and added, "We will keep your dream for you until you return."

Johnny was in one of his favorite places, sitting on the rear deck of the ferry to Sausalito watching the water churn away from the big paddle wheel and thinking. Jinx was lying on the seat beside him, seeming to enjoy the view. Today was his last trip to the ranch and he knew he would miss it as much as anything they were leaving behind. The train was getting steamy, and within minutes of landing he was watching the scenery passing from the railroad car window. Black was waiting for him at the station stable, and even in the rain, he enjoyed the short ride to the ranch.

Handy and Gray were sitting on the porch waiting for the lunch the ladies were preparing when Johnny rode up to the barn and handed the reins to Bits. Jinx leapt from his shoulder to the railing and disappeared into the kitchen where he would try to cozen an appetizer. Johnny joined his friends on the porch.

"So, this is your last trip?" said Gray.

"Yeah. We're supposed to leave next Friday morning after the get together at the store," replied Johnny. "Y'all'll be there won't you?"

"We've hired a new man to work with Bits and they'll be here," said Handy. "We plan to come down a couple of days early and stay at the mansion." He looked around stealthily. "Don't tell Rebecca I said it, but I wouldn't mind going with you. When we came through Los Angeles we changed trains but didn't see much, although I sure did like the weather."

"I'd like to have you along. The plan is to set up in each town and stay a few days. If all goes as planned, we should be in San Diego the first part of June. Annaliese should be there soon after and we can settle in."

Lunch was served, and because he was leaving, the ladies had made an effort and it was special.

When they were back on the porch after, Handy said, "Seems the only time we get a good feed is when you come up." He winked at Johnny.

"Well, I never," said Rebecca, exasperation in every word. "Handy Josephson! You know that's not true."

"I was just joshing," said Handy. "I wanted Johnny to think we thought he was special so maybe he wouldn't leave."

Johnny smiled ruefully. "It's a new life, but it's one we talked about coming across the desert. Lemuel's idea was to continue to travel, leaving books wherever we went. I love how he puts it - 'like seeds in plowed ground'.

"Of course, I'll miss a lot of things, but it'll be a beautiful way to spend a couple of months.

"Coming up here every week has been like a cool drink of water when you're thirsty. I'll miss the peace and beauty of the place, the work I have to do, the people, and most of all, the smithy," he smiled. "That's where I go to be with Pa. We've had some good talks out there."

He stood and turned to face them. "If things work out as planned we won't be back here for a while, maybe never. So, if y'all agree, I'm going to sell you my share. As much as I hate to do it, it's not fair of me to be a partner from five hundred miles away. You can pay me when you get it or never. I don't really care."

"I thought maybe that's what you'd do," said Handy. "And since I sort of expected it, we have all talked it over and we accept. We've thought about where we want to go with the place and felt we had a better chance that way."

"Think you'll look for other partners?"

Handy looked at Gray and Gray said, "We'll be open to offers. Over the years I'm sure it will change, but right now we have an idea of where we'd like to be in ten years. We also realize how we get there, or even if we get there, depends on life. My mother used to say, 'Man proposes, God disposes'. What you're doing helps us bend more easily if we have to.

"Something else I've wanted to say before you leave. I appreciate how you helped us when my brothers came along. Actually, you didn't help so much as you handled it. I can imagine how different our lives would have been if they'd moved in here."

"I must admit I've wondered whether you look at me differently since I killed your brother," said Johnny.

Gray shook his head. "No. He was asking for it. If you hadn't done it someone else would have."

Johnny stretched and said, "I'm going to see what work I've got in the smithy."

Handy raised a finger. "The fellow we hired is a smith of sorts, so he's got everything caught up."

Johnny smiled at him. "I'll just go visit for a while".

A little later Handy saw some puffs of smoke from the smithy.

When he walked by he saw Johnny sitting by the bellows, chin on his fist, staring at nothing.

Greta had given Roy the letter the night before and told him to read it on his day off. The next day she had trouble thinking about anything else. She wondered what he'd feel about it and how he would behave when he came to work the next day. She was so distracted she asked Sun Li to work for her. She sent Mrs. Keane home and spent the day with the children.

That night in bed she was more aware of her body and how it felt than any time since Jed was killed and lay running her hands over it until she fell asleep.

But her sleep was fitful, and before morning light she was sitting on the edge of the bed thinking about Jed, how she had loved him and how he had kissed her and how they had made love. She bent forward and sat, head in hands, trying to understand what was happening to her and what she could do about it.

It was somehow wrong to think about a love that was gone when she just asked another man if he loved her. If her future with Roy was to have any chance for the two of them and the children, she couldn't allow Jed to come between them. But how could she keep it from happening?

Besides, she didn't want to give up her memories of his love and what it meant to her. She just wanted it not to interfere with what she felt for the new man in a new life.

She shook her head, and her thoughts became chaotic for a while. What would Annaliese say? Whatever it was it would help; she knew that. But this was her life, not her friend's, and she needed to find her own way forward.

Suddenly she heard Annaliese's voice as clearly as if she were in the room. "Jed's gone, Greta. Don't let a loyalty to his memory keep you from seeing happiness when it comes along. He wouldn't want that."

She smiled to herself. Yes, that's just what her friend would say.

When she came downstairs the next morning Roy was sitting in the backroom staring into a cup of tea.

He looked up and said, "Morning, Greta. Can I get you some tea?"

"Good morning, Roy. Yes, thank you." She could hear a strangeness in his voice. He was nervous too. Her stomach felt as though a dozen butterflies were flying around in a very small space and she smiled to herself thinking he probably felt the same. Somehow realizing he was as nervous as she made her feel better. She took a deep breath and plunged in.

"Did you read the letter?"

"That's all I thought about all day yesterday," he said. "I must have walked ten miles after I read it."

"Did it surprise you?"

"Not surprise so much." He hesitated. "I was hoping you felt the same way I did, but now I know, I don't quite know what to do next."

He reached across the table and took her hand. "Maybe this is a good way to start."

She felt a warm wave rising in her chest, then into her head, and was a little breathless. She got to her feet, moved around the table, and held out her hands. He took them and stood up.

"Kiss me," she whispered, and it felt as good as she remembered. Fortunately, no one else was around early because the kiss lasted a long time, and they learned a whole lot about each other just that quick.

Whenever Rebecca and Maxine came down from the ranch they would go to lunch with Greta and Sun Li, usually at the City of Paris, one day during the week. They sat and talked afterwards, usually about all sorts of things. This noon, however, it was all about Roy and Greta.

"I don't really have any idea what two people do when they're in love but not married," said Greta. "I mean, Jed and I did a lot of different things together, but we were just working and living our lives. It just so happened we were living together.

"I'd say we're probably not the best people to ask," said Rebecca. "Handy and I got married three months after we met, and for most of that time we didn't see each other."

She looked at Sun Li. "Don't look at me," said Sun Li. "If it wasn't Jimmy or my father around all the time it was my sisters. I took things I cooked for him to the livery stable and we'd sit and talk while he ate. That was all the time we had together until we got married. I didn't kiss him but once before our wedding night."

Maxine chimed in. "Gray and I were like you and Jed. We worked together for a year before we became engaged, and most of the time I thought he was immature and a pain in the rear."

"Roy's like Jed in some ways," said Greta, "but not in others. I don't really know much about him. What would be some ways to find out what he's like when we're not at work?"

They were quiet while the food was served and then Sun Li said, "You could take walks. There are lots of places to walk and talk down by the bay and in the Presidio, and have you ever been to Golden Gate Park? I read somewhere that in the first ten years it was open they planted over 150,000 trees there."

"For that matter, you could come here for lunch," said Rebecca. "I don't mean with us girls, but just you and him. And, since they built the spur line from Sausalito, you all could come up and spend the day at the ranch. You and Jason could come too, although I don't know who'd run the store if you all came. If you wanted to stay the night we could put you up. We've got plenty of room."

"It all sounds wonderful," said Greta. "I've never been on a ferry either. I imagine there are many places we could go around the bay."

"It sounds like being engaged could be a lot of fun," said Rebecca. "I'm sorry I missed it."

When they finished talking about Roy and being engaged, Rebecca took her friend's hand and said, "We have so much fun together I sometimes forget you're my sister-in-law, but I want you to know I'm so glad you found someone to love, and I knew Jed well enough to know he'd be glad too."

Johnny woke up early, and instead of lying in bed thinking, was out and dressed before Annaliese even turned over. She watched him hurrying through his morning routine and finally said, "Excited?"

He hadn't known she was awake, but now he leaned over and kissed her good morning.

"Everyone will be here by ten and we'll be ready to go not long after. Yes! I'm excited."

He sat down on the bed and took her hand.

"I didn't want to tell you, but I guess I have to. I'll be wearing the Colt on the trip, and I'll have it on when I leave this morning."

She shrugged. "I'm not surprised. It's something you might need on this kind of a trip." She leaned over and kissed him. "You'll never know how much I appreciate that you stopped wearing it around here because you knew I didn't want you to. If it will help keep you safe on the trip, I want you to wear it, even use it if you need to, to protect yourself and your friends."

When they went downstairs, she stood in the doorway of the office and watched him strap on the Colt. "I must admit, it does look like it belongs right there on your hip," she said.

They opened at nine and within minutes their friends began to come in. Will Smith and his wife and half a dozen people who worked for him were first through the door. Hank Rose came in with Bev and Dr. Brown. Annaliese's friends from the study group came in together, husbands in tow, and Jonas Burke was there with Sarah and Madame and everyone from the mansion. There were even several other people from City Hall. Johnny talked to everyone, said goodbye so many times and had his hand shaken so many times he was hoarse and couldn't feel his fingers.

About noon he climbed enough of the steps so he could see everyone and called for attention. He hesitated while people from around the store gradually filled up the room.

"Lemuel's the talker in this partnership, but I want to say something. We opened the BookSeller with the idea it would be a place where people would come to learn more about each other and the rest of the world. Seeing all of you here makes me believe we've succeeded. It will still be here, and Greta and Roy and Jason and Sun Li will make sure it keeps on being the kind of place we wanted. We will see you again, I'm sure. There are too many here I love for me to stay away." He looked at Lemuel who had come to the foot of the steps. "Anything you want to say, Lem?"

"No, I think that says it all."

The store gradually emptied, and afterward some people remained in the back room.

"Johnny, I'm really sorry to see you go," said Madame. "You and your friends have made this city a better place, and since I live here, I like that. But I see why you're going and also see you're leaving it in good hands."

Annaliese joined them. "I remember the first time you came in," said Johnny. "I thought you were the kind of person we wanted to come here. I still feel that way."

"It will be strange, not having you here," said Greta.

Lemuel took her hand. "Are you afraid?"

"Not afraid, but I'll miss you. We have always been together, but I know I will be fine."

"Greta, there'll come a time when I won't be around anymore. This will help you learn how to handle that. I'll be back, and if things work out, I may spend part of my time here and part there. And there may come a time when you and the children live in San Diego part of the time too."

"Don't forget about Roy. He may be there too."

"Is it that serious?"

"I think it is, and I'm happy about it."

"Then I'm happy too."

"Make sure you read my column when you get a chance." Herschel was shaking his hand. He lowered his voice. "I'll keep an eye on the place in case they need any help."

Johnny held his hand for a moment. "You know, I don't think I'll ever quite understand how we got to be friends, but I'm glad it happened."

He turned to his wife, embraced her, and said to Lemuel over her shoulder, "If we don't go now it'll be tomorrow before we get out of here." He looked at Wash and his friend nodded. Lemuel mounted the seat of the wagon. Wash untied the horses and Johnny swung up on Black behind Jinx, already in the saddle. He looked at his wife, at her red hair shining in the sun, at her bright eyes, almost teary, then turned, and with Wash beside him, led the wagon down the street.

Chapter Seventy-Six

They had done this before, so they just naturally fell into the routines on the trail necessary to keep them moving forward. At first their way led them along the Camino Real, south out of the city and through the towns and villages of the Peninsula. They had decided not to stop until they were beyond San Jose, and once there, they turned eastward aiming for the valley of the San Joaquin.

The towns which grew up there to buy and transport what the farms around them grew were their targets and the first of these was Modesto. In the great valley to the south of there along the rails of the Southern Pacific, towns had sprouted about every thirty miles or so. Lemuel believed a few days in each of them would be good for selling books. As their stock dwindled, they could telegraph the BookSeller to have restock shipped to a town farther south to be held until called for.

Later in life, when he thought about it, Johnny believed this time traveling the valley, selling books was among the most rewarding of his life.

They would pull into Modesto (Spanish for modest) or Merced (Spanish for mercy) or Tulare, and within an hour there were people milling around the wagon looking at books and talking about books. At each town, first thing, they would buy any newspapers printed there and read them so they would be able to talk with people about local issues of importance to them.

Usually by the middle of the first day there was a steady stream of customers, and in many cases their stock would be so depleted by one town they would have to order restock for delivery at the next.

People wanted good books. History and biography, religion and philosophy; novels too, but good novels, Dickens and Thackery, Poe and Cooper and even the new fellow, Mark Twain. Since people didn't have many books, they seemed to want good ones. They also bought books for their children.

Back in Kansas, with the long cold winters, people read by the stove in the evenings and shared what they read. Here the weather was more congenial, but people were still the same, always seeming to find the time to read and loving to talk about what they read.

Johnny remembered his Pa saying the first people to come west were so busy surviving they didn't have time to read. The second generation found the time and wanted more of it for their children.

Usually by the third day business slowed, so they would pack up and move on. Nearly every night in nearly every town there would be a meal in someone's home, and talk till bedtime, which was usually later than normal. There was good food, good talk and good humor, and Johnny met some wonderful people and learned much more than he taught.

From Modesto in the north, to Bakersfield at the south end of the valley, it was just over two hundred miles. They took a month to travel it and then spent a week in Bakersfield. Madera, Fresno, Tulare, Vaisala, all towns with a future because of rich land and hardworking people, all a little better because they had been there and sold some books.

Chapter Seventy-Seven

Greta was lying on the bed, but her mind was far away. Beside her Roy's deep, even breathing told her he was asleep. Tonight was the first time they made love and she was thinking about Jed and how different it was than the first time with him.

For several weeks they walked and talked, had lunches together and shared their pasts and thoughts about the future. They both believed they would be happy together, and the things they shared on the walks and ferry rides made her feel good. What she felt was happiness, just as it should be when two people join hands to walk through life together.

But for her there was another on that path, there and yet not there, a ghost or a vision as it were, and she knew it would always be there. Tonight, it had been. The lovemaking was exciting, and she enjoyed it. She could feel Jed looking on but couldn't see his face and she had no idea how he felt or what he thought about her reaching out for happiness with someone else.

But she was. She remembered what Annaliese said about the big rock and how, as she walked away, it would become smaller, part of the landscape of her life. It was out there, and she was aware of it, but had made a conscious choice to leave it out there and not let it intrude.

She turned onto her side, ran her fingers across his face and kissed him. He awoke, smiled beneath the kiss, and reached to take her in his arms.

"Again?" he asked.

She smiled and said, "No, not yet. I want to tell you something." She sat up in bed. "I enjoyed tonight, but I want you to understand something, and you may find it hard to accept. We can only make love when I say so."

She paused but he didn't speak, so she went on. "One night Jed and I made love, and that night I knew I was pregnant; somehow, I just knew it. It seems like I can feel things inside me that other women can't.

"As much as I love you, I don't want to have any more children yet. With the twins it's all I can do to keep them safe and care for them.

"What I'm saying is, I can feel when I can get pregnant. I don't know how or why, but I just feel it, so we can make love only when I feel I can't conceive. If I make a mistake and it happens, then of course I'll love and care for the child, but I need for you to trust me and make love only when I feel it's safe. Can you do that for me?"

He looked at her in silence. "Is it because you're blind? Is that why you can feel it?"

She shrugged. "I don't know. I just know I can."

"Do you want to get married?"

"No, at least not right now. With Papa and Johnny leaving and the twins and the store, I have enough to think about right now. Let's wait a while, say six months, and see if we still want to. Is that alright?"

He took her in his arms again. "Well just so you know, I love you and don't plan on marrying anyone else. Does all this mean we can do this again tonight?"

She giggled and kissed him. "And again, if you want to."

He did.

Annaliese was listening to her friends. They had come to The City of Paris for lunch and for a celebration, but all knew it was also an ending. This was the last time they would gather together as students.

The first time they saw each other was the day Dr. Brown advised them the road they were committed to traveling would be easier if they shared their strengths. So they had.

They worked together for three years, helping, cajoling, encouraging one another, sharing heartaches, disappointments, and triumphs; and finally, tomorrow they were finished. They could call themselves doctors now and that frightened them a little as well as making them proud of what they had accomplished. Now each would go her own way, and though they would probably drift apart over the years, they would always be friends.

"You're awful quiet," Tudie said to her.

Annaliese smiled. "Just thinking back, remembering the day we all met."

"Been a long, hard three years," Tudie said. "But we've made it through, and now everyone's leaving. Ginger and Henry are moving to Bakersfield. He bought into a mortuary there and she's going to open a practice. Jess and her brother are headed up to Seattle, Maggie and Charlie are moving to Chicago, and you're headed south. I'll be all by myself around here."

"All of us are beginning new lives. I wonder where we'll be in ten years?" said Annaliese. She grinned at Maggie who was listening. "What kind of smart remark are you going to make?"

"You know, when I do that it's usually because I'm nervous or afraid," said Maggie. "Helps me not be afraid so much. So, I'm not afraid of school anymore, but tomorrow I'll probably have a hundred new things to be afraid about."

"Have you heard any more about the thing in Chicago? What did they call it - an internship?" asked Annaliese.

"It's more school I reckon, but I think I'll be watching them do surgery, then they'll be watching me, so it's not like it's just more classes or anything."

Jess and Ginger stopped talking and were listening.

Annaliese shook her head and took a deep breath. "When I was working with the Doctor or here at school, there was always someone there to help me if I didn't know things. After tomorrow I'll be by myself; just me and my patients. It's a little scary."

"We must do the best we can with what we know and keep learning," said Ginger. "We may never be the doctors we want to be, but we should always keep trying. Those researchers Dr. Rose talked about, they'll keep finding out new things and we need to make sure we keep in touch with the new things they find out."

When it was time, they parted, and the tears in their eyes were of sorrow and friendship.

Roy, just back from the post office, handed Annaliese a small square envelope. It was addressed to Dr. Annaliese Fry, and in the corner the name and address of Hannah Grimes was written in what she thought was Sarah's handwriting.

Dear Dr. Annaliese Fry,
*   You are invited to dinner at 6:OO PM on Monday next*
at the home of Mme. Hannah Grimes.
*   Please do not RSVP, just make damn sure you show up.*
Yours truly
Mme. Hannah Grimes and
Mrs. Sarah Travers

She threw back her head and laughed.

When she walked into the dining room at the mansion, the room was full of people and they applauded as Sarah led her to the head of the table.

When she was seated, Madame at the foot of the table, tapped her knife on a water glass and said, "Your friends and family would like to congratulate you on a signal achievement which will benefit all mankind."

Everyone raised their glass. "Here, here," they chanted in unison, and all drank.

"Thank you, everyone," she said. A quick count showed twenty-one people at the long table. She'd never seen this room in her visits to the Mansion.

For the next hour everyone ate a delicious dinner, and then they moved into another room even larger than the dining room, and she began to circulate among her friends and Johnny's.

She was pleased to see her anatomy teacher and his wife talking to Maggie and Jess and joined them.

"Hello Dr. Rose." She nodded at his wife who said. "Surely you can call him Hank now."

Annaliese grinned at her. "Hank then. I'm glad to have a chance to say goodbye and let you know my ambition to do research was thwarted in Los Angeles. The school is in an old winery, and I didn't see hope of doing any research there for a while. That's one of the reasons we decided on San Diego instead."

He waved his hand. "Don't worry about it. That's the same speech I give to all new classes. You've plenty of time to get into that later if you choose. I understand you bought a practice?"

"Yes, although I don't know how it will work out. Most of the patients are in the Mexican community, and I may drive them away with my horrible Spanish. The doctor I'm taking over for has been there since the early 1840's, so I'm replacing an institution. Fortunately, he's going to be there to help me get started and introduce me to my patients."

The other members of the study group had joined them, and while they were talking with Bev, Hank pulled her to one side and said in a low tone, "Is your friend Mr. Josephson here? If so, I'd like to talk to him."

She had seen Handy towering over everyone at the table and now spotted him talking to Gray and Madame in the corner. She caught his eye, and he came over.

"Well, looks like you've made it. Congratulations," he said. "When do you leave for San Diego?"

"Day after tomorrow," she said. "Handy, this is one of my teachers, Hank Rose. Hank, Handy Josephson. He'd like to talk to you."

She spent the next two hours talking to her friends, and as people began to leave, she found herself shepherded into Madame's dressing room with Sarah and Rebecca.

When she was seated before the bay window, Sarah produced a large package wrapped in brown paper and an envelope and handed it to her.

The note was from Johnny.

Dear Dr. Annaliese,

The second day we were selling in Merced, a fellow asked if he could set up a display next to us and take advantage of the crowd to sell his wares. He was a wood carver, and when I saw what beautiful work he did I decided to have him make this for you. Hope you like it.

Johnny.

She unwrapped the package and was looking at a beautifully wrought sign made of wood with a metal frame and painted in green and gold. It read, Dr. Annaliese Crawford Fry, and below, Doctor of Medicine.

For a minute she had trouble seeing through the tears forming in her eyes. She held it so her friends could see it.

"It's beautiful, Annaliese," said Sarah. She read the note and handed it to Madame.

"Well, I guess that makes it official," said Madame. She poured champagne into four flutes, and they drank a toast to absent friends.

"Have you heard from him since he left?" she asked.

"I got one letter from Fresno and one from after they got to San Diego. They're all fine, and Woman got there a few days before they did."

"So, tell me how you feel after all this preparation for something," said Sarah.

"Only that I hope I'm up to the challenge," she said. "And Johnny makes enough to keep us from starving for a while."

"The BookSeller should help," said Madame. "Johnny told me they were going to give Jason and Sun Li a third interest in the store. From what I know about them, things should keep perking along."

Chapter Seventy-Eight

There was a stunning view on the long hill leading down the southside of the San Gabriel Mountains, but they were too busy keeping the wagon from running over the horses to appreciate it. If the wagon, heavy as it was, got out of control on that steep grade it would probably leave death and destruction in its wake and spell the doom of any hopes for their futures in the book business, even if they lived to tell about it. In the end, the strength of the horses and Lemuel's skill and experience handling them brought them safely into the Los Angeles Basin.

From what they could see of the towns scattered around the Basin, if they ever grew together, this place would be a sprawling city, probably bigger than San Francisco. They debated whether or not to stop and sell here, and when they finally came into the city itself, decided to try it for a few days. Business was good, but even with all the people, not as good as it had been in the valley. Either the people didn't read here, or they had plenty of other places to get their books.

After four days they left Los Angeles and camped the first night on a bluff overlooking the ocean. They were up and on the road early the next morning. Wash was scouting ahead, and Johnny was riding beside the wagon when they saw four men crest the hill they were approaching and come down toward them.

Something about those men made Lemuel pull the wagon to a stop and pick up the shotgun from where it lay on the seat beside him. The closer they came, the more he felt it, and he said to Johnny, "Watch this bunch. They make me nervous."

Johnny slipped the loop from the Colt and moved a little away from the wagon. "It's your call," he said quietly.

As they came closer, one man moved a little ahead and Lemuel realized he was the reason for the feeling of unease. The man was an albino; white hair, pinkish eyes, and skin so pale he looked ghost-like even in the bright sunshine. And he looked evil, more evil than any man Lemuel had ever seen.

The man nodded and spoke. "Noticed you picked up the shotgun when you saw us. No need for that." Lemuel just looked at him. The man cast a measuring glance at Johnny and then said, "That sure is a pretty wagon; stout looking too. We were wondering what you've got in it."

"Books," said Lemuel and gestured at the sign on the side.

Suddenly the man's face hardened. "You got no call to point a cocked shotgun at me. We ain't doin' nothing."

Lemuel smiled but didn't lower the gun.

From a small wood to one side of the four men came the sound of a Sharp's being cocked, and their heads turned toward it. Beside him Brutus growled and showed his teeth.

"Yes, and between the two of us here and my friend in the woods there, we want to keep it that way. I'd suggest you ride on."

The man gave him that same measuring glance, slowly nodded his head, and said, "There'll be another time, old man." He nodded and Lemuel could feel a wave of evil emanating from him. "Yes, another time."

A twelve-gage buckshot cartridge fired from ten feet will make a mess of a man. The albino flew backwards off his horse and was likely dead before he hit the ground. Lemuel had been aiming high to avoid hitting the horse and there wasn't much left of the man's face.

The shocking suddenness of the blast seemed to freeze everyone in place. By the time the rest of them brought their horses under control, Lemuel had shifted his aim to a point between two of them.

"What'd you shoot Whitey for? He wasn't doing nothing," said one of the men plaintively.

"He threatened me. I don't like to be threatened." The Colt was out, and Wash had come out of the woods and sat on his mule, dead on their flank, Sharps ready.

"Gawd mighty. You can't go around shooting people like that."

The shotgun was steady. "I'd apologize but he doesn't seem too worried about it." He chewed on his bottom lip then said. "You know when you threaten a man you gotta expect something like this. You might remember that in the future."

He gestured at Wash. "That fellow's our scout. Pretty good at it too. If he should see you trailing us…" he paused. "Well, he might just be waiting for you one night when you go out to answer the call. He shaves with that Bowie he wears and he's awfully hard to see in the dark." They turned and saw the long sheath hanging from Wash's belt.

As the three men rode away, Lemuel called after them, "Aren't you even going to bury him?"

One of them turned and said, "Nah, I never liked the bastard anyway."

After the men were gone, Johnny asked, "You think we'll see them again?"

"Not a chance in hell," said Wash.

They rode in silence for a while.

"I reckon I was as shocked as they were when you pulled the trigger," said Johnny. "I'm not complaining, you understand, just curious. Why'd you do it?"

Lemuel looked at him thoughtfully. "Ninety-nine times out of a hundred I wouldn't have. But that man looked to be as evil a man as I've ever seen, and I could tell he'd try to make good on his threat. I'd no appetite to wait. Lots of trees and rocks to hide behind and shoot someone around here. Besides, from the looks of him and his friends, he likely deserved it.

"I heard little Phil say more than once, 'there's a time to talk and a time to shoot' and rather than leave him behind me with a grudge, it seemed to be a time to shoot. Now I won't have to worry about him and his friends shooting at us from ambush."

The next place on their way was Laguna, a pretty little oceanside town, and they stopped at the town marshal's office and reported the shooting and the body they had left lay where it fell.

"You say this fellow threatened you?" the marshal asked.

"He did, and I felt he would likely be waiting somewhere down the trail and shoot from behind a rock or something. I decided not to wait and give him a chance."

"You say there were four of them?" the marshal asked, and when Lemuel nodded, he continued, "What did this fellow look like?"

"Albino, pale skin, white hair, pink looking eyes, although I doubt you'd recognize him. There's not much left of his face. One of them called him 'Whitey'."

The marshal nodded his head and said, "Whitey Aleshire. He's a bandito and we've had some trouble with his bunch before. I'd say you were probably right. He'd have been waiting for you somewhere down the road. I'd bet a dollar he'd want to find out what was in the wagon. You say you just left him lay there?"

"We figured if his friends didn't want to bury him, why should we?"

"Well, I think you should at least foot the bill to plant him."

Lemuel considered that for a moment. "How much?"

The marshal pulled at his chin. "Make it two dollars."

Lemuel handed him the bills and asked, "Mind if we set up to sell some books here?"

It was a small place and there weren't many customers, so they moved on the next morning.

As they left the town behind, Lemuel chuckled,

"Well, with the cost of burying Mr. Aleshire, we just about broke even in Laguna."

Later Johnny was riding beside the wagon, and he asked Lemuel if the killing the day before bothered him.

"Naw. I felt about him the way you felt about the fellow in the saloon. You knew he'd try sometime and decided not to wait. Just looking at him I knew he'd be waiting somewhere down the road with all the advantages on his side. Didn't make sense to wait. I saw too many good men killed in Virginia to worry about someone like that. There are people in the world that need killing. From what I saw and what the marshal said, he was likely one of them."

"That's pretty much what I felt about Clement Grayson. If it hadn't been me someone else would have done it. There are some who seem to go around asking for it.”

Kate Sessions was watering the flowers and shrubs in front of the nursery when she saw an odd-looking wagon turn the corner and come lumbering down the street toward her. She set the watering can down and shaded her eyes to see better. A familiar figure spurred his mount to come on ahead.

She was smiling broadly when Wash swung down and shook her hand.

“I thought I’d be seeing you before long,” she said.

“She’s here then?” he asked.

“Got in a couple of days ago.” She held his hand. “Glad you’re back in town, Wash. When you going to work?”

He threw back his head and laughed and she joined him. “If you need me special, right away, but I’d kind of like to get my friends settled. Might be a couple of days.”

“I’ll hold you to that,” she said, “but you can’t have her. I’m getting used to having her around again.” She raised her voice. “Woman, someone here to see you.”

Wash and Woman were saying hello in the doorway when Lemuel and Johnny pulled up.

“Since Wash seems to be busy I’ll do the introductions,” said Johnny. He swung down. “Kate, this is my friend and partner Lemuel Waters. Lemuel, Kate Sessions.”

“Woman told me you planned on June first, so you didn’t miss it by much,” said Kate.

“We stayed over in Bakersfield a couple days, by popular demand,” said Lemuel.

“When is Annaliese going to be here?” Kate was running her hands over Black’s neck when she saw Jinx in the saddle and stepped back, startled. Then she laughed. “Wash told me about him, but I forgot. Can I pet him?”

“Go ahead. If he doesn't like it, he’ll just turn his head.”

“So, this is the famous Jinx, the horseback riding cat,” she said. She ran her hand along his back and then scratched behind his ears. “He didn’t bite so I guess he likes me.”

She stepped back and looked at Black. “He’s a big fellow.”

“One time I’ll tell you how I got him,” said Johnny. “To answer your question, it should be early next week,” replied Johnny. “She’s in a hurry to get started doctoring, so she'll probably go to work the first day she's here."

"I saw Dr. Clark yesterday. He's getting anxious about her getting here," said Kate. "She's taking on a load. I hope she's up to it, fresh out of school and all."

"She worked with her father for ten years, so she's got a start on most things, and she was top in her class. She's ready. Of course it will help having Dr. Clark around for a while. Give her a chance to find her feet."

"Kate, any ideas where it would be best to park the wagon?" asked Lemuel. "I'll be sleeping in it most nights, so I'm not worried about safety, but I don't usually drive it much in town. We're going to sell out of it until we get a store ready, so we want to find a place with good traffic."

"If I were you, I'd go down to city hall tomorrow and talk to John Weatherby. He's the town planner here and he'll be able to tell you all you want to know. You can just park it here for a while until you decide." She indicated a spot just inside the fence surrounding her yard. "You can put your horses in my barn."

Later, she watched them ride away until they were out of sight around a curve in the road.

"Good," she said, nodding her head vigorously. "Good."

Chapter Seventy-Nine

Wash spent the next couple of days helping his friends get settled in, then he was back at the nursery, and when he walked in remembered how much he loved working there. It was great. Woman and Kate had become friends, and soon she was sort of an assistant to the boss, in charge when Kate wasn't there.

The day after he returned, Kate came into the potting shed where he was wrapping trees in burlap.

"Take a ride with me," she said. Wash glanced in the back of the wagon and saw three trays of seedlings and several bags of feed. He climbed into the driver's seat and asked, "Where we headed?"

"You remember Ger Schweder's place, don't you?" she asked.

He resisted turning to stare at her. He nodded and started the horses onto the street.

"I've got a surprise for him, and I want to take it out myself."

"How's he coming along after that shooting?"

"Joaquin told me he was sitting on the porch some days now. He's got a big fellow who helps him get around. Had he lost the leg before you left?"

Wash shook his head. "Not that I recall."

"Well, it got infected, and they took it off, right here." She drew her finger across her leg halfway up her thigh.

He pulled the horses to a stop and got down. "Looks like he's limping," he said. He lifted the horse's front leg and examined the hoof. There was nothing wrong with the horse, but he wanted to give his heart a chance to slow down and some time to think how to carry on a conversation he wasn't expecting.

He got back on the seat, and they started again. "Just a stone in his hoof," he said. "What were you saying about his leg?"

"I hear he's got a fellow to lift and carry him, and he's ordered a wheeled chair from a company in San Francisco. He thinks it will help him get around. He'll still need the helper, but he'll be able to do more for himself."

They rode in silence for a while.

"Looks like they're getting things going up on the hill already," she said.

"Lemuel's not one to let grass grow under his feet. He decides something and then pitches right in. We have to keep up with him as best we can."

Wash dropped Kate at the big house and took the wagon into the barn to unload the supplies and seedlings.

"Hey Joaquin, where do you want this stuff?" The foreman pointed and Wash positioned the wagon, then turned to watch Kate and the man in the rocking chair. She handed him an envelope, and he opened it and took something out.

After a few minutes she whistled, and he drove the wagon up to the porch. He started to get down to help her up, but she snapped, "Stay where you are." She turned back to Schweder and said, "I don't have to tell you what to do with those, but I want to know how they take hold." She climbed up on the seat without any help, and when Wash started the wagon, she waved goodbye.

"I got those lemon tree cuttings from India," she said. "If anyone around here can make 'em grow it's Ger."

Lying in bed next to Woman that night, he could see the empty pant leg when he closed his eyes and knew he'd have trouble sleeping.

Sarah was reading the paper when Madame came into the sitting room and dropped into her chair.

"Good morning," Madame said.

"Morning," replied Sarah. She rustled the paper. "Did you see this piece about the banquet for some visiting diplomat?"

"No, tell me about it."

"Jonas wants me to go with him. I told him I had nothing to wear to such a shindig so he's going to take me out this afternoon and buy me a new dress."

"Didn't you know? That's what men do for their mistresses. I've had a few bought for me over the years."

Sarah laughed. "So, you say. He's taking me to more and more of these things. I'm liable to have quite a wardrobe eventually."

Madame looked at her for a moment, a smile on her face. "So, are you getting used to having a man in your bed again?"

"Yes, it's nice to have him for that, and for other things, and still have all this." She looked around the room.

"Is he still reading the erotica stuff to you?"

"Once in a while."

"When he stops doing it, you'll know the honeymoon's over."

Sarah laughed. They were quiet for a few minutes, both reading the paper and sipping coffee.

"It was nice having Woman here for a while," said Sarah. "Do you know if Johnny and them got down there yet?"

"Haven't heard. She doesn't write much."

"You miss her, don't you?"

"Every day, but she's like a bird; if you hold her too tight, she'll suffocate, too loose and she'll fly away. I've learned over the years to get it just right, so she always comes back."

"Are you in love with her?"

Madame sat so long without answering Sarah wasn't sure she was going to. "I don't know if I'm *in* love with her, but I love her. I think there's a difference. She gives me something I haven't gotten from a man in many years, not since I was first married back years ago."

"I've thought about the two of you in bed."

Madame smiled at her, "Oh you have, have you? And what have you thought?"

"I don't understand what you get out of it with her."

Again, Madame looked at her for a long time.

"Please understand, I have no desire to create a problem between you and I. We have something special, and I don't want to do anything to hurt it. But, if you really want to know, I'd love to show you."

Sarah looked at her, a thoughtful expression on her face, then she smiled. "Not just yet. I need to think about it for a while."

Madame stood up. "I have to get ready to go out." She bent over and kissed Sarah lightly on the lips. "Let me know what you decide," and she was gone.

Chapter Eighty

They were sitting on the new porch Wash built on the front of the cabin, talking about the new bookstore.

The question was, where did they want to site it? Johnny and Wash felt a place close to the New Town business section would be best, but Lemuel wasn't so sure.

"If we're going to build it to be a bookstore, maybe we should spend some time and energy looking for a good spot instead of putting it where someone put up a building." He let that hang in the air for a moment, then said, "That's pretty much what Annaliese said, and I agree. This town is small enough we'll have many choices, so why not make it special enough that people will come no matter where we put it?"

They sat thinking for a minute.

"The BookSeller in San Francisco was special, not just because we sold books, but because of the things we did to draw people to it."

"You mean the open houses and the speakers we invited, things like that?" asked Johnny.

"Exactly. Back home it was the center of a movement to clean up the city and then people who wanted to communicate new ideas about improving the city came to speak and to talk to others about their ideas. They also came to buy books.

"I think Annaliese was right. We don't want to assume the

things we did in San Francisco will necessarily work down here. We should, however, examine things that worked there and see how they apply here, but we should also look for new ideas, ways to draw the people of our new city to us."

"I don't know if I'd call it a city quite yet," said Wash.

"That's the point. It will be one day, and we can help make it the city we want it to be with the store and how we do business."

"What you're talking about is strategy, and I agree," said Wash. "Before you begin to build, it would likely help to know what you're aiming for."

"Exactly," said Lemuel. "When we open a store here it shouldn't be just to sell books. We need it to be a place people come for information, a place to learn and grow, a place to help our city become what we want it to be. We want people to come because it's worth the trip."

They sat silent for a while. Finally, Johnny said, "You've convinced me. So, it looks like every decision we make will trace back to the idea 'because it's worth the trip'. So how does that affect what we need to do tomorrow?"

"I think the first thing will be to follow Kate's advice and see the town planner," said Lemuel. "We need to get set up and selling as soon as we can, and we'll need to order some books too. Also, it might be a good idea to see the lot you bought first and see if it fits what we think we'll want going forward."

Later that night, after everyone else was asleep, Johnny and Jinx went for a walk. He came to the flat rock, sat down, took Jinx in his lap and thought about what Lemuel had said. The phrase 'because it's worth the trip' echoed through his thoughts and new ideas came rushing into his brain. It was late when he finally walked back to the cabin, lay down, fell asleep and dreamed of his wife.

Five days later he kissed her 'hello' on the station platform. "You are Dr. Annaliese Fry, aren't you?" he asked.

"Yes, I am, at last. Anyone around here need a doctor?" They laughed together. He relieved the porter of her carpetbag, and when everything was recovered from the baggage car and in their new carriage, said, "Welcome to San Diego, your new home. This is the city where you will live, but I'm afraid the house itself is still on the drawing board."

"Where is everyone? I thought they'd all be at the station to meet me."

"Wash and Woman are working and Lemuel's minding the store."

"You mean you're up and running already?"

"Not exactly. There's a fair bit I need to acquaint you with. We've made some plans, but I'll tell you about them once we're there. How's everyone at home?"

"We're going to have to be careful using the term 'at home' for a while so we'll know what we're talking about, but everyone's fine. Store's doing great. Rebecca and Handy came down to see me off, and Greta and Roy are talking about marriage. Jason and Sun Li are doing fine, and the children are all OK.

"Hank and Bev came to a little going away get together at the store the other night and it appears Hank might be the new partner at the ranch."

Johnny's face showed astonishment. "Really?"

"He heard you were selling out, so he made an offer and they're going to meet this week to work out the details."

"Well, that's a surprise," he said. "Hank's not going to sell their place, is he?"

"I don't know the details but I'm sure you'll hear about it soon. Where are we going?"

"We got a refund on the lot we bought, and Lemuel and I picked out another one."

She could see the wagon now sitting on a low rise looking down into the city. It looked as though a small tent was in front of it, but as they got closer, she saw it was a large umbrella placed to keep Lemuel out of the summer sun.

He was talking to a customer when they pulled up but excused himself and she gave him a hug.

"So did you flunk out?" he asked with a grin

"I'm officially Dr. Annaliese Fry, MD, and anxious to get started."

"Come let me show you something," he said, and led her around the wagon to where strings were tied to stakes clearly outlining what would be a large house.

"Of course, this is all dependent on your approval, but this will be the store and your house and, if you want, your office; and while

I can no longer build it myself, I'll be working with the builders to make it exactly what we want it to be."

Johnny came up beside her. "If you walk to the top of the hill over there," he pointed, "you can see Presidio Hill and the mission. Dr. Clark's office is just beyond the mission.

"We picked this spot because it is halfway between Old Town and New Town. If you put your office here your patients from the Mexican community won't be too far away, and neither will the people from New Town if they need a doctor. We'll have one foot in the old and one in the new."

"And this is where you want to put the store instead of down on the main street?" she asked.

"I didn't at first, but Lemuel suggested we build a store so special people would come because it was worth the trip. I agreed with him and here we are."

He took her by the shoulders. "Of course, only if it's OK with you."

"I think it sounds wonderful, but I need to get over to Dr. Clark's and talk to him before it's too late."

"We knew you would," said Lemuel. "And since I want to meet him, I'm going to close up shop and come along."

"If you don't mind, I'd like to talk to him by myself for a while. You and Johnny can come with me in the morning, and we'll chat."

She tied the horse to a post by the dry fountain in the square and sat on the wall looking at the door to the office.

When she was thirteen, she told the Doctor she wanted to be a doctor. From then on it was accepted and he had been a constant presence she knew was there to guide her when she didn't know where the path was, to help her when she had blood up to her elbows and someone died anyway, to guide her when she was helping a mother bear her first child, and to hold her when it all became too much and she cried her eyes out.

Now, though hundreds of miles away, he was still at her shoulder, and when she remembered that she got to her feet, took a deep breath and strode resolutely across the square to the door. She raised her hand to knock but the door opened suddenly, and Dr. Clark was standing there smiling. "You don't have to knock, Dr. Fry," he said.

About the Author

All my life I've wanted to write a book. One morning in March 2019, at age 76, I woke up and started writing. The BookSeller is the second novel I've published since then and there is a third in progress. I'm Virginia born, married Mary Lackovitch, the love of my life in 1964 and she and our twin daughters, Diane and Samantha, followed me around the country for 45 years until she died of cancer in 2010. I lost one of the twins in 2015 and the other, Samantha and Lily, my granddaughter, live close by my present home in Gresham, Oregon where I live with my partner Bev and her two cats and a little black cat named Jinx.